A WOMAN'S WORTH
SPAWN OF DARKNESS

S. A. PARKER

A Woman's Worth (Spawn of Darkness Series)

Copyright © S. A. Parker, all rights reserved.

This series is a work of fiction. Any resemblance to characters and situations is purely coincidental and not intended by the author.

Edited by: The Editor & The Quill

❦ Created with Vellum

CONTENTS

NOTE FROM THE AUTHOR   vii

Chapter 1   1
Drake

Chapter 2   17
Dell

Chapter 3   23
Dell

Chapter 4   31
Dell

Chapter 5   41
Dell

Chapter 6   50
Sol

Chapter 7   55
Dell

Chapter 8   62
Dell

Chapter 9   72
Dell

Chapter 10   89
Dell

Chapter 11   93
Drake

Chapter 12   97
Kal

Chapter 13   113
Dell

Chapter 14   122
Dell

Chapter 15   142
Dell

Chapter 16   148
Sol

Chapter 17   156
Dell

Chapter 18 *Dell*	163
Chapter 19 *Dell*	172
Chapter 20 *Dell*	191
Chapter 21 *Dell*	205
Chapter 22 *Dell*	213
Chapter 23 *Dell*	223
Chapter 24 *Dell*	237
Chapter 25 *Dell*	252
Chapter 26 *Dell*	261
Chapter 27 *Kal*	271
Chapter 28 *Dell*	276
Chapter 29 *Dell*	295
Chapter 30 *Dell*	303
Chapter 31 *Dell*	310
Chapter 32 *Dell*	320
Chapter 33 *Aero*	329
Chapter 34 *Dell*	341
Chapter 35 *Dell*	349
Chapter 36 *Dell*	364
Chapter 37 *Dell*	373
Chapter 38 *Kal*	380

Chapter 39 *Dell*	385
Chapter 40 *Dell*	398
Chapter 41 *Dell*	412
Chapter 42 *Dell*	426
Chapter 43 *Dell*	435
Chapter 44 *Beasty*	444
Chapter 45 *Drake*	447
Chapter 46 *Beasty*	451
Chapter 47 *Dell*	459
Chapter 48 *Dell*	465
Chapter 49 *Edom*	475
Chapter 50 *Dell*	492
Chapter 51 *Dell*	502
Chapter 52 *Drake*	507
Chapter 53 *Dell*	512
Chapter 54 *Kal*	522
Chapter 55 *Dell*	526
Chapter 56 *Dell*	533
Chapter 57 *Dell*	543
CHAPTER 58 *Dell* Ten Months Later	560

CHAPTER 59	575
Sol	
One Year Later	
Chapter 60	580
Aero	
The End	585
Chapter 61	586
Cassian	
Acknowledgments	593
Spawn of Darkness Series	595
About the Author	597

NOTE FROM THE AUTHOR

This is the last book in the four-part Spawn of Darkness series and cannot be read as a standalone.

Although integral to the story arc, some of the situations that occur in the Spawn of Darkness series are brutal.

This story is not for the faint of heart.

It contains content which some readers will find triggering and is intended for a mature audience aged eighteen years and over.

Content warning: sensitive and taboo subjects, offensive language, explicit sexual content, graphic torture scenes, violence, and miscarriage from a secondary character.

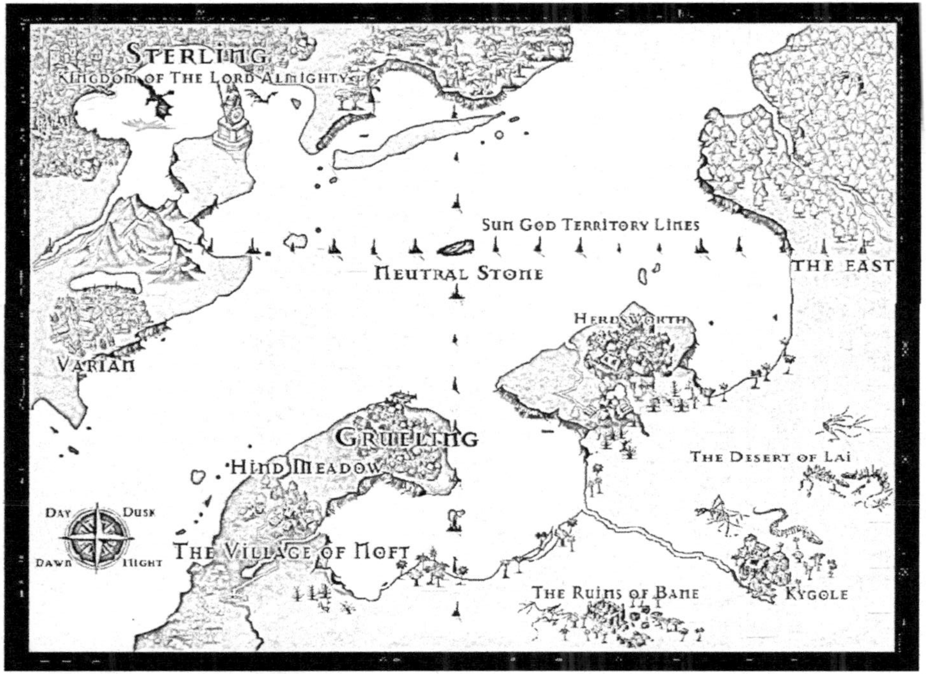

Sterling
Kingdom of The Lord Almighty
Varian
Sun God Territory Lines
Neutral Stone
The East
Herdsworth
Grueling
Hind Meadow
The Desert of Lai
Day
Dusk
Dawn
Night
The Village of Noft
The Ruins of Bane
Kygole

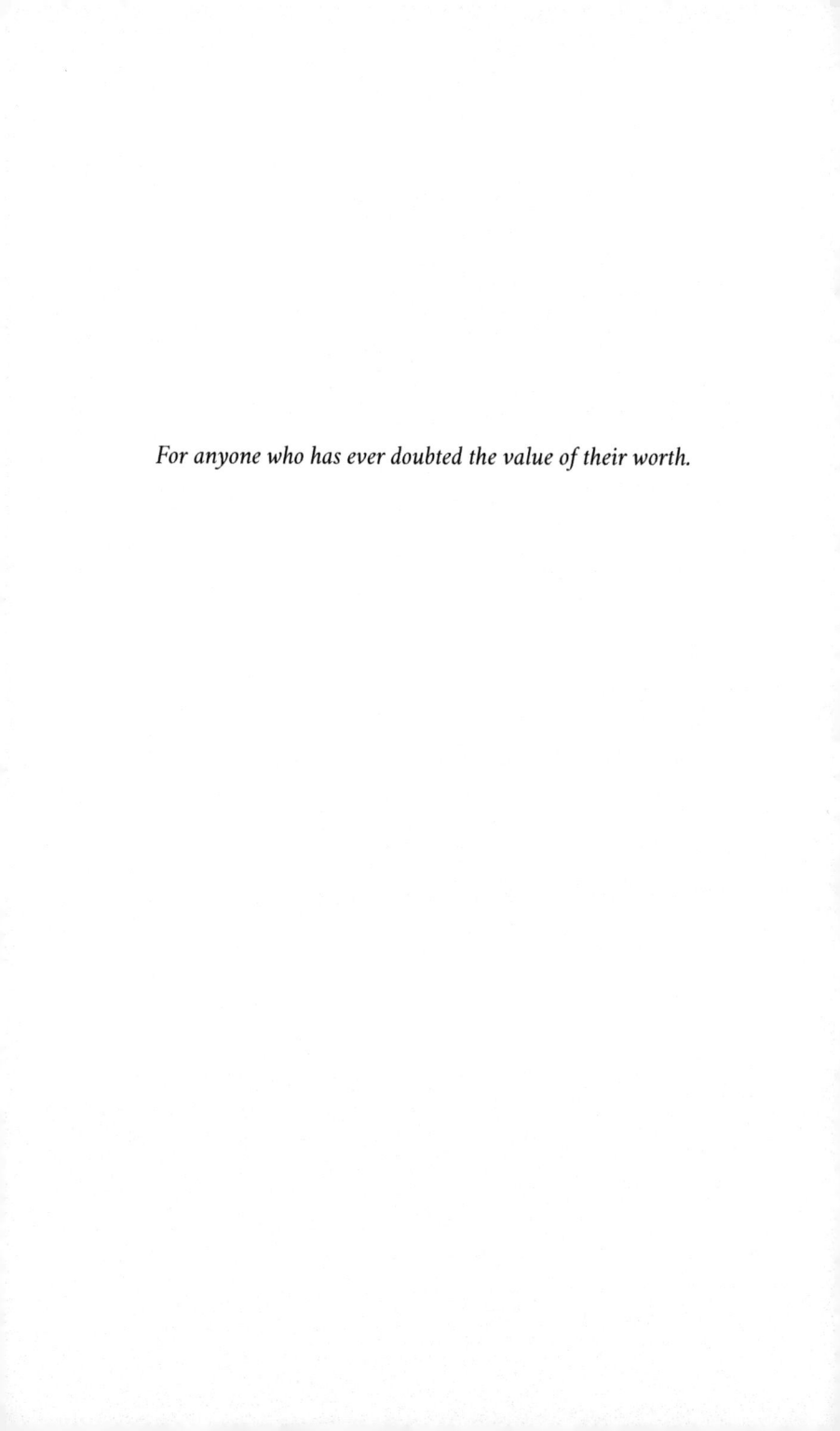

For anyone who has ever doubted the value of their worth.

CHAPTER ONE
DRAKE

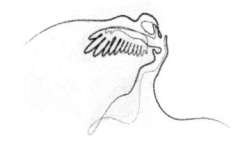

*H*er pain haunts us.

The intermittent, blinding bolts that carved phantom lines in the most delicate places. It haunts our wings, our stomach, our *fingertips* ... only sips of what she went through because she was *shielding* us from the worst of it.

The sensationless hours that have dripped by since mean she's either strengthened those fucking walls or she's passed out somewhere.

We can't decide which is worse.

We roar loud enough to challenge the howling wind, punishing the air with a violent beat of our wings. When we find her, she's going to learn the real meaning of 'no personal space', something she'll have to come to terms with for the rest of her immortal life.

We shake our head and bank, darting through a ravine; its sheer walls pierced with hollow dwellings that once belonged to a colony of High Fae. We scent the remains of a fragile existence, but no sign of anything living.

She's not here.

We drag blunt nails across our chest, clawing skin that barely feels like it's holding us together.

For the first time in a long while, my beast has free rein. He's more animal than man, more instinct than rational thought. But if anyone's going to find her, it's him.

Island after island, town after town; deserts, forests, villages ...

We've searched. And searched. *And fucking searched.*

Shooting from the ravine, we scan the desolation that fans beneath us. Soon the entire world will look like this: crumbling, infertile land scattered with the bones of creatures that once thrived.

Nothing could survive out here now. This is a dead end.

We tuck our wings in tight and we free fall, careening towards an old, wasted sentry tower.

Fuck lot of good it was against Edom Sterling.

We propel our fist through its pallid face and rip through the Bright, landing on the outskirts of Varian—wings settling around our body like a cape and blood dribbling from our shredded knuckles.

It's so quiet, only the shriek of wind whirring around corners of decaying buildings. We throw our wings back and scowl at the sky ...

Still fucking dawn.

It's been like this for a while; the entire world's basking in a relentless morning glow, never giving way to the crisp, clean light of day.

It tells me we're running out of time.

We take a few steps towards the lethargic city nestled at the foot of Mount Stalis—a settlement I used to worship when it was a cultural hub brimming with creativity.

Too bad it's so close to the capital. So close to *him*.

Much like the rest of the world, this city no longer has a pulse.

Our nostrils flare, tasting the air for signs of life aside from the scavenging vermin. We follow our nose between scattered houses on the outer rim, coming across a young boy with straggly hair and wings the colour of dirty wool. He tiptoes down the street carrying a fishing rod and basket—ragged clothes clinging to his slight form and bladed shoulders bunched around his sunken cheeks.

I step out of the shadows.

His face blanches as he drops into a low bow, forehead kissing the cobbled ground.

A fish flops across the pavement.

My beast approves; puffing our chest and extending our wings to their full majesty.

Vain fucker.

"M-milord. Can ... can I help you?" The sharp scent of his adrenaline is a potent tang.

"I'm looking for a woman. Small with long, white hair and determined eyes. Have you seen her?"

The voice, multi-layered with a devastating cadence, is not my own.

The boy shakes his head, tilting his wan face and glancing up at us. "N-n-no, milord. I'm sure I'd remember a w-woman like that."

Yes, he fucking would.

We turn, intent on searching every cobbled street of this labyrinth city.

"M-milord?" he asks, his voice as high as his balls undoubtedly are.

My beast glances back—his temper a thin sheet of ice prone to shatter. But the boy might have information. "Yes?"

There's a light shift of his expression, the scent of his fear morphing into something much sweeter.

Something akin to *hope*.

I haven't smelt *this* scent in a long time. Well, aside from the moment my brothers and I watched the ocean toss a white-winged Dell onto the shore at our feet—a pretty, irresistible parcel of what the actual fuck.

"Is ... is it true?"

"Is what true, boy?"

He stands and bridges the space between us, his voice little more than a whisper. "Is she coming to save us all?"

"Who?"

He cups his hand around his mouth, motioning for us to lean down. We crouch, casting him in the dark lump of our shadow as the boy's calloused hand brushes the side of our face.

His words are the flick of a delicate paintbrush against our ear. *"The Little Dove."*

Fucking hell.

Our wings flare and a sharp snarl has the boy pressing his face flat against the road, his urine weaving through the cobbles.

We didn't mean to frighten him. We certainly didn't mean to make the poor kid piss himself. But *fuck* ...

Our disobedient, drunk little mate flicks her wings out in front of no more than five High Fae for half a fucking second and the world perks its pointy ears.

So much for keeping her father in the dark.

Our head starts to pound with the urge to give the boy hope. Anyone who's not accepting cunt like it's candy is fine by us. He's a seed which could spawn a movement and shed some light on this dank world ...

But we can't. Even if Edom's wards weren't gagging us, this world is not his problem to fix.

We turn from the untainted child pressed flat against the ground. "Be careful who you trust, boy," we toss over our shoulder before tearing through the Bright.

He wears his hope on his sleeve.

It'll get him killed.

We step out of the Bright and scan the wreath of tall, gangly buildings peering down on us—finding nothing but the barren scent of desolation. We're about to make another rip when heavy footsteps echo throughout the pallid town square ...

My aching heart sinks into the pit of my empty stomach; we'd know that languid stride anywhere.

Motherfucker.

The steps draw closer and a chill crawls up our spine. We consider running, but then he'll rightly assume we have something to hide. Something small with pearly skin, a crimson pout, and hair that's just as unruly as every other fucking part of her.

The King steps into view, shelled in pearlescent armour and white leather pants, his wings dragging along the ground behind him—feathers *pristine* thanks to his ever-present shield.

While the world rots, this man continues to thrive.

I wrestle my darkness, but he just bats me away and snarls—perhaps forgetting we're no longer equal opponents. Not since he painted his wards with our blood and turned us into his little band of bitches.

Edom quirks a brow, sharp cheekbones complimenting the feral awareness seeping from his chilling gaze. "You lost, Golden Boy?"

"What do you want?" my beast asks on a sneer, his words poisonous.

Destructive.

He has a fucking death wish I certainly didn't agree to.

"Come, now," Edom purrs, a lazy smirk curling the corner of his mouth. "Is that any way to greet an old friend?"

We bare our teeth and that smirk sharpens.

I wrestle my darkness, managing to lock him down before he says something stupid. He doesn't know how to ride the fine line between being a cunt and getting a spear through our chest.

I step into control and study the immaculate cape of Edom's wings. "You preened for me. I'm flattered, really."

Black, oily marbles watch me with keen precision. "It's been a while since I've seen your dark side come out to play, Drake."

Where the voice of my beast is multi-layered, Edom's is not.

It's hollow. Empty. A menacing timbre that radiates the power dwelling beneath his alabaster skin.

There's little left of the man I used to know ... the man I once cared for.

I wipe blood on my pants and study him with feigned boredom. "What coaxed you out of your foreskin?"

Edom strums his pearly breastplate, brow cocked, studying me ...

On second thought, maybe my beast is better off in charge.

"One day, Drake, I'm going to cut that flapping tongue right out of your mouth."

I clamp my mouth shut. He would do it, and I need my flapping tongue; I've yet to show Dell how truly skilled it is.

Besides—if I can't speak, I can't complete wish cycles to feed my dissipating power. My resources will dwindle until I can no longer initiate dusk, the world will eventually burn to a crisp, and he'll be the King of ashes and nothing more.

This bastard is walking the line between power and mass extinction.

"Why don't you bring your beast back out? I'd like to know what's got his feathers in a fluff."

I bite my tongue, really fucking hard.

Don't say it.

Don't say it.

Don't say it ...

"Well?" he snaps, eyes narrowing. "Cat got your cock?"

Screw it.

"I don't let my beast ride me like a little bitch."

I may have good control over my inner darkness, but my mouth runs its own mission.

A suicide one.

The blow hits harder than I expected it to; a sizzling ball of energy colliding with my chest, sending me careening into a sandstone wall and splitting a building precariously in two.

Somehow, I'm the one that always gets embedded in a fucking wall.

The monster prowls towards me with flared nostrils, tasting my damage with deep, exaggerated breaths while I peel my limbs from the crumbling reinforcements. "You like provoking me, don't you?"

The likelihood of escaping this encounter on two feet is next to none, but every minute he's entertained by lobbing me around is another he's not potentially hunting *her*.

"You know I love it when you shake your tail feathers for me," I grit out, dusting myself off. "It gets me all huffy."

"As much as I enjoy listening to your dribble, how about you bring your beast back out for a chat?"

I flick chalky hair out of my eyes and throw him a winning smile. "He said you can go fuck yourself."

Edom squares his shoulders and my beast sharpens his talons ...

"Are you going to make me do this the hard way, Drake?"

Here we go.

I sigh, slipping my serious face on. "What do you want, Lord?"

My tone is flat, suggesting I'm disinterested.

I'm not.

I need to know how much he knows ...

His features turn stone cold and his lips curl back, exposing the length of his canines—revealing the full face of the monster he's handed himself over to.

The monster I've come to hate with every beat of my bitter heart.

"You know why I'm here," he says, seeping an air of malice that can only be maintained by someone far beyond redemption. "You know who I'm looking for."

My heart skips a beat. I can't fucking help it.

I struggle to keep my features neutral with my inner darkness thrashing against his restraints, snarling for me to drop my hold.

"Enlighten me."

A knowing smile twists the corners of his mouth. "I'm looking for the same thing as you. The same thing Sol was searching for before I twisted him in iron and threw him in my dungeon." My chest grows heavy as I watch him lift his chin. "I'm looking for my daughter."

The words hit harder than any physical blow ever could.

My beast breaks loose, and I let the fucker fly—his answering roar shattering windows, raining glass all over the pavement.

"There he is ..."

We lurch forward, cracking against his sparkly fucking shield. We beat it with our fists; our immortal strength meeting his impervious power over and over again.

My beast isn't stupid. He knows when he's battling a lost cause, but he only gives up once we're doused in our own fucking blood.

We pace, drawing sharp breaths.

Edom knots his arms over his chest and watches us with piqued interest. He knows we can't kill him, but that doesn't mean we can't make him hurt. And we're very good at *that*.

Pain.

We only need to get our power past his fucking *buffer*.

"Drop the shield and fight like a man!"

"Then I'd have to execute you for punishing my organs and being a thorn in my arse. I still need you to bait my Little Dove back to her nest."

I'm instantly sobered, hauling my beast beneath my skin. "She doesn't belong to you."

She belongs to nobody.

His brows reach for his hairline. "She has my white wings, does she not?"

I don't answer, unwilling to speak about my mate's glorious wings in front of the bastard who thinks giving Mare some seed allots him the title of Father.

"I'll take that as a yes. You thought you could pull a feather over my eyes, Drake? You're all idiots if you think I'm that stupid." He takes another step forward and presses his forehead against the shield so we're eye to fucking eye. "I control this world." He smacks his head against it. Hard. "*Me!*"

His roar is the war cry of a monster.

This is the Edom who's spent the past two centuries destroying our world ... the Edom who's *beyond* reason.

I step wide and anchor myself ...

Shit's about to get ugly.

I pour out of the Bright, stumbling into a rainforest that smells like decaying vegetation with only sparse light filtering through the dense canopy.

I'm perched, muscles poised ... heaving.

Four seconds and I'm in the clear.

Three.

Two.

One ...

The Bright claps open.

Edom stalks through the rip, smeared in the scent of his twisted enjoyment like this is some perverse game of hide-and-go-fucking-seek.

I sigh.

"You're weak, Drake. Surely you don't think you can outrun me anymore?"

Worth a fucking shot.

"When have I ever handed you my balls on a platter?"

I'm offered a half smile as I edge backwards over a fallen tree.

He follows, like Death stalking that final heartbeat. "Never. But you must know by now that I rather enjoy the chase."

Oh, I do.

"Well, no need to ruin your fun." I launch skyward, bludgeoning my way past sharp branches that shred my skin and thin my feathers.

Once I break through, I tear into the Bright, emerging on a small atoll in the middle of fucking nowhere. I careen into sand—my vision blotted with rage, pain, and frustration.

One.

Two.

Breathe.

Three ...

The Bright yawns and I don't have time to brace before a crushing bolt of power strikes, tossing me towards the ocean. I collide with unforgiving waves—the impact causing a sickening crunch in my right wing that has me sucking water.

Everything from my waist up feels like it's been set on fire.

I battle the current until I gather enough concentration to rip through the Bright, emerging drenched, still choking, teetering on the edge of a cliff.

The angry ocean churns around jagged rocks below, promising a swift and brutal death.

My stomach roils.

I turn just as a ball of wild energy strikes my chest, propelling me over the edge with a shower of fat stones. A split second before I'm set to be skewered, I make the tear, landing in a groaning heap on the outskirts of a small village.

A boulder lands on one crumpled wing, but I barely register any pain as I taste the air, wild eyes scanning my barren surroundings ...

I can smell her.

My breath catches and my fists clench. I can smell her blood.

Her *agony.*

Her fucking *fear.*

My beast starts to claw at my skin, trying to slice to the surface so he can hunt her down and take away her pain. I grip the boulder with clawed hands and heave it off my wing, clambering to my feet, arms raised.

Edom emerges fresh as a fucking daisy, and I throw the rock.

He raises a hand, shattering the boulder into razor-sharp shards that hang suspended for the beat of a heart. With a flick of his wrist, those chips slice towards me ...

There's no time to run, no time to *blink* before they hit—

lacerating exposed flesh and shredding my wings. An invisible hand clamps around my neck, blocking my airway, obsidian eyes painting me with death.

I drop to the ground.

Motherfucker.

He paces around my flailing body, stopping next to one of my limp wings sprawled across the dirt. He unpockets a pair of mesh gloves, slips them on, then reveals a thick ring made of a dull metal I know too well ...

Iron.

My vision starts to blur as I watch him pry the ring apart then spread my laden wing across his knee, feeling around the gristle and bone. "This will hurt, Drake."

He takes a blade from his belt and I become all too aware of what's about to transpire.

I can only watch, every cell in my body screaming for air.

He stabs through soft tissue and bolts of red flash across my fading vision. The ring is threaded through the hole and hot agony rips through me—a deep, searing pain radiating from where iron meets flesh.

I sink to the earth, feeling myself drift. The pain loses its lustre and I embrace the approaching darkness, cradling Dell's tether, praying that Aero or Kal are still out there ...

That they'll find her. Hide her. Keep her far away from this cunt.

Suddenly I'm sucking air, dragging lungful after lungful of sweet breath. "I didn't realise you wanted to get so close," I rasp through the bitter tang of defeat. "You'll forgive me, I haven't preened today."

"Don't worry, I'd only rough them up again anyway. You know I'm not the gentle sort." He strides behind me, curling my wing by the anchor of his iron handle. I choke on a scream when he stabs the blade through my other wing, plunging it deep into the fleshy soil.

I hiss, stomach heaving, arms shaking with the effort to hold me up.

"How long do you think it'll take my daughter to come flapping after her boy toys?" he purrs, jerking the blade free. I groan through blinding agony while he brings my wings together and slides the ring through the fresh wound, linking them in such a way that if I strain, I'll shred them to fucking pieces.

I roar to the wind, the earth, the sky, and the motherfucking sun as that iron ring takes eager gulps of my dwindling energy stores. "You're one twisted *fuck.*"

Edom kneels, his wings sitting high on his back. He twists his fingers into my hair and tugs my head to the side. "She mated with *two* of you?" I feel his blazing trail of perusal over the spot I doused in saltwater, preserving her mark. "What a greedy little slut."

My wings try to spread, causing the iron ring to tear through flesh. *"Fuck you."*

"And harbouring my offspring, Drake? One whose veins pulse with *my* power? Well, that truly is unacceptable."

"She has no powers."

The invisible hand hauls me to the ground, sprawling me at Edom's feet, pressing my face into the dirt with a faithless bow. A thick line of fire rips along my left wing and I release a strangled roar.

"Then how did she mist my men, hmm?"

Mis—

Oh ... *fuck.*

I twist my head and stare up at him through a veil of crimson, seeing the truth in his eyes.

My girl found her powers.

"Oh, you didn't know?" His black eyes dance. "They hacked up her wings before she dealt her own dose of justice and silenced some of them for good."

Fuck.

I gag, the void of my stomach clenching.

"Did you think she was above losing herself to her inner darkness, Drake? That she was *better* than me?"

Does he think I give a shit that she dished a cold serving of karma? I'm only concerned about her poor fucking *wings*, and her fucking mindset. My baby doesn't cope well with the stain of blood on her hands. And having her wings hacked up *again?*

It makes me want to rip this fucking world in two.

"Don't speak about her like you know her."

Edom huffs, reaching over my shoulder. He grabs the iron ring and jerks it forward, causing blinding pain to lick around the expanding holes. "But I do, Drake. I know her more than you'll ever realise. And take it from me," he whispers, his lips almost close enough to graze my ear. "If she can mist someone, she can damn well do less than that. Her beast *chose* to spill their blood because she's *my* daughter."

"She's *nothing* like you."

He laughs—hard and coarse and dripping malice. "What makes you so sure? You thought you knew me, too, but you know *nothing.*"

This cock's crow isn't as loud as he thinks it is. I know the girl I fell in love with. She's the missing piece my soul has been searching for since the dawn of fucking time.

I hope he lubed his arsehole real good this morning because I'm about to sodomize him with some hard truths.

"Because you, *Dom*, were born in the light. Somewhere along the way you got lost, and now you're one fucked up bastard who's managed to bring an entire world to its knees, all because your beast made you his *bitch.*"

His lips twist and he tugs the ring, pulling my wings at an odd angle. "I think we're done here."

"Not until I'm finished," I rasp, leaning back, *forcing* the ring to tear through feather and flesh until it collides with bone. It'll be a miracle if I fly again, but I bet it's *nothing* compared to having your wings sawn off at the tender age of four. "Adeline. Dell for short. Did you even know her name?"

His left eye twitches.

"*Dell* grew up in a whore house in motherfucking *Grueling*, so she knows what it's like to live in the bowels of your world."

A bitter breeze whorls, kicking up fragments of her scent ...

She's so close.

It's a fiercer form of torture than the one shredding my wings, and I cling to that white tether like her life fucking depends on it.

"She belongs with *us*, not with a father who failed to protect her. You can take that thought with you to the grave."

Edom tugs the ring, grinding iron against bone, curling my body forward until I'm face-planting the earth. "Don't underestimate me. I've waited *years* for her, and I'll get what I want, Drake. One way or another."

I growl into the hard-packed ground kissing my cheek with unpassionate vigour. "You have no right to call her your daughter. You've given her nothing but a world that fucked her until she was broken. You are no father. You are no man. You're a pathetic shadow of someone who was once great."

He jerks my wings, making me scream. "Run your mouth again, boy, and I'll order Kyro to hunt that wee golden drako and fry her up for his midmorning snack. He's quite partial to the taste of his own kind."

My beast cuts free and we buck and heave and roar.

Nobody threatens my fucking baby.

Edom smiles, stretching his wings to their full, overwhelming breadth. "There he is ..."

"*I'm going to rip your fucking wings off!*"

The invisible hand squeezes our neck.

Hard.

From my spot in the shadows, I'm aware of a terrible pressure behind our eyes as though our brain is about to erupt through the sockets ...

"I'd *love* to see you try."

He grabs the iron ring, tears a hole in the Bright, and drags us far away from the ghost of Dell's tortured scent.

CHAPTER TWO
DELL

A deep, raspy roar pries me from a cold, dark room that smells like ancient death ...

My eyes snap open, my heart a hammer in my chest.

A nightmare, Dell. It was just a terrible nightmare.

I draw in a rattling half breath, wincing when a bolt of pain strikes my ribcage, realising I should have stayed asleep as the events of the last few days come surging back ...

I whimper.

Dark room.

Probing things.

Blood on my hands.

Nope. Fuck no.

I slam *everything* deep in a shadowy corner so it's not right in my fucking face, and frantically check my mate tethers, breathing a shallow sigh when I find the gold and silver threads still clinging to my heart ...

I really should have collected the full set ... now I'm going to be imagining the worst until I see for myself they're all okay; that the attack was only aimed at *me*.

My hand throbs a deep, dull ache, and I haul it up,

recalling the grossly oversized spider that used me as a pin cushion. The wound slowly comes into focus—a pustular bite oozing green, pungent fluid ...

"*Dammit*," I croak, crinkling my nose. It's definitely infected, or ... something.

I try to roll up and out of the dense mud and let out a pitchy wail when I disturb my wings' despondent coma. I give my snoozing beast a prod, but she just yawns and bats my hand away with a lethargic paw.

Lazy bitch. She's only ever around when it suits her. Too bad if I need some motherfucking pain relief.

Sinking back, I roll my head to the side, seeing a roaring waterfall I must have fallen down. Fuck, I'm surprised I'm still breathing. I try to spot its turbulent beginning through the shifting mist and glimpse the sky—a fleeting gift of vibrant colour ...

Dawn.

Aero ...

A sob bubbles out of me and the scabs across my breasts split, plaguing the air with a coppery tang ...

Pull yourself together, Dell. You can fall apart when you're dead.

Gathering my remaining scraps of energy, I manage to haul my mangled wings behind me like laden fishing nets and plunge my face into the river—drawing greedy sips of crisp, clean water. I submerge my festering hand and agitate it, ignoring my reflection—too afraid I'll see a fractured face with real cracks and missing pieces.

I crank myself into a wobbly kneel and splash my mud-caked body until the grime is gone, revealing a maze of fermenting lesions ...

Fucking ... shit. Definitely should have stayed asleep.

If I've learnt anything from my Sun Gods and their ... *tough loving*, it's that I can't leave filthy wounds to fester.

Unfortunately.

Not wanting to see more of the devastation carved across my body—over my fucking *scar*—I stab my gaze down river and get to work scrubbing the caps off my wounds. Grinding down screams, I put extra elbow grease into the brand on my arse while picturing my Gods diving into this dirty ditch and wrapping me up in their strong arms ...

They don't see the residue of rape and torture on my skin, because it's not there.

They don't see it in my eyes.

They don't see me as weak or a victim, and they certainly don't see the blood on my hands.

I grit my teeth and scrub an open wound, blind to the raw, pink flesh warming my hand. Roiling power simmers in my gut—a smouldering pit that has its own violent pulse—watched over by a beast who seems to have the conscience of a stick.

I remember the moment she *poofed* those men, her terrible cock-ligraphy, and the feel of Feather Plunger's colon dragging through our fingers ...

I almost hurl.

What happened in that dungeon broke what little innocence I had left. I became a *monster* ... much like the one I'd seen in the man who killed my mother.

The tears come quietly, burning my cheeks.

I'm not like him.

I can't be. This world needs to be fixed, not fucking *misted*.

My hand falls and I shudder, rolling my head to the side. I peek at the filthy remnants of my wings ... and instantly regret it.

Dammit.

My moody Night God isn't going to think they're so gorgeous anymore. All that's left is long, exposed bones draped with patches of gnarled flesh and spindly feathers. They're ruined, my feathery G-spots are ... *gone*, and I doubt I have the tendons left to keep them from dragging around ... through the dirt ... while they get infected ... no. That won't do at all.

Looks like we're doing this the organic way.

I wiggle my fingers and lift my shirt, but my vagina's giving me a grumpy-old-man face and I immediately cover her up again.

Guess that's a no.

I sigh and glance around, looking for clues to discern my location. Perhaps if I knew where I was I'd be able to find a way back to my Gods. Even find a spot to rest for a few days so my body has a chance to ... not look so mangled when we reunite.

Probably wise.

The waterfall crashes into a turbulent pool, feeding a river that cleaves the land in two. Coconut trees hang from muddy banks that carve up and disappear into low-hanging fog ...

I've never seen this place in my life, which is hardly surprising since I spent most of it in a whore house.

I stand and take two agonising steps before something *whines* at me, and I scan the muddy bank ...

A long, slimy thing catches my eye. "*Weeeehhhhhhhhh.*"

Well, fuck me. There's a baby penis serpent stranded in the mud—its tiny dickhead waving back and forth.

The small ones are a lot less intimidating.

I lower into a stiff kneel, reaching out to stroke the little guy who's longer than my forearm but nowhere near as girthy. He peers up at me with wide eyes and emits another sharp plea.

I lay my hand flat in the mud. "You're a bit far from home, aren't you wee man?"

He slithers onto my palm and curls into a tight ball.

Ahh ...

"You're a cute cock, but I can't take you with me, buddy."

He tucks his head into a penis ball and starts to ... *purr?*

Great.

Just great.

My uterus never anticipated becoming a mother at the tender age of ... well, zero. And me? I've already got my hands full of Godly cocks. Can I really add this willy to the mix and give him all the affection he deserves? What if I forget to feed him and he eats one of my Gods?

No. That just won't do at all.

I submerge my hand in the water, letting it flow over my fingers invitingly, but the squiggly fucker slithers up my arm and curls around my neck.

Actually, he's quite an efficient neck warmer.

Sighing, I resign myself to the fact that I've obtained another cock. "How am I going to keep you lubricated, Little Willy? I don't know about you, but in my experience a dry penis is never a good thing."

No answer.

Not sure why I was expecting one, I'm talking to a fucking penis serpent.

I scan my surroundings, searching for something I can use as a pail, and spot a coconut shell in the mud with a hole large enough for Willy to slither into. I fill it up, cradle it close to my chest, and my little diddle slips in without hesitation—his purr making the shell vibrate.

"Look at that, Willy! That coco-cunt fits you perfectly."

I'm excelling at this mother shit.

I inch up the embankment, using my free hand to latch onto weeds and rocks while bolts of blinding pain threaten to send me rolling back down the hill. The fog thickens, a suffocating blanket that muddies my vision and chills me to the bone, but I keep climbing—reopening wounds, dirtying the ones I just cleaned.

The world opens up and I crest the rise, discovering a vast, bronze desert stretched all the way to the horizon …

Well … fuck me. Perhaps it's the one near Grueling?

Guess there's no time like the present to make a run, or in my case a half-naked hobble for the East. Too bad I have the physical stamina of a slug unless I'm lying on my back with my legs spread.

I draw a deep, rattling breath and drop my internal walls, then take a shaky step towards the sandy sea ahead ...

I've threatened to run to the East plenty of times over the past couple of months. Hopefully my Gods were paying attention.

CHAPTER THREE
DELL

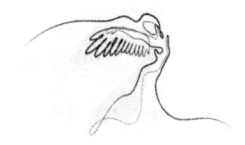

The dawn kaleidoscope presses down on me like a curse, every step through this barren wasteland seeming to bring me closer to a sandy grave.

Licking my parched, cracked lips, I study a giant drako skeleton—its head the size of a house, ribcage clawing at the sand.

These decaying beasts litter the desert like old thoughts cast aside; some missing large chunks of skull as though something much bigger than a spear-wielding Fae brought them down.

Thinking of Sap, I realise with a flip of my queasy stomach that *this* one must have been ancient to have grown so large ...

Nothing is safe.

I crumble against a canine the size of a small tree, the knowledge that something has happened to Sol sitting like a rock in my stomach.

I just need to know they're okay.

He can't take them from me, too.

My fucking eyes start to leak again—a serious waste of

resources I really can't afford right now. Not when I haven't seen water in ... a very long time. I tug Willy's home against my chest, ignoring the persistent throb of my oozing hand, allotting myself a few minutes to regain my strength ...

Just a few minutes. Then I'll pull myself together and carry on.

I wake with a start to a turbulent, bitter wind battering me while tiny teeth nibble on my clavicle. "You couldn't wait until after I'm dead?"

Willy peers up at me through slitted eyes and emits a pitiful whine.

"*Weeehhhhhhhhh.*"

In all my years, I've never known a penis to be so high maintenance.

I close my eyes to the wind and the grit, but he does it again though this time those tiny teeth go all the way through to the bone ...

This dick.

"Don't bite your Mumma, Little Willy! I raised you better than that!"

I swear the fucker cocks a penis serpent brow.

What a brat. I'm about to send him back into his coco-cunt to think about what he's done when I catch movement in my peripheral, dragging my lethargic gaze north ...

A winged creature is darting around in the distance.

I blink, trying to focus through a haze of fatigue, imagining I'm seeing honey wings tinged with auburn, pink, orange ...

My heart stops.

Aero?

No, it can't be ... Aero wouldn't fly here; he'd tear through the Bright like the fancy bastard he is.

Damn. I always thought my colourful imagination was my saviour, but now it's just being cruel.

Wait ...

The pretty mirage moves closer, a muscular form coming into focus ...

Those rosy, ochre wings aren't just *dipped* in the morning glow ... they're *dawn incarnate*.

Aero.

He's okay.

I attempt to stand but succeed only in flopping around with my poor wings crumpled beneath me.

He turns one way, then another while I try to remind my limbs how to function properly.

"Aero!" I rasp, managing to prop myself against the canine. "Aero, I'm over here!"

Wow, he's not going to hear that. I can barely hear that.

'I'm over here!' I shout internally, and it's not until he starts flying in confused circles that I notice I wasn't very specific with my directions. *'Cold, warm, much warmer! Cold again ...'*

He tosses his hands up, then turns and soars in the *opposite direction* ... towards another contingent of dead drako skeletons.

I groan.

'Freezing. Your balls have just turned into ice cubes.'

I swear I hear him roar.

He hovers, scans the horizon, and finally looks my way ...

'Hot! Scalding! Your dick is on fire!'

Those massive, magnificent wings beat at full strength as he blazes through the sky ...

And here I was thinking men weren't good at following directions.

My wings pry themselves free and flap around in a

valiant attempt at being joyful, even as I let out a sob that cleaves my chest right open.

He's coming for me.

There's a thunderous clap, a searing flash of light, and Willy darts right back into his coco-cunt with a sharp *weeehhhhh*.

The harsh light bleeds away, and I stare in horror at the colossal pair of alabaster wings, the shock of white hair, and the cruel stance of a monster hovering in Aero's path.

My father.

My throat constricts, my heart thrashing in my chest like a caged criminal. It's been nineteen years since I watched that man slice my mother's throat open. Nineteen years since I saw the depthless hollow of his eyes ...

The two men hover, Aero's bearing strong as he faces the man who haunts my twisted mind with a reign of terror. Tears seem to gouge my cheeks, but I'm not crying for myself ...

I'm crying for my Dawn God.

I prod my beast, but she's flat and lethargic with barely enough energy to lift her feral head. She snarls, then whimpers, and my sandy wings come to rest around me ...

Hiding me.

"*No*," I rasp, barely managing to part frayed feathers with gnarled fingers so I can stare out at the scene unfolding ...

I'm four years old again, peering through the crack in the door.

Small.

Powerless.

'*Go, Aero!*' I'm giving him the only thing I have to give right now ...

Permission to flee.

Because I can't go through this again. I can't.

'*Get away!*'

Aero claws at his throat, and my heart plummets when he drops several feet, a groan escaping my split lips. My beast unravels on shaky legs—spine curved, teeth bared.

It seems the bitch is back and ready to maul some white feathers, even if it drains us entirely ... and I'm all in.

"That's it, Beasty. Let's do this."

Our canines lengthen and my pain fades until it's nothing but a dull ache. Even my tender heart becomes a stone in my chest as I slip into the shadows, waiting for her to protect what's *ours*.

I'm expecting her to go all savage and roar like the monster she is.

I'm expecting her to reach past me and haul a great cauldron of fiery lava to the surface with her.

She doesn't.

She lifts our trembling hand, reaching for our choking Dawn God through our feathery camouflage, then lets it fall back to our lap ...

My mouth drops open and I choke on a wisp of shadow.

That's it?

That's all you've got?

She's unwilling to give what we have left and put an end to the man who's responsible for letting this world rot. Once again, I'm failing someone I love.

But this time it's not because I'm powerless ...

It's because my beast is a *coward*.

The thought knifes me in the chest.

I ignore her keening mewls, dragging her back by the tail as Edom moves closer to my Dawn God. "*No!*" I rasp, but my rusty whisper is torn from my lips by the howling wind.

And then I'm alone with nothing but a fading flash of bright light that shatters my will to survive.

My head flops to the side, the pain comes slicing back,

and I drift into a darkness that threatens to swallow me whole.

Featherlight fingers dance across my skin, my hair, my wings ...

I see a blur of moving figures through a sliver of sight. Hear the soft murmur of female voices.

My teeth feel like they might break apart against each other.

I'm so cold.

My eyes close.

"Gently ..."

Someone's trying to tuck my wings behind me, but the spindly things are hugging me too tightly.

"They won't budge. Can we carry her like that?"

"We have no choice. We can't leave her ... she'll die."

If I had the energy, I'd tell them not to waste their time. I'd tell them I'm already too far gone.

Everything hurts.

I feel like all my organs were ripped out of my chest, put through a meat grinder, then stuffed back inside me with careless hands.

A dry, grating moan fights its way out of me.

"Shhh," a warm voice coos. "We've got you now. We'll take care of you."

Their tender touches are too soft; their skin too supple.

I want to be wrapped in big silver wings. I want my hurts to be soothed by a man with sapphire eyes and a seductive smile that pretends to be intact. I want my tears to be kissed away by pillowy lips that leave a chaser of citrus and sage. I want to weave my fingers into flaxen locks while a gruff voice tells me everything's going to be okay ... even though some innate part of me is screaming that it's not going to be okay at all.

That something is very, very wrong.

A wetness dribbles onto my lips. "Open up, honey. Come on, you're not dead yet."

I am.

I fucking am.

Fingers pry my mouth open and water trickles down my throat. I gag, then choke it back. "There you go. That's it, honey. You're okay ..."

I'm not. I don't deserve this. I want to tell them to leave me here ... that I've failed.

Again.

I want to climb onto my knees and apologise, to beg for their forgiveness, because I can't be what they need me to be.

My wings hug me tighter.

"I've never seen wings behave that way ..."

"I have," a distant, brittle voice states, and something about the way she says it has me prying my eyes open, trying to scan the hazy, distorted figures.

A damp cloth soothes my brow. "Rest, honey. You need rest."

I close my eyes, feeling myself drift, vaguely aware of Willy's coco-cunt being lifted off my chest. "No!"

"You can't carr—" there's a jarring squeal before something *thwacks* onto the ground next to me. "The coconut *bit* me!"

"Wehhhhhhh!"

"I don't think it was the coconut, Lucy ..."

My territorial peen slithers up my arm and coils around my neck as I start to drift towards the beckoning void of silence, lulled by the gentle sway of our journey.

It feels like I'm floating, but I know that's not the case ...

People are carrying me because my body's too broken to carry itself.

As I drift in and out of consciousness, I'm vaguely aware of the glowing sky and clouds etched in pink. I'm haunted by black, unforgiving eyes and the crushing knowledge that it's *still fucking dawn.*

My father has my Gods ...

I failed them.

CHAPTER FOUR
DELL

Minutes, hours, days drip by as I follow the endless corridor; the darkness broken only by sparse orbs illuminating pockets of the snaking passageway.

Honestly, I have no idea how I got here ... but the deeper I go, the closer I feel to *him*.

Long, lethal talons slash my insides, my entire body shuddering as I fight to keep my beast contained. She doesn't understand why I'm taking so long to find him—thinks she can do a better job.

She might be right, but she's untrustworthy.

A coward.

She's the reason we lost Aero in the first place.

My nostrils flare as a familiar scent cuts through the dead air, and every muscle in my body goes taut. "Aero ... are you here?"

Nobody answers, just my desperate echo followed by more aching silence.

I heave a strangled sob, suffocating under the sense of oblivion, when I'm tossed against the pillow of my internal shadows like a sack of grain. I'm still choking on shock as my beast sprints into the cold, dark unknown, cutting our feet on broken cobbles.

I leap forward and snarl at her, but she just bats me into another shadow with a well-aimed kick to the tit.

What a bitch.

Our foot catches on something and we're thrown forward, our body scraping along the ground. Beasty glances over our shoulder, seeing a shard of peach and purple light shooting out of the ground from the hole we just created ...

Our nostrils flare.

Aero.

She rips at it with bare fingers, tearing off fist-sized pieces of rock and tossing them aside. More light gushes through the expanding hole, and she tips us forward, diving into it like she does everything else ...

Thoughtlessly.

We plummet towards an imminent death, and my beast hightails it back to her shadow nook with a smirk on her face, leaving me no other choice but to take the motherfucking reins.

I scream, flailing through a myriad of peach, purple, and orange mist, landing on a cushion of clouds that drag me into the subtle warmth of their sun-kissed belly.

Cradling me.

All I can smell is dew, virgin air, and the zesty spark of a new day. The morning sun caresses my face, making my skin prickle ...

Dawn.

The most beautiful dawn I've ever seen.

But it's not like I'm witnessing it from the edge of a cliff—watching it break across the horizon and spill out to meet me.

I'm in the heart of it, *captured* by it, feeling it pulse all around me.

I leap up and spin, a smile splitting my face. Then I see *him*—looking at me with wide eyes and a face drawn of colour, his stretched wings almost blending with our scenery ...

He's not breathing.

His face is stone.

Looking at him hurts.

"Aero ..." I whisper, and his features shatter, making my bottom lip wobble and my knees give way.

He catches my weight, crushing me against him, his body all hard heat and unyielding strength. There's the sound of shuffling feathers before a deeper sense of safety settles around me ...

"How are you even *here?*" he rasps, crushing me with a kiss before I have the chance to respond—an urgent clash of teeth and tongues.

I claw his shirt, drawing closer, wishing I could bury myself inside his heart ...

Stay here forever.

Aero breaks our kiss, holding my face like a prayer while he looks down on me like I'm the answer to every question he's ever asked. His amber eyes consume me, nurture me; make me feel like I've never truly been *seen* before this very moment ...

But it's like being presented with a beautiful rose only to have the thorny stem twist around my heart and cut deep into the fragile flesh.

Because deep down, I know this isn't real.

That I'm lying somewhere, lost and broken, while my dreams taunt me with something that seems so utterly unobtainable.

He doesn't argue; doesn't tell me I'm wrong.

His gaze turns sad as I clench my eyes shut, feeling warm tears dart down my cheeks ...

I lean forward and rub my face on his shirt. I'm not sure when I became so emotionally unstable but, hell, I think I prefer the Dell who couldn't cry. Her vagina had a particularly foul mouth but at least her eyes weren't leaky.

"I don't know what to do, Dream Aero."

"Yes you do. You don't give up," he growls with a deadly tone that makes me shiver. "You keep fighting, just like you always have."

"Easy for you to say, you're a pretty figment of my imagination. A feathery dream that smells good."

"Who's to say I'm a dream?" he asks, wearing a frown that's so indignant I roll my fucking eyes. "Don't roll your eyes at me, or I'll fold you over my knee and give that pussy something to blush about."

I open my mouth, then close it, squeezing my thighs together to stifle the sound of my mewling vagina.

He thrusts his hands into my hair and grips tight, anchoring me against him—the action making my beast writhe and squirm and snarl for release.

She loves it when we're handled like we're unbreakable.

"Let her out." His words strike my face and I flinch, feeling the effect of his request pressing down on my chest.

He has no idea what he's asking for.

"No. She might hurt you."

I have no interest in seeing Dream Aero go *poof*. I doubt that's a vision I could recover from.

His eyes spark, and in one swift movement he has me sprawled in a cloud, caught between the cushy, pink fluff and his powerful dream-body. Those glorious wings palp, stirring the mist into a swirl of colour and light. "I can handle her."

I try to make myself smaller—consider digging through the clouds so I can hide from my sins.

He doesn't get it. She's a killer.

Aero frowns.

His hand cups the side of my face, astute eyes scouring me until I'm raw from his scrutiny. "You're not like him, Dell. You're not."

My lungs snag.

Fuck.

I feel like he just unwrapped me, only to discover my withered soul inside.

"What if I'm worse?" I whisper, the brittle words laced with my deepest fears which are so hideously exposed.

"You're not the villain, Dell."

Perhaps not. But that same darkness plagues me, I can feel it. The potential to unravel.

"I'm not the hero, either. Heroes aren't built from twisted minds and broken pieces. Heroes don't spawn from dark places that threaten to swallow you whole."

Aero tucks a flossy curl behind my ear. "Well, perhaps they should ..."

He sounds so sure of me.

"I am sure of you," he growls, his eyes the blazing orbs of a new day, and I watch him pluck a long, handsome feather from his sleek collection. It's got a perfectly tapered point, and when light catches on the different angles, it shifts from soft pink to a deep, vivid orange.

"Nice feather ..."

"You like that?"

I really do.

His eyes glimmer as he brings it to my lips and paints the rise and fall of my cupid's bow with the silky tip. The sensation fills my lungs with hot breath, and my beast arches her back like a cat lazing in the midmorning sun ...

"Let her come out and play," he whispers while scrawling silent secrets over my cheek. There's a languid lilt to his tone which makes my spine curl—pressing my hips closer to the God hovering over me.

"Why, Dream Aero?" My words are soft like the flick of his feather dancing over the canvas of my skin; over my lips, my chin, down the line of my throat ... leaving a trail of pebbly skin.

He tilts my head to the side, drags the feather down the length of my neck, then swirls it over the artery screaming to be bitten into ... before he speaks in a voice that's not entirely his own. "Because I want to make her fucking *purr*."

I quiver from the tips of my toes to my fluttering lashes and a soft sound of surrender falls from my lips ...

Beasty lunges, dissolving all our lazy lust. She wraps our limbs around his waist, growling into his mouth while he tames her with his tongue.

His hands.

His hips.

"There's my girl," he grates out, his voice a crushed melody of dark, wicked things that punctuate our kiss. He holds our wrists above our head with a hand reminiscent of a big, violent paw, and tears our shift straight down the middle.

He pulls back, a smug look dragging across his face as he sinks a canine deep into the flesh of his lower lip. A messy ribbon of peach, orange, yellow, and purple dribbles from the wound, down his chin, and drips onto the swell of our breast ...

Our nostrils flare, scenting a medley of springtime and crisp morning air.

"Now, be a good girl and stay still," he murmurs, dragging the tip of his feather through the pretty colours pouring from his self-inflicted damage. Twin onyx orbs pin us in place while he decorates our nipple with vibrant circles—luring it into a hardened peak that aches to be nipped and sucked.

The strokes don't feel surface level ... they're *inside* us, dancing along our nerves and setting us on fire. The feather is flicked along our ribs; each stroke edging lower and lower. He swirls the tip around our belly button, the sensation digging deep into our flesh, coiling around our womb.

It's delicious, aching, exquisite ... and our hips buck as our knees spread of their own accord.

We need *more.*

A throaty sound spills from his lips while that feather paints a line down the inside of our thigh. We spread our legs further, our hips rolling in search of phantom friction ...

"More," we berate, feeling the sharp tips of our canines prickle our chin.

"Beautiful, greedy thing ..." He flicks the feather up, up, up ... before tickling the edge of our panty line.

Teasing.

Taunting.

Aero groans, finally focusing on the coil of nerves that has its own heartbeat, drawing tight circles that stir our insides.

We whine, the torturous heat flooding our core ...

But it's not enough.

We want him to tear the barrier of our panties away. We want his blood dribbling down our throat, coating our insides. We want to feel his flesh yield to our bite as he gives himself to us entirely ...

"You want me, baby?" He leans in and flicks his tongue over the barbed tip of our canine. "Then fucking *take* me."

We strike with a snarl, capturing his bottom lip and biting

down. Warm blood spills into our mouth and Aero's eyes flash with unveiled euphoria. His liquid-life is gulped back, painting everything in its path with the light of a brand-new day ...

There is nowhere to hide.

He's *everywhere*.

He's stitching us up from the inside, airbrushing our seams ... leaving us hanging on the edge of a dream-blowing orgasm that will probably make our nightmares blush.

We drop his lip and our hands are set free as he pushes our hair aside—exposing our carotid that's pumping hard, delicious beats. "How did you find me, Dell?"

The question is spoken by a quivering voice I recognise ...

Aero.

Not his beast.

That feather flicks against my nub and I wrangle my own inner minx, dodging slashing paws and snappy teeth. "I ... I didn't. My cock-biting ... beast ... did ..."

"And why did she do that?" His words are fractured, the feather pausing—an unspoken demand.

I'm not getting this orgasm until I answer his dream-riddle.

My shackled beast slams her response down our mental link, and panic explodes in my stomach.

What if he doesn't feel the same way?

He snarls and I flinch, swallowing the lump in my throat. "Dell, *answer me*."

Shit. Shit. Shit.

This is happening.

"Because she *loves you*," I yell with my eyes squeezed shut, buffering myself from the threat of rejection ...

The silence is a chasm between us for three entire heart-beats before Aero drags the spine of his feather up the length of my core—a taunting lick that holds no heat, but somehow sets me on fire.

My body curls and I thrust my breasts skyward.

"And you?" he asks, his voice rusty as he dips into the crook of my neck, the tips of his canines making dimples in my flesh ...

My breath catches.

"Do it ..." I whisper, craning, giving him a stretched canvas.

"Do *you* love me, Dell? I'll only have you if I can have every part of you." He applies more pressure and every drop of blood seems to rush to the spot, as if eager to spill out and meet him. "All of *her* ..." My nipple is pinched and I cry out, vibrating. "Fucking *everything* ..." He does it again, in tandem with a vigorous feather swirl that tips me over that edge; a dominant wave of warmth tearing through me as my pulse thumps through my pussy ...

"Yes! I fucking love you!" I cry, and he strikes—my entire body jerking as he sinks his teeth into my flesh, emitting a low rumble while he draws and draws and draws ...

A thrumming sensation spreads through me, my beast purring like a sated lioness while a myriad of morning colours dance across my vision. The roots of an auburn tether dig into my heart, magnetising into every fibre of my being, and I gasp as if it's the first full breath I've ever taken ...

As if I just slipped out of the motherfucking *womb*.

What the fu—

He laps at the two puncture wounds on my neck, then kisses the hurt and lifts his head—drowning me in ochre eyes half hidden behind a flop of auburn hair.

A pearly shimmer is smeared across his lips and chin, blending with the peach, purple, pin—

Oh, fuck.

It's not my actual blood he's devouring like a starved animal ...

It's my fucking *essence*.

This is real. This is happening.

Aero just mated with my fucking *soul*.

He gives me a coy smile that makes the dawn spectre behind him look dull in comparison. *"You're mine."*

CHAPTER FIVE
DELL

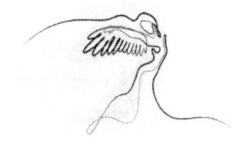

He's alive.
He's safe ... ish.

I release a shuddering sigh and pry my eyes open, enjoying three seconds of post-orgasmic bliss before I realise I'm lying on a makeshift bed in the middle of a crowded room, surrounded by wide-eyed women on their knees ... *praying.*

To me.

My sheets are damp, it smells like sex, and I'm still trembling from my soulgasm. I realise with absolute horror that everyone just watched me writhe in pleasure while Aero tickled my dew flaps with a feather.

"Hi," I croak, trying to ignore the overpowering scent of my climactic release.

Someone clears their throat.

My cheeks heat.

I'm used to getting off with a crowd of witnesses but this ... this is some next level shit. I feel like I just peed all over their deity.

Pretending my vagina isn't still clenching around sweet

fuck all, I glance around with feigned interest, taking note of every minor detail in an effort to avoid making eye contact with anyone.

The room seems to be carved from solid timber with tiny windows pricked in the undulating amber wood ...

I'm inside the hollowed belly of a *tree*.

"I think I made it to the East," I mutter, taking a punt to brave the sea of onlookers, hardly believing my eyes when I recognise a few faces from Kroe's ...

One I know *very* well—framed with a pixie cut of burnished locks that suit her delicate features.

Alert, healthy eyes meet mine and I almost forget how to breathe. *"Leila ..."*

She jolts like I just slapped her, then glances down my body. I follow the trail over my tattered wing blanket ... and close my eyes.

Fuck.

That's right. I look like I've been put through a meat grinder.

I exhale my angst, coming to terms with the fact that I have an entourage of spectators looking at my white, raggedy wings. No wonder they were *praying*. They probably think I'm the sum of their vaginal liberation.

Sol's going to be *so* pissed when he finds out my wings have been flaunting themselves in front of a crowd like common hussies ...

Thoughts of my Day God have me checking my mate tethers, and I almost whimper with relief when I find them all intact. My heart swells when I see the confirmation of my brand-new Aero link—a semi-boner that will require some in-person petting to reach full mast.

I narrow my internal gaze ...

Drake's tether is thin and wispy, not pulsing with its usual lustre, and my beast snarls from her place coiled next to it.

My golden God is hurting.

And Kal? I have no tether for him. Nothing to indicate whether he's okay or not.

A deep groan escapes me and I try to sit up, but my cobweb wings refuse to unravel and my bandaged hand becomes burdened with a wild, excruciating throb.

I hiss and hands are upon me, stabilising me, perching me against straw-filled sacks. "You need to take it easy, milady."

"Don't *milady* me, Leila. I'm still the same person." I glance sideways, seeing Willy's coco-cunt discarded on the side table next to a bowl of water. "*Oh no* ... has anyone seen my dick?"

Someone in the back clears their throat. "Risa took him outside the moment you started—"

I flap my hand around, "No need to finish that sentence."

An older lady with greying hair and a wiggly spine ushers everyone out the door and into the blushing forest. Many are missing body parts, but their eyes are sharp with determination—no longer hollow shells pinned to painted faces.

These women have *hope*.

The elderly lady closes the door and steps into a shaft of light, igniting my memory and my heart as I recognise the younger women beneath the unfamiliar wrinkles.

"*Marion*," I cry and her features contort.

Hers was the only friendly face I saw for *years*. My only friend in that bland room, aside from the darkness of my own thoughts.

She tended my wounds, gave me herbs that helped me sleep through the nightmares. She soothed my vulnerable, aching soul ...

Then, she disappeared.

Marion drops to the bed and tugs me to her ample bosom, taming my hair in smooth strokes just like she did when nobody was watching through the grate in the door.

They were quiet moments that tried to wipe Kroe's insidious touch from my body, and though I never asked for the hugs, she must have known I needed them.

"Adeline," she soothes, rocking us back and forth while I break apart.

I thought she died. I *mourned* her ...

Blamed myself.

Wondered why I poison all the people I love.

I peer up, looking into pity-filled eyes framed with the markings of a hard life.

"How?"

How is she still alive?

She offers me a soft smile that's a pin through my heart. I lean back and she sighs, allowing me to twist away.

"Where to start ..." She smooths her apron patched with little pockets, and I can see that her hands are shaking. "I was at the markets collecting supplies for Kroe when a heavily pregnant breeder approached me; said her master was a brutal man who killed her last baby because it was female."

I swallow the lump in my throat, hating the tremble in my shoulders. "Go on ..."

"She was a wee frightened thing. Only a babe herself and carrying triplets she'd dreamt were female. The rest happened so fast. An elderly woman heard our conversation and dared hide us in a fishing crate. We were loaded onto a barge and jumped free once we hit the eastern seas and drew close enough to land."

I can barely breathe through the dull ache in my chest that's threatening to cleave me in two. It must show because Marion shakes her head, the creases around her eyes deepening. "She couldn't birth and care for them on her own, child. And not many people live long enough to gather my knowledge of herbs."

I nod my understanding, feeling more like a child than a

woman as old scars rise to the surface. "But you left me ... alone with that monster."

My words are monotone, devoid of the emotion screaming for release. I know they're selfish thoughts, selfish words, and I understand why she did it ... but it doesn't stem the pain.

I really needed those hugs.

She shakes her head, studying my wings. "No, Adeline. I could see it, even then. Something hibernating beneath your skin. You weren't alone. Hiding from yourself perhaps ... but never alone."

My eyes widen and I rear back. "You ... you *knew?*"

I swear there's an ocean of pity in her eyes. "No. Not this ... *these*. I just knew there was more to you, child. The burn marks on your wee back were too convenient. I could tell someone had gone to great lengths to protect you as a babe." She brushes her thumb across my cheek, giving me a sad smile that doesn't reach her eyes. "Kroe didn't keep you in that dark hole because you were breeder material. He kept you there because he knew you were something *more*. Something *special*. Even at such a wee age you had the fight of a caged queen."

I flash my teeth, I can't fucking help it.

I don't want to be associated with that man.

My father.

"I am no queen."

"Then what are these?" Marion gestures to my wings with a weathered hand.

I look her square in the eye and prepare to slap her with the truth I've been hiding from for far too long. "The wings that got my mother killed."

My voice cracks on the last word and Marion's chin falls to her chest—a sign of respect for their fallen Queen who lost her life because I couldn't control my wings.

Because all I could do was stand there and *watch*.

I snatch the bowl of water from my bedside table and gulp the cool liquid back, feeling the heat of Marion's gaze trained to my trembling hand. I try to place the empty bowl on the table top, but send it clattering to the ground; the commotion no doubt the cause of Leila storming back through the door on high alert.

She stops by the side of the bed, and I focus all my attention on the woman who risked everything to rescue our girls. "If I stay, these wings are a death sentence for your sister. For every single one of your friends."

"Your friends, too."

"How can you say that, Leila? You lost your *hands* because of me."

She raises what were once stubs, now fitted with curious looking prosthetics; one a sawing device, the other a lethal looking fork.

Something tells me any man who tried to give her an unsanctioned dicking these days would end up, well ... sans the ability to procreate.

My vagina claps her hands.

"Others here are far worse off than me," Leila states with a sense of finality.

"Which strengthens my point."

Her ardent gaze burns like the brand on my arse. "It led me to you, didn't it?"

Fucking hell. I need to get out of here before they start sacrificing virgins in my name.

I push my legs off the side of the bed, the movement tugging my scabs at odd angles.

"I'd forgotten how stubborn you are," Leila mumbles as I try to stand. My legs crumble and I fall back to the mattress in a feathery heap. Pain lances every inch of my skin and the air becomes thick with a metallic tang.

"My legs aren't working," I snarl, riding the wave of pain.

"That's because you've been out for three weeks," Marion says on a deep sigh, filling a wooden bowl with water from a bucket by the door.

I almost choke.

Three.

Fucking.

Weeks?

The world burns in perpetual dawn, and I take an extended *nap*. I swear to shit, this is the last time I fall into a coma while my loved ones get tortured, brutalised, or killed.

Some heir to the throne I am.

Marion drops a piece of cloth in the bowl and sits on the bed. "The bite, I haven't worked out what sort of spider it's from, but I've been able to slow the spread of poison. I think it's stemming your ability to heal properly."

I glance at my bandaged hand pulsing with a fiery heartbeat ...

"We've been feeding you soup in small increments as you fevered in and out of consciousness, and changing your sheets thrice daily," Leila interjects.

"That's just a kind way of saying I've been pissing myself," I mumble, trying to come to terms with the fact that I'm stuck here until I can move on my own.

Three fucking weeks. My captive Sun Gods probably think I've abandoned them.

Marion pinches my chin, snaring my attention. "It's nothing to be ashamed of. When they found you in the desert, you were half dead. You took a beating, child."

I took several, actually. But she doesn't need to know that.

"Bite or no," I grind out, "my other wounds should be healing faster than this." I've never healed this slow in my entire fucked up existence.

"Tha—"

Leila's silenced by a sharp glare from Marion. Blushing, she excuses herself and leaves the room, feigning some excuse about needing to shine her fork.

"What was that about?"

Marion gives me a tight-lipped frown and eases me back, shifting some of the straw sacks to the floor to give me room.

I sigh, trying to rub the ache from my chest. "I can't just lie around, Marion. I need to build my legs up again. I have shit to do."

Gods to rescue.

"You need to heal first. I have guards stationed at your door, so don't get it in your head to leave until you're well enough to use your wings."

I think back to my rash attempts at flying, and aside from ending up splattered across Kal's juicy abdominals, both yielded pretty unsatisfactory results.

"I don't know how to use them," I murmur, and Marion raises a brow.

"You've never flown?"

"Never had the chance when I was little, then I lost my wings. I haven't had them back long enough to learn."

The skin around her mouth tightens and she gets to work assessing my wounds, applying a green balm to my pierced fingertips that almost numbs them entirely.

She doesn't ask how I got my wings back. She doesn't ask how I lost them in the first place.

I appreciate that.

"They're not usually so ... tatty," I mumble, and they wilt ...

A boulder of guilt lands on my chest because Kal was right. They *are* sensitive.

"They're *lovely*," Marion states, and the poor things proceed to part, creating an opening so Marion can access my bleeding abdomen.

I close my eyes as she dabs my wounds with a cold cloth,

making me flinch. It's hard to ignore the sting she paints across my lower abdomen—the curls and lines that take me back to a murky place that reeked of death.

The moment they defiled a scar I'd come to *love* ... and can no longer bear to look at.

"You'll be fine, child. You'll see. You just need a wee bit of time to heal."

A response plays on my lips, but I don't want to spit in the face of all the hard work and *prayers* committed to keeping me alive. I certainly don't want to trample on their budding hope. But the truth is, I don't know what will become of me if I lose my mates ...

I have no link connecting me to Kal; Sol and Aero have been captured; Drake's tether is fragile; and I'm *bed-bound*. Once again, all I can do is sit back and watch while the people I love suffer.

It's a recurring cycle that makes me sick to my stomach—makes Beasty pace around a turbulent cauldron of power I have no idea how to control.

But *she* does ...

For all I know, these women could be resuscitating a monster.

Marion plugs my wounds with something that smells like crushed herbs and chicken shit, making me burn for a moment before the flesh turns numb.

If only it could numb my conscience.

I saved some of the women who've found refuge in this place, and now I'm putting them in danger just by being here.

As soon as I'm well enough to walk a reasonable distance without falling tits first into the dirt, I need to leave this place and hunt down my Gods ...

Nobody else will die because they care too much about a broken whore with shredded wings.

CHAPTER SIX
SOL

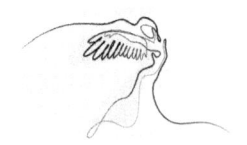

Water drips on my shoulder, sluices down bunched muscle, and traverses the chains twisted around my body—a scalding iron fist that's sucking the light out of me.

My nostrils flare.

The water smells like piss, but it doesn't stop me from twisting my head and opening my mouth. A fat droplet lands on my tongue and I wince, jerking away from the foul liquid that will probably rot my insides.

Aero's eyes snap open, revealing two pools of amber restraint.

Safe.

Controlled.

"Good to have you back," I mutter, jerking my chin to where he's lumped against the wall—the same spot his beast collapsed what seems like days ago.

Aero sighs, rubs his face with a hand caked in blood, and gives me a noncommittal drone; as if he'd rather still be locked inside himself like he has been the past few weeks while his beast raged.

"You slept a long time ..."

He tilts his head, resting it against the cobbled wall. "Still no mention of Kal?" he croaks, and I shake my head.

"He must be out there still. We have to trust he'll find her, then do the right thing and keep her well the fuck away from here."

"He's going to have his hands full ..."

Yes, he fucking is.

She'll be due to go into heat, so she'll be a fucking riot. I won't let myself think about the alternative ... I trust our brother will find her.

Safe.

Alive.

Kal doesn't know how to fail.

A fat rat scuttles across the floor and plucks at a plate of food with greedy claws, nibbling the meal that was meant to be our breakfast, lunch, and dinner.

"Fuck, sorry." Aero pushes off the wall and shoos the rat while Drake mumbles in his sleep from the cell across the hall; his silhouette barely visible in the meagre light.

"Don't apologise," I mutter, scenting the air for any insight into Drake's deteriorating condition. "I still feel sick from the last tray of shit they dished us. Let the vermin feast. If we get desperate, we can eat the fucking rats."

Aero shuffles back to his spot against the wall and jerks his chin in my direction. "They chafing?"

I glance at the chains twisted around my torso. Not for the first time, I wish my beast had set out with a top on that day. "Not as bad if I barely move. Or breathe."

He closes his eyes and sets his fists on bent knees. "Mine absorbed the last of my power a while ago."

I glance at the grisly cuff around his ankle—the flesh there peeled to the bone.

Aero's beast has done more damage to that ankle than the

fucking iron has; thrashing around, almost skinning his foot trying to slip it off.

It wasn't pretty.

The brazen rat creeps out of his hole in the wall, inching towards the plate of sludge that was already mouldy when it was pushed under the gate six hours ago. "My tank is empty, too."

It's the strangest feeling, having a hollow in my chest that used to roil with power. I can't scratch the innate itch to answer the sun's plea to initiate day and it's twisting my insides up.

The world can hold out for a while, but eventually things will get messy out there.

Silence stretches, my attention pinned to the rattling rise and fall of Drake's chest and the rodent fattening himself up —an impending sacrifice to our cause.

My beast coils, poised to pounce, black eyes pinned on the nugget of meat that's unaware of the two predators sharing its cell.

This is so messed up.

"What dragged you out?" I ask, trying to distract myself from the fact that I'm salivating over a fucking rodent.

"I don't want to talk about it."

I study the hard panes of his face, taking in the tense set of his shoulders and the shadows bruising the skin below his eyes.

His beast may be leashed but he's carrying something.

"This is no time to keep secrets, Dawn ..."

"And the walls have ears," he sneers, cutting me a lethal glare.

I snarl.

It's about *her*.

This fucking place. It smells like death and ancient

secrets, but as long as we're here, Dell's safe and hopefully far from this shithole.

I cradle that wispy, white tether, willing it to stay rooted in my heart.

She's not going anywhere.

Heavy footsteps echo down the hall, and my nostrils flare, my wings itching to burst out of my back ...

Aero starts to growl.

"*Easy*, Dawn."

The footsteps draw closer, and the king steps into view wearing simple clothes and a bland expression. His wings are hidden, white hair pushed back from his sharp face. Nostrils flaring, he sweeps his chilling gaze over our cage before turning to unlock Drake's cell.

He kneels, pressing a hand against Drake's forehead, and I try to burst out of my fucking chains. "Don't touch him!"

"He can't die yet, Sol." Edom pulls a tub from the bag slung over his shoulder, unscrews the lid, and smears a potent goo on Drake's wings.

It smells like the bog of shit we threw Dell in, and the memory grates my cold, black heart.

Drake doesn't even shift in his fevered sleep as I watch with narrowed eyes and bated breath, waiting for the fucking token to drop.

Edom finishes, locks the cell door, and leaves us to dwell in the wake of his sadistic game.

"I thought he was lucid for a minute there," Aero drones—a comment I refuse to respond to, choosing instead to close my eyes and listen to Drake mumble in his sleep. "Remember the dinner party? I keep thinking about that night. It wouldn't have taken much to manipula—"

"*Don't.*" I open my eyes in time to watch Aero rear back from the blow of my tone.

"Don't *what?*"

"Don't go there," I hiss, my rage finally sinking its teeth into an outlet. "He's ruined this world, Dawn. *Ruined it.* There is no coming back from that."

"You think I don't know that?" he snarls, branding me with his own wrath. "I was just making conversation, you prickly motherfucker! My mind is a fucking graveyard right now."

I grunt, reining myself. "We owe it to the man we used to know to put him out of his misery."

Aero doesn't argue, because he knows I'm right. Edom's lost within the beast—a casualty of some internal war we weren't privy to.

But we can't kill the callous monster without killing ourselves.

The only hope we have is finding some way to get past his shield and slice his chest up ... and now we have no power. Dell may be rich with untapped potential, but there's no way I'm letting her near that man. Not if I can fucking help it.

I've lost her twice, I won't let it happen again.

I stroke that white tether, willing it to strengthen ...

Willing it to fucking *glow* again.

"And if he gets to her first?" Aero asks, his voice darker than before.

I draw a chest full of air, causing my iron sheathe to press against my skin. I force myself to endure the pain, imagining I'm siphoning it straight from *her*. "You already know the answer to that, Dawn."

I'll die before I let him hurt the woman I love.

CHAPTER SEVEN
DELL

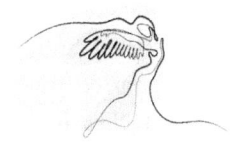

A soft knock makes the dick draped around my neck lift his head in lazy curiosity. "Come in," I call, giving him a stroke.

He nuzzles back down and starts to purr.

I'm going to tell my Sun Gods I want 'Penis Whisperer' added to my official title. They'll either love it or hate it. Sol will be the latter because he's a big fun sponge, but his dick will probably side with me.

I rest my bandaged hand directly over my heart—two parts of me that are throbbing with painful, destructive force …

I need to get the hell out of here.

The door cracks open and soft, blushing light spills through the room. A stout, mousy haired woman shuffles in backwards carrying a tray stacked with food.

Gods, that smells *good*.

I draw a deeper whiff, giving Willy a scratch below the nob when he suddenly swells and cuts off my air supply. I watch the woman's powder blue eyes widen while I claw my throat and gasp …

"*Milady?*"

I wave her off, peel Willy away, and heave a breath into my starved lungs. "Don't worry, it's not the first time a penis has choked me," I grate out, trying to reassure the poor woman. "*Bad Willy.* That is *not* how you treat your Mumma!"

He turns floppy in my hand, then shrivels up like a post-coital slug.

I should have used my safe word.

My visitor clears her throat and lowers the tray to a bedside table made from gnarled tree roots. There are all sorts of colourful goodies stacked high, and the sweet scent of roasted root vegetables makes my stomach rumble.

It also makes me want to ... *vomit*.

"Thanks for the food," I say, swallowing the excess saliva pooling beneath my tongue. "You don't happen to have any meat lying around for my little friend, do you?"

Her eyes widen and she slides back a step. "He's, ahh, what's he doing?"

I follow her line of sight, seeing Willy folding over himself at the edge of the bed. He flicks into the air, exposing rows and rows of pin teeth lining his gaping maw, and lands like a tumbling dickweed before wrapping that deadly cavern around a small, unsuspecting mouse that was tiptoeing across the ground ...

There's a strangled squeak, a dusty quarrel, and a few unfortunate jerks from the mouse's hind legs before Little Willy throws his head back and gulps it down ... leaving nothing but a small, grey tail hanging from his peen slit.

"Well then ..."

The woman gapes, watching Willy work the rather large lump down his body. Surely he's going to choke on that thing? Either that or it's going to take the rest of his life to digest it.

"I, ahh ... just came here to deliver your food, milady. And to check if you need anything?"

"What's your name?" I ask, trying to ignore the muted squeaks coming from Willy's body.

"Manilla." She bows awkwardly, and I repress the urge to cringe.

"Manilla, don't bow for me."

A deep crease forms between her large eyes. "But ... you're a *God*, milady."

So is my father.

The man directly or indirectly responsible for the squiggly scar that runs from her left eyebrow to her cupid's bow.

"Let's try a different tact. Don't bow for me unless I've earned it, okay? I was born like this." I gesture to my frayed wing cocoon with my throbby-hand that feels like it's about to split some seams. "It doesn't mean I *deserve* your respect."

She nods, twisting her hands into the folds of her dress. "Okay ... m-milady."

I sigh, watching her eyes dart to my side table. She takes a large, calculated step around the cock-carnivore trying to digest his meal, then reaches for Willy's coco-cunt propped next to my food tray.

"I need that to keep my dick lubricated."

Her dark brow shoots up. "You know those things can survive without water ... right?"

Ahhhh ...

"*What?*"

"The grown ones venture inland to lay eggs in the sand, then stay through winter to guard their nests. We try to avoid the desert during those months because they're *very* territorial ..."

"Well ..." I gulp. "That's fucking frightening." I wonder

how many unsuspecting whores have made their escape across the desert, only to wind up being eaten by a giant penis serpent? The irony isn't lost on me.

She nods, wincing when a sharp crack comes from Willy's bulging abdomen. "They're not the sort of animals people usually keep as ... as *pets*."

Willy rumbles, sucking up the thin, twitchy tail like a piece of string.

"Can't imagine why."

And to think, I'd been feeding him flies. No wonder he tried to eat me—the wee fuck was starving.

"The babies seek waterways and streams once they hatch, then head out to sea to grow big and mate."

"Right ..." And I lugged the poor thing across a desert which almost killed us both. He was probably just hoping I'd find him a more adequate trench to slip down. "Any streams nearby?"

"One on the western side of the camp. It runs pretty well."

I peel back layers of woolly blankets, revealing skin that looks like it's been dabbed from a pallet of blue, red, purple, and brown.

My wings insist on cuddling me, so I bare my teeth and growl at them. They actually listen for a change, flopping down either side of the bed with a painful *thunk* that makes me see little red dots.

"Do ... do you think it's wise to get up?"

"If I don't move around, I'll fuse with the bed."

I rise from the straw-filled mattress, gritting my teeth as my scabs stretch and tug. I'm healing slower than a Lesser at the moment ... much slower. Seems even Karma's taking a turn at fucking me in all the wrong ways.

Standing isn't easy, neither is walking. I resort to taking short, shuffling steps, dragging my listless wings behind me.

"Do you need help finding the way?"

"I'll be fine," I say, scooping Willy up into a ball against my chest. I step into the slice of light, using my throbby-hand as a shield against the warm glow of dawn. When my feet sink into the mossy ground, I draw a deep breath and savour the cool, smoky ai—

"*Stop.*"

Shit, I didn't consider the fucking *guards*.

I spin, blinking at the girl standing by my door with eyes the colour of sea grass. Her skin's the most sensational shade of burnt umber, but it's the familiar face that makes my heart thump harder.

"Talia!" I breathe, using a nearby boulder to steady myself. I thought she'd taken her life when she disappeared a year ago ...

She offers me a shy smile and tucks a rope of hair behind her ear. "Hi, Dell ..."

The words are whispered, like she's afraid I might flick my shredded wings and try to flutter off.

"Hi ..."

She steps from foot to foot, twisting her hands around her makeshift spear. She's missing two fingers ... and a thumb on the other hand.

I try not to look.

An awkward moment stretches, her eyes darting between my face and the broken wings slumped on the ground behind me.

"I'm, ahh, just going for a walk. I doubt I'll last long, but I need fresh air."

She tugs the spear closer to her body which is soft in all the right places; a full, healthy figure that suits her much better than the sharp, sallow one she wore at Kroe's.

I think she's about to tell me to hobble back into my tree like a good little hoe, but instead she curls her lips and offers me a crooked smile. "I'll keep the wolf at bay for as long as I can. Don't cross the stream, there are traps there that would mess you right up." She points to my poor, threadbare wings. "And I wouldn't try to fly with those if I were you."

I glance over my shoulder and sigh. If they'd tug into my body I wouldn't stick out like such a sore whore. "Hadn't planned on it."

"Be quick. Marion's assisting a labour, but she'll be done soon."

I nod and continue my hobble through the forest, heading towards the distant sound of babbling water.

The trees are thick and ancient, casting heavy slabs of shade across the mossy ground, the odd blade of light breaking free to cut the space into segments.

Small dwellings have been carved into the base of many trees, and roots have coagulated to form others. Even nature is doing everything it can to provide these people shelter.

No wonder they've gone undetected.

I enter a busy part of the forest with people mulling about, some with babies strapped to their chests while they toil vegetable patches. I even see the odd male helping around the village ...

They were probably born here; unexposed to the psychological plague twisting the rest of the world into believing you need a dick to have a voice.

People pause to watch me stagger by and anxiety fills my chest cavity like an oily shadow. But where I expected to see at least the odd hateful glare stabbed towards my white wings, instead I see something very different ...

Hope.

They smile, whispering in their children's ears, bowing their heads as I pad past.

They're *worshiping* me. Not because I'm the brood of a God, but because I spawned from the same darkness they did.

Perhaps they believe that makes me different from my father? Well, I fucking hope so, because I'm coming to realise the fissures I've collected don't hinder me at all.

They make me stronger. More lethal.

They make me a weapon.

CHAPTER EIGHT
DELL

*F*at, speckled fish swim idly against the current, visible through crystal clear water that glitters in the morning light.

I ignore the foreign reflection of the white-haired woman staring back at me and drop my foot onto a ledge of dirt, holding the little dick close to my nose so I can look him in the eye. "This is it, wee man."

He pouts, and I swear to shit, it's the strangest thing I've ever seen. But I get it. Facing the world on your own can be terrifying.

"I'm sorry, I wanted to keep you, too ... but perhaps this is for the best? Maybe you can come for me when you've grown up to be a really *big* Willy?"

That makes him stiffen up. He rubs his head against my face, leaving a dampness smeared across my cheek that I have trouble convincing myself is *not* his penis serpent pre-cum.

I'm going to have a hard time explaining this to my mates.

"Okay, time to go; else you're going to be so engorged you can't wiggle through the water properly." I'm already questioning his ability to swim stuffed full of dead rodent, but at least I'm not sending him off with an empty stomach.

That wouldn't be very motherly of me.

I dip low, my wasted legs trembling as I drop my hand into the icy water. It barrels over my skin, lifts Willy off my palm, and sends him floating off down the stream.

I release a deep sigh. I'm used to needy penises but having one physically attached to me was a whole new kettle of cocks.

"You got rid of the finger biter, then?"

"Huh?"

I turn to see Leila standing above me, donned in leather pants and a white linen top that floats on the handsy breeze. She has a loop of rope draped over her shoulder, strung through the eyeballs of about twenty dead fish.

She shrugs, making the fish wobble. "He was wrapped around your neck most of the time you were passed out, but we had to keep the fucker fed. The girls drew straws ... a few of them almost lost fingers."

I gape, almost vomit, then grab a fistful of grass to haul myself out of the trench. "This was probably for the best," I sputter breathlessly from the two-step ascent. "Who are the fish for?"

"The griffins."

"You have *griffins?*"

I've only seen depictions of them embossed on the back of tokens.

She nods. "Lots. They seek the protection of the trees. A couple of the big ones even let the girls ride them occasionally."

My ears perk up.

"How interesting," I muse, trying to hide my enthusiasm. "Can I see them?"

Griffins have wings.

I need wings because my own are shot to shit and I have my harem of Gods to rescue.

She gives me a quick once over. "It's a bit of a walk, Dell ..."

"And I'm tired of sitting on my arse."

She shakes her head, but I can see the ghost of a smile tugging the corner of her mouth.

I trail behind her down a bedraggled track with gangly branches that pinch my hair, rasping each breath as my exertion takes hold and doesn't let go. By the time we reach a dense waterfall of vines, my legs are brittle and I have a sheen of sweat dappling my brow.

Leila turns, frowning when she takes me in, no doubt seeing the fatigue I've lost the heart to hide. "You look like shit."

"They better be fucking impressive," I heave, ignoring the incessant throb in my hand.

Anyone else would probably insist I hobble back to my whore hut.

Not Leila.

She just pushes her fork through the veil of vines, creating a small opening which she summons me through.

The world opens up, revealing a wide, glistening pond the colour of starlight. It perfectly reflects tall, gnarled trees hugging the water's edge and tawny griffins sipping from the pond with big, hooked beaks. Others loiter, pawing undergrowth with their front claws.

They're twice the height of a regular Fae with beige fur covering their bodies and proud manes of rich, golden feathers embellishing their necks. The sight has me stroking Drake's frail tether that looks like it could snap off at any moment, and my stomach flips at the thought ...

I don't have time to cover my mouth before a thick spray of vomit comes surging out, smattering the leafy ground with the remnants of my last meal and a green smear of bile.

"Shit," Leila murmurs, dropping her fish in a potent heap. My stomach twists again, more vomit spraying as I cough and choke and gag.

By the time I'm finished, tears are streaming down my face and I'm lumped on the ground, trembling. A wetness crawls over my skin in places, and I just know I've reopened wounds.

Leila turns around, putting her arse in my face.

"What are you doing?"

"These are my roommate's pants; mine were dirty. She carries a cum-rag in her back pocket out of habit, but I can't get it without slicing off an arse cheek."

Of course.

I pull out the cloth, give it a sniff, and use it to wipe my mouth before rolling my sleeve to tuck it in my bandage for safekeeping. My eyes widen when I notice a black stroke painted up the inside of my arm—like a rotten, festering vein ...

I lift the material higher ...

The line stops just shy of my elbow.

Shit.

I'm tucking the sleeve around my wrist when Leila turns, offering me her saw which I gently nudge away.

"Oops, sorry ... sometimes I forget."

I nod and stand like the rising dead, trying to ignore the fact that my stomach is threatening to spill itself again.

"You good?"

Does she know I can't lie?

"I miss the sun," I say honestly. I don't mean the *actual* sun, but she doesn't know that.

"Yeah ... I don't understand why it's been dawn for so long. Something's not right."

"Yup," I say, popping the 'p', stroking the silver tether attached to my heart.

Something is very fucking wrong.

I galumph towards the water, the distinct musk of fowl shit hanging in the air, the smell is reminiscent of the goo Marion smeared on my wounds.

Lovely.

The griffins flick their serpentine tails, tracing my movements with keen, black eyes ...

They're probably wondering why I smell like their shit. I'd be curious, too.

Leila spears the loop of fish with her fork and walks deeper into the clearing. I watch her slice through the rope with her saw-hand and scatter them about ...

Massive, powerful limbs pound the ground and make it shudder; golden wings churn the air; beaks *snap*, rip, and caw. A fish head is flicked through the air and quickly snatched up with a strike of wild dexterity ...

I've never felt as small as I do standing next to the writhing mass of their violent feeding frenzy.

"There's more sun up there if you miss it so much." Leila's words are a challenge, eyes sharp with mischief as she points towards an abrupt cliff face with steps carved up the harsh terrain—its destination somewhere above the cap of towering trees ...

I look at it much like I did the regurgitated remnants of my last meal. Why would I want to do that to myself?

"You'll have more luck luring me back to the whore house. What about the griffin riding? Where do we go to see that?" I ask, scanning the clearing, trying not to sound too desperate.

Leila jerks her chin at the steps.

No ...

"Up there, *milad—*"

I hiss at her.

She smiles, stepping away from the throng of honking creatures and the smell of exposed fish guts. Bitch is trying to rile me.

I look forlornly at the stairs ...

Fuck me.

"How many steps are there?" I bite out, trying to come to terms with the fact that *this is fucking happening*. More than once. If I'm going to steal a griffin, ride it to the capital, and rescue my Gods, then I'm going to have to make those stairs my bitch.

Leila shrugs. "Never counted them before. No time like the present to rebuild the muscles on those chicken legs though, hmm?"

I scowl at her.

Once upon a time, I pushed her to save the lives of our fellow hoes. Now she's pushing me back—betting on the horse with frayed wings and a broken body.

I sigh and lumber towards the stairs. "I'll go first. If I fall, try not to prod me with your fork-hand."

She huffs as I push past her and begin the seemingly impossible task of inching up the embankment.

I'm gasping for breath after the tenth step; knees wobbling, cheeks flushed.

By the seventy-fifth, I'm pondering the effectiveness of Leila's fork if I were to 'accidentally' fall backwards onto it.

"*This is ... messed up*," I wheeze, curling over my knees, looking at step number seventy-six like it's a separate fucking continent to the one I'm standing on now. Leila hasn't even cracked a sweat. "*Marion's ... going to ... murder you ... for this.*"

She hacks at a fallen branch with her saw while she bides away the moments of my torture. "Only if you tattle though something tells me you won't."

I heave another breath, contemplate taking a nap, think better of it when I picture my Gods rotting in a cell somewhere, and force myself further up the motherfucking stairs.

By the time I crest over the top of the final one, lights are darting across my vision and my entire arm is blazing. Falling into a heap on a grassy platform, I use my bandage to mop my forehead while I marvel at the vast chasm before us ...

The hike almost killed me, but the view is worth all the feathers I lost on those stairs.

The gorge is so deep that it fades into oblivion, the steep walls littered with fluffy shrubs and large, bulging nests heaped with yellow eggs the size of my head. Some even hold nesting griffins.

Trees still bow overhead, but it's more of a loose netting that allows chunks of morning light to highlight the mousy-haired woman perched atop a proud griffin on the opposite ledge ...

She looks tiny on his back.

He canters forward and leaps off the edge, stretching his massive wings and catching the wind as the rider tucks her body flat—hands wrapped around twin handles of a little leather saddle.

They curve and twist, arch and dive, and I can't look away. His wings are a slightly smaller version of Drake's ...

I knead my chest, wrestling the ache threatening to split me open as I monitor that wispy tether.

You better not die on me, you big golden goose.

My lip curls back as my wings lift and stretch, reaching for their full span in a painful attempt to fly.

It breaks my fucking heart.

"I don't think they're ready for that just yet. They took quite a hit ..."

I clear my throat.

Dark room.
Smells like piss.
Things that made me bleed.

"Everything makes so much more sense now," Leila says with a dreamy lustre that makes me want to vomit again. Instead, I dangle my legs over the edge, rip a wiry weed from the ground, and toss it to the wind, watching it flutter into no man's land.

"I'm still the same person."

"I know that, Dell. That's what gives them hope. Those women would do anything for you; and it has nothing to do with the wings on your back."

I won't be letting the people in this community do *anything* for me that might involve putting themselves in harm's way, not that I'm going to tell Leila that.

They're finally free. I would never dream of taking that away from them.

The only person who can help me is *myself.*

"Did you have them when we were at Kroe's?"

"No ..."

Leila looks down at her prosthetic ... weapons. "How did you get them back?"

I inhale a sharp dose of her desperation, hating that I can't answer her question. It's a tale twisted with my Sun Gods, and while those wards are still active, I won't risk jeopardising them.

I won't risk their safety more than I already have.

"I wish I could tell you ..."

She offers a gentle nod, looking forlornly at the griffin swooping through the air.

"I understand. And like I said, I'm luckier than most. But sometimes ... sometimes I just miss being able to wipe my own butt."

Salt perfumes the air and I glance away, giving her privacy ...

One day, I'll give back the things he's taken.

I shuffle, agitating the brand on my arse, sucking air through my teeth as a fresh well of warmth pools beneath me.

Leila eyes me warily. "Do you want to talk about it?"

"What do you think?"

She lifts a slight shoulder. "Just thought I'd ask. I often wished other women had the voice to ask me the same question."

I tuck a curl behind my ear, watching a stout woman saddle a griffin on the other side of the gorge. There appears to be a full tack shed over there. My gaze sways to the right, and I spot a rope bridge about a hundred metres down the way ...

Good to know.

"I'm not one to dredge up emotions. You know that."

Leila closes her eyes and tilts her head back, the wind twisting through the short tufts of her pixie cut. "You can't just stuff it all away, Dell. Sooner or later you'll have to open up to someone, otherwise you'll always be living in the past, never moving forward."

"When did *you* stop living in the past?"

She cracks a single eye open, peering at me sideways. "When a woman with skin of steel and a heart of stone put her life on the line to save fifty-seven women who'd barely spoken a word to her. And when I realised that woman did it knowing *full well* she wouldn't make it out of there alive."

I break our eye contact, preferring to peer at the bottomless chasm than into her perception of the truth.

"Well, I did come out alive, so—"

"Barely."

She's trying to bait me into talking. I wonder how

someone who'd hardly uttered three words before her escape learnt to be so diplomatic.

"Kroe didn't do this to me, Leila."

She shifts to face me fully, slender brow arched. "Then is he dead?"

I roll my eyes.

"I'll rephrase," she states when it becomes obvious I have no intention of answering. "How long did it take you to figure out you couldn't bring yourself to kill the bastard?"

I pluck another weed from the healthy soil and, with a deep sigh, I throw it off the edge of the chasm. "I had the blade at his throat ..."

It's a decision I don't doubt will come back to haunt me. It's plagued me ever since—the thought that one choice could possibly implicate more than just myself.

"You should have done it, Dell."

I know.

My head starts to pound and I turn my attention to the cliff we just ascended. "We've got to go back down those stairs now, don't we?"

Leila sighs and prods her fork into the unsuspecting soil at her side, making me wince. She uses it as leverage to haul herself up, then sashays towards the slut-killing stairs. "Yup. You go first. I don't want you taking me out when you faint halfway down and turn into a giant, feathery whore-ball."

CHAPTER NINE
DELL

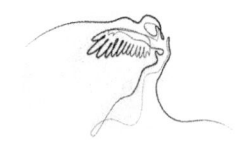

If the slog back to my little hut wasn't bad enough, Marion almost murdered me the moment I walked in the door.

She bruised my ear, probably the only part of me that wasn't previously discoloured, then herded me into bed where she mummified me in blankets and told me that if I didn't eat my cold root vegetables *right now*, she'd shove them down my throat.

It took her a good hour to clean my wings and reapply the 'healing serum'. Despite the fact that I now smell like I've been rutting around in a grotto, the whole charade had part of me wishing I could stay here with Marion forever …

Although she's not my mother, she's caring for me like a mother would. But I can't stay.

Just as Marion left me all those years ago, I have to do the same, and pray our paths will cross again.

My door's been buttered with an extra layer of security—two badass bitches with spears and a burly boy with a kind face who looks impenetrable. Everyone but the guards went to bed hours ago.

Not me.

I'm lying here, wrapped in smelly wings with a blazing arm, plotting a way to sneak out and coax a griffin into flying me to Sterling. First things first, I need to find a way to knock the guards unconscious ...

Unfortunately, that rules out my unpredictable beast, who's likely to mist first and think later. The only viable plan I can think of involves Willy's coco-cunt, a stick, my chamber pot, and a mouse ... but I think my wee dick ate the only one living in my hoe hut, which means I'm back to square one.

Sighing, I pluck a small berry from my tray and pop it in my mouth, moaning at the burst of sweetness that explodes across my tongue. "Woah! Fuck. Me. That's some good shit."

A deep throat clears from just outside the door.

I don't usually like berries all that much but, hell, I think I'm sold.

I go back for another, this one a bright pink globular thing that gives me a straight mouthgasm the moment I chew into it. "Ohhhh yeah, that's it ... that's the good stuff."

A ferocious snarl makes the entire hut shake and my body locks up, the berry falling from my mouth.

I really hope that's not Willy's real Mumma come to reprimand me for doing a shit job of raising him. I'm in *no* state to battle a big dick right now.

I hear a loud thud and my wings tighten their spindly grasp as a burst of panic explodes in my chest, my mind churning with possibilities. They all end with me dead on the floor and my Gods rotting in a cell for eternity.

Nudging my sleeping beast with my internal foot, I pull the blanket around my face, watching the door shudder as something thumps against it ...

Fuck. Fuck. Fuck.

It swings open, spilling dawn into the room, and my beast

starts to wail—dragging razor-sharp talons down my insides and bleeding little puddles of light everywhere.

A tall, topless silhouette of rolling muscle fills the entryway, wearing nothing but black pants, kick-ass boots, and a brown leather strap that snakes from shoulder to hip.

My lungs seize as I meet the wild, azure stare of a heaving Kal, shadowed by the peaks of majestic black wings folded behind him ...

His face is full of thunder, but the moment we lock eyes he breathes a raspy sigh, those proud shoulders curling forward. He closes the door, then drops his head in his hands and groans—the sound a chilling mix of relief and devastation.

He's *here*.

This is real.

He's okay.

"Fuck, Dell," he grates, and I cry out—my shock shattered by the sound of his deep, velvet voice. I fucking gorge on it; my chest almost cracking open as my heart tries to launch right at him.

My vagina tries to do the same.

My wings reach forward, and I climb out of bed on unsteady legs, trip over tangled blankets, and go lurching straight into Kal's awaiting arms. I'm tugged against his chest, the rowdy hum of my pain drowned out by a deep-seated need to be *surrounded* by him.

Jasmine and verbena ... I want to *bathe* in his scent. I want it inside me, washing away the men who took me without permission.

Trembling hands smooth my hair while Kal mutters soft words like a motherfucking prayer. *"Geil de na vej, tai ma ten jiorn estan ... dej navi la!"*

I nuzzle his sweaty chest, coating myself in his musk. "I can't understand any of that, Midnight Snack ..."

Though I intend for my voice to come out strong and fortified, it's a soft, fractured whimper.

"*Tas, tas, tas ...*" Kal soothes, wrapping me in the shade of his magnificent wings.

I expel a shuddering sigh.

Home.

This is home.

He nuzzles into my hair, draws a deep breath, and then his grip tightens ...

Significantly.

"*Geil de na vej ... druca teis ...*"

The words drop around me like shards of broken glass.

Sharp.

Fragile ...

"*Klash dos nav!*"

I have no idea what he's suddenly so pissed about but it makes me smile ...

My moody God; he's okay ...

He's fucking *okay.*

He brushes a tender spot on my wing before jerking his hand away, and my shoulders grow heavy ... the weight on my back feeling more like a curse than ever.

For a moment there, I'd forgotten that I'm ruined.

"Dell?" Kal threads unsteady fingers through my hair, like he's worshiping his deity. "Dell, look at me."

His words are a blazing command and my throat turns arid—each breath sliding through it like poison.

"*Look at me!*"

I shake my head, refusing to pull away and look him in the eye. I can't stand to see the pity staining his perfect face.

What if it's worse. What if he's *disappointed?* He used to think my wings were so beautiful ...

"What happened?" He tilts my head forcefully, but my eyes are squeezed shut. "Dell, *please.*"

What I can't see won't hurt me.

Hissing, he wraps strong hands around my thighs and hoists me up so my legs are draped around his trim waist. My wings give him a lopsided, quivering hug, and I put a tooth through my tongue in an effort to distract myself from the blaze of pain.

Kal lowers to the bed and drops me into his lap, causing the brand on my arse to split a seam. I let out a pitchy wail, the hot lick of agony dragging my eyes open in time to witness Kal's gaze turn into a wild, fearsome thing.

A fierce energy rolls off him—something almost tangible—making the skin all over my body prickle. Suddenly, this room feels far too small for the God it's trying to contain ...

Fuck.

I lean forward, resting my face over his hammering heart.

"Calm down, it's okay ..." I use my good hand to pat him like a puppy, trying to soothe the memory of my knee-jerk reaction right out of him. "Calm down, Big Man ... I'm right here."

The sharp scent of his anger stains the back of my throat. I count his laboured breaths, making it all the way to fifty-three before his body no longer resembles a boulder, his unsteady hands settling on my hips and anchoring me in place.

"I need you to tell me what happened."

That doesn't sound like Kal.

My head snaps up and I take in the sharp face of an ancient, primal darkness.

Kal's features have become a weapon in their own right, causing my heart to falter a few beats from the shock of being so close to those obscure eyes, whetted cheekbones, and the savage cut of his mouth.

My breathing turns idle. Everything about him screams *predator.*

"No," I state and lift my chin, meeting his dominance head on, pretending my body and soul aren't shattered.

If I give Kal's beast the answer he's seeking, the backlash could rip this hut, this *village*, to pieces.

I'm sick of all the bloodshed.

"*Now!*" he hollers like a crack of thunder, making the hairs all over my body stand on end.

Beasty lifts a brow, tail twitching. It seems she's not opposed to a quarrel with the God of Night.

"What's done is done. I dealt with it."

Kind of. I did leave a few stragglers behind, marinating in their own shit ...

His hands tighten. "You really expect me to just let this go? Are you serious?"

I nod, pinning his beast with a glare that would send lesser men running for cover. "I do. Now, lock your beast down before I do it myself."

He fucking snarls at me, baring his canines at my throat before the black recedes from his eyes. They return to the safe star-flecked blue that has me folding forward, nuzzling into the crook of his neck, breathing him in ...

Home.

"Happy?" he rumbles in a deep, familiar timbre that's stained with a sarcastic tone, almost earning him a ticket straight to the sin bin. But I wouldn't do that to him right now, because he's still shaking ... and I get it.

I probably look like death warmed up; I sure as hell feel that way.

"Yes," I murmur, preening one of my raggedy wings. "The people here have been looking after me. The last thing I need is for your beast to shred this place in a fit of rage. Surely Aero filled you in while I was gone ... I don't need to go over it again."

He twists his hand into my hair and tugs so hard I'm

forced to look up at the rigid disappointment smeared across his face. "He was only getting filtered *bits*."

I open my mouth, snap it shut.

They picked up on that, then ...

"*Oh*."

Those pillowy lips thin into a sharp hook. "Yeah. Expect that conversation when you see him next."

Goddammit. I was hoping that would just sort of ... get brushed over like no big deal.

I clear my throat, trying to ignore my blazing arm which feels like it's melting. "I've probably had it coming for a while now ..."

Kal nods and I almost punch the bastard in the arm, but I don't want to draw attention to the fact I'm favouring one hand. I doubt he'll be impressed by my little black line, and right now? I just want to enjoy being in his arms ...

Feeling safe.

Knowing *he's* safe.

I gnaw my bottom lip and a few pasty feathers fall into my lap—smelling like griffin shit and dried blood. "So ... what *do* you know?"

His eyes spark dangerously.

He brushes the feathers to the ground as if he can't bear to look at them, grabs my wrist, kisses the pierced tips of my fingers, and tucks my preening hand against his chest.

Guess that answers *that* question.

My heart does funny things ...

Is he ... repulsed by the idea of mating with me now? I mean, I know I'm a little more broken than I used to be, but I thought—

His wings tighten, brushing against my tattered ones, smothering them in a protective layer of ink. "I know that you were held captive. That they weren't going to let you out alive." His voice cracks on the last word and I swallow thickly ...

Guess my walls weren't as sturdy as I thought they were.

"Edom began rounding us up," he says on a rueful sigh. "Starting with Sol. I received his distress ping while I was searching a ruined city for any sign of your scent. I figured Edom tracked him through the rips in the Bright, so I resorted to hunting you by air."

Kal's statement takes root in my heart and germinates—a heavy burden growing with each stroke of the picture he's painting ...

The *King* took my mother from me. Now, he's fucking with my Sun Gods. I can't help but feel that caring for me is a death sentence.

"After *weeks,*" he grits out, "I finally found your scent on the outskirts of an abandoned village ... as well as Drake's."

He says his name like he's handling an injured bird, and I almost forget how to breathe ...

He was so close.

Kal twists a curl around his finger, expression wan. Even his shoulders appear heavier than usual. "I couldn't find your ..." he clears his throat, "*body.* I figured the only place you'd go from there would be across the desert to the East, seeing as you were always threatening that shit."

My poor, long-suffering Gods. They put up with so much.

"Drake's not doing too great," I whisper, checking his tether, my stomach twisting at the sight of it.

It's growing more frail by the hour.

"There was a lot of blood," Kal murmurs. "Did you see him?"

"No. But he's deteriorating, and I'm not sure how much longer he can hold on. We need to find them. I know I'm fucked but we can't wait."

He frowns, tucking the curl behind my ear. "Aero will find us soon, Little Dove. I need numbers if I'm going to break Sol and Drake free without landing myself balls deep in shit. I can't do it alone."

Fuck.

He doesn't know ...

He also seems to think he's doing this without me, but I'll blow that cock right out of the cooch once push comes to shove.

"Kal, my father has Aero ..."

His eyes go from warm summer night to cold winter darkness. "*What?* How do you know?"

"I saw him get taken," I admit, scrunching my nose as a familiar sensation starts to worm its way through my sinuses. Some lone dust particle must have found its way into my face.

I don't have time to turn or cover my nose before I sneeze all over Kal's shoulder, feeling like I just got flung against a tree. My cheeks heat at the sight of all my spit now smeared across his skin.

"Sorry," I mutter, pulling the cum-rag from my bandage to wipe his shoulder clean.

Kal's nostrils flare, his astute gaze narrows, and he snatches my right hand—those deft fingers dancing over the gauze binding, no doubt searching for a tail ...

My heart leaps into my throat, sheer panic locking my spine. "Ohhh, I wouldn't do that if I were you ... Marion will be so pissed off if she has to rewrap my hand." I waggle a finger at him. "And trust me on this. You *don't* want to get on her bad side, Kal. There's a reason I smell like griffin shit."

"I'll take my fucking chances," he rumbles, his voice laced with so much warning even my beast cowers.

Pussy.

He begins unravelling the dressing and dread flays me from the inside.

"Did you know anxiety has a sharp taste?" he muses, glancing at me from under black brows while his fingers work. There's so much accusation dripping from his tone, I could drown in it.

"Really?" I rasp, trying to calm the erratic beat of my heart. I could be stressing over nothing—the black line could've disappeared entirely.

Kal reaches a layer sodden with yellow fluid and releases a low, warning growl.

Damn. That doesn't look like nothing ...

I stroke the side of his face while I watch him work, reallocating my efforts towards damage control as he unravels the last of the bandage. It's tossed to the side, revealing the bulbous, throbbing welt that's starting to turn a bright shade of green.

I suppress a gag. No wonder my arm feels like it's been dipped in a vat of lava.

"Oh," I feign, trying to ease the brittle tension stretched between us. The man's not even breathing. "Would you look at that ..."

He rolls my sleeve, every vein in his muscular arms bulging, revealing the trail of black that now goes *well past* my elbow ...

It seems to be some sort of trigger.

He sneers, ripping the neckline of my dress in one sharp movement. "Hey! Marion made this especially for me!"

Firm hands push and pull both fabric and skin until he locates the head of the line now sitting just shy of my armpit.

This time, my blatant shock isn't feigned. That sure did escalate quickly, though I think I should keep that tiny detail to myself.

"*Glein de taj!*" Kal snarls, lips pulled back from his canines.

He leans forward and gives my hand a sniff, making my stomach churn again.

I don't need to dip my nose near that thing to know it doesn't smell good, and I'm not sure how he isn't gagging. I want to hurl berries all over him just looking at it.

There's a long, heavy silence while Kal rolls my hand around, studying the wound, and it feels like the world is holding its breath. "Kal ... remember to brea—"

"*Don't,* Dell." He snatches another bandage from my side table and peels it around the welt. "Just ... *don't*. You need to heal."

I roll my eyes. "I've been trying to do that for the past three weeks. It's gotten me nowhere. Obviously."

He finishes wrapping my hand in record time and lays me on the bed so fucking gently that I feel no pain at all. My shredded ladies try to pull him down with us, and I'm seriously impressed with their fortitude. The bitches are threadbare and they're still herding Sun Gods.

Kal shucks out of their spidery hold and turns towards the door, exposing a long sword sheathed down his spine—the black hilt crowned with a big, blue rock that harbours its own sparkling heartbeat.

I frown.

"Wait. Where are you going?"

He stops, his shoulders rising with the rhythm of his heavy breathing, his midnight wings vibrating like they're itching to take flight. "The people here can't see me, I can't risk setting off the wards." He doesn't look back, the unforgiving timbre of his voice directed at the door. "I need to collect the root of a rare herb to settle that bite, but it only grows on a small atoll in my territory that's half a day's flight from here."

"Great," I say, sitting up, pushing my blankets off. "Let's go, then."

An awkward silence stretches, and I pause with one leg dangling out of bed.

"Wait, you're planning to go ... *without me?*"

Surely not.

Kal spins, a black tornado exploding into action, his eyes pulsing with their own heartbeat. "I have no choice. You're too weak to make the trip, Dell. You need to remain stationary, and I'm not budging on this so stop punishing me with those fucking *eyes* ..."

He pleads the last words, but they're lost on me.

"We go. Now. Both of us. Or I steal a griffin and find my own way there." Though my words are calm and fortified and fucking *final*, they seem to be an ember to a hayfield.

"You don't even know the way!" he bellows, and another few bodies thump to the ground outside the door.

"Exactly my point! But *you* do! Now, you come over here and pick me up, I'll nuzzle into your chest, and we can flutter off together—"

"I do not fucking *flutter*."

"We'll make a *pit-stop* on your atoll," I continue, unperturbed by his little outburst, "then you can fly us to Sterling and we'll hunt down the others. Simple, but more importantly? You don't piss me off when I'm *this close* to going into heat and turning into a crazy hormonal bitch." I show him just how close I mean with my thumb and forefinger, but he just clears his throat and tugs his wings into a tight parcel.

"You're not going anywhere, Dell. Not yet."

"Why not?" I yell, trying to stand.

"You really want to know?" He glides forward, towering over me like a tree. "That bite is from a *Fae Fury*. That black line is headed straight to your heart, and if it makes it there? It will kill you and th—" he pauses, clamping his mouth shut, chest rumbling with a growl threatening to explode.

"And what?"

"Druca teis me ... zas ta!" He tears his hands through blue-black hair and drops into a crouch. *"Fuck ..."*

We're getting absolutely nowhere.

I brush his cheek, trying to placate my moody Night God who seems to have fallen off his perch. He's being entirely irrational. He says I need to stay stationary, but I can do that in his arms. And it's not like I'm heavy to carry around. My wings are a little handsy, so is my vagina, but they're all pretty sedated right now ...

"Dell ..." he breathes, brushing my hand away, his shoulders falling along with my heart.

He can't even bear to have me touch him.

I swallow the lump in my throat, watching him pinch the bridge of his nose. "That's not all, is it ..."

He's disgusted in me. Either that or he *pities* me, and I honestly don't know what's worse.

"It's not," he grinds out, rancour swirling in his throat, sharpening his voice into something that maims. He lifts his gaze, and what's staring back at me is that time of the night when all your worst fears seem to grow a pulse. "What will I see if I look beneath that shift, Dell?" He gestures towards my entire body. "What made you wince when I set you on my lap, hmm?"

"Stop ..."

"No. I won't stop." His hand is suddenly cradling my cheek, his breath hot on my face, those midnight eyes stripping me. "Not now, not *ever*."

I almost fall over. Probably would if he weren't anchoring me in place. But he's focusing on all the wrong things.

"This isn't about *me*, Kal. Stop making this abou—"

"*Really?* Why do you think Edom left me, huh?" He gives me a little shake. "So I could *comfort* you? No. Somehow, he knew you'd need help getting to Sterling. He's trying to lure you ... Always. One. Step. Ahead."

I squeeze my lips together, drawing blanks. He's my father, yes. But I don't know the man from a puckered arsehole.

"In his mind, he's already won, Dell. And you're already dead. Or worse."

"I've dealt with *worse* my entire life. I'm sick of bending over and taking *worse*."

Kal flinches and I instantly regret saying it.

"You have no idea what he's capable of," he grits out, gutting me with a glare. "He's warded, untouchable, with an army of legionnaires at his disposal. And you and I both know they aren't fucking *gentle*."

He drops my face and takes a step back.

I sneer.

Desperate, low-fucking-blow.

It's not enough though. I've faced those barbarians and survived; I'll face them a million times over to save the people I love. "I'm not staying here while Drake, Aero, and Sol decay in a dungeon somewhere." I take a step towards the door, lifting my chin, standing as tall as I can manage. "I'll walk there if I have to."

Kal cuts in front of me. "They'd flay me if I let you go in there without the proper precautions."

He almost looks repentant, but he's still standing in my fucking way.

"Then they obviously don't know what's good for themselves, and they need a whore with shredded wings and a wayward fucking vagina to put them in their place."

His lips peel back and he widens his stance, splaying his wings.

My eyes almost bug out of my head.

It's as if a mask has been ripped off his sultry face. There's suddenly something *more* about him ... something *foreboding*.

A darkness that calls to my own.

"You're not doing this."

The command falls upon me like a weight, making the walls shudder. Making the very *air* shift. Making every single cell in my body stand to attention.

The words aren't spoken from the man, they're spoken from the God.

It's an order.

Final.

Not that I give a shit.

I lift my chin further. "Try to stop me."

His lips twitch, but it's the only warning I get. "I wish for you to fly by yourself for an hour *straight* before you go searching for the other Sun Gods."

What.

The.

Fuck.

I'm smacked with a bolt of warmth, making me cry out as I feel it fuse with my very being ... with my fucking *soul*.

I stare at him through a blanket of red-hot rage, catching a slice of regret staring back at me from those star-flecked eyes.

Kal just gave me an impossible task. My poor, shredded wings can't catch a *break*, let alone a motherfucking updraft!

"What have you done," I whisper, but as the words fall from my lips, I realise the voice is not my own.

It's a voice warped with callous vengeance. The voice of a beast who went rogue in a dungeon—misting two men and gutting another ...

She snuck in like smoke in the night, ready to choke the room with her fury.

My beast steps forward with a flick of our hips, reeling from his betrayal. She wants him to fear that cauldron of lava tipping heat through our veins.

"Dell ..." he coaxes, hands up in submission, taking a step forward when he should be doing the *exact opposite.*

"Dell's in a shadow ditch. You may call me *Mistress*," we purr as a soft glow emits from our body, dousing the room in *light*. Our fingers become laden with a molten smoulder, and she splays our palms at our sides ...

From my spot in the back seat of my own body, I can see what the bitch has planned and clamber for control, screaming at her to *stop*.

It's useless.

Our lips curl into a sharp smile, and she pumps our fists, sending one wave of power barrelling towards the wooden side table ... the other straight at my fucking *Night God*.

Kal's going to go *poof*, and there's not a damn thing I can do to stop it.

Our wings curl around our body as the table detonates, and wooden bolts erupt with a strident scream—shredding everything in their path.

We barely manage to protect our face with the back of our hands.

It's not until the brutal assault comes to a silent finish that we notice Kal is standing inside a shimmering shield, absolved from the scene of a million broken, bloody pieces of wood and fabric and feather.

I almost weep from my spot doused in darkness.

She protected him.

Kal's features are contorted by the wrath of his own beast while he beats his fists bloody.

We take a step forward, planting our feet directly in front of him. "*Stop.*"

He does.

Instantly.

He falls to his knees like a deflated shadow, and we look down on him with blood peppering the ground at our feet.

He rests his hands on his knees, palms facing up, chest and shoulders heaving ...

When we drop our shield, we're assaulted by the sharp scent of his desperation.

"How dare you," we scold. "How fucking *dare* you."

All that stares back at us is bone-chilling anguish.

Beasty sneers and coils back, leaving my body entirely bare of *any* controlling entity while I stare at her in utter disbelief ...

She's a fucking psycho.

'You can't just go around blowing shit up!'

She pops a feral shoulder as if to say *whatever, hoe; I did you a favour. I'll take my thank you in the form of five severed dicks and a virginal blood sacrifice.*

'No God cock for yo—'

Darkness.

CHAPTER TEN
DELL

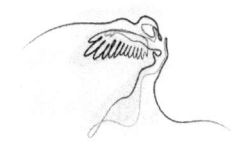

The warm body cradling me makes the bitter wind chill feel like an afterthought. As does the inferno in my heart ...

Thud-unk.

Thud-unk.

I'm fucking *flying*.

Well, not me specifically.

I open my eyes, looking up at the stretched neck and prickly shadow staining the lower half of Kal's face. His wings are beating the air like they have a point to prove—cutting through the blushing sky so fast it's almost impossible to catch my breath.

Anxiety lances my chest, a garnish to the liquid fire swishing through my veins ...

Poor Marion's going to walk into my tree hut and wonder what the hell went on. Beasty left it in tatters, smothered in bloody feathers ...

She'll think the worst but at least their vagina sanctuary is safe now I'm no longer hobbling around, luring unwanted attention.

I nuzzle into Kal's chest, drawing on his scent for comfort. He's being so gentle, carrying me like I'm some glass dolly ...

"How did you wake up?" he croaks over the howl of the wind, and I glance up to see him watching me—black brows reaching for his hairline.

"Opened ... my eyes?"

He swears under his breath and shifts his gaze back to the sky, guiding us into an updraft.

Wait ...

"Did you put me to *sleep* again?"

The muscle along his jaw pops. "I had no choice, Dell. Look at yourself."

I glance at my hands curled between us and make a small choking sound.

Fuck.

I look like I've been dipped in a vat of red dye, and my *wings* ...

"*Oh,*" I whisper, eyes sweeping shut as my sizzling heart hacks away at my ribs. "Maybe we should, ahh ... keep this to ourselves. You officially have my permission to throw me in the bog. I won't even toss you in the sin bin for it."

I open one eye, only to suffer the wrath of Kal's berating glare. "You want me to hide this from the others?" he thunders, and I make a small squeaky sound, clenching my butt cheeks, preparing for a brutal dose of verbal sodomy.

He shakes his head and sighs. "What happened back there, Dell? I need to know what we're dealing with."

The question is a punch straight to the tit. The spawn of a monster, that's what he's dealing with.

There is no pretty way to say it.

"My beast likes to throw her weight around ... if it suits her."

Only when it suits her.

I clear my throat as thoughts of a dark room that smelt like death and piss and vomit twists my stomach into knots.

"Have you done that before?" he asks, his voice much softer this time.

Blood on my hands.

"I don't want to talk about that."

"Well, okay ... where did the *warmth* radiate from?"

That's much easier to answer. "My hands."

"*What?*" I literally hear Kal's heart skip a beat, his eyes midnight moons that can't seem to take enough of me in.

"My hands? Well, my fingertips actually."

All the colour drops out of his face. "Your fucking *fingertips?*"

"Well it sure as shit wasn't my vagina!" But how awesome would that be? I'd totally wipe my father out with a beam of vagina rage and kill him with irony.

He finally blinks, then shifts his attention back to the emptiness before us—nothing but pastel clouds for as far as the eye can see.

"Where are we going?"

"Night Kingdom," he murmurs although it seems I've lost his attention. "Get some more rest, we're still a few hours away from the Atoll of Jal."

I glance at my chest, half exposed from Kal's earlier abuse towards my poor shift. Beneath the thin smear of blood, I can see the shadow of that septic line now creeping across my right breast ...

Kal's arms tighten and I lean into the hand cradling my head. "What if I don't want to rest?" I whisper, all too aware of the blazing beat of my heart.

If I go to sleep ... I might not wake up.

Kal sighs, presses his lips to the top of my head, and an

eclipse slips over my consciousness. I mentally chastise myself for leaving my shield down before I fall fast the fuck asleep.

CHAPTER ELEVEN
DRAKE

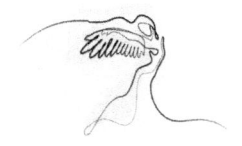

She looks so fucking beautiful standing there, framed by unruly curls that shimmer like spun gold in the burnished glow of my soul's heart—the last place I thought I'd *ever* see her.

My aurous clouds churn around her feet, climb up her legs, and leave gilded smudges on her skin while I try to calm the fierce sledge in my chest ...

Dell's presence could only mean one thing.

"You shouldn't be here, babe."

She shrugs, her lips set in grim determination. "Yeah, well. Neither should you, Sunset."

Fair point.

Nobody else has seen this place. The fact she got in just reaffirms she was made for me. That her soul calls to mine, just as mine calls to hers.

She takes in my quintessence, and my chest bubbles with nerves ... hoping she likes what she sees. I watch with bated breath as she draws deep, cramming her lungs full of the metallic dust veiling this place—my fucking *essence*.

It doesn't make her sneeze.

Every cell in my body vibrates with *that* slice of knowledge, and my chest swells with the satisfaction in her gaze when she trains it back on me—lumped on my arse, hands hidden behind the fall of a cloud ...

Unmoving. But not by choice.

If I weren't anchored by precious cargo, I'd be all around her, in her, fucking *saturating* her.

Her tongue darts out, tasting the golden sheen that's settled on her lips, and her eyelids flutter, making me want to tip my head back and groan.

"Dell?"

"Hmm?"

I open myself, baring my chest, careful to keep my hands hidden by the swirl of clouds. "Why are you not in my arms already?"

She winces, teetering from foot to foot like she's about to pee herself, hands hiding behind her back. Her teeth chatter, her next breath out a little puff of white. "Are you ... angry?"

She thinks I'm angry at *her?*

I almost snarl as the knowledge flays my fucking heart, but that's the last thing she needs to see. At this moment, all she needs to focus on is *being here.*

"Furious, babe. But not at you. Now get over here."

Her face softens and she nods, hands still behind her back as she shuffles forward and wilts between my legs. I flinch as her little body folds against my chest—a cold, listless lump that barely has a pulse ...

Shit.

Nuzzling into her neck, I weave an arm around her—wishing I could swallow her up with the motion. I'm desperate to sink my fingers into her hair; to tilt her head back and sweep my thumb across apple-red lips that make me weak at the fucking knees ...

But I won't.

I'd have to let go of the dull, sooty tether fraying in my grip and barely rooted in my soul; the one that's usually a crisp, clear white.

I'm worried there'll be nothing left for me to grab again ...

I tighten my fists, push my wings out, and wrap her in another layer of *me*.

Safe.

Protected.

Mine.

"Why are you here, babe?" The words are ground out because part of me doesn't want to hear the answer.

"What, I can't soul-visit you in your dusky wonderland?" she asks, her muffled voice a pretty ruse wearing a fluffy mask.

She wriggles to get more comfortable, and a burnished cloud falls away, revealing her fists bunched around the faintest glimmer of something gold ...

Her knuckles are bone white.

Strained.

Just like mine.

I try not to balk at the confirmation that she's holding onto me, just as I'm holding onto her.

I close my eyes and dig my nose into her hair. "If you let go, I'm coming with you. You know that, right? We're not through, you and I."

My words are guttural, and they hold a sharp edge of warning ...

A command.

Am I playing on her love for me?

Yes, I fucking am.

Are they dirty tactics?

Probably.

But I'm willing to dip as low as it takes to keep her

drawing breath. And if that doesn't work? I'll ride her lily-white arse all the way to the motherfucking afterlife.

"I know," she whispers, snuggling in, getting nice and comfy in the crux of my soul. "Just don't give me a reason to slap you and we should be just fine."

CHAPTER TWELVE
KAL

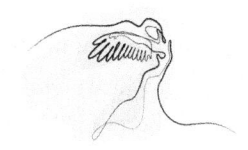

"Dell?" I cut into dewy air and settle on the wide lip of a terrace pool, one of many jutting down the dormant volcano my kingdom is perched on. She's limp in my arms, her breathing shallow, skin clammy from a raging fever—her body's last-ditch attempt at saving itself.

I pull my wings into my back and give her a shake, hating the way it makes her head roll.

Lifeless.

"Come on, Little Dove ..."

I stopped using my power to keep her asleep while I was digging up the root of a mung herb on a small atoll just west of here. It may neutralise Fae Fury poison but it's useless unless I can get her to consume it.

And she won't wake up.

I'm regretting putting her out, but every time we tossed words her pulse would race, giving the poison a fucking leg up on its journey to her heart.

If she dies ...

My beast snarls—a warning sound sharp enough to slash my insides.

We *both* know what happens if she dies.

I sink into the smallest white mineral pool I can find—turquoise water soaking the pants I've been wearing for the past three and a half weeks. They smell like sweat, panic, and desperation; something I'm more than happy to wash away along with the blood masking Dell's skin.

I need to get a good look at the damage my girl's been trying to hide from me.

"*Dell?*" I brush my hand across her forehead and watch her lids flicker, making my heart worm its way into my throat. "I know you're in there, Little Dove. Come back to me ..."

I set her box on the lip, thankful I'd stored it in my fucking bedroom. There's a pottle of something acrid enough to bring a God to his knees in there, and I really hope it's a sample from the healing bog and not just a vial of crap.

I rummage until I find it, tarnishing all her bits with my desperate, bloody fingers ...

Fuck it. Her life is more important.

When I pop the cork, I'm smacked with a pungent musk that makes me gag.

Definitely the right stuff.

Saying a little prayer, I plunge my finger into the muck and swish a large blob through the water, turning the pool transparent brown. I set the pottle next to her box and unravel shreds of bandage from her right hand, encouraging water to flow freely across her broken body ...

The red veil dissolves, revealing starlight skin mottled with marks old and new.

My blood boils.

"*Geil deh mi. Geil deh mi.*" A moan escapes those pillowy lips, and I mirror the sound. "*Geil deh mi ...*"

Don't leave me.

I grit my teeth and fight the innate urge to hold her tight, wishing I could gift her my fucking essence; make her whole again.

I wouldn't think twice.

Long moments drip by and I can't bring myself to look away ... studying every inch of her body, her wings; searching for the slightest tell this shit is working.

Perhaps it's wishful thinking, but I'm *certain* the swelling in her hand is going down ... but it's not happening fast enough.

Fuck it.

Forgive me, Little Dove.

I reach for the pottle when her eyes pop open, limbs flailing, sending shit water splashing. She shrieks, her eyes wide and wild, wings snapping out in a desperate attempt to grab hold of something while my heart smacks against my ribs.

Thank the *fucking* sun.

My own wings break out of their cage, scoop her up, and I feed her a drop of calm—posturing myself so she knows I'm not a threat. "Dell, you're okay. Relax, Little Dove ..."

I see the moment her eyes register, and her body softens, wings losing all their rigidity. I cradle her closer—watch her lashes sweep down to rest on cheeks that lack the colour they usually hold. "Sorry," she rasps, nuzzling into my chest. "Post-traumatic stress from that time you threw me into a pool of shit. The smell of arsehole brings back memories of me wanting to swing you around by your dick."

My balls try to suck up into my body. My girl has such a way with words.

"Well, this one's diluted ..." I mumble. "It may not work as well."

She opens her eyes, appraising me, and I watch recognition settle over her face like a dark storm cloud. "*No ...*" Her attention snaps to her box mid-yawn and the half-used bottle of shit. "*You ... You ...*"

"I had no choice. I'll use the other half if I have to."

I'm trying to sound empathetic; it's just not coming out that way.

"No. No more." She starts to wriggle, and I lower her feet to the ground of the shallow pool, allowing her to pull away, my narrowed eyes like fishing hooks piercing her flesh.

I can barely bring myself to blink, tucking my wings into my back as she drops her wilted shoulders below the water. The wet hair glued across her face makes her look like an ivory water nymph; those big, round eyes like fading stars looking at anything but me.

She needs space. Fine, I can do space. Just so long as she's not asking for more than two fucking metres, we'll be right as rain.

I unbuckle my sword, setting it next to her special box while I watch Dell smear her face with water—no doubt trying to mask the salty scent of her tears.

Too late, baby girl. You can't hide shit from me.

That bottle of crap was precious to her, and I hate that I've betrayed her trust by using it without her permission, but my priority is to keep her alive and healthy.

And she's not there yet.

I reach for the jar. "Dell, it's not working fast enou—"

"*I said no!*" she bites out, making me pause like she has my balls in a vice.

I clench my outstretched hand, feeling my canines lengthen as I fight the urge to spread my wings, puff my chest, and assert my fucking dominance. "You're pushing my limits, Little Dove ..."

She rolls her eyes. "Calm your feathers, Nightcap. This is my first warm bath in weeks, and by the smell of you ..." she scrunches her nose, "I'd say it's yours, too. Let's just enjoy it."

I grunt.

News flash, baby. We both smell like we've been balls

deep in a dirty arsehole. Besides, her sassy mouth just doesn't hold the same bite when she looks like she's been tossed through a meat grinder.

I scratch my chin, watching her curl shredded hands around the hem of her shift. She pauses, narrowing that regal gaze on me. "Don't look."

Fuck no.

I bite my lip so hard I taste blood, attempting to stop myself from spewing words I'll regret later.

She's not asking me to give her privacy so I don't see her naked. I caught those hands trying to preen her shredded wings for me earlier—a sight that split my chest clean open. I know she wants to bite into me and give me every tangible and intangible part of herself. That's not the fucking issue here.

She wants privacy because she's been using that shift as a shield, hiding her damaged body. Damage I've been scenting since I first laid eyes on her in that hut, tucked under a mountain of blankets.

Damage that wasn't created by fucking *table shrapnel.*

My beast claws at his bonds, snarling for release. The shady bastard's not okay with sitting back while Dell comes to terms with what happened to her. He wants to use whatever means necessary to draw the information so he can hunt the culprits, feed them their own cocks, then drown them in blood.

I doubt her beast left much for him to play with, but I wouldn't allow it anyway.

Dell deserves more than a savage who would leave her side when she's at her most vulnerable because he can't control his own darkness.

"Fine," I grind out, reaching into my pocket and tossing the gnarled root at the water, making a small splash. "But I need you to chew on that."

The filth we're swimming in should fix her up but fucked if I'm taking any chances.

She plucks it up, sniffs it, then scrunches her button nose. "Smells like shit."

"I could force feed you," I offer, face stony. "Up to you."

She sighs, then indicates for me to spin around.

I gesture for her to take a fucking bite.

She rolls her eyes and slips the girthy end between her lips, her cheeks hollowing into the perfect blowjob face ...

My cock twitches, finally springing to life now that she no longer seems to be in mortal danger. There's nothing like seeing your woman haunted physically and mentally to cut the circulation to your dick.

She sinks her teeth into the root, making a loud crunching sound, and for some reason my cock gets even harder.

I clear my throat.

I'm so fucked up.

"Now, turn around," she says around a mouthful before swallowing, making a bold show of not twisting her face up.

I grunt my approval and I spin, glancing out across the ocean, ears tuned into every movement she makes.

She's doing better than I did when I had to chew on that rancid root about three hundred years ago. I vomited five times before finally keeping some down.

I hear her shredding material, then the resonating 'plop' as she drops her shift on the edge of the terrace pool.

Times up, Little Dove.

I turn, seeing Dell's arms bound around her body like a shield while she eases onto a shallow step of mineral rock, wincing when it no doubt bites whatever the fuck is caning her arse. Leaping up, she searches for some place more suitable to perch while I internally congratulate myself for not being all over her like a fucking rash.

Feigning a relaxed bravado, I lower my arse onto another shelf and recline, using the edge of the pool as a back rest. I watch her contemplate the best position to rest so her entire body is submerged, waiting for her to realise *I'm* the best solution to that fucking problem.

Her attention shifts to me, and I've never seen her look so timid. "Can I ... lay on you?"

I spread my arms, exposing my chest which is doing a pathetic job of containing the achy organ inside it. She clears her throat, inches forward, then floats down, resting her cheek on my chest with her legs dangling between mine.

I quiver at the contact, resisting the urge to wrap her in the cage of my arms and pin her to me. I should be given one of her gold vagina stars for all the restraint I'm showing right now.

Her limbs are sharp and angular, her hips like razor blades protruding into my stomach; such a contrast to the swell of her breasts pressed against my blazing skin.

She's lost a lot of weight. Just more ammunition my beast uses to gut me from the inside.

I drizzle water over her exposed shoulders, trying to ignore the fact that her wings are oddly perched over her bum. Perhaps she doesn't know just how shredded they are, because honestly? They don't hide shit ...

And that ... that's a brand on Dell's arse cheek—as if she's nothing more than livestock.

Darkness swarms through my body like a locust plague, leaving nothing but the harsh, barren bones of something that used to be so full of life.

My beast isn't ... normal. He's dark. Savage.

Broken.

Cursed by his own secrets.

Our arms slide around Dell's back, locking her in place

with corded muscle and feral fortification. "Tell me what happened."

Her head snaps up at the crackling echo of our voice, eyes wide and wild with her desire to flee ... like a finch caught in the claws of a wild drako.

"Kal ..."

She tries to move, her mouth popping open when she no doubt registers she's trapped—forced to remain submerged while we condemn her with a glare.

"What. Happened?"

She shakes her head and our answer is a sharp hiss that makes the surface of the water vibrate.

"Don't make me say it ..."

We can taste the tartness of her fear, see it in her eyes as she tries to make herself smaller.

"You can't ignore it and expect it to just *disappear*."

Her gaze ignites with a spark of challenge, like a fire in her belly just sprung to life. "That's exactly what's happening." Her eyes dart to the murky water and back again. "It's *disappearing!*"

We walked right into that one.

Nobody else would dare give my beast lip, but our little Queen does whatever the fuck she wants. It makes our cock swell as we picture her with a crown on her head, taking shit from no one; using that fierceness to protect our future offspring ...

We jerk our hips, seeking her valley of warmth, and she sucks a sharp breath. "Too late, Kitty. I already *saw* it."

Our voice is a guttural promise of violent things she's certainly not ready for ...

Shit.

I wrestle my darkness down before he tries to fuck the memory of whatever she went through right out of her, though my cock continues to wage a war against my pants.

Her body softens, those doe eyes peering up at me as she swallows so loud I can hear it. "I'm not good at ... *this*."

Because she's never had anyone to rely on before.

The thought is a fucking pike to the chest, my beast desperate to sink our teeth into her flesh and call her his own.

But she's not ready for that. Not yet.

"You don't have to be good at it. But I'm here, telling you I want to share the load. And it's not just because I want to fuck those cunts up. Something tells me they've already been dealt with anyway ..."

Her face remains impassive despite the tang of her anxiety biting my tongue.

Perfect fucking game face.

Interesting.

I narrow my eyes, my beast prowling towards the surface. "Have they been dealt with, Dell?"

"I—" she starts, then sputters on her words as she tries to lie through her teeth rather than let me take some of the fucking weight.

My beast flings himself against the shell of his restraints, making my entire body shudder as I taste the bitter bite of my own disappointment. "Hard habit to shuck when you've spent your life running from the truth, isn't it?"

Her eyes widen.

It's harsh but, *fuck* ... I refuse to stand by and watch her buckle under all the weight when I'm standing right here with empty hands.

She stutters over jumbled words again.

"Heil neig ta den da, jasta. Geis heil na ta vest mi kaft heil."
You bow to no one, baby. But you have to let me lift you.

I gently pick her up, lower her on the shallow ledge, and turn to get out of the pool.

"*Kal* ..."

"No." I spin, chiding her with a glare. "I'm here for you, Dell. We all are. Stop pushing us away and hiding shit from us when we'd do *anything* to make sure you're safe. That you *feel* safe."

"That's just it," she murmurs, her shoulders bowing forward.

The sight puts a pin through my bubble of anger.

I take a step towards her through the dick-deep water. My cock's going to smell like shit for the next week.

The things we do for love.

"That's just what, Little Dove?"

"My problem. Why I'm afraid to let you all the way in." She clears her throat, arms wrapped around her body. "The people who care about me do it at their own expense. Every time I let someone in, I lose them. And I'm *sick* of it."

My cold, black heart softens as she finally shows her underbelly. It's soul candy, and I gobble it up like a starved child, then smack my tongue against the roof of my mouth at the caustic aftertaste.

"Dell, you're not going to lose us ..."

Her face hardens.

Wrong thing to say, apparently. Go fucking figure.

"You can't promise that," she growls with a dominating undertone that makes my skin pebble. Makes *his* lips curl back. "Here I am, in a healing pool while your *brothers* are in a cell somewhere. What if one of them dies, Kal? What if we lose the sun cycle because you regard my safety over *theirs?*"

I take a step forward, my wings nudging at my skin. They're desperate to unfurl and crowd over her, but I need to know what happened.

I need to hear her say it.

"They're stronger than you think, Dell. That's not going to happen."

"How do you know?" she sneers, her words aimed to maim, distract, and deter me from seeking the truth.

Nothing she says or does could turn me away. I'll take the good, the ugly, the evil ... I'll take all the sad pieces pretending to be sharp.

We can be broken together.

"What happened, Little Dove?"

"Fuck you," she snaps as she stands, white hair clinging to her shoulders, arms dropping to her sides. I draw a sharp breath at the sight of full breasts riddled with long, fading slash marks, and waning scabs from the word 'whore' sliced across the fading scar I know she fought to keep ...

My wings explode from my back.

Motherfuckers.

I put my knuckle between my teeth and bite until I taste blood. I used to think I was strong for surviving some of the shit I've lived through, now I know I didn't even grasp the *meaning* of the word.

I sense Cassian's arrival and fling my bristling wings out to give her privacy, snatching her ruined shift off the edge of the pool. But she just shoves past me and begins to climb out of the water, her body only half mended.

I pitch the garment at her. "Put it on!"

She catches it mid-air and slams it in the pool with a sharp, feral sound that ignites a fire in my belly.

Fucking hell.

Cassian clears his throat, making his presence known from the terrace above. Dell halts with one leg still in the pool, and I watch all the blood rush to her cheeks.

I fish the shift out of the pool and hand it to her. "Put it on. Now."

There's a riot of movement while she wraps herself in the shredded garment, avoiding my gaze and filling the space with uneasy silence. "You need to heal. Stay in the pool, I'll go."

She needs this shitty water more than she needs me right now.

I snatch my sword and leap to the upper terrace, signalling for Cassian to follow before bounding from level to level, propelling myself up, up, up ...

Stopping close enough that I can still see her, I wait while my insides get shredded by the big paws of my pacing beast.

Cassian advances, climbing the terrace pools, eyes slanted with confusion. "A little warning next time you plan on disappearing for a month?"

"I pinged you ... numerous times."

His brows dig in. "You know that's like piecing together a jigsaw puzzle blind." He sighs, shaking his head. "Whatever. There's a prisoner in the dungeon that requires judgement. That's if Kova hasn't taken it upon herself to castrate him already." He jerks his thumb over his shoulder. "And what happened to he—"

I shake my head and he snaps his mouth shut. "What do you need?"

"Another pair of eyes I can trust. Cling to the shade. I'll just be on the training slab so she feels like she has some distance."

"And if she *does* try to get out prematurely? In my experience, she's a loose fucking feather."

"Language," I growl, but Cass just rolls his eyes and knots his arms over his chest. "She's got the poison of a Fae Fury in her system," I say with a sigh. "If she tries to get out too early, ping me. I'll coast down and put her to sleep." *Fuck the repercussions.*

I stretch my wings, but his hand wraps around my wrist. My attention snaps at it, dragging up to his angular face—sharp, brutal, and almost punishing to look at. "What is it?"

"Have you told her about me yet?" His voice is a dark, husky rumble; velvet allure derived straight from *her*.

"No."

He combs thick, ebony waves back with his fingers, stuffing his other hand deep into his pocket. "You going to blow that shit out of the water soon, or what? I'm no expert, but I'd say your window of opportunity is shrinking. Pretty soon her hormones are going to start clouding her judgement."

I study him, *really* study him—my gaze shifting to Dell, then back to Cassian. "What do you mean, *exactly?*"

"You know what I'm talking about, I can smell it from here despite the rotten shit she's soaking in. Wait ..." he narrows his eyes. "She doesn't know?"

Well ... *fuck*. Seems his senses are more in tune than I thought they were.

"No." I scrub my face, feeling a headache coming on. I need time to think through my next move, lest I screw it up entirely. "And we're going to leave it that way."

"But wh—"

"She's not ready, son. *Leave it.*"

He flinches like I've just assaulted him, and it fucking kills me. It's so uncommon for him to show pain openly.

He's always been a closed heart—I've never even seen him cry. Not even as an infant when he was in need of the wet nurse.

It's like part of him slipped away all those years ago.

There's a moment of stillness where we watch each other, both testing the limits on this relationship that's only ever bloomed in the shadows.

"That's not it," he mumbles, head cocked to the side like he's listening to a voice I'm not tuned in to. "There's something else."

Astute spawn of my loins ...

"Now's not the time." I turn to leave, but his hand grips my arm again, though this time it's a sizzling brand against my skin.

I snap my attention to his face; his pupils thickening, canines lengthening as massive, feathery silhouettes uncurl behind him ...

Shit. I'd forgotten how big his wings are.

I stand a bit straighter, letting my own wings rise. "Son ... *contain it.*"

He shakes his head, blinking the beast away until black fades to icy violet.

When he was a child, I was so enchanted by those eyes that would just stare and stare and never fucking cry. They broke me.

Every. Fucking. Day.

They still do.

I sigh, shaking my head, trying to see the man and not my little boy. "She was raped," I concede, watching Dell bathe her wings while avoiding her reflection in the water's glassy surface. "She won't confirm it, but I know it's true. I can see it in her eyes."

"Go on ..."

I swallow hard, then meet his frigid stare, preparing to rip the bandage off us both.

The moment I voice it, there is no going back.

"Father?"

Fuck.

"I doubt the cub she's carrying belongs to either Sol or Drake."

His eyes widen, all the colour draining from his face and his gaze swivels towards the pool. I watch him watching her, wishing I could scour the filthy aftertaste of the words I just spat out.

My shoulders curl. "Put your wings away. You can trust

her, but if she sees the tips she'll get the wrong idea. She has history with the Legion."

"But I have nothing to do with them," he grits out, and I blow a deep breath.

"I know, son. Just ... put them away."

I give him a tight smile, clap him on the shoulder, and shoot into the sky. I spent most of Cassian's early years telling him to put his wings away, and every single time I hated myself a little bit more.

He deserves more than a life where he's forced to hide who he really is.

Clear of the steam billowing off the terrace pools, I let my darkness shed to the surface. We gnash our teeth, thrashing our fury against the air—my beast scratching our skin like he can hardly stand the feel of it holding all the ugly in.

Once we're hanging high above the training slab perched atop my Kingdom, he retracts our wings and we plummet, feet first, landing with so much force that a hairline crack weaves through the black marble. Large, black birds with fearsome, hooked beaks scatter, as if they know my beast is something to fear ...

Damn straight. Even I'm scared of him.

He's brutal.

Punishing.

He blames himself for shit he'll never be able to atone for, wearing the burden like a cape of malevolence.

He'll always fear the fate of the woman who fell in love with his darkness, and lost sight of the light. He's afraid the same fate will fall upon the first woman he's ever loved—the first woman he's *chosen*.

He draws our sword, tosses the sheath, and notices a brand in the distinct shape of our son's hand wrapped around our forearm ...

It's tempting to cake it in salt so we're left with the scar, something we'd truly treasure.

But if Edom saw it, he'd ask questions; he'd find out about our son.

That's not an option.

We stalk towards the training dummy carved from onyx. Its shoulders are broad and it's tall enough to pass as a depiction of me.

My beast.

Requiem is forged from fortified darnium; the strongest metal aside from iron. And coupled with the feral strength of our inner turmoil?

Death incarnate.

We slash the dummy shoulder to shoulder before leaping high and slicing it directly down the centre ... all in the space of a few split seconds. We land with our back to the victim, breathing even as the distinct sound of stone sliding against stone forebodes the thunder of onyx crashing to the ground.

We grunt, rolling our shoulders.

Sol thinks my spare time is spent getting my dick wet, but he's wrong. I allow him to believe the veiled lie that hides the fact that I'm deeply scarred.

Tormented.

But more recently? *Frightened.*

It hurt losing a woman I once considered a friend. Losing the woman I love?

It would fucking *destroy* me.

CHAPTER THIRTEEN
DELL

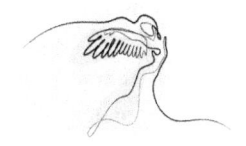

I roll my shoulders, arc my back, and stretch my wings—looking left and right, watching them rise from the pool with water streaming from their alabaster tips.

"Hey, pretty ladies ..."

Nice to have you back, again ... again.

My spine tingles and I shudder, *whuffing* them forward, getting a face full of shitty water.

They can fucking *move* without hurting ... or, like, shedding everywhere. And hot damn, I'd forgotten how beautiful they are. Kal's going to be so impressed. Not that I care since he's temporarily sin-binned, but that's not going to stop me from waving them in front of him.

I peel my shift up and glance down at my stomach, seeing clear, pearly skin ...

My heart turns to stone.

No exit-womb scar.

Seems the water didn't discriminate between the hate carved into my skin and the mark I'd come to treasure.

Swallowing the lump in my throat, I lift my chin and refocus my energy on what's really important.

This fucking *wish*.

I stalk to the edge of the pool and climb out using steady legs that no longer buckle, seeing a folded towel on a shaded lip of the pool right next to my special box and a big, black knapsack.

"Ohh, gifts!"

I hope it's food.

I glance in the bag as I dry myself, finding a skein of water, a stack of clothes, and a cloth parcel I can't catch the scent of over the wafty smell of arse.

Glancing up, I see a huge, marble door pierced into steep terrain above the upper terrace pool ... probably leading to Kal's castle crowning the volcano.

I frown.

Guess that means I'm scaling these motherfucking terraces.

There's nothing like marinating in shit for over an hour to make you appreciate fresh air in your lungs and clean, dry clothing that doesn't smell like crap. And by the fit of these black leather pants? Someone in this kingdom knows the shape of my arse much better than I do.

I sway down the hallway, my bag of things slung over a shoulder, the little cloth parcel waving back and forth in the vicinity of my nose ... smelling like the lovechild of every single one of my culinary fantasies.

My stomach rumbles.

I unwrap the cloth, reveal a big disk of golden goodness, and stuff half of it in my mouth ...

Fuck.

Me.

A sweet yet salty taste laced with *just* the right amount of creamy richness *explodes* across my tongue, almost bringing me to my knees.

What the fuck is this and how do I get more?

I take another blissful bite, weaving through corridors doused in watercolour light, my wings floating around me like pretty, fluffy clouds.

They do a shimmy, appreciating my internal compliment.

I'm taking them on a tour of the Night Kingdom, hunting for the perfect spot to die. And by that, I mean the perfect spot to learn to fly.

I know they've only just risen from the grave ... again, but I have a wish to conquer, so the tarts better get in line. Drake's tether may be looking a touch more perky, but I'm not taking any chances.

Scarfing down the rest of my snack, I round on a framed entrance to the coliseum I'm all too familiar with. I pause and look out across the spectacle while my wings get an airy boner, naïve to the fact they're about to *wish* they were still shredded.

I nod to myself. "This'll do."

The coliseum is half drenched in soft morning light pouring in through the open roof; the other half cast in deep, melancholy shadows. Dropping my sack at the door, I glide into the open arena ...

Blood-curdling screams echo through my memory; the sickening grind of saw on bone as Kal's beast hacked the pastel blue wings from that man's back.

I shiver, glancing skyward.

Kal's majestic throne hangs over me like a monolith of his power, and I gauge the distance from the ledge to the very hard ground my feet are currently rooted on ...

This is going to hurt.

I climb the stairs and step out onto Kal's dais like I'm walking a fucking plank. I make my way to the edge, close my eyes, push my wings wide, and leap into the air; picturing myself as a delicate, softly falling petal—one that's going to glide towards the ground in a remarkable show of natural finesse.

Fucking *wrong*.

The useless tarts don't even flap.

I plummet like a feathery boulder, arms and legs flailing, my wings trailing behind me while my heart tries to worm its way out of my arsehole. I'm internally cursing Kal and his whore-killing wish when I land in a crumpled heap of feathers and limbs atop a warm body that makes a dramatic *'oomph'* when I flatten it.

"You're a fucking nutter," the body groans in a deep, velvet voice I recognise—one resonating from my *vagina*—and it takes three breaths too many for me to register that I'm currently face-deep in a pair of testicles ...

Cassian must keep fairly well tended in the scrotum department because, I have to say, this is probably the most fragrant pair of balls I've ever drawn a whiff of.

I'm not sure how I get myself into these situations, but I doubt Kal's going to be impressed if he finds out I've been using Cassian's ball sack as a landing pillow for my face.

"And you're swiftly becoming a pain in my arse," I grumble, uprooting from my spongy cushion, clamouring off Kal's second-in-command in case my Night God walks in and gets all huffy about this unintentional sixty-niner.

I dust myself off, quietly impressed Cassian's cock didn't even twitch for me. It's hard to find a man who isn't governed by his dick these days.

"Now, do you mind?" I ask, spinning, tucking my useless wings against my back. One of them flicks out again and waves around. "If the fear of death isn't actually there, I won't be able to figure this shit out in time to rescue the rest of my harem."

Cassian grunts and peels his body off the floor. Either he's suffering some serious internal damage or he's uncomfortable with the casual mention of my collection of prime cocks. "*Kal* asked me to keep an eye on you while he attends some business. If I hand you back with broken bits, he'll be pissed."

I frown. Of course he organised a chaperone. Why would I expect anything else?

"Yeah, well. You can tell him your balls softened my landing. He only has himself to blame for ... *this*." I gesture at my wings who're flapping about forty-nine seconds too late.

Unfortunately, my testicle taunt doesn't have the desired effect of sending Cassian fluttering off so I can get back to my insurmountable task. He simply rubs his thinking face with a big hand. "You're going to have to fill in the gaps, I'm afraid."

I sigh, turn on my heel, and start up the stairs again. "I can't rescue the others until I've learnt to fly and have satisfied Kal's wish."

My distaste is palpable.

Don't be bitter, Dell. Be *better*.

"*Really?*" He sounds more amused than shocked, the bastard.

I turn, copping a surprised wing to the face that almost knocks me out. "Why else would I be throwing myself into the air from an obscene height when my wings are *obviously* too pretty to be of any use?"

He lifts a brow but doesn't spare a single glance at my fetching feathers. "I can give you some basic tips."

My mouth drops open, locked and loaded to toss a rebuke, but then I snap it shut.

Actually, that's exactly what I need.

"Is that going to get you in trouble with the big boss?"

He shrugs. "I'm just not in the mood to watch you snap

your neck on the marble when you land wrong. Which you were about to do, by the way, before I softened your landing with my dick."

Rude.

Not only was he not affected by my dick taunt, he's throwing it straight back in my face.

I feel oddly disarmed.

He strides towards me with a predatory gait, and I can't help but stare. He's a mountain of muscle, but he moves like a cat—silent and precise.

Deadly.

I quiver. No wonder Kal keeps him close.

"So, do you want to break your neck, or not? Your choice. I don't really give a fuck."

It *has* to be why he keeps him around, it's certainly not for his jovial attitude.

"You're assuming I don't know how to land. You didn't even give me a chance to prove myself before you decided to become a big ..." *dick pillow, dick pillow, dick pillow,* "safety net."

"I panicked. Babysitting isn't my thing."

"I'm not a baby!" I snap, stomping my foot to emphasise my point.

"You are to me." He slips his hands deep into his pockets and yawns, like he's about ready to settle in for a midmorning kip.

I narrow my eyes and study his nonchalant gaze pretending to be sharp ...

He's purposely being a cunt, using it as some sort of shield.

Interesting.

I think I like him ... in a platonic 'he's sexy, but I'd only use his dick as a pillow' sort of way.

He rolls his eyes and runs a hand through his hair. "Look, just throw your fucking wings out. I've got shit to do."

Yes, sir.

I do as I'm told. I've got shit to do, too. Namely Sol, Drake, and Aero once I break them out of Sterling ... and maybe Kal, so long as he stops treating me like a flight hazard. "This okay?"

Cassian scowls. "Can you keep them still? Or is that just ..." he waves his hand in their general direction, "them all the time?"

I'm tempted to knee him in the nuts.

"This is what you get. You up to the challenge or not?"

He studies my wings, looking like he just got asked to lick an arsehole. I think he's about to choose option B, just to be super cunty, but he huffs a sigh and nods. "Yeah, sure. Fuck it. I'm up to the challenge."

Well then.

I stand a little straighter; even my vagina slips her game face on.

"Show me your movement."

"My ... movement?"

"Yes, you need to get the movement correct. Like this." He presses his wrists together, rolling his hands and fingers like mirrored waves.

"Oh ..." He's talking about *wing* movements.

Whew.

I concentrate really hard, trying to mimic him, though I think my wings have become accustomed to being gammy. "Umm, like this?"

He cocks his head to the side. "Ehh, close enough."

I blink at him.

He changes the 'movement' his hands are making, putting more focus into the flick of his fingers. "Now, when you're coming to a stop, the motion is more like this ..."

I sigh and give it a red-hot crack.

Finger flick.

Finger flick.

Finger flick.

He scrunches his nose, throwing my rhythm entirely.

"*What?* Am I not doing it right?"

"You look like you're trying to lay an egg."

This dick.

"Why don't you just show me?" I blurt, gesturing towards the absence of his wings.

I watch his throat bob, all the colour dropping from his generally olive complexion as a certain hardness falls over his face. Avoiding my eye contact, he strides over to my sack and strangles the hessian neck in his white-knuckled grip.

"What are you doing?"

"Taking your shit to your room, *highness*." He drops into a low, cunty bow, rises with cold eyes, stuffs his spare hand in his pocket, and stalks away.

Ummm ...

"You said you would help me!"

He starts up the stairs while I gape after him. "Lesson's over. Don't kill yourself."

"But what about my shitty *movement?*"

He doesn't answer, just continues on before disappearing out of sight.

What a douche canoe. I should have kneed him in the balls when I had the chance.

My shoulders slump forward.

Moody bastard. Perhaps he's been spending too much time with my Night God? Kal's emotional whiplash is rubbing off on him.

Oh well, looks like it's just me, my vagina, and my limited supply of common sense.

I continue back up to the dais where I practise the 'movements' Cassian just showed me with his fucking hands. Once

I think I have it at least *partially* down pat, I draw a deep breath and throw myself off the edge.

Finger flick.

Finger flick.

This time, the landing is somewhat buffered by the small amount of air my wings manage to scoop, and I almost land on all fours. Probably would have, too, if I didn't lose balance at the very last second—the mild impact absorbed by my face and achy pre-heat breasts.

Cassian's balls were far less hostile.

I sit up, pinch my fingers all the way down my nose, and breathe a sigh of relief when I find no broken bits. I doubt my gag reflex could handle another stint in that shit pool.

Smoothing my clothes, I toss my hair over my shoulder and stand, giving my wings a pat. Positive reinforcement is the only way forward here. Don't want to hurt their feelings, then end up with a fractured spine because they're pissed at me for calling them out on their incompetence.

CHAPTER FOURTEEN
DELL

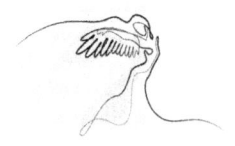

I peel off the ground, arms quaking, thankful the only witness to my shame is a sea of empty seats staring down at me.

Fucking wings.

I know the lazy tarts were sawn off at the nub when I was four, but seriously? This is getting ridiculous.

"I think that's enough."

Peering under my arm, I see the upside-down vision of my topless Night God emerge from the shadows; folded wings peeking over the breadth of his shoulders like twin claws. My own wings do a flirty flick and my elbows give way, flattening me against the ground with an *oomph*.

I groan.

Hussies. It's the most effort I've seen from them all day.

"How long have you been there?" My words are distorted, my cheek flat against the cold marble offering my sweaty skin a touch of reprieve.

Kal's badass boots thump towards me, pausing in front of my face where I study his loosely tied leather laces. "Since Cassian left." He reaches out a hand. "Time for a break."

"But I'm not done yet," I mumble, making no effort to move. At all.

"You need food and sleep. You can come back when you've had a rest."

"I don't want to rest!" I arch my body off the ground and clamber into an unsteady crouch. My wings wilt like a blanket, pouting at the mere suggestion they have to do more physical labour. If you could even call it that.

I sigh.

They may be pretty, and I'm glad they've been restored to their former glory but fuck me ... they're really only good for hugging Gods and gaining unwanted attention.

I'm hoisted to my feet like a *child* before he starts to knead my useless wings. "You need a rest, or these ..." he rolls his fingers along the muscles bunched at the root of the inept appendages, "are going to be too sore to make any progress for the next *week*."

Hot damn, those hands are pure *magic*.

I moan, pressing into him, preparing for the mind-melting, vagina-blowing wingasm that's *well* overdue, and will make my flirty feathers ... *disappear*.

My eyes pop open and I jerk away, hissing over my shoulder while I stomp towards the stairs. At least that's how I picture it. In truth, it's more of a languid skulk while I drag my bratty wings along the floor, deflating a little with each soul-destroying step.

"I know what you're trying to do." I wipe the sweat from my face, focusing on the colossal staircase in front of me—one of the many that segment the rows and rows of staggered seating. "You're trying to put my wings into a coma so I have no choice but to take a break. That's just dirty tactics."

I hear the booming beat of Kal's wings before he falls from the sky, landing in a warrior's stance on a wide step before me—blocking my path with his massive wingspan.

I yelp, almost tumbling backwards down the stairs, but Kal's hand fists into my top and saves my life. I roll my eyes when my wings rise from the ground like a fucking soufflé, rubbing all over his shiny, black feathers ...

He smirks.

I frown.

"*Move.*"

"No."

"You're being an arse."

His brow jacks up. "And you're being stubborn."

Is he serious?

"Because I have three mates to rescue!" I holler, wiping that smirk clean off his perfectly rendered face.

Kal drops his grip on my top, his sapphire eyes like crystal chips. "You don't think I want to rescue them, too? You have no idea how much I want that! How much I *need* that. But you need to be able to fly if you insist on coming along so you can protect yourself should something happen to me! Right now, you're too tired and weak to make logical decisions. You need to eat ... sleep ..."

My beast is pacing a hole in my frail outer shell, snarling at the mere *suggestion* we should take a fucking nap. Ironically, she slips free of her feeble restraints, practically setting Kal's point on a plaque.

My teeth lengthen, pressing past the full flesh of my lower lip as I'm shoved into a pile of shadows, my wings snapping into a tight parcel of discipline.

What the fuck?

If only they listened to me even half as much as they listen to my cock-biting beast, we'd be on our way to Sterling by now.

"We slept for three fucking weeks." We sway forward a step, poking a finger at Kal's broad chest. "We've done enough *sleeping!*" Our roar is as turbulent as the heat pouring through our veins—the cauldron overflowing, filling us with dense, delicious *power*.

Not this again.

Kal presses his body flush against the full wrath of my inner bane, his eyes soft and reassuring, painting our cheek with delicate strokes of calloused fingertips. "It's okay, Little Dove. You're okay ..."

It's not okay. It's so far from okay. Drake, Sol, and Aero are likely trapped in a cell and I'm stuck here, hammering myself against the ground like a faulty catapult. But he's cooing to us like we're a baby ... and it's kind of working.

We crack our neck to the side and any heat siphons back to the cauldron which calms to a light simmer. My beast softens enough for me to shove her down and clamp her in chains, but they're weak and frail ...

She's not.

"It's not okay," I say through clenched teeth, stepping backwards down the stairs while I fight to maintain control.

Kal follows and my hands dart between us.

"Stop. *Please*. I don't want to hurt you."

"Why?" His voice is silk, his movements composed, like he's hunting a wild animal. "Why do you think you might hurt me?"

I know what he's asking.

Tension clogs my throat, a ball of venom threatening to spew corrosive truth all over his perception of me. He needs to know what I've done—what I'm capable of—so he knows to keep his distance when the bitch is loose. He may be twice my size, but she's unpredictable.

A killer.

I take another step down the stairs.

"Because I'm a weapon," I blurt before I can second guess myself. "Because I blew two men up and gutted another. Because I thought my beast was going to blow *you* up in the

East and there was nothing I could do to stop her. Because I can't control myself when the bitch takes over."

"You *gutted* one of them?" he asks, raising a brow when he should be fucking *quivering*.

"He swallowed the key!" I scream, feeling oddly defensive. I wasn't exactly jumping for joy when she sliced through Feather Plunger's shit-chute, and that's exactly my point. I'm worried my inner darkness has no moral compass.

"Okay, it's okay ..." Kal implores, his eyes a tranquil, starry night ...

My shoulders shake with the continued effort to contain my darkness. She's eager to prove she can take care of us *all* —while I'm out here trying to convince myself I'm not a fucking monster.

"It was self-defence ..."

Kal wraps me in his shadow, cups my face with both hands, and I draw on the scent of jasmine and verbena like it's my fucking lifeline. "I know, *jasta* ..."

"I'm not like him, Kal. I'm not."

Voicing it feels like solidifying the statement. Like saying it aloud will make it true.

Kal swirls his thumb around the sharp of my cheekbone. "That's like telling me the stars come out at night, Dell. *I know ...*"

His words are a balm to my tender heart, and I wish I could fall into him—curl up with his inner darkness and hide from the uncertainty.

The fear.

But, I can't. There's too much to do.

"Just tell me we're going to rescue them. Promise me you're not just making me waste time learning to fly because you know they're a lost cause ..."

Tell me something I can use to grout myself together until I see them again.

Kal's grip on my face tightens. "We're going to fucking rescue them. I promise."

The words feed my hungry heart and I deflate, a shuddering sigh pulling from my lips as my beast burrows away ... trusting him.

Kal's eyes fix on my lips and he pinches the bridge of his nose, taking a step back, cleaving us apart with too much bitter air.

He looks exhausted.

Pained.

I frown, feeling how much space this entire situation has put between us.

We've done nothing but argue since he found me in the East, all because I was so busy worrying about my other three Gods that I overlooked the one right here ... trying to keep me alive and hurting in his own way.

Shit.

I've been so *selfish*.

Straightening my shoulders, I rise to the tips of my toes and grab Kal's scruffy face, pull it down a notch or three, and press our lips together.

The kiss only lasts a fraction of a second—not enough for me to taste him like I really want to, but hopefully enough to show that I recognise I've been a bit of a dick.

"Thank you," I whisper, bundling everything into a few small words I hope will portray my sporadic burst of sentiment. "For saving me."

Kal's barely responsive, still bent over, staring at me ...

Unblinking.

It's like I just kissed a stone sculpture and not the real thing.

Have I been wrong to presume he's still interested because his dick got a bit stiff in the pool? It doesn't mean his *heart* belongs to me ...

Shiiiit ...

Here I am, stealing kisses when he probably just feels duty bound to my white wings which are currently getting handsy with his muscular arse cheeks.

Suddenly self-conscious, I clear my throat and take a step back.

The energy shifts.

Kal's strong arms band around me, smooth and lethal, and he takes my mouth in a bruising kiss that folds me into him. Every movement is exquisite and precise, as if he's visualised this moment a million times over.

I moan, threading my fingers into his hair, his tongue sliding against mine in a primal dance of thirst and rage and heartache.

But it's not enough.

I want to show Kal just how much I care about *him*. I'm practically salivating at the thought, my body gaining some newfound strength ...

I break the kiss and shove him back.

He catches himself on the stairs, lain out like a Night God banquet; wings spread, lips swollen, chest heaving ...

Straddling him, I align my core with the hard, throbbing bulge in his black leather pants, and he growls; a primal rumble that sets my blood on fire. *"Dell—"*

I silence him with my lips, sweeping my tongue into his mouth while I reach between us, unbuttoning his pants with tremulous fingers.

It's not quick, and it's certainly not dignified. Mainly because I'm not used to fumbling with buttons while I consider all the ways I *want* to pleasure someone.

The woes of being a hoe.

"Fuuuck!" The word pours into my mouth like a hex. "Dell, stop ... *we can't.*"

I pull back and frown at his tight face, my burrowed hand

inches from his cock. "What do you mean we *can't?*"

He sits up, refastening his pants, the air thick with the scent of our arousal ... and something else that's sharp and tangy.

Anxiety.

His.

"I have something I need to talk to you about before we go any further."

"What's it about?" I ask, sitting a little straighter.

He clears his throat, his fingers digging into my hips like he's trying to hold me down, and I can see the cogs turning behind those midnight eyes ...

"*Cassian.*"

I arch a brow. I'm not sure why we're talking about Kal's sex-on-a-stick sidekick while I'm cradling his cock between my thighs. *Unless ...*

Shiiiiiit.

Maybe he saw me face-plant into Cassian's balls.

Fuck. Fuck. Fuck. There is no pretty way to say I didn't mean to sniff his dick!

"Mmmhmm." I plaster a nonchalant mask on my face, my galloping heart making me feel like I'm going to hurl my meagre guts up. "What about him?"

His face hardens, gaze narrowing like spears pointed at my flailing conscience. "You're nervous. Why are you nervous?"

Because I used his dick as a pillow.

Son of a tit.

"Am I?" I squeak, trying not to pee myself while I marinate in his ancient perusal. "Perhaps your sensors are malfunctioning. Keep going." Get it over with so I can lock my silly arse in the sin bin for the rest of eternity.

His eyes narrow further. "My sensors do *not* malfunction, Dell ..."

"Well," I say, sultry smooth, "aren't you a clever boy."

Gods have mercy. I'm making this worse.

Should I sniff *his* dick, tell him I like the smell? Butter him up a bit? I see no other way out of this mess.

I'm just about to bend down when he blurts, *"Cassian's my son."*

I choke on my next breath, my thoughts dissipating into mind dust as my vagina turns into a fucking raisin.

No way. Not possible.

"Bullshit ..."

But even as I say the word, I'm thinking back to the first time I saw them walking side by side: strides alike, their hair so black it almost looks blue, the same tight buns ...

Fuck. Me.

The whole *penis-sniffing* thing just got a shit ton more awkward.

My wings snap into my back and I shake my head, ambling out of his lap. No more flying lessons until I can coax them back out again, *dammit*.

I step over Kal, clamouring up the stairs.

"Dell, wait ..." he pleads, his steps echoing in the wake of my bafflement.

I'm beelining for some fresh air. I know this coliseum has an open roof but *hell* ... it's sweltering in here.

"Jasta ..."

He grabs my arm but I shake him off, peeling down the hall and into the communal walkway with unperturbed views of the crater village.

"It's not what you think ..." he implores, sliding in front of me with his hands up in a supplicating gesture.

I jerk to a stop, almost slamming into him. "I sniffed your son's testicles."

There. I said it.

Kal rears back, massive wings flaring—two angry alter

egos staring down on me. *"Dell! What the fuck?"*

I prod his puffed-up chest. "Don't spread your wings at me, you big, moody bastard! You lied to me about having a son, so you have to forgive me for the junk-sniffing thing. That's the rules!"

He shakes his head, face ashen. "Why the *fuck* would you smell his nuts?"

"I fell on them!" I screech, throwing my hands in the air. "They softened my landing! And I swear Kal, I swear! His thunderstick didn't even twitch for me. Not once. It was as soft as a slug snuggled up against my face. So calm your wings, okay? They're giving me a complex."

Now *I'm* all puffy.

"Wait ..." he says, sliding forward a step, his hands suspended between us like he's afraid I might sniff *his* wrinkle purse, too. "So, it was an accident? You didn't actually walk up to him and ask to smell his balls?"

"What the hell do you think I am?" I shriek, throwing my hands up.

He winces.

"Hor"—I narrow my eyes—"monal?"

Wow, he's really lucky. I thought he was going to say something entirely different, and he was about to be blessed with a pair of bruised balls.

And he's right, I'm not feeling myself. I'm almost positive I'm not reacting to this news like a normal person would.

Kal's a daddy.

I tilt my head to the side, picturing a smear of satisfaction on his face while he cradles a newborn baby to his naked chest; those long, corded muscles wrapped around the small bundle of womb-fruit ...

My uterus just wobbled with excitement.

I groan and wiggle my hips while observing all that paternal Night Godliness, ripe and ready for the penis-plucking, my hungry gaze roaming down, down, dowwwnn ...

Bingo.

I balk, shaking my head. My mind's on a rampage, and not a very pretty one.

Poor Aero.

I'm definitely going into heat. I need to get away from ... all *that* before I end up inseminated. What a disaster that would be. To really drill the point home, I slap my own cheek —a reminder that semen is the devil in disguise—before cutting a path under Kal's wings.

"Where the hell are you going?"

"I need to move," I mutter, following my feet down the corridor.

"Nobody knows he's my son, Dell! Nobody except the Suns and his Electi." His words are a whisper-scream I can't run away from quick enough. "It could put his life in danger if the news got out!"

I groan, walking even *faster*.

A protective father doing everything in his power to keep his son safe? My vagina has her own personal paddling pool.

"Dell, wait. Let's talk this through. I don't want you doing anything impulsive."

That's why I'm walking away—before I screw him in the middle of the hall while I scream for all his daddy-jizz. "I can't believe I preened my feathers in front of his *son*," I mumble to nobody but my own stupid self. Honestly, someone should confiscate my vagina.

"Yeah, that was unfortunate," Kal says from right behind me, making my heart leap into my throat.

I spin, glaring at him. "I can't believe you didn't tell me sooner. How am I ever going to look him in the eye again? I mean, I literally thought to myself *this man's testicles smell nice.*"

"*Dell* ..." I swear I hear his knuckles pop. "For the sake of this building, can you stop talking about my son's balls?"

Wow. He's oddly protective over them.

"Sure," I mutter, wiggling my hips. I wonder how he'd fare if he knew my vagina was in Cassian's face while I was nuzzling his dick? Would he be just as protective over my little honey hole?

"I'm far more interested in *your* skin twins, just so we're clear."

He blinks at me, his eyes glazing over. "Did you just ..." he clears his throat. "Did you just call my testicles '*skin twins*'?"

I nod enthusiastically, welcoming the change of subject like a breath of fresh air. "You're welcome to use it any time. I think it has a nice ring to it."

He opens his mouth, looking like he's about to say something profound before he deflates, offering me a pinched smile that looks a bit forced. "Thanks, Little Dove. That's really thoughtful of you."

I swell with pride.

I'm also great at coming up with masculine nicknames for his meat candy. As far as potential mate candidates go, I'm a straight ten.

He stalks forward, strong thighs tensing ...

I lick my lips.

"Look," he purrs, pinching my chin, reigning my full-ish, partially divided attention. "I know I fucked up. I'm really sorry, Dell."

I gape at him, stunned in the wake of his most humble and heartfelt apology. Sol, the hard bastard, could learn a thing or two from Kal in this regard.

Actually, so could I.

"No, it's fine. I'm just embarrassed. And frustrated, and really, *really*—"

"Horny?"

I cross my legs and almost tottle over. "You can smell it, can't you?"

He gives me a lopsided shrug, those azure eyes glimmering. "They can probably smell it all the way down in the village."

My cheeks heat. My vagina's literally cock-calling.

"What's wrong with me? Is this the normal reaction to finding out my ..." I wave a hand in his general direction, "has a full-grown man-child who's probably hundreds of years older than me? Because I'm concerned."

"Nothing's wrong with you, Little Dove. You're just hormonal ..."

The fuck?

I widen my stance, narrow my eyes, and knife him with a sharp, serrated sound.

My uterus does the same.

How *dare* he blame my raging hormones. I know I just did the exact same thing but ... *how dare he!*

"*Dell,*" Kal hushes, dropping into a low crouch so I'm looking down on *him* for a change. "That wasn't a dig ..."

He looks even better from this angle—where I can study those strong shoulders in all their glory. And don't even get me started on those big, baby-guarding arms ...

"Of course." I sigh, tugging him up and dusting him off, paying extra attention to the V pointing straight to his dick. "I'm about to start spitting blood everywhere. From my vagina. You know, the spot between my legs that's open for business ..."

He starts to say something but he's disrupted by the distant cry of someone ... well ... *climaxing.*

I turn so fast my surroundings blur, then follow my vagina's nose straight down a shadowy corridor.

"Dell ... *shit*. Hold up ..."

I locate a door that's stifling pleasure-pitched wails,

throw it open, prance inside a dimly lit room, trip over a petrified penis, and go sprawling forward.

Luckily, I'm caught by a pair of muscular arms.

"Whoopsies," I chirp as I'm tugged against Kal's hard body and wrapped in the cape of his glorious wings. I pat his feathers, sniffing the air. "Thanks. But you can let me go now."

"Apologies!" Kal bellows, backing us out the door while I pry his wings from my face, trying to catch a peep at whatever smells like a cocktail of *very* happy vaginas.

"Stop, I want to see all the hap—"

"*Shh*, Dell. We just busted in on a private party. We have no right to be here."

I pout.

He herds me towards the door when a woman's voice cuts through the wailing symphony of moans. "Stay if you want! Let the pretty lady have some fun."

She sounds cheeky.

Kal turns into a fucking stone statue and I peer up at him through my lashes, catching his wild, penetrating gaze.

His face seems to say *it's up to you* ...

I gnaw my bottom lip, nipples puckering. "Was it one of them?" I ask with a stage whisper.

"No, Dell."

Good answer. Gold vagina star for him.

"Did you love her?" I brace myself for a response I don't want to hear.

"No." His reply is swift and sincere. Brutal, in fact. For a moment, I feel the sting she no doubt felt at the rejection. "Though I tried to, wished I could meet her on that level. I've lived with that guilt ever since."

I run the tips of my fingers down the grain of his silky feathers. "You can't always choose the people you love ..."

Hell, I know that all too well.

He holds my stare for a few tense moments, gives me a sharp nod, and I know he's done with that particular subject.

That's fine, I won't push him on it. He'll talk to me when he's ready.

I clear my throat and fold my fingers over the edge of his wing ... holding his gaze. He lets them fall and I offer him a small smile, shifting my attention to the room full of writhing female bodies.

The lighting is soft and warm, the room swathed in black velvet furnishings perfect for draping bodies over. Kal steps closer, his body flush with my back, and he traces little circles over my hip bone.

Heat pools in my core as I watch a woman with waist-length hair the colour of coal ride the face of someone I can barely see, except for splayed legs and her flushed pussy between them glistening with arousal.

Their movements are carnal and desperate—breasts bobbing, spines rolling, the energy spiked with wanton *need*.

From the smell, I can tell at least five of these women are in heat, and I figure this must be one of those 'in heat slumber parties' my mates were talking about ...

Seems much more pleasant than biding the time wearing a chastity belt that chafes your gooch.

I go to take a step forward but Kal holds me steady, tapping his finger to my hip. "Are you sure, Dell?"

His words blow against my ear and make my skin prickle, but they hold a tentative timber, like they're haunted by some sort of ghost.

Am I sure?

Yes.

I need to see this raw, natural display of simply enjoying someone for the sake of it. I need to be reminded that it doesn't always hurt. That it's not always *taken*.

"My wings are too tired to work," I croak, prying his hand

off my hip and towing him deeper. "Besides, I might learn something ..."

I drag Kal towards a lounger, gesture for him to sit, and am about to take a seat right next to him when he grabs my hips and I land in his lap with an *oomph*.

"What are you—"

"Shh," he breathes, gripping my chin, turning my face to the tangled exhibition.

I wiggle my hips, nesting into my lap-saddle with a built-in dick.

How convenient.

He slides his hands between my thighs, widening them ... the smell of sex and sweat intoxicating me a little more with each sharp pull of breath.

"Do you like watching?" Kal's voice is liquid night that trickles over my nipples, slides past my navel, and pools between my legs.

"All signs point to yes," I reply, watching a woman with cutting eyes and a hard, toned body disentangle from the mob of writhing parts.

Her hair is messy scribbles contrasting creamy skin and sumptuous curves. A black, see-through robe falls from her waist in long, gossamer ribbons, gifting flashes of naked flesh ...

Her honey gaze casts a blazing trail down my body, and all the blood rushes to my cheeks. She tugs a naked woman with bright, dreamy eyes from the crowd and lures her towards us—their full breasts bobbing with each swaying step.

I stiffen in Kal's lap, stuck somewhere between not wanting to look and being unable to peel my eyes away.

"This is Sasha, and I'm Nina," the woman with ochre eyes purrs, her words silk with a lilt of *I could play your vagina like a pussy-lute*.

It's hard to ignore the blush of Sasha's cheeks and lips standing out in stark contrast to the rest of her. A saucy smile lights up her face when she notices my attention.

"I'm Dell," I rasp, half tempted to introduce my vagina, seeing as she seems to be the one in charge of this little detour.

"Dell ..." Nina whispers, her tongue slipping out, running a slow, wet trail over her lower lip. "Would you like to join, Sweetness?"

Sweetness?

My vagina bows, taking the compliment I'm not entirely sure was meant for her.

I swelter under the heat of Nina's gaze. "Do you mind if we just ... watch?"

For a fleeting moment, I think she's going to whip me off Kal's lap, clamp my nipples, fold me over a chair, spank my pussy, and make me cream all over her face for giving the wrong answer. She just has that imperious look about her.

Instead, her eyes dip to my lips before dragging back up. "Of course, Doll." She winks and pinches Sasha's nipple, making her entire back arch as a moan slips out. "We like an audience. Watch all you like."

They saunter back to the group, hips swinging while I lift my fucking jaw off the ground.

A low rumble of laughter spills into the crook of my neck, Kal's hand squeezing my thigh. "You should see your face. So shocked."

"Well ... in my"—*extensive*—"experience, these situations are never instigated by a female. And they're certainly never about female enjoyment."

Quite the opposite. Unless you've twisted your mind in a bid to survive.

Robust tension hums off Kal, warming my skin wherever we connect. "I'm from a time when sex was primal, and sexuality was whatever the fuck you wanted it to be." He tucks a curl behind my ear. "Lean back ..."

I do as he asks, Nina watching as she threads her fingers through the black ocean of Sasha's hair, taking her mouth in a gentle kiss—the slow rhythm of their sliding tongues a dance I can't look away from.

I don't realise I'm grinding against Kal until he rumbles in my ear, the sound low and grating. "She's thinking about you ..."

Yeah ... I was starting to suspect that.

His hand wanders low and he flicks my buttons open, one by one.

"Wh-what are you doing?"

"Shhhh," he whispers, nudging down the front of my pants, making my pussy throb. He touches me, slides *through* me, and rumbles a sound of primal satisfaction. "You're fucking *drenched*."

I make a soft, mewling sound.

He pinches my aching clit and I buck my hips, Nina's gaze still locked on me as she starts to kiss a trail down Sasha's neck ...

Kal gently nips my neck while he swirls taunting circles around my entrance, teasing me into a sizzling frenzy.

I suck a shuddering breath and nudge against his hand, trying to catch him.

"*Kal* ..."

"Watch," he growls, the word hot on my neck.

I whimper but do as he says, and I'm gifted a single digit sliding into my aching heat as Nina peppers soft, gentle kisses past Sasha's navel. She lifts her leg, slings it around her shoulder, and opens that blushing pussy ...

"Watch her tongue," Kal whispers, adding a second finger as Nina takes a long lick up Sasha's swollen slit, her face getting lost between creamy thighs.

My hips roll, reaching for more.

Craving more.

Sasha's puffy lips pop open and she releases an airy moan, tipping her head back, gouging Nina's hair with desperate hands.

"Look how she's chasing her," Kal rumbles, stroking my G-spot, swirling his thumb around the coil of nerves smeared in my own slick juices. "She wants that hot tongue to fuck her little hole ..."

Sasha's eyes squeeze shut as she cries out, and I notice Nina's hand undulating between her own thighs in tandem with the beat of her jaw, matching the movement of Kal's fingers sliding in and out of my pussy ...

Fuck.

My skin is barely containing all the sizzling heat that wants to spill out of me.

"Kal," I moan, pleading with the desperate rock of my hips.

"Don't fight it, baby." He nips my ear, winding deeper ... adding another finger and stuffing me full.

I watch the woman curl and quiver, her knuckles turning white, lips stuck in a silent scream. Her posture becomes rigid as Nina coaxes her into a blaring climax while I grind against the heel of Kal's palm.

One final flick of my clit has me coming apart, my walls clamping down, my back curling forward ... a rinse of cloistered energy spilling out of me.

Kal plants a kiss on my neck and pulls his hand out of my pants, leaving me achingly empty, his entire chest vibrating as he sucks me off himself.

My cheeks burn.

"Learn anything?" he whispers, refastening my buttons like a true gentleman.

"Yeah," I breathe, jutting my hips to give him better

access. "You're really good at finding my G-spot. One cock-coin for you. To be used at my discretion."

I feel him smile against my neck, but I'm not joking. He should put a flag on it and claim his territory because that was some next level finger-fucking.

"What's a cock-coin?"

I'm so glad you asked.

I brush his hands away, drop to my knees between his legs, and start to pop his buttons.

He arcs a dark brow and scans the room. *"Here?"*

"Don't pretend they haven't seen your cock before. You've staked your claim; I want to do the same."

I give him a wink and watch his eyes flare.

"Besides," I say, wiggling his pants down a notch, "that woman over there?" I jerk my head towards a girl receiving a rim job, her mouth trapped in a perpetual 'o'. "I recognise her from a specific pre-drink gathering, which suggests she's pretty good at giving head."

And damn, she probably looks good giving it, too.

Kal's thick, angry cock jerks free, slapping against his navel, and I salivate over the sight of it—desperate to feel that meaty girth slide between my lips. I glance up through my lashes, spit on it, then lick him from base to tip with my wide, flat tongue ... moaning when a salty bead of pre-cum smacks my buds.

He releases a throaty groan, staring down at me with eyes as vast as the midnight sky, his face drained of all its colour.

I smirk.

That's right, Big Man.

I remember *everything*. I forget *nothing*.

And right now? I'm preparing to prove that *I'm* the best blowjob he's ever fucking had.

CHAPTER FIFTEEN
DELL

I sweep my tongue over my upper lip and moan.

I can still *taste* him ... and it's the only reason I'm not *poofing* some fucking tables right now.

"I require at least ten more opportunities to prove my superior blowjob skills in front of that woman," I snip, making each step down the hallway sound like the beat of a war drum.

I'm hoping Kal will register just how irrationally grumpy I am now that my post-orgasm blush has worn off, and ... well ... I don't know. But nobody should be even remotely happy when I feel this way.

"I'm sure that can be arranged," Kal states, sounding super chill now that his balls are no longer blue. The man withholds information and I reward him with the best blow job of his very long existence. What sort of precedent am I setting?

Not a very good one.

I hold my breath and bear down, expelling a long, straining grunt ... garnering a weird side-eye from my Night God.

"What?" I snap, ready to slash his nuts off. I don't care that his face is beautiful enough to evoke tears of joy; he's looking at me strangely, breathing in my direction, and, like ... *existing*.

He shakes his head, casting his attention down the curling hallway. "Nothing, Little Dove. You just look like you're trying to lay an egg."

Bastard.

He's definitely Cassian's father.

"For your information," I heave out as I bear down again, "I'm trying to push out my wings. I have work to do."

Kal snatches my wrist and spins me into his personal space, making my hair whip around my face.

Brave man. He mustn't value his skin twins very much.

"Your wings are tired, Dell." He brushes my hair back from my face, the morning light leaking through wide open windows making his hair look almost navy. "Give them a break, they've been working a lot harder than it may seem."

I draw a deep breath, ready to blast him with barbs straight from my vocal cords, when I'm tugged sideways into a sprawling chamber with a view of the crater lake far below. I instantly salivate at the smell of *everything* heaped on the black table stretched down the centre of the room ...

A bowl of berries bigger than my head, a pile of steaming bread rolls, jugs of bubbly water, a chalice of wine at each of the three table settings ... *the list goes on.*

I refuse to blink in case it all magically disappears.

"Like I said, *jasta*. You need to eat."

I try to talk, but it comes out as a garbled mash of words while I picture my face buried in that pile of mashed potatoes.

He pulls out a seat at the head of the table, steers me into it, then takes a spot down the length of the table while I reach into my pocket and readjust my newly acquired petrified penis so it's not prodding me in the hip.

Having a dick must be a real pain in the arse sometimes.

I wiggle my fingers then dig a ladle into a vast assortment of berries. "I've been craving fruit all day. And roast rabbit liver. Do you have any? I have a hunch it'll taste great mashed together with yoghurt and a sprinkling of dried chilli."

Kal makes this weird sound that resembles a smothered gag.

"What?"

"I'll ... see what I can arrange," he says, taking a sip of his water.

Cassian breezes through the door with his hands in his pockets, dressed in black leather pants that highlight the impressive size of hi—

I clear my throat and look *anywhere* else.

The cucumber didn't fall far from the, ahh ... patch. I think I'll keep that thought to myself seeing as Kal's so protective over his son's family jewels.

Poor Aero. Perhaps I should do him a kindness and put my walls up.

"Speaking of fruit, here's the fruit of your loins. I'm sure he'll confirm our sixty-niner was unintentional."

Kal's wings flare and he snarls so loud my vagina shrivels up.

Fuck.

I curl away from his threatening glare and stuff my mouth full of berries before I dig myself a hole too deep to crawl out of.

Cassian's brow almost jumps off his face. "You *told* her?"

Family dinner discussions. How fun.

Kal's wings drop slower than the fading night while he takes another long draw of his water. By the time he's drained the entire glass, he no longer looks like he's questioning every life decision that led him to this point.

He sets the cup down and spears a glance at his son. "I did, yes."

Cassian's eyes soften as if he's ... *relieved*. If I weren't paying such close attention, I would have missed it.

He gives a curt nod, takes the chair opposite Kal, and stacks his plate full of food while I glance between the two of them ...

Honestly, I'm surprised I didn't notice. Same blue-black hair, same thick brows, same olive skin and broad shoulders. They're even filling their plates the same way. Though Cassian has a surlier appearance, with dark tattoos peeping above his collar. His hair is longer, currently held back by a leather band, and he has slightly more bulk to him.

But his eyes are ... *striking*. They're opalescent violet—the colour of a twilight storm cloud—and if you look hard enough you can see a sprinkling of black that glimmers like burning coals.

"Don't call me 'son' and we should be fine," Cassian grumbles, not even looking up from his food, reminding me that he likes to be a little bit cunty sometimes.

He shoves a piece of fleshy meat in his mouth, just as Kal does the same.

"So long as you don't call me *'mother.'*" I glance at my wine, contemplating the merits of downing the entire thing in one shot. "I won't be ready for that shit until ... I don't know. Maybe never."

The world is too fucked up.

My hand veers towards the promise of some mind-numbing alcohol and Cassian clears his throat. Kal snatches my goblet with his lightning reflexes, throwing the contents back in one large gulp.

I blink at him, hand still frozen mid-air.

"Sorry." He winces, refilling his water glass from a sweating jug. "I need it more than you right now."

"I highly doubt that," I mumble, wondering why he didn't just drink his *own* goblet of wine that's sitting right in front of him.

Although ... perhaps it has something to do with my drunken adventure in the Day Kingdom that got us all into this mess.

Yeah, that has to be it.

Sighing, I start stacking my plate full of food—custard, a meat that's bloody, a sprinkling of grains, a glob of mashed potato, and a yellow, fleshy fruit that's sliced into big moons and dripping liquid sunshine. I also jam a bit of black cake on there, all too aware of the men sitting either side of me, studying my growing plate of food ...

They're probably jealous I got all the prime cuts of meat—but where I come from, you snooze, you starve to death.

I start scarfing down my meal, guarding it with my elbows, replacing the dents with more delicious treats.

"Wo mearl ith thith?" I ask around a mouthful of food.

"Nobody really knows anymore," Cassian answers, watching me from the corner of his eye. He picks up something round and crumbly and takes a bite. "They've just been serving up a bit of everything."

My nostrils flare and my gaze hones on a platter stacked with discs *just* like the one I found in my sack of goodies!

I dive across a bowl of custard, snatch the tray, then place it right next to my cache of food. "What's this ... disk thing called?" I ask, waving one around before taking a giant bite.

Fuck. Yes.

My eyelids flutter as I chew through the most tantalising mouthgasm I've ever experienced.

"A cookie," Kal rasps, dropping a slice of apple back to his plate.

"A *cockie?*"

Cassian chokes, but I'm too busy mouthgasming to bang him on the back and help him breathe again.

"No, Little Dove. A co—" There's a long pause—time I utilise by stuffing my mouth full and trying not to moan too loudly.

Kal clears his throat. "Sure ... a *cockie.*"

I swallow and throw him a wink. "No wonder they taste so *delicious.*"

Cassian slaps his fork to the table with a *clunk.* "Fucking hell."

"*Language,*" Kal berates, adjusting his pants before reaching for the bread roll I was just eyeing up.

I snarl at him, flashing my sharp teeth.

He jerks his hand away. "Yours, Little Dove. *Yours* ..."

Too right that bread roll is mine.

Cassian and Kal exchange a *look*, and I pat myself down to see if I've smeared food anywhere unusual, other than the twin globs of custard oozing down my breasts from my peaked nipples.

"*What?*"

"Nothing," they both reply before chugging their water in unison.

I shrug and perch the roll atop my mound of food.

Perfect.

CHAPTER SIXTEEN
SOL

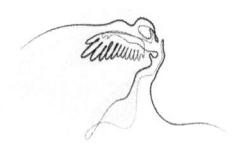

The legionnaire swaggers in front of me, smelling like rotten arsehole and things that have been dead for far too long.

Sick fuck.

He's walking around like he owns this shithole, dragging me like a dog, strutting past large doors with inch-thick layers of dust perched precariously on their handles.

Perhaps Edom doesn't have any servants left. By the state of the chandeliers dressed in grey, stringy cobwebs ... I'd say not.

Dell would be sneezing her tits off in here; just another reason she needs to stay the fuck away.

The red-winged pervert leads me up an endless trail of stairs I barely have the energy to climb, finally rounding on a large set of doors I know too well.

The throne room.

The doors fly open, revealing Edom, solid and ancient and draped on his robust, glistening throne. Kyro's curled behind him like a black smudge, watching me over a claw tipped in talons longer than my wingspan ...

Fuck me, that drako's gotten huge. At his age, he should only be the size of a mule, not bigger than three large houses jammed together.

Edom's been using the Bright in all the wrong ways. Bastard should know better.

I'm dragged forward to the tune of Kyro's coarse rumble, every movement traced by that keen, ruddy gaze. "What's this about?" I drone, listening to my voice echo back at me.

The legionnaire kicks me square in the back, sending me flying forward, and I land with a clanking thud beneath the throne—my chains finding fresh meat to sink their iron teeth into.

I peel myself off the ground, seeing Edom dressed in a loose top and black leather pants to match his depthless eyes.

He looks nothing like the man who used to sit on that throne. This one is almost painful to look at—the shell of a man who sold his soul to a monster.

He balances the pointy tip of a pin blade on the pad of his finger, the ruby hilt glistening in the morning light. "Time to strengthen these wards, old friend."

I curl my hands into fists. "Is your memory finally fading? You did it last month at our ... *dinner* party."

Once a year is more than enough, and he knows it.

Edom stands and lifts a lazy shoulder. "Can never be too careful, Sol; not that I have to explain myself to you." He puffs his chest, spreading his wings, barely stopping short of whipping out his cock and pissing on me. "You're below me on the food chain."

I bite my tongue so hard I pierce fleshy muscle.

Dell would throw something ridiculous in response to that, and she'd say it with such sass I'd want to bend her over and fuck her pretty pussy right there on the spot.

My balls tighten and I have to physically focus on taming the thrashing organ in my chest.

I fucking need her.

I need her crushed against me so I can feel the rise and fall of her chest; need to see for myself that her fortified tether isn't some trick of my morose, thirsty mind.

I need her looking up at me through those big, unapologetic eyes while I wrap her hair around my wrist and anchor her to my *fucking* body so I can never lose her again.

Edom stalks down the dais and my wings itch to unravel, upper lip trembling while I resist the urge to snarl.

I refuse to give him the satisfaction.

There's only one Sterling who can break me, and she has long, white hair, eyes like diamonds, and a bratty mouth that gives me *life*.

He lifts a brow. "Why the long face? I thought you enjoyed a bit of pain."

I like *control*, and I don't have it right now.

This bastard does.

"My face is long because the only arsehole I'm interested in looking at is your daughters'," I drawl, then stifle a mock yawn. "Yet here you are ..."

His eyes widen and I smile—a twisted, vengeful sort of smirk that'll probably get me killed one day.

He thrusts his hand into my hair, tilting my head, flicking his painting blade along the base of my throat like he's paving the path of a killing strike. "Always such a *cunt*." He whips his hand back and slashes the sharpness across my chest, slicing an inch-deep gash through the thick muscle.

For a moment, it feels like I've been sliced in two. Like my top half is going to slide off the rest of me and thud to the ground.

I seethe through the pain, allowing it to fuel my hatred for this monster. "Is that why you like sticking your pointy thing in me?"

He watches the blood ripple down my body, his head

cocked to the side. "Maybe I just like to crack you open, Sol. You always were so thick-skinned. This seems to be the only way to watch you *spill*."

"I think your daughter would disagree," I say on a forged smirk. "Perhaps you should ask for some tips."

All I get is a grunted response and I know I've hit some twisted nerve of his. "You're talking yourself into a hole today ..."

I know I am, but that fucked up part of me wants to feel whatever pain he's ready to dish, picturing it as *her* pain I'm eating. Not my own.

It's an ugly craving that makes me want to do ugly things ...

Things there's no coming back from.

Edom rips off his shirt, exposing a body embellished with snippets of the ancient language. A web of wards that keep us at his mercy.

Blood magic shouldn't be tampered with.

Ever.

The idiot digs his painting blade into his flesh, following previously etched paths while liquid life trickles down his inflated muscles. "The things I do for you," he grinds through gritted teeth.

I don't think that was directed at me ...

He swipes a finger through my raw wound, using my blood to paint the tracks of his scars. Sighing, I fill the time by glancing out one of the far-off windows, catching a glimpse of the stale dawn begging for release ...

"I thought I'd draw a new ward today. *Glaft de fals.*"

"But that means—"

"Oh, I know what it means." He fingers my wound, hooking the edge of my lesion and tugging—*hard*—ripping me all the way to the fucking *armpit*. "It renders you incapable of producing an heir."

I heave through the pain, bleeding all over the throne room floor.

I shouldn't have provoked him.

"Where should I draw it?" he asks, surveying his torso for space.

There is none.

I clear my throat and push my shoulders back. "If you can scribe small enough you could probably fit it on your dick."

"Careful," Edom growls, the inky depths of his eyes seeming to thread down his cheeks. "Those are brave words coming from someone who fucked my daughter, then *mated* with her." He brushes the two tiny puncture marks I slathered in salt water to preserve Dell's claiming, making me flinch. "*These* are punishable by death. You took something of mine without my permission. I should skin you alive, then feed you to Kyro."

The colossal drako uncurls, *tripling* in size. He unfolds his leathery wings and releases a barrelling roar, exposing a mouth full of gnashing teeth that reek of death.

I should be scared, but he's not the most dangerous predator in this room. I can tell by the metal cuff locked around his hind leg.

"Don't pretend you care about her."

Edom shrugs, finding a small spot along his ribs where he starts slicing '*glaft de fals*' into his pearly skin. "Part of me cares. The same part that cares about you."

There he goes, trying to sprinkle me with droplets of false hope, perhaps forgetting I'm already *drenched* with loathing.

"But that man is *weak*." He goes back to his carving, finishing the phrase, narrowing his eyes on my wound. "I'll need more blood than *that*, Sol."

I glance down. "The fuck are you talking ab—"

He lacerates my chest and I choke on the blinding pain

that threatens to spill my insides everywhere, my pulse roaring in my ears.

Motherfucker.

He swipes his finger through the fresh wound, then paints the words he just inscribed with slow, precise strokes; rendering my balls useless.

I wish he'd just castrate me. Because I know ... I just *know* I'll still continue to *hope*.

It's all part of the twisted games he likes to play.

I lift my chin while he does his little finger painting—just more ammunition to break those wards and put him out of his misery.

Once completed, he cleans my blood off his hand. "You're going to need me dead if you want to sire a child with my daughter. And this ward here," he points to a series of symbols carved across his pec, "means you can't kill me."

I clear my throat, a bit lightheaded from all the blood loss. "You do like your games, don't you?"

Edom studies the damage he just inflicted—cuts that are going to be a pain to heal while I'm wrapped in iron.

"Eternity's boring without them." He jerks his chin at the legionnaire. "Take him back to his cell."

About fucking time.

We're almost at the door when Edom roars, "*Wait*," and I'm spun around in time to see him disappear through the Bright.

Sigh.

What more could he want? I'm already struggling to hold my guts in.

He returns a moment later with a pail of water, wearing a sharp smirk I want to carve right off his face. "Salt water," he announces, setting the pail on the ground at my feet.

I stare at it. "And?"

He dips his painting blade in the bucket, jostles my head

to the side, and puts the tip against my throat ... not too far from Dell's *mating bite*.

I snarl ...

"You know, you and my daughter aren't too dissimilar," he mumbles before he starts to slice a deep circle of ownership around my precious mating scar.

This fuck.

"Just thought I'd put this here as a reminder that you both belong to *me*." His arm momentarily grazes my iron chains and he sneers, eyes darting to the fat welt now staining his elbow ...

My iron chain penetrated his shield.

I strike, sinking my teeth into his shoulder, growling against his flesh like a rabid dog as blood bubbles between my lips and down my fucking chin.

If I kill him, I die, but I'd be an idiot to waste this chance. I could save Dell a world of pain—right here, right now.

I'm just about to rip a chunk of meat right off his shoulder when something sharp and pointy slides between my ribs and scrapes against my heart. *"Arrrgh ... you fuck!"*

Edom leaves the blade hanging in my chest and brushes his wound, flicking red at his restructured shield while I huff through the pain.

"You *missed*."

His hand snaps out and wraps around the ruby hilt, making every cell in my body freeze lest the blade hook my heart and slice it open. "I intended to," he drawls, caressing the vulnerable organ with the pointed tip while I choke on the invasion. "You're not allowed to die. *Yet*."

His gaze drags to the circle he sliced on my neck, likely similar to the one my little mate wore on her palm before she was tossed in the pool of shit and exposed for what she really is ...

Everything.

He pulls his blade out of my chest.

"*Oomph* ..."

"No food for the next two days," he sneers, turning on his heel, stalking towards the dais while I bloody up his floor.

I grunt.

It's a good thing I've grown accustomed to the taste of rats.

CHAPTER SEVENTEEN
DELL

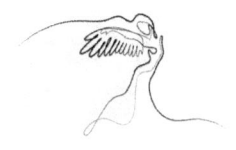

*K*al might insist I need sleep, but there's no way I'm getting a peaceful dawn's rest with *two* wilting tethers. Just looking at them hurts; my mind racing with different scenarios—each more nauseating than the last.

I peep at my Night God currently lumped on top of the quilt, dead to the world. Looks like he passed out on contact and hasn't moved since.

Screw it.

If he has a problem with me disobeying orders, he can take it up with my sulking beast. I'm sure she'll be a joy to play with right now.

Not.

I slip out of bed, assessing the back of my short nightdress in the large, gilded mirror—the fabric like a crushed night sky weighing little more than a few loose feathers.

Thin straps meet the scooped back just below my waist, leaving enough space for my wings to pop through without shredding the flimsy garment. I can't imagine Kal would be too impressed if he caught me fluttering around his kingdom naked.

I ease past the heavy door and tiptoe down the corridor, my chest tight when I verge on an open doorway leading to a familiar balcony. It juts from the palace, hanging over the crater city far below—the pool at the centre glistening like a dawn-kissed turquoise jewel half dipped in perpetual shade.

I tease the tips of my toes over the edge, hating the way my stomach shrivels at the sight of the rocky ground hundreds of metres below ...

Fuck me, that's a long way down.

"Dell ..."

I turn to see Kal poised in the doorway; his hammering chest far from temperate. The ball in his throat rolls as he tries to bridge the space between us with his outstretched hand.

My vagina almost leaps into his palm.

"Don't," I warn, hanging my heels over the edge. "I need to do this, Kal. It's the only way I'm going to learn."

All the colour drains from his face, his wings twitching behind him like nervous shadows. "You do realise I can't use the Bright?"

That's the point.

"You don't need to. I'm going to fly, and I need you to stay right there. If I think you'll save me, they won't work."

His cool regard snaps and he waves at the blank space behind me. "*What* won't work? They aren't even out!"

Negative Night needs a taste of his own happy web.

"I'm sure they'll pop out when I fall," I blurt—an attempt to lull him into a false sense of security.

Honestly, I have no idea if this is going to work. But my gut tells me my wings need to be taught their limits under extreme, life threatening duress.

I'll call it tough love.

Kal slides forward a step. "I can't just sit by and watch you throw yourself off another cliff, *jasta* ..."

The statement puts a noose around my battered heart.

"Do you trust me?"

"I—" His answer trails off and my lips thin. He's a far cry from a cheer squad.

"I need to see that you believe in me, Kal. Or you'll be washing white feathers off the rocks below." He flinches, looking like he's about to launch straight at me. *"Don't.* You and I both know, one way or another, *I'm doing this."*

I'm not asking, I'm telling.

He pinches the bridge of his nose and I almost cringe at the sound of his teeth grinding. "Sometimes, I feel like you were put on this world just to test me, you know that?" He snarls the words, like I'm causing him some sort of internal damage.

I feel bad about that.

I'm still going to jump off this cliff.

"Please don't be angry at me ..."

Kal's eyes harden and he finally gifts me a sharp nod.

I relax into my fate, allowing relief to course through my veins and ply me with the same fearlessness I once wished for. Only now, it's *organic.*

I offer Kal a soft, resigned smile. "I love you."

His eyes widen and he jerks forward as I fall backwards into the void ... and *plummet.*

Gravity, the relentless bitch, grabs hold and doesn't let go—dragging me down, cool air assaulting my face and shoulders.

Sweet baby Dell pancake ... I'm going to die.

"Do your thing!" I scream to my cowering wings, waiting for them to pop out of my back as a grizzly, rocky doom races towards me. I can almost picture my innards smeared across those razor-sharp stones—a feast for the circling crows.

Fucking hell.

"You really want to die this way you *lazy tarts?*"

Nothing. Not even a probing feather curling out to pat me on the back and offer condolences for my impending doom.

I crunch my eyes shut, refusing to witness the moment I skewer myself, when my entire length of spine *tingles*.

My wings erupt with gusto, my entire body jolting as if I just dove into a body of water, and I choke on a scream. They bank our course, thump, thump, thumping away, working hard until I meet a warm up-draft and begin to glide ... *precariously*. "Holy-fucking-shit-motherfucker-shit!" I rasp, cutting a shaky path over the crater city.

I'm *flying*.

I hear a booming thud and Kal soars up beside me, a wide grin splitting his face, but it swiftly fades into a scorn darker than the night sky. "I'm going to get skinned alive for this."

"I'm sure they'll forgive you when they watch me slice through the sky like a well-trained arrow," I say in a chipper tone, watching the world slide past. I probably look like a gammy bird, but my wings need all the positive reinforcement they can get.

"No, Dell. Drake will make me think my cock's on fire and leave me pissing blood for a week once he finds out I let you jump off that cliff."

I peer at him sideways, wiggling through the sky. "He's done that to you before?"

"No, but he does it to Sol whenever they're both *manst*rating at the same time."

"*Manst—*"

What have I gotten myself into?

We pass the water's edge and I'm slapped by the reflection of a woman pretending to be whole, yet I can see the lie in her flat gaze peering back at me ...

Dark room.

Smells like piss.
Probing things.

I close my eyes, hold my breath, and attempt to calm the thrashing organ in my chest ...

You made it out. You're okay.

You survived.

"Dell, straighten up," Kal hollers, and it takes me a moment to realise I'm careening sideways ...

Fuck.

I straighten my achy wings that are starting to lag, a flailing attempt to regain control.

"Dell ..."

"I'll be fine," I snap through gritted teeth, though to be honest? They *are* starting to turn a bit numb. "I'll ... I'll be *fine,"* I whisper, and I realise I'm not trying to convince Kal. I'm trying to convince *myself*.

I've only been flying for five fucking minutes and my impotent wings are ready to throw in the feather.

"Dell!" Kal warns again, and I'm just about to give him the middle finger when my wings lose all rigidity and disappear into my back.

Poof. Gone.

Just like that.

My mouth drops open and I plummet towards the lake like a fucking boulder.

What. The. Twat.

We were doing so well until my tarts decided to take a vacation *mid-flight*. Who does that?

Kal tucks his wings in and dives, but not fast enough. I pierce the water like a pin, going so deep that I'm swallowed by the inky void, almost losing sight of the distant smear of light above.

At least I didn't fall into a vat of lava.

I come to a floating halt and start pedalling towards the surface though I can't shake the feeling that I'm not alone ...

Probably just my imagination finding new and inventive ways to fuck with me.

I break the surface and gulp air, treading water, glad I had this serene lake to pillow my landing. Kal's reaching for me, beating the air with his mighty wings, the glassy surface scribbling from the onslaught ...

"Take my hand!"

Does he think I'm deaf?

I landed that fall like a pro. He should be congratulating me with a wee vagina pat.

"Relax, Midnight! It's actually quite refreshing after all that hard work! Won't you join me?" I roll onto my back and float my body to the surface, reminded of a simpler time when my definition of pain was stubbing my toe on uneven floorboards.

Kal hisses, grabs my arms, then beats his wings violently, hauling me out of the water like a thrashing fish on a line. *"What the hell!"* I scream over the thunderous drum of his wings.

But then I hear the muffled sound of something pounding below the water ...

Thump.

Thump.

Thud-ump ...

I look down just in time to see the surface of the lake *explode*; a red, bulbous head bursting forth, wide maw splitting to reveal rows and rows of sharp, serrated teeth. Its scales are glistening in the morning light; its big, bulging eyes like orbs of fucking *fire*.

I squeal and tug my feet up. "Faster, Kal! *Faster!*"

He releases a sharp, ferocious sound as the monster's jaw snaps shut just shy of my feet. It falls back to the water, creating a wave three metres high that rolls towards the shore and explodes against the nearest embankment.

Fucking hell.

"What ..." I shake my head and clear my throat, dangling back and forth. "What was that?"

I shriek as Kal flings me into the air, then snatches me up in a more convenient position pressed flat against his chest, his arms a cage of muscle.

"That," he snarls by my ear, his angry breath making my skin prickle, "was a *baby* lava monster."

Gulp.

"A ... a *baby?*"

"A baby." His arms tighten. "And *you* almost became its dinner."

Yes ... yes, I did.

"Well ... good thing you were there to pluck me out of the water!"

He grunts a half-assed response, and I take the opportunity to snuggle into him, drawing on his scent while he glides towards the crowning city.

He can't stay mad at me forever. I repeat the notion to my vagina who's giving me the stink eye.

I may have pissed off my Night God and almost became lava chow, but what's most important is ...

I *flew*.

CHAPTER EIGHTEEN
DELL

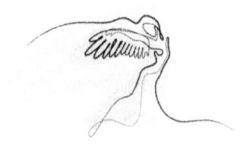

Kal yawns, rubbing his eyes, splayed on the black velvet seater with his taut abs on display for my wandering eye.

I've never seen him look so ... *ruffled*, and I'm half tempted to ride his fac—

I shake my head, trying to get my mind out of my vagina.

"You look tired." I stretch one arm over my head, then the other. Not that my arms are going to be doing any flapping, but I need all the help I can get.

"That's because I'm not a morning person," he grumbles, looking ready to fall back to sleep.

I frown.

"But it's perpetually *dawn* at the moment ..."

Kal yawns so wide his face looks like it's going to split in half, then levels me with a half-lidded glower. "Exactly."

"Well, I would have left you sleeping, but I knew you'd be pissed if I went without you after yesterday's ... *experience*. Aren't you happy I'm communicating for a change?" I throw him a wink as I arch to the side, stretching my abdominals.

Kal blinks vacantly, then yawns for the third time in less than a minute, like he didn't hear a single word I just said.

I roll my eyes. I'm finally in a good mood because I'm making *progress* and my Night God has digressed into a state of semi-stasis.

"Aren't you sore?" he asks, adjusting his slacks when I finally start to stretch my wings. Seems not *every* part of him is sleepy ...

I run my fingers over a few rogue feathers, making sure they're super smooth. I want them to look their very best while I'm cutting through the air on the odd chance Kal's looking my way.

I'm silently smug when he clears his throat, palms his swelling bulge, and picks at a plate of food I personally requested. Though he's only touching the blueberries—ignoring the mash of anchovies, buttered peanuts, and garlic flakes entirely.

I guess we can't all have superior taste buds.

"Yes, I am sore," I say, reaching for my sack of goodies. I find my box, crack the lid, and locate my little vial half-filled with shit, cradling it like a precious jewel and not excretions from the world's pungent arsehole.

All the sleepiness dissolves from Kal's demeanour.

"That's why I need you to rub some of this into my back."

"Are you sure, Little Dove?"

I nod. Leila was right ... I need to stop living in the past and start moving forward.

Kal reaches for the pottle and I spin, stretching my wings. He uncorks the vial and we both gag in unison.

Good god, that's some heady shit. "I don't recall it smelling quite so ... *potent*."

"Block your nose."

I hold my hand over my mouth, the other clutching my

stomach as I try to contain my jerky gag reflex. "Too late ... it's already *in* me."

"You okay?"

I nod, shake my head, nod, then start to gag again ... only this time, I can taste the fishy tang of my anchovy breakfast which is nowhere near as appealing the second time round.

I toss myself towards a potted plant with big, blue leaves and retch all through the soil, my eyes feeling like they're going to pop right out of my head. Kal holds my hair while rubbing small circles on my lower back, likely kicking himself for following my scent to the East.

This is fucked.

I'm not sure what I did to offend Karma and deserve all this heaving. Maybe she hates the word 'vagina'? Hmm. Perhaps she has a *lonely* vagina? Maybe her vagina just needs a good cuddle?

Now I feel bad for Karma and her sad vagina.

The retching subsides and Kal hands me a cloth to wipe my mouth. "I feel much better now." I steal a glance at the plant with my spew frothing around its base. "Though I think that will need repotting ..."

He leads me away from the overwhelming scent of regurgitated fish. "I can get that taken care of. But in the wake of all that vomit, I think you need to go back to bed."

"Are you *kidding me?*" I jerk away, causing my freshly preened wings to startle. Now I need to fancy them up again, dammit. "I'm at least a boob lighter. I'm ready to roll!"

Kal places his hands on my shoulders and anchors me in place with his steely, star-flecked eyes. "Dell ... you just vomited all over my rare Labius Dicotum plant."

"It was just the overwhelming smell of ass! Don't pretend you didn't gag too! I just took it to the next level."

His grip tightens. "I have my limits, Little Dove ..."

I step closer with a flick of my hips, fingering my feathers.

"You want to see my pretty wings slice through the air again, I know you do ..."

As if on cue, my wings stretch and ruffle. Kal's colossal black ones burst out of his back as the bulge in his slacks receives a second wind.

I hear him swallow.

I step into the corona of heat surrounding his body and trace the outline of his rock-solid cock, watching him twitch for me.

The air between us seems to charge.

"One small, *itsy-bitsy* flying lesson ..." I glance up, catching his stifling gaze through my lashes. "Then we can come back"—*brush my teeth*—"and I'll put you straight to sleep, hmm?"

With my mouth.

A warm zap travels straight between my legs at the mere thought of giving my Night God another record-breaking blowjob.

"You're playing a dangerous game, Dell." He slides his thumb over my bottom lip and drags it down. "If I'd had the opportunity to bed you already, you'd know not to taunt me like ... *this*."

My vagina blushes as I reach down and cup his balls, then give them a gentle squeeze.

His eyes darken ...

"Fortune favours the bold, *Big Man*."

A low rumble rolls off his chest, that already ample package swelling in my palm, telling me that *this* time his cock has made the decision for him.

"Turn around," he grunts, seemingly pissed off by the amount of sway I have over his dick.

I do as I'm told, trying to repress my budding smile.

He totally wants my mouth again.

This time when he uncorks the pottle, I block my nose and try not to squirm while he paints my back with crap.

I hear him replace the cork, enjoying the warm tingle that laces through me as the shit-paste works its magic. I tuck my wings into my back and spin, squaring my shoulders. "Okay. Now that we both smell like rotten arsehole and all your blood's hanging out in your cock, let's fly."

Today's the fucking day.

---

*T*oday is *not* the day.

Kal flew beneath me lest I end up in the belly of the lava monster who followed our path; its red, floppy dorsal fin cutting jagged lines through the water.

I lasted fifteen minutes before I fell out of the sky like a feathery fuck up, right into Kal's awaiting arms. I convinced him to coax my wings back out with the absent promise of a wingasm, then made it all of five minutes before they folded again.

We called it a day.

My mind's been a riot ever since. Not even an entire platter of freshly baked cockies was able to lift my dampened spirits.

I stare at the roof while Kal sleeps like a rock with his hand splayed across my lower stomach ...

My wings are too fucking errant.

Maybe they need a firmer touch to whip them into shape? Because what I'm doing sure isn't working, and I refuse to wait another day to rescue my mates.

I nod to myself and close my eyes, intent on getting a few hours of sleep. I'm going to need all the energy I can muster. Because when I wake up?

I'm unleashing my beast.

"Need more of this?" Kal asks, waving the shit pottle at me.

"Nope." I stride out of the room clutching a teardrop vial of aromatic oil, on a beeline down the hallway haunted by blushing light.

Kal slides up next to me as we approach the balcony. "Dell ... I can feel your anxiety like a brick in my stomach. Stop putting so much pressure on yourself. Learning to fly takes time, but you *will* do this. Eventually."

My lips curl into a cloying smile and I glance sideways, studying the naked panes of his chest. "Oh, *I know*."

"You're up to something ..."

I shrug and step onto the balcony with Kal close on my heels, bathing me in the scent of jasmine and verbena. Taunting me ...

Taunting *her*.

He brushes past me and turns, hanging his heels off the edge like a cat expertly perched—his hair a flickering, black flame fuelled by the bitter, howling wind.

His eyes narrow as I do a casual sweep of his body—all muscle and tone and dark, sexy allure. "You wouldn't happen to know anything about all my missing tops, would you Little Dove?"

"That's a very bated accusation, Muscles. Why would I empty your entire drawer of tops over the edge of a volcano?"

Since I can't lie, my new tactic is to attack him with the truth.

Outcome still pending.

He blinks at me for a good few seconds, scratching the back of his head ...

Night God successfully stunned.

I step forward and uncork the vial I found in the washroom cupboard, then drizzle the contents all over his unclad torso while I chew my tongue in concentration. I'll steer him in the direction of his lost wardrobe once he's lured my beast out of the shadow lair she's burrowed into.

Unbeknownst to Kal, he's beast bait.

I slide the empty vial into my pocket and massage his chest and stomach, stopping just shy of slipping my hand down his pants and sheathing his semi-hard cock with the same lubrication. I think I deserve special recognition for showing such restraint when every cell in my body wants to climb this man like a greasy pole.

Beasty nudges out of her den and licks her chops, then probes further, eye-fucking Kal's biceps and his impressive collection of abdominal muscles.

She's so predictable sometimes. Oil a prime piece of Sun God meat, make it look *extra* tasty, and her and my vagina both drizzle everywhere.

I look up in time to see Kal arc a midnight brow. "If you wanted to get me half-naked and baste me, you only had to ask. I would have been more than happy to oblige." He clears his throat and splays his wings, creating a striking image ...

I step back and tilt my head to the side, assessing my masterpiece.

My beast does the same.

Kal smirks as my wings explode from my back—all fluffy and flirty—as if they've been summoned to high tea, butter puffs, and a side of well-oiled Night God.

Little do they know, they're about to be *broken in.*

"You ready?" Kal asks, just as I drop the shadow leash. Beasty swoops in like a punitive plague, taking absolute control over our body.

She sneers at our wings, making them snap to her command like a couple of fluffy foot soldiers, and a frown sweeps over Kal's face. He probably thinks we're about to blow something up, then ride his oily body all the way to the afterlife.

"Yes, I'm *ready*." My thirsty beast throws him a seedy wink that makes me shudder. She steps forward and slides our fingernails down strong slabs of muscle while sizing him up like a three-course meal.

Just when I think she's about to take a chunk right out of him, she ducks his outstretched wing and dives off the ledge.

We free-fall like an arrow shot to *kill*, and for the first time since I started this flying thing, I don't feel like my life is in danger as we hurtle towards sharp rocks.

My beast wants to do more than just fuck that prime piece of Godly meat; she wants to prove she can wrangle these feathery toddlers and teach them how to be big-people wings. She wants to show Kal she's a respectable *mate choice*, and if I weren't counting on it in the first place, I'd be rolling my eyes.

Our compliant wings snap at the air, sending us shooting across the crater lake city. We soar through the sky in a seamless motion; every flick of our wings fuelled by something dark and primal ... the innate urge to save our mates.

Each beat rings with a resounding echo.

Protect.

Protect.

Protect.

I feel the moment the wish is happy, like a weight lifting from the shoulders of my soul.

Take that, Wish! You needy fuck.

My beast wastes no time carving a sharp corner, slicing a straight path back to the ledge where we drop onto the sturdy stone. I battle her down and give her a pat on her feral head.

Kal lands beside me with a thud that makes the ground

tremble while I soothe my hair back from my face. "*Veis de klash!* Dell ... you did it!"

He's *totally* impressed by my passenger-seat flying skills.

I tuck my wings into a tight parcel of pretty and toss my hair over my shoulder. "I'm allocating myself four cock-coins. Let's go pack some bags." I swagger inside like a badass bitch with a pocket full of penis.

I did it.

Beasty rumbles from her place in my shadows ...

Well ... I *sort of* did it.

CHAPTER NINETEEN
DELL

"Fuck it's cold," Kal hisses, the heavy thump of his wings like a toiling heartbeat, "Even for me."

We glance sideways and lift a brow, watching him rub his arms as we slice two parallel lines through the sky. "Why do you think she let me take the helm?" my beast purrs, the ominous undertone of her voice making me quiver from my toasty spot cushioned by internal shadows.

Seductive death.

But she's not wrong ...

Enjoying the front row seat on this flight across the ocean was *not* worth freezing to death over, so I handed this crazy bitch the reins. Now I can't feel *shit*.

Kal shakes his head, seemingly unperturbed by the deadly beast who's likely picturing all the dangerous ways she wants to wrangle his cock. "One of us needs to stay ... with it. And you haven't seen my beast in his prime. Trust me, he's not very fun to be around."

Beasty grunts and from the lewd thought she flashes through the shared segment of our mind, I'd say she's eager to test that theory herself.

We glance down at the angry ocean—a thrashing, *living* thing.

"That's a nasty storm ahead," Kal states, studying the mass of black clouds barrelling towards us—incandescent veins scribbling across its ever-mutating skin.

"We should fly around it," my beast barks, already banking our path. "We can make it in time."

All of a sudden Kal's right in our face, blocking our way with his churning wings, forcing us to do some fancy feather work and straighten back up again.

"Don't be fucking *ridiculous*. It's too big and it's moving too fast and you need to stop and *think!*" he bellows, his voice more intimidating than the clapping thunder.

I gotta hand it to him, the man must have balls of steel to speak to her like that.

I nuzzle further into my toasty shadow nest, put my feet up, and recline, wishing I had a bowl of snacks for the imminent show.

"I *am* fucking thinking! I'm thinking we'll fly the fuck *around* it!" she roars, and Kal cuts her a seething glare that I'm thankful isn't directed at *me*.

Oh, you two. Just bang already.

"Dell, we need to find *shelter*. There's a shore that way." He points to the West and Beasty sneers, likely because it's in the wrong direction and will add precious time to our journey. "If we fly fast enough, we may outrun the storm and make it in time to bunker down."

The man's right. I've never seen a storm move that fast, and if we don't make shelter we're not going to make it to the capital at all.

Wow ... logic is *so* much easier to see when I'm disengaged from my traumatised heart.

Maybe I shou—

Nah. It's cold out there. Surely she's not going to fly us into a *storm*.

"It's *Mistress* to you! And we're not finding *shelter!*" she roars, propelling us forward while Kal hollers for us to stop.

Oop, fuck.

We shoot through the sky as I scramble into an offensive stance, and we're suddenly in the thick of it—getting tossed around by powerful gusts that try to rip our wings from our body. Rain lashes us in a constant sheet, making it hard to see anything but the scribbling bolts of sharp, fluorescent light.

I pin my beast down, slamming a shadow over her feral face so she can't distract me while I find a way out of this cold, wet mess.

A bolt of lightning illuminates an angry face of water rolling towards me, the irate ocean about to swallow me whole and pound me into a feathery, breathless pulp.

"Shit."

A menacing roar is the only warning I get before Kal careens into me like a rock, knocking me sideways, sturdy arms cloaking me and my frazzled wings into a tight, convenient package.

He shoots across the rolling ocean with me tucked against his hammering chest while I gulp air, and actually, I think this might be preferable to reclining in my shadows.

I thread my hand up and cup his face, but he rips his chin away, pins me with a menacing glower, and *growls*.

Oh, boy. I swear to shit, it's like the entire weight of the night sky hammering down on me.

I'm in trouble.

We converge on a shoreline after a long flight haunted by awkward silence, and Kal drops onto the sand; his sturdy legs absorbing the force with expert ease.

"Well done," I say, patting his chest.

No answer.

"I'll just ... ahh, climb down then." I try to wiggle out of the cage of midnight muscle, but all that does is agitate the delicate direction of my sodden feathers and drag my achy boobs up around my chin. "Umm ... do you mind?"

He sets me down and I huff when I see the sorry state of my wings. "Dammit, they were looking so pretty, too. Did you really have to be so rough with them?" I glance up and let out a sharp breath.

Yyyyyikes ...

Water trickles into Kal's eyes from his inky hair, black clothing clinging to every swell and rivet of his body. His wings are giant, dripping shadows staring down on me and my two trembling tarts.

My wings yank away from my preening fingers and tuck flat against my back, abandoning me, and I'm not even mad about it. Hell, even *I'm* discreetly scanning the shoreline for something to hide behind so I can escape their feathery glower.

"What?" I ask, hands on my hips. "You *cannot* hold me accountable for that!"

"You're saying it wasn't *you?*" he bellows, and I cringe.

Ehh ... it was *partially* me. The crazy, psychotic part. Though I'm sure arguments could be made that condemn the rest of me to the same title.

"Look," I plead, flicking my hair out of my face and trying not to shiver. "I know I have no regard for my safety most of the time, but *that* was ridiculous ... even for me." I gesture towards the storm that chased us here—a swollen, black smudge rolling towards the shoreline with angry shards of light forking off its face. "I'm an innocent bystander."

He shakes his head and huffs out a sigh, wings sinking. "They're going to murder me," he mumbles, stalking towards the limestone cliff face lining the shore.

Poor Kal. He really does have his hands full. No wonder

my Gods are so keen on time-sharing my vagina ... I've run Kal ragged in the short span of a few days.

The rain hits, washing everything in white, and there's a blinding flash that makes my heart leap into my throat. In one blink, Kal's right next to me—sword in hand, liquid obsidian seeming to web across his cheeks.

He's perched for battle, surveying the barren beach like he's looking for something ...

"You ... okay?"

His jaw ticks, sharp eyes doing another sweep of the shore before black fades to blue. "*Fine.*"

He doesn't look *fine*.

I trail him towards a waterfall bellowing off the edge of a cliff, flowing into a short stream that feeds the ocean. Those grand, swarthy wings puff and quiver every so often, doing well to make my nipples harden.

My head tilts and I chew my lip, not realising I'm being led behind a rock until Kal turns and tucks me out of sight— pressing the hilt of a dagger to the palm of my hand. "Ahh ..."

"Wait here," he commands before stalking off.

I pinch the dagger, dangling it as far from my body as I can possibly manage, watching Kal edge around the churning waterhole before he slips through the raging sheet of water and *disappears*.

I squeal, wriggle out of my little den, and dash forward, following the same sketchy path he just took. I'm about to dive in after him when glossy black wings slice a hole in the waterfall, creating a large pocket of peace.

"I see you were following my instructions," he bellows over the turbulent roar.

I shrug, acting cool, calm, and collected as I mosey into the mouth of a hidden cave, still dangling the dagger at arm's length. "You kn-know me better than th-that, surely. Also, I don't know how t-t-to use this thing. You'd be better off handing me n-n-nipple clamps."

Kal grunts and seizes the dagger, tucking his wings against his back and shutting us off from the world, enveloping us in the musky scent of ... *charcoal?* And something else I can't place.

My gaze is drawn to the roof, to bioluminescent globes hanging from long, spindly fingers of calcified stone. "Wow, look at all the p-pretty blue b-b-alls," I grit out, giving my wings a not-so-subtle preen. "You're g-going to feel right at home."

"They're glow bugs." He glances at my preening hand for a sharp second, and I certainly don't miss the corner of his mouth twitching. "Don't eat one, they make your skin turn blue."

Why the fuck would I *eat* one?

I watch him pluck pieces of driftwood off the stony ground, piling them in the centre of the cave. "Know from experience, d-d-do we?"

He gives me a roguish smile, cracking that tense demeanour he's been wearing since my beast almost drowned us all.

"About seven hundred years ago, Sol thought Drake could do with some pretty blue skin to make his golden eyes pop."

Of course he did.

"I'll get the fire started," Kal mutters, that smile disintegrating as he rakes me with a sharp scrutiny.

"We're waiting out the s-s-storm?"

He nods and goes back to collecting wood.

Right. Guess I better make myself useful.

I set my empty water skein aside and open my bag, excited to get changed into something soft, warm, and dry ...

Until I see the meagre contents.

That's right. I forwent the change of clothing for a few bags of cockies and my wooden schlong. Seems my priorities are all up the twat.

"What's wrong?" Kal asks, reaching over his shoulder, tugging the wet top over his head. The flickering flame shades his carved body in all the right places, and I almost combust at the sight.

I clear my throat, watching him drop his top to the floor with a wet *plop*. "I ... ah, forgot a change of clothes."

His brows knit together and he reaches out, giving me the grabby-hand.

Sigh.

Cheeks burning, I hand over my pack, watching him rifle through the contents while I twiddle my thumbs. "I packed a lot more than this, Dell. The only things in here are the lock pick, a fuck ton of cockies ... and," he waves my petrified penis at me, "*this*."

I chew my nail in a weak attempt to mask my red-hot schlong-shame. "Yeah, that sort of just ... wormed its way in there."

He drops my bag, rises to his feet, then begins circling the fire ... *and me.*

Gulp.

"So, let me get this straight," he rumbles, dragging the 'tool' across my freshly preened wings and making them shiver all the way to the tips. "You removed the clothes I packed for you—the ones that would have kept you warm—and replaced them with *treats* and a large, wooden *cock*?"

"Treats are important."

"And, pray tell, what were you planning to do with this?" he asks, slapping the shaft against the palm of his hand and making my vagina flinch.

"I'm, ahh ..." *Good question.* I've never had one before, but I get the general idea ...

"Look, I don't know if you can tell, but I'm constantly—"

"Horny," he finishes, slapping the penis against his palm again.

The delicious warmth pooling between my legs begins to throb. He runs the phallic object along my overexcited wings again, making them get a bit fluffy, and I see the satisfied glint in Kal's eyes at their flirty show.

"Dell?"

"Hmm?"

"Answer my question, Little Dove."

Oh!

"Yes," I blurt, nodding enthusiastically. "I'm horny."

Did that answer it?

He stops behind the crackling fire, looking down at me perched on my knees in my sodden clothing. "What am I going to do with you, hmm?"

"Was that a rhetorical question? Because I have a few ideas in mind ..."

He rumbles low, his wings rising, casting half the cave wall in obscurity.

I moan.

Look. At. That. Wingspan.

"Take off your clothes."

I gulp at the dark challenge in his star-flecked eyes, the hard cut of his words.

Well then.

I twist my fingertips under the hem of my soggy top and peel it over my head, groaning when it brushes past my hard nipples. I toss it on the ground, peeping up as he draws a tight breath ...

That's right, Big Man. I didn't wear a chest wrap on this wee excursion of ours. Mainly because I'm hoping for some group nipple action the moment we rescue the others. But I'm not opposed to kicking things off early, considering we're trapped in this cave with nothing to do but pretend like we're not falling apart at the seams.

I stand, perhaps a bit too eagerly, and unbutton the latch at my belly button, attempting to wiggle out of my wet leather pants. Inch by stubborn inch, I manoeuvre them down until I'm panting and standing over the brown, strangled heap that resembles a pile of shit.

I'm really doing the hard yards for this cock.

Kal's looking at me like I'm the sun itself. Maybe my little strip tease didn't look half as awkward as it felt ...

"You have two options," he grinds out, giving his dick a tight squeeze through his pants. "You either get me or my beast. But if you choose *him*, I need you to know he's a kinky sonofabitch."

Interesting.

"Does he harbour all your darkest desires?"

His face is suddenly cold. Hostile. "He harbours a lot of shit, Dell. And the way he fucks ... it's an outlet for him."

I study his almost battle-like stance and wonder if he *needs* this. To hide for a bit.

I know all about that.

My heart thrashes and I draw a deep breath, about to tell Kal I'm ready to become acquainted with his beast when he cuts me off. "You have to be firm with him."

"Huh?"

"You haven't met my unrestrained beast ... not really. He's been waiting to have you for so fucking long that once he gets hold of you, he'll struggle letting go. I need you to promise you're not afraid to use force if you're feeling trapped."

I nod.

I need this—to be at the mercy of Kal's brutal half and be reminded that I *chose* this. That I'm not in a dark room stained in piss and vomit and death.

That darkness doesn't have to mean pain, suffering, and a sad vagina.

"Your word," he bellows, and I roll my fucking eyes, glancing down to flick a stray ember back into the fire.

"I promise I'll 'use force' if it becomes too much," I mumble, and a low growl splits the air. I peek up to see Kal's beast staring down at me ... that perfect face made even more striking by sharpened features and extended canines reaching well past his full bottom lip.

Fuck.

There's very little essence of Kal left in the cave; replaced by a sinister, deadly version. Even his wingspan seems to have grown.

He starts circling, his stride slow and powerful. "Lay down."

The raw timbre of his voice makes my breasts ache with the need to be licked and sucked by his feral tongue, and I do as he says, wings splayed, using Kal's water sack as a pillow.

"That's good, Kitty. Now spread your legs for me."

He smirks when I automatically comply, and I can see the meaning behind those dark, perceptive eyes ...

It's unlike *me* to be so compliant.

He taps that carved, wooden cock against his thigh, pausing in front of me with a front row seat to everything I'm offering between my legs. His nostrils flare, eyes roaming from my face, over my breasts, past my navel, and right between my thighs ...

A smooth, appreciative rumble makes my hips buck. "You're dripping."

I know.

His cock is hard and hungry, the outline of it so distinct on the surface of his leather pants. "Spread that pussy. I want to see what I'm doing to you."

Sweet, starry night babies.

There's a loud crash and the ground shakes as I walk fingers past my navel and reach my swollen lips, taking the opportunity to stroke my clit before parting myself—showing Kal just how hot and wet for him I am.

His teeth grind, gaze sizzling, and he makes a sound like thunder. "Good girl." He spits in his hand and lubricates the wooden cock before handing it to me. "Now, show me how you like to be fucked."

A sharp thrill shoots down my spine. "You're going to stand right there and ... and *watch?*"

He folds his arms, making his biceps pop as he stares down at me.

Guess that's a yes.

Rising to the challenge, I swirl the wooden cock around my entrance, slapping it against my swollen clit—making a wet sound every time it hits. My hips buck and I ease the toy into my pleading heat, thrusting to a slow beat—getting used to the intrusion before I fuck myself *just* the way I like ...

Hard. And fast.

Kal's muscles bunch, nostrils flare, his attention darting between my eyes and what's going on between my legs. I strum my clit, back arching, slick sounds filling the cave as sensual heat floods my core ... and I know I'm close.

So *fucking* close.

Kal starts to growl and I can't help but smirk. "Are you jealous of this big wooden dick?" I moan, lids fluttering. "It feels so *fucking* good, Kal."

Am I taunting his darkness?

Yes.

Perhaps I want to see how hard I can push him. See how much control I *really* have.

"*Stop.*"

There's so much fervour in his voice that I automatically comply.

He drops to his knees. "Take it out."

This time, my compliance is a *tad* more reluctant ... *I was so close.*

Fluid fingers unbutton his pants and I swallow.

Shit.

This is happening.

"Good luck, Shadow Man. Those things are hard to get off when they're wet, and fifty percent of your blood is now sitting in your dick."

He manoeuvres them off with persuasive hands, and I frown. Why does he make everything look so easy?

His large, angry length is released and I swallow the nervous lump in my throat ...

Even his dick looks bigger.

He tosses the petrified penis aside with a snarl, hooks me behind my knees so my feet are pointing at the roof, and stretches over me—that obscure gaze inches from my face. "After I'm done with you," he says, his voice barely restrained chaos, "you'll never be satisfied by that fake cock again."

I open my mouth to say something, but it leaks out in a throaty scream as he sheathes himself with one long strike of his hips. He doesn't give me a chance to catch my breath before he's driving out, then back in; every hard, claiming stroke a promise and a plea.

He smacks me with a kiss and I thread him a whimper, his pleasure storm ravaging my body ...

It's fierce. Violent.

Destructive.

It's a cleansing sheet of water to wash away my sins, and I have nothing to do but hold on for dear life.

"I need you to tuck these pretty wings away so they don't get hurt," he grits out, teeth bared while he fucks me hard, fast, and rough. "*Now.*"

I clamp down around Kal's intrusive cock, my orgasm slashing through me like a bolt of lightning. With a *swish* of white, my back is bare and pressed against the cold stone floor.

"Good girl," he purrs, striking me with a sharp kiss. He tugs out, flips me onto my hands and knees, and nudges my legs apart until my arse is poking up. A big, powerful hand snatches my wrists and pins them behind my back ...

I'm not given a single moment to catch my breath before he grips a fistful of hair, arches me off the ground with a commanding tug, and drives into my flushed pussy like a wild shadow.

My mouth pops open, neck stretched, core spread and at his fucking mercy. I bite my lower lip, trying not to scream ...

"*Don't hold it in,*" he chides, his hard, girthy cock staking claim with deep, primitive strikes. "Show me what I'm doing to you."

A whimper bubbles out ...

"That's it," he says on a rusty growl. "Give me *all* the pretty sounds. *Louder.*"

I moan, the noise interrupted with each violent thrust; the sting of my scalp making those muscles low in my abdomen knot.

Tingles start in my toes, trek up my legs, and seem to grow their own roots right where his cock is stamping his claim ... and I just know this orgasm is going to ruin me.

"Look at you," he rumbles, fucking me like I'm unbreakable. "Taking me *all* ..." He yanks my hair and my spine locks, eyes rolling into the back of my head. "Now be a good girl and *cum*."

My nerves *explode* and I draw on Kal's savage cock while he continues to thrust through the wetness dribbling down my legs ...

Fuck.

Me.

Dead.

I just *squirted* everywhere. I've never done that before.

He frees my wrists and drops my hair, firm hands spreading the globes of my arse. "What a good Kitty," he rumbles, before sinking his tongue into my core with a deep, husky growl that vibrates *through* me.

I'm ... fucking ... putty.

His tongue digs and probes with undomesticated hunger, like I'm a fresh kill he wants to savour. I press my breasts to the chilling floor, opening myself, when his canine scratches against the hot flesh of my core.

I jolt as all the blood in my body rushes to that small spot of contact, *begging* for him to dig past the flesh and claim me. "*Bite!*" I scream, pressing my arse back into his face.

His teeth scrape down ... around ... start to dig *in* ...

He rips away with a growl—leaving me on my knees and on the fucking edge.

Breathless, whimpering, I flip over and gasp—seeing Kal resting on his heels like a forest cat, looking at me like I'm *dinner* ...

"*Kal—*"

"*Run*, Kitty. Get your pretty claws out and *hide*."

The words spur between my legs like they're fucking *tangible*.

"But ... I don't want my beas—"

He snarls—this coarse sound that's wild and unbroken. "Last chance. Otherwise ... you're *mine*."

I flinch.

He said the word like it's some sort of *curse*.

"*Run!*"

The word crackles through my veins and I scramble back like a crab, thrill blazing in my belly, eyes wide and darting. I clamber up and bolt—my heart a hammer in my chest as I dart down a wiggly side tunnel that's almost entirely sponged of light.

I amble along on shaky, post-orgasm legs that threaten to cut out from under me, searching for somewhere to pretend to hide.

There's a distant rumble that smacks me right between the legs and almost makes me crumble ...

"You'll have to hide better than that. I can smell your wet pussy from here, Kitty ..."

Shit.

Fucking vagina's terrible at this game.

I scoot to the side, fold into a little nook of shadow, and curl up with my back pressed against the stone, thrill shooting through me like a drug.

"Do you have your claws out?" His voice bounces off the walls and turns my nipples into little pebbles ...

My beast yowls inside me but I gag her with a shadow.

He wants me to punish him—wants to scare me away ...

Well, fuck that. Nothing could frighten me off.

I can feel my pulse beating through my pussy, and I let it drown out my nerves—waiting—trying not to think about the dark place where I lost myself ...

Iridescent eyes flash green, and I gasp as big hands clamp around my ankles. I'm manhandled into the light of a single glow-bug, pinned between a wall of stone and a wall of man, and I think the weaker of the two is probably the rock at my front ...

"Got ya ..." His sharp words graze my ear, his hand sliding

around my throat and forcing my chin to lift, my tits stamping against the cold, unforgiving stone. "You're not scared of me, are you?"

"No."

Never.

He lets out a primitive purr, kicks my legs apart, then spears up into me—making me cry out. Those big, powerful wings stir and I press my arse out, presenting while he fucks me hard and fast, his fingers stoking the wet flame between my thighs ...

He nudges my head to the side, canines prickling my skin, his breath a punishing promise. "Mine," he rumbles, hovering. His dick swells with each deep grind, and he pinches my clit ...

My third orgasm crashes violently.

"Say it."

"Yours," I moan, "I'm *yours!*"

He strikes on a snarl—pinning me to the wall with his teeth in my neck. My eyes roll back, his venom igniting a blazing trail of carnal *need.*

My knees almost give way.

His cock swells up and starts to pump, and he grinds through his own release, growling into my flesh, his wetness dribbling down my inner thigh. My neck is released and he digs his nose into my hair, jerking my head to the side while calloused fingertips swipe through his seed ...

"Mine." He paints my stomach and my hard, peaked nipples with his cum—sniffing long and deep and making my neck prickle. *"Mine."*

The word zaps through me—makes my body jolt and sends a bead of venom dribbling down my chin. "Yours, Kal ..."

No takesies backsies.

He fists my hair, jerks my chin into the air, and takes my

mouth, his entire chest vibrating against my back while he battles my tongue.

I can *taste* myself ...

My blood.

My pussy.

I twist at the waist, suck his bottom lip between my teeth, and bite down, spilling his rabid purr ...

He's *everywhere*.

Digging into my heart, tucked in my chest and stretching me from the inside. I drop his lip, my kisses greedy—all sharp canines and the coppery taste of *mine*.

But I want them *both*, not just Kal's darkness ...

"Let him out ..."

"*No*."

My warning growl is sharp enough to slice. "You don't want to test me ... I'll confiscate your new favourite *plaything*."

My vagina clamps down on his cock like it's a fucking chew toy.

I try to churn in his arms but his grip tightens, trapping me between his hot chest and the cold stone wall like a prisoner of love—as if he believes he could keep me here forever.

Protected.

Guarded.

Despite the fact that I'm in this safe place with a man I trust, that stained part of my mind starts to panic ...

Darkness.

Vulnerability.

Fear.

No.

I reach between our legs, find my dangling target, snatch his balls, and *squeeze* ... not hard enough to hurt, but hard enough to establish a line in the fucking shadows.

The sound that powers out of him is corrosive. "I

wouldn't damage them if I were you. The seed of our future child is in there ..."

Wrong thing to say to me right now, motherfucker.

I squeeze a bit harder, making his wings pound the air like an excited dog wagging a tail.

"Give. Him. To. Me. Or your *planting* days are over."

His wings speed up their turbulent pace and I look back over my shoulder, seeing his lips hooked in a lopsided grin that barely fits his sharpness. "You're *perfect*. You light up my darkness like a fucking *star* ..."

All the breath whooshes out of me.

The hardness seems to bleed from his muscles, wings disappearing, his eyes beginning their gentle fade to the deep, striking sapphire I've come to know and love.

I drop his balls and spin, chest heaving, pussy *throbbing*.

"De—"

I shove him back and he takes the hit, sprawling across the ground, naked and glorious and fighting for breath. His gaze darts to my stomach—to the mess smeared over my breasts—and his nostrils flare.

He exhales with a rumble, cock *growing*, those midnight eyes flashing with so much emotion I can't keep up ...

One is more potent than the rest.

Yearning.

How deep did his beast push him down? Was he here for *any* of that?

I drop down and straddle his trim hips, guiding his thick length inside me, his breath hitching when I settle into his lap—holding every stretching inch.

Our breathing slows, eyes locked and barely blinking. The only movements are our rising chests and the frequent twitch of his dick.

"I never thought I was capable of love," he rasps, finally breaking the silence. "For so long I wanted to love Sel ...

Cassian's mother. I even prayed for the sun to warm my heart towards her. I just couldn't."

"We don't have to talk about thi—"

"Then I met *you*," he continues, "and I realised I wasn't broken after all. You may believe we're fixing you, Dell, but it's the other way around. You piece us together a little more each day just by *existing*."

A hot tear rolls down my cheek as Kal's tongue sweeps in and claims my mouth, emotions clashing like a storm we couldn't escape even if we tried.

I break the kiss, tip his head to the side, and sink my teeth into his neck ... because I want him to know that I want it all.

The dark.
The light.
And everything in-between.

CHAPTER TWENTY
DELL

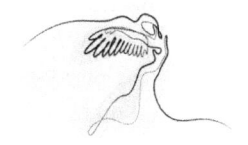

"*D*ell ... wake up, Little Dove."

A crack of lightning makes the entire cave shudder, and I groan, curling deeper into the soft jumper I'm practically swimming in. "Still stormy. Why can't I keep sleeping?"

"Because I'm impatient. You've been asleep for twelve hours and there's something I want to show you."

Well, shit. Apparently the remedy for insomnia is a goodnight kiss from my Night God—right between the thighs.

"Something to show me? Is it your dick?" I pop my head out and crack an eye open, seeing Kal sitting on his heels with mussed-up hair and a cocked brow. Fully clothed.

I frown.

A coarse chuckle rolls out of him, the sound rousing every nerve in my body. "Greedy girl. Get up. Now."

Ugh.

Waking me for anything less than his cock is a risk. "This better be good ..."

"I'm not one to disappoint."

Oh, I know.

I stretch and yawn ... observing Kal while he takes a draw from his drinking skein. He's wearing a tight black top and loose pants strung low on his hips. I can even see the outline of his dick hanging heavy between his legs ...

I bite my lower lip, replaying everything that body did to me, tracing his delicious lines until I see a knowing hook of his lips and realise he's watching me.

All my blood rushes to my cheeks and I try to smooth my errant hair ... unsuccessfully. Oh well. He bit my neck, he's stuck with me and my vagina's pervy-eye forever—even if I do look like a hot mess hacked up by a rabid street cat.

"Did you sleep?"

"Too close to Sterling." He winks and tosses me the skein. "I had precious cargo to monitor."

I'm practically a puddle at his feet.

I guzzle some water while checking my tethers, and all that postcoital happiness bleeds straight out of me ...

Sol's link seems to have improved, and Aero's little half-nub is healthy ... unlike Drake's tether which is now a fragile wisp—as if he's losing the battle to hold onto me.

I flatten my palm against my chest. *'Don't you dare leave me, you golden bastard! Our deal still stands; if you let go, I'm coming with you. We're not through, you and I.'*

"They okay?"

I shake my head and take Kal's hand, letting him tug me up. "I wish this storm would fuck off."

"Soon, Little Dove." A warm blanket of calm settles over me and I've never been so thankful for his gift as I follow him down the throat of the cave, sniffing around, peering over my shoulder every few seconds.

"Where are we going?"

"It wouldn't be a surprise if I told you."

I frown. I don't particularly like surprises. They usually end up biting me in the not-so-proverbial backside.

The further into the belly we go, the more I feel like we *just shouldn't be here*. The ground is too smooth—almost like it's been worn down by something ... *heavy*.

The cave takes a sharp turn, yawning to reveal a colossal room heaped with mounds and mounds and chaotic mounds of gleaming *treasure*.

My mouth pops open as I scan ... everything.

Well, fuck.

"That's not all." Kal scales the disorder, gesturing for me to follow, sending a golden goblet and numerous coins clattering down the slope.

My left eye twitches.

I scan the dunes with distaste swirling in my stomach, then narrow my eyes on my beaming Night God. "How can you stand to surround yourself with so much ... *disorder?*"

His face falls and he makes a weird choking sound. "Wh—what do you mean?"

Of course he doesn't understand.

I wave a hand and start sorting tokens into a tidy pile. I clump a few emeralds together, then some silver drabs that could do with a polish once I'm done stacking them.

"Go on without me. I have treasure to stack and jewels to categorise into a colour-coordinated sequence. It should only take about—"

"Three hundred years."

I catch sight of Kal's dancing eyes and scowl. "You know what? I don't appreciate your tone. Or your face. This is a serious issue! *Look at all this mess!*" I gesture towards the entire cavern. There isn't a single thing I don't want to change.

He slides forward a step, making a stream of gems scuttle down the dune and stampede my progress. I gasp, long and accentuated, my eyes going so wide they almost pop right out of my head. "Look what you just *diiiid!*"

His hands fly up like he thinks I'm going to mist him. "That was an accident! I'm sorry! I didn't mean to undo all your ..." he clears his throat, "hard work."

"I can't work under these conditions, Kal. Just ... *go.*" I throw an arm over my face and point in the direction of anywhere but here. "You've caused enough trouble."

I start re-building my towers from fucking *scratch.*

Unbelievable.

"Little Dove ..."

"Look, Nightmare. Unless you're going to feed me a cockie, I suggest you heed my warning and flutter off."

"How about I promise to show you something small and really cute?"

My ears perk and I glance at him warily. "*Really* cute?"

He nods, eyes twinkling. "Really, *really* cute."

I do like cute things. And small things.

"How small?"

"About yay big?" He shows me the general size with his hands and the sight pleases me so much I stand and dust myself off.

"So, like ... the size of a wee baby Faeling?"

"Yeah," he croaks, the corner of his mouth twitching. "About that size."

Good size, good size ...

"So, you coming up?"

I chew my bottom lip, scanning the colossal mess I've somehow inherited, and sigh. "Fine. But we have to come back to this chaos eventually. I won't be able to relax until I know it's organised."

He nods, giving me his come-hither hand. "One day, *jasta.*"

I scramble to get a foothold in the mountain of mess and Kal hauls me up by my wrist. I fall into his arms, clutching his biceps like pre-dinner rolls.

My wings pop out and my Night God-sized top that was swimming on me a moment ago is suddenly dabbling in non-consensual breath play. Kal laughs and spins me around, sending an emerald the size of my head rolling down the dune.

Sigh.

He shoves his arms through the slits and guides the tips, setting my tarts free to roam.

I gasp for breath.

"Thanks. These impromptu wing boners are a pain in my arse."

Kal gives me a nudge towards a dark corner of the cavern and waggles his brows. "If you want, I can distract your arse with a different sort of boner."

Any trace of amusement is strangled to death when I notice we're headed towards a treasure cliff that slopes into darkness. The ceiling dips low, almost touching the coins and gems cascading into the unknown—meaning the only way down that thing is to *slide*.

"No. No way. My pretty wings will get roughed up. They've been through enough already."

Kal grabs my other hand as well as my full attention. "Your pretty wings happen to be at the top of my priority list. Besides, it's fun. And if you stay here, you'll miss out on the really cute, really *small* surprise ..."

God-fucking-dammit. The man has me by the ovaries, and by the curl of his lips I'd say he knows it, too.

"I miss the good old days when we used to flash everywhere."

My eyes widen ...

Kal's face hardens. "No. Not happening."

"Who the hell are you? *Aero?* You don't even know what I was going to say!"

He scoops me up, and in one swift motion I'm hanging

upside down by my ankles, my wings clawing the air in a mad flap. I'm stunned silent, dangling with a face full of dick as he sits on the edge of the drop. "You want to learn to use the Bright."

He lays back, claps my knees around his ears, and then we're shooting down the golden slide of *doom* head fucking first. Kal's got a prime view of my vagina, my wings are stretched like they're *soaring*, and I'm screaming at the top of my lungs while riding my Sun-God-sixty-niner-sled into the abyss.

I have to admit, it is kind of fun. Mainly because my face is so close to Kal's cock.

We come to a halt amongst a cushioned carpet of shrub and I sneeze. Clamouring up, I study the large cavern we just plummeted into. It's not colossal like the one that feeds into it, but it's cosier and way more sheltered.

There's a heaped hill of sticks and leaves in the centre of the room and I sniff the air; trying to place the odd scent that's so much stronger in here.

"You good?" Kal asks, brushing my sides and belly.

I prod him in the chest with my pointy finger. "Why won't you teach me how to use the Bright?"

He sighs and plucks a twig out of my hair, eyes softening. "It's too dangerous to use at the moment. You know that."

"But what if the situation is dire?"

His brows knit and he cups the side of my face. "Dell ..."

"No, Kal. You know I need this, you're just too busy wrapping me in your sexy wings to admit it to yourself. You're teaching me, or that little sleigh ride will be the last time you come face to face with my fanny sandwich."

"*Fann—*" He closes his mouth and grunts, holding my stare—iron will to iron fucking will. It's a drawn-out moment before he breathes a long-suffering sigh, and I know I've won.

"If I do this, you must promise not to use it unless the situation is *dire*. Unless your life is in enough fucking danger that it warrants risking a run-in with your father."

"Okay, sure. Whatever you say."

His eyes narrow. "Don't make me regret this, Adeline ..."

Ooh. Serious name calling.

He's totally going to regret this.

He drops my face and mutters something in that language I can't follow. I wonder if he's regretting biting my neck yet?

"Close your eyes," he finally huffs. "I need you to dip inside yourself."

I cock a brow.

He winks, then jerks his chin at me, slipping his hands into his pockets. "Hurry up."

I do as he says, going to the dark place inside me. "Now what?"

"What's your beast doing?"

I spot the feral thing in the corner, fast asleep under a blanket of shadows. I give the toiled feline a prod and she responds with the flick of an ear ...

That's it.

"Sleeping. She's probably pissed I left her out of our bonding fuckfest."

"You need her to be awake and cooperating. She should be guarding a kernel of light about the size of a pea."

He's got to be kidding.

I pop my eyes open and glare at him. "You want me to convince that savage thing to *cooperate*? Are you serious?"

"Do you want to use the Bright?"

Well, I'm screwed. I'm saddled with a psycho who's hot one minute, comatose the next, and occasionally blows shit up. She's probably going to gut me from the inside.

I sigh, close my eyes, and give her a shove ... which is

useless. She weighs as much as my aching soul. "She's too heavy," I whine, watching her tail twitch ...

She's enjoying this.

"Find a way to lure her," Kal suggests on a light baritone. At least he's finding some enjoyment in this shit show.

I muse over the few times I've received a valid response from my beast without getting turned into a proverbial pincushion first, and it's generally when there's a Godly cock up for grabs. If she responds to the presence of their dicks so keenly ... I wonder how she'd respond to an extended *absence* of said dicks?

"You know what, Kal? I'm considering going celibate."

"*What?*" he squeaks, then clears his throat. "Ahh ... I mean ... why's that, Little Dove?"

Aww. He's trying to act all gentlemanly despite the scent of pure, undiluted fear I just got smacked in the face with.

Cute.

My beast's tail is no longer twitching, one round, attentive eye visible over the crook of her curled limb.

Bingo, bitch.

"I don't know. This whole 'sex with my Gods' thing seems to be coming between my beast and me. Perhaps it's for the best if we purge her obsession with your cocks by going cold turkey?"

The wild thing launches so fast that I jump back unnecessarily, forgetting I had the tart on a chain. She starts to pace—leaving a pea-sized bead of bright, colourful light nesting in the shadows, entirely unguarded ...

I squint at it. All of this for *that* tiny thing?

Kal clears his throat again. "Look, if it's important to you, we—"

"Shh!" I hiss, dodging shaded memories. I shuffle forward, shortening my beast's chains so she can't maul me while I ponder the pretty. "I found the thing. Do I touch it?"

"The kernel of light?"

Why does he sound so surprised? "Yes. You should have seen how fast she moved when she thought I was giving up your dicks."

"Guit te geize kruiten ..." Kal mumbles. "Yes, Dell. Touch it."

I scoop the drop of light into the palm of my hand, peering into its floodlit depths webbed with brighter, pulsing veins ...

Suddenly, it morphs into a massive wall of throbbing light draped before me. "Holy hand job!"

Kal makes a choking sound as I drag my hand across the waxy surface, leaving a path of iridescent light mottled with every colour of the rainbow.

"What do you see?"

Good fucking question.

I frown, watching the strange skin quiver in the wake of my touch. "Hard to explain ... is this thing *alive*?"

"It's not *not* alive. The Bright's a separate plane only a God or Goddess can sense. Can you see veins webbing the surface?"

I nod, running my hand up a particularly thick and throbby one. "They're everywhere. They glow a few shades brighter than the rest of the skin."

"They may look like veins, but they're actually weak seams in the skin we take advantage of. Anywhere else is too thick to rip."

I snatch my hand away. "Well that sounds fucking brutal."

"We're not hurting it, Dell. Drake and I have only ever sensed pleasure and happiness during a rip. It's so brimming with light that if it's been underused, a build-up can cause the Bright serious discomfort. Every time we force a tear, we release a little pent up energy. If anything, we're helping it."

Oh ...

"Once you're in," he continues, "it's as simple as focusing

on where you want to go. If you have a clear picture in your head, it will take you right there."

I nod, taking a step back towards my outer conscience. I almost trip over my beast curled in a ball on the floor at my feet, growling.

Temperamental bitch.

"That sounds simple enough," I say, reaching down to give her a stroke, but she snaps for my hand.

I scream, launch into my outer self, and look straight into Kal's very serious eyes.

"It sounds easy, but it's not. You'll find regular rules don't apply in the Bright. Time moves at a crawl and gravity abides by no laws." He rubs his thumb over his bottom lip, making me want to bite it. "Tearing into its flesh leaves a temporary scar that lasts for three seconds. For those who carry the Bright's seed, if we tune in enough, we can determine when it's being used and follow the rip ... so to speak."

"Which is why you're avoiding it at the moment?"

He nods tersely and I pop all the information somewhere safe inside my never-ending memory bank. "Okay ... anything else I need to know about it?"

There's a pregnant pause before he nods. "If you go in without a destination in mind, you'll just ... *be*. And if you settle on the surface for long enough—touching the grass, swimming in the phosphorescent water, mulling with the creatures that live there—you'll eventually be affected by *ignis infernum*."

"And what's that?"

"When you lose all sense of time or self. You could live for millennia there, then pop back out and only a day has passed in our time. It can be tempting to stay, forget about who you are and what your purpose is. Press pause on life. It's addictive, just ... letting go."

I swallow the lump in my throat, the information settling

on my shoulders like a weight. He steps closer, plucking a black feather from my hair. "People *lose* themselves there, Dell."

"That's why you didn't want to show me how to use it," I whisper, and his face softens.

"One of the reasons, yes."

"I wouldn't leave you all like that ..."

His wings explode from his back and sweep around me. "We would hunt you down if you did."

I've never heard someone mutter words so soft yet still thread them with such a possessive decree.

Kal slips my pinkie between his teeth and nips the tip, making a small sting. He suckles my blood, tongue warm and smooth as it rolls over the hurt ...

I squeeze my legs together.

"How do you know?"

"About?"

"Ignis infernum ..."

All the colour drains from his face and he sighs. "That, my Little Dove, is a story for another time."

I open my mouth to say something more when he tucks his wings behind his back and turns, leading me up the small mound of twigs.

Guess that's the end of *that* conversation.

We reach the top, peering into the well in the peak of the knoll where four eggs are resting against each other ...

My womb literally *throbs*.

"No way ..."

"Yes way."

Three of the eggs are wrapped in the same overlapping scale-like texture, like rows and rows of blunt teeth. One is black and dusted with gold, the other two a deep forest green with the same metallic dusting on the tips of each scale.

The fourth egg is smooth and white with thick flaxen

veins webbed around it—feminine compared to the other three.

"Are these what I think they are?" I whisper, trying to ignore their stone-cold chill when I touch the surface of the smoother one.

Kal really delivered. My hormones are having a party in my womb, dedicated to this cluster of cuteness.

"Drako eggs," he rumbles, kneeling next to me. "I haven't seen any in *years*, and not from lack of searching. They stopped breeding when Edom started hunting their kind."

"Why would he do that to such beautiful creatures?"

"His beast is power hungry." Kal rests his hand on the black, red, and gold one. "Kill or use, that's his rule of thumb these days."

"But the cave ... it's abandoned." I think back to my stroll through the desert; to all the skulls and bones I walked past, rested against, and almost fucking died next to. "The mother's probably dead. We can't just leave them here."

There's a soft sort of candour in Kal's eyes as he puts his hand over mine. "We can't take them, Little Dove. Edom has a black drako named Kyro who's been trained to sniff out and kill his own kind. They wouldn't be safe with us."

"Then what do we do?"

He glances back at the nest. "Leave them. Hope for the best. They can sit in stasis for eternity. If they're supposed to hatch one day, they will."

A cool shiver crawls up my spine ...

Something inside me wants to fluff my feathers, wiggle my bum, and nest until they crack open and start breathing fire everywhere. But, then what? I'd have four Drako babies following me around, calling me Mumma and roasting things that ought not be roasted.

I sigh. That just won't do at all.

But *look* at them ...

"Come on." Kal kisses the top of my head. "Let's climb out of here. Hopefully the storm's passed."

I stuff the last of my snack in my mouth, moaning ... That's some tasty cockie.

The ocean roars while Kal pulls on his form-fitting leather jacket, pushing his wings through slits in the thick material before wrestling the buttons.

Looks like it's shrunk, not that my vagina's complaining.

"Did you order Cassian to stay behind?"

"No. He protects the Kingdom in my stead. He also knows how important it is to keep his fucking head down." The last part is said with such zeal, I can't help but wince.

"Because Edom doesn't know about him?"

"And he won't learn about him either." Kal buckles the sheath for his sword like he's preparing for war. He does the same with a baldric across his chest, then kneels in the sand and starts to tie my laces. "I'd go to my grave protecting that secret."

I know he would, but I'd never allow that to happen.

While he's preoccupied with my boots, I slip the petrified penis into my tight-fitting pocket, hoping Kal won't notice the extra appendage I'm packing and make me leave it behind.

You never know when a spare cock might come in handy.

The only things we're taking are Kal's weapons, the lock pick, my half-filled vial of shit, and our water sacks—namely, this large pouch hanging across my chest on a string.

I pinch its neck, inspecting the unique object. I've never seen a skein like this before—so soft and malleable. I give it a sniff then rub my cheek on the wide surface, enjoying the silken texture. "What are these made from?"

Kal finishes the complex knotting system and glances up. "Camel scrotum."

I blink at him.

And again.

"You're fucking with me, right?"

"Unfortunately not. The *fucking* part, I mean."

I drop the thing so damn fast ...

This entire time, I've been carrying a testicle like a trophy strung around my neck, drawing from it in ravenous slurps. I even used this extra-large one as a pillow while my Night God fucked me flaccid.

I really need to start asking more questions.

Kal kisses my knee and stands. "The storm may be gone, but it's still fucking cold." He spears a glance towards the clouds—dark, angry, and still rolling with electric scribbles.

"How far off are we?" I ask, handing him my pack.

"Not far." He pitches both our bags through the waterfall's enraged face before branding me with his foreboding astuteness. "You ready?"

I slide my hand over my tender heart and nod.

Yes, I fucking am.

CHAPTER TWENTY-ONE
DELL

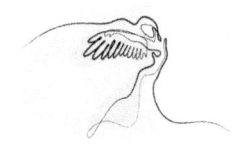

I catch fleeting glimpses of the city through pink, fluffy clouds; thousands of whitewashed buildings pieced together like a flat, soulless puzzle. I glance at Kal who's scanning the ground, bashing the sky with his imperial wings. "Isn't this the capital of the world? Where is everyone?"

A muscle in his jaw tightens. "I don't know. I haven't surveyed Sterling since The Fall began. This is *his* kingdom."

His.

My father.

How could a city built to sustain so many be so empty?

"Our descent needs to be swift in case there are any scouts in this area." He glances at me and I can see the unease he's trying to mask with his rigid demeanour. "It's a *hard* manoeuvre ..."

Lucky for me, I have a knack for hard things. "I've got this, Kal."

He nods, tucks his wings into his back, and dives. I watch him grow significantly smaller as he plummets towards the city like an arrow. "Fucking hell."

I have *not* got this.

I mimic his movements, squinting against the brisk air as I try to follow his path towards a brassy roof. Kal flicks his wings out and drops onto a small patch of overgrown lawn before slinking into the shadow of a building.

As I draw closer, it becomes apparent that I've botched my trajectory. Not only am I heading straight for a pointy spire, but I'm also travelling too fast to remedy it.

My arms and legs begin to flail and I plummet like a fallen vagina star.

Kal shoots into the air and wraps me in a torrent of black feathers that mask my resounding grunt. He lands like a fucking feline, and I'm hauled—breathless and quivering—into a pocket of shade.

"I f-fannied that u-up, didn't I ..."

Kal presses his lips to the back of my neck. "We'll work on your descents, Little Dove."

Such a nice way of saying my flying skills are still a bit shit.

"Where to n-now?" I ask, trying to smooth my hair. I can't be looking like a mangy hairball that was tugged out of a blocked drainpipe when I finally see my mates.

Kal grabs my hand and tugs me behind a large shrub, then down some uneven steps that curve into a tunnel I would never have guessed was here. Only a trickle of light follows us into the tight, cavernous space tainted with the distant tang of pain.

I quiver.

All I can see is the faded outline of uneven walls and Kal's silhouette leading the way.

"Where are we?" I ask, my heart thrashing like it's trying to bust out of its cage. Tight, dark spaces make me nervous—reminding me of the years I was helpless, weak, and enslaved to a man who took absolute advantage of me.

Kal's grip tightens. "Shh, Dell. Words carry in these tunnels."

My heart slows, my taut shoulders slump, and a wash of relief tamps my erratic thoughts ...

Sweet, sweet happy web. I've missed you, old friend.

I squeeze Kal's hand, thanking him for the touch of power stumping my nerves. At least until a warm glow begins to lift the oppressive darkness, illuminating the roof —barely three feet from my head—clotted with fucking *cobwebs*.

All my happiness fizzles as I stop and stare at the webs, hoping to hell they don't belong to those Fae eating spiders I'm far too familiar with.

Kal spins, grabs my chin, and pinches so hard I'm forced to look into his star-flecked eyes. *'It's okay,'* he mouths. *'I've got you.'*

And *I've* got a sudden urge to pee myself.

I point to my hand, the one the spider gnawed on while I was trapped in that dark place.

Kal winces, then ... *nods*.

Motherfucker.

"Are you kidding me?"

His eyes widen and he stamps a finger on my lips, but I'm too busy drowning in a metaphorical sea of fangs and hairy, probing legs.

Deep, alert voices echo all around us ...

Oops.

Kal sighs, running a tense hand down the length of his face.

"Sorry ..." I whisper-yell.

"Stay here." He spins and storms towards the source of light, leaving me entirely alone with my impending doom ...

Nope, nope, *nope*.

I step forward but receive a scalding glare that bears the

entire weight of the night sky. "The spiders are knocked out. All of them. Sit the *fuck* down and wait for my signal."

Well then. I adjust the wooden dick in my pocket and sit cross legged on the ground, deciding to let his shitty attitude fly on the basis that knocking hundreds of spiders out must be exhausting.

I rock back and forth, trying not to look at all the black lumps pretending to hide behind loose drapes of web ...

I'm a big, brave girl.

I'm a big, brave girl.

I'm a big, bra—

I hear the stark sound of *swords* clashing. Bones pop and snap, my body jolting with each disturbing splinter of sound.

No ...

Don't worry, Kal. Backup's coming!

I clamber up and dash in the same direction he went, the cave becoming so tiny I have to wiggle on my stomach to save my wings from a rocky assault. A chilling silence ensues as I emerge in the shelter of a mammoth boulder and scramble up, peeking over the top ...

The dreary hallway branches left and right, clogged by a pile of dead legionnaires. Heads are severed, necks are bent, there's gore everywhere ... and Kal's standing over them like death incarnate.

Bloody.

Still.

"I see you were being a good girl and waiting for my signal," he scolds, and I flinch, watching him sheath that grisly sword down his spine in one swift motion.

"I thought you needed backup ..." I whisper and instantly regret it.

He definitely did not need backup.

"Are they"—I gag—"all dead?"

"I had no other choice." He scratches his temple and peers sidelong at me. "Jump out of the way, I'll stash them behind the rock."

Fucking hell.

I do as he says, watching Kal stack one lifeless body after the other, blocking my nose against the overwhelming stench of shit, piss, and layer upon layer of brutal, bloody rape ...

It doesn't make it any easier to watch their entrails spill everywhere as they're dragged along the ground with flat, wide-open eyes.

I quiver.

Once they're successfully tucked away, Kal takes my hand and we continue down the long, curling passageway in heavy silence until we reach a junction; one hall curving to the left, the other descending into darkness. Kal sniffs the air and I do the same, picking up the faintest hint of Sun Godly musk from the scarcely lit stairs ...

"That's a dead end," Kal grinds out, jerking his chin towards the stairwell. He unclicks the baldric, pressing the sheathed blade against my chest.

I glare down for a sharp second.

I'm not sure how many times I need to say no to that dagger for it to really sink in, but apparently we're not quite there yet.

"There's a heavy scent of foot traffic through this hall, and we have nothing to mask your ..." he clears his throat, "*scent.*"

I frown.

"Are you saying I smell?"

"Yes," he snarls. "You smell *feminine*, Dell. And it's really fucking strong. I'll need to stand guard and stop anyone from taking this turn, otherwise every legionnaire in this haunted city is going to be hunting you like a hound."

My mouth pops open and I blink at him, taking the weight of the dagger.

"Put your walls up. I don't know how the others are going to react to you being here."

"Shouldn't we just ... stick together? Splitting up is a recipe for another lost Sun God. If we run into anyone, you can just play Sandman and put them to sleep."

Kal draws a deep, unguarded breath. "Dell ... I can't."

My eyes widen, realisation booting me in the kidney. "You're running low ..."

"No, Little Dove. I'm all out."

My wings sink.

"How?"

"I've been low for a while, and I whittled the last of it trying, and failing to put those rapist pigs to sleep. But my body's a weapon. If more legionnaires show, they'll siphon into that tight hall where I can dispose of them. We don't have any other choice."

I watch him haul that crimson-clad sword from the sheath down his spine while I frantically search for my lady balls. The weapon looks so comfortable in his hand, like it's an extension of his arm.

I'm holding mine like it's going to leap out and bite me.

"Use your beast if you have to. She'll protect you."

I almost fucking laugh. I can't rely on that bitch. She'll either paint the walls red or quiver in a corner while everyone takes stabs at my vagina. There is no in-between.

"And the blade?"

"Precautions." Kal points to a spot below one of my left ribs. "Right in here with an upward tilt to put it straight through the heart."

Gulp.

He folds his hand around the side of my neck, right over his mate-bite. "The Legion are a different breed of High Fae with a certain level of bloodlust that's unexplained. Don't hesitate. They sure as fuck won't."

Dark room.
Smells like piss.
Death ...

"Dell ..."

I nod, my grip on the dagger tightening. "It's okay."

Kal presses our foreheads together, holding me so close we're mixing harsh breaths. "Remember what I told you about the Bright. Once you've made the tear, all you have to do is step through and picture where you want to go. And *focus*. Make a triple rip to muddy the trail, then find somewhere safe to hide."

I lean back, seeing frigid darkness trying to chase the light out of his eyes. "Why would I use the Bright? You said it's not safe."

He sighs and splays his hand across my heart. "If I tug on this link, you have no choice. Do you understand me, Dell?"

I nod ...

I know exactly what he's asking me to do, and I'd rather skin myself with this blade than follow such a bullshit order. I'm not collecting three Sun Gods only to lose another.

"Good girl," he whispers, taking my mouth, treating my lips like he's pouring his dying wishes between them. I respond in kind though we undoubtedly have different reasons for our desperate surge of passion ...

He's preparing to sacrifice himself for the majority. Me? I'm just shit at apologies, and this is my way of pre-lubing his arsehole before he's sodomized by my blatant disregard towards his very stupid request.

We're broken apart by the distant thud of heavy boots. My heart grows laden as Kal buckles the baldric to my chest, securing it right between my boobs.

"Kal ..."

He kisses my nose and nudges me down the steps, stoppering the exit with his intimidating frame. "*Go,*" he rumbles, and it's only when I hear the tortured timbre of his voice that I realise Kal is no longer in control ...

His beast is.

CHAPTER TWENTY-TWO
DELL

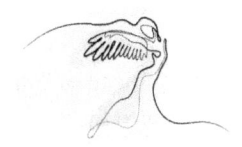

The stairwell spits me into a wider hallway that splits both left and right with intermittent Fae orbs creating sporadic pockets of light. Their Sun Godly scents are so much stronger down here, filling my chest with hope ... at least until I hear footsteps approaching from the left.

Shit.

I dart back and press flat against the damp stone while I steady my heaving lungs, the unfamiliar weight of Kal's dagger now clutched in the palm of my hand.

The footsteps draw closer.

Whoever it is smells like freshly baked bread with a side of 'I like to stick my cock in corpses'.

Dark room.

Smells like piss.

Rape ...

No, Dell. No.

I sheathe the blade and palm the long, hard bulge that's pointing down my thigh.

I'm no assassin. A blade feels awkward in my hand, and to

be honest, I don't trust myself to finish the job unless my beast is in charge. But she's nuzzled so deep it's almost like she doesn't exist.

Slipping my hand in my pocket, I grip the smooth shaft ...

This is a weapon I'm familiar with, though I'm usually on the receiving end of the abuse—which is going to make this act of rebellion that much more *satisfying*.

The legionnaire steps into view as I draw my schlong-sword, raise my arm, and strike his temple ...

His body crumbles into a heap of muscle and feather; the wooden knob discarded next to his body.

I toss the shaft aside and tut. "What a waste."

Stepping over the lump of man, I follow my nose down the dimly lit hall for a good five minutes until I come to another fork in the road.

Dammit.

Perhaps I should have asked that legionnaire for directions before I fucked his temple with a dose of irony.

Incorporeal fingers use my vertebra as a ladder, and I spin, scanning the gloom ...

Nothing.

This place is creepy as shit.

Turning back to the decision before me, I draw a deep whiff. My vagina does the same.

Left. Their smell is definitely strongest to the left.

I follow my vaginal instincts, walking past cell after cell— all rotten, hollow, and smelling like long-forgotten death.

I start to run, each cage flashing past me like a silent threat.

What if they've been moved?

What if I'm *too late?*

I round a corner, seeing a dramatic end to the dingy hall, and my heart twists in my chest ...

Fuck. There're only a few cells left for me to scour.

Every step and sharp turn of my head accelerates my pulse until it's a surging wave between my ears, screaming that I'm *too fucking late*. I reach the last two cells and peer to the right, seeing Aero and Sol lumped in separate corners of the tight space ...

I crumble to the ground, my hands clapping over my mouth in a desperate attempt to stifle my relieved gasp.

They're here. They're fucking *here*.

They're okay.

Kind of.

I crawl towards the cell as silent tears track down my cheeks, studying Sol's chest smothered in dried blood and a rank smelling goo. There're two half-healed wounds across his chest and chains wrapped around his naked torso, his slumbering scowl half hidden by a flop of filthy hair.

There's a circular scar carved around my claiming bite ...

He gave him a fucking whore mark.

Beasty pokes her head out of her shadow lair and snarls. My vagina does the same.

My father's a dead man walking.

I swivel my gaze to Aero, his ankle tethered by a grizzly looking shackle. His knuckles are shredded, his hair matted, and the skin beneath his eyes is smudged black—a total contrast to his pallid complexion.

He looks ... *haunted*.

I spin, turning to liquid when I spot Drake sprawled on the ground in the opposite cell—his rotten wings twisted unnaturally. His chest rises and falls with each shallow breath and a sheen of sweat dapples his gaunt face.

Tight, shaking fists hang by his sides ...

I crawl forward, grab one of his cell rods, and hiss, jerking back when it sizzles my palm. "Fucking ... *ouch*."

Iron.

"Dell?"

My wings flare at Aero's sharp whisper, and I pivot, seeing him perched by the bars of his cell. Gripping them. Not pulling away despite the fact that his flesh is sizzling.

His eyes are wide and wild, scanning every inch of my body. "What are you *doing* here?"

"Saving your arses," I sob, shuffling forward, digging the pick out of my pocket.

He draws a deep, exaggerated breath, nostrils flaring, eyes going round like the sun. He drops the bars and stumbles back onto his arse. "Oh, *fuck* ..."

"What?" I bark. "Do I smell bad?"

I sniff my armpit ...

Okay, so I don't exactly smell fresh, but there's no need to be so fucking rude about it.

"De—"

"I just crawled into the grey arsehole of Sterling to rescue you, Morning Glory! So what if I've perspired? This is stressful stuff!"

Now I'm self-conscious.

"You need to go," he growls, the black in his eyes threatening to expand. "Right now."

I gape at him.

"I'm not going anywhere. Not until you're all free!" I whisper-yell at the disrespectful bastard. I'm not sure who taught him his manners, but they didn't do a very good job.

I stand and reach for the lock.

Aero's hand darts through the divide and snatches my wrist. "Dell ... baby, please. You need to go. This is a trap. You need to think of nobody but *yourself* right now."

I roll my fucking eyes.

"I think you're forgetting who you're talking to," I say, switching the pick to my other hand. "And I'm ambidextrous, so eat this."

He reaches through and snatches that wrist, too.

Bastard.

I hiss through the rods, my beast adding a little extra *zing* in a show of feral fortitude.

He returns the sentiment—his canines sharp and ... longer than mine.

Rude.

"What the fuck is she doing *here?*" Sol's groggy, slashing voice cuts through the air and my knees wobble when our hot gazes meet like fire and brimstone. A thousand emotions flit between us, the look in his eyes telling me *everything* ...

He knows. At least to some extent.

Dark room.

Smells like death.

Probing things.

The ground seems to well up beneath me, my wings wilting like a storm cloud loosening its load. Perhaps Sol blames himself ...

I close my eyes, squeezing them tight.

"Let her go, Aero."

What?

I stare at Sol with my mouth hanging open while Aero makes a deep, abrasive sound. "She has to leave!"

"Calm your sausage!" I whisper-hiss.

"My sausage *is* calm!"

"You've *clearly* never seen a calm sausage. Your sausage is the opposite of calm."

Sol shakes his head, his jaw stiff enough to bounce a token off. "You know her better than this, Dawn. She won't leave without us. Let her go."

Well, knock me down with a petrified penis ... Sol just earned himself a gold vagina star. I never thought I'd see the day.

"*Heil de na vej, al mei ten a veil jarva tes!*" Aero spits out, making me go immediately cross-eyed.

"What was that? Speak louder, and *normally.*"

"*Ves da vi!*" Sol snaps in a sharp baritone that makes my vagina weep itty-bitty happy tears. "*Vas jan e tami, de nei ve hes!* Kal *de ma glutz!*"

"Oh! Kal! I recognise that word!"

They ignore my enthusiastic outburst, probably pissed I'm doing such a great job of decoding their language because soon they won't have their fancy words to hide behind.

Aero rolls back on his heels and drops my wrists.

Huh.

Having the big alpha dick on my side is mighty helpful.

"Thank you. I'll get back to saving your arses now, if you don't mind."

I jam my pick into the lock and start flicking it around, just like Kal taught me. But it's hard to hold my focus when I've got two caged Gods scouring every inch of my skin.

I heave a sigh when the device cracks open.

Aero's hand reaches through, plucks the heavy bolt off the hook, then drops it to the floor with a thud. He boots the gate and I wince, glancing down the hall when the un-oiled hinges squeal at us ...

Too loud.

I launch at the cuff gripping Aero's grisly ankle and almost coo when he strokes my face, tracing all my angles with the tips of his burnt fingers. "You and me, Dell, we need to have some serious words."

His voice is sweet venom.

"Yeah, well ..." I meet his condemning gaze when the lock on his cuff clicks open. "It'll have to wait."

He flicks the iron off, threads his hand around the back of my neck, then pulls me so close our foreheads are kissing. His eyes close as he draws on our shared breath, making a low, rumbling sound. "You're a naughty girl." *His grip tightens.* "And you're officially in the fucking *sin bin*."

"That's not very nice!"

He snatches the pick and gets to work on the lock securing Sol's chains. "Now you know how it feels. You should have stayed the fuck away."

Somebody needs a hand job.

Sol's cerulean gaze is fixed on me like the mid-afternoon sun on a hot summer's day. The moment that last ring of chains drops, he's on his feet, wings exploding from his back as he wraps me in a devastating embrace that makes my heart pop.

"I thought I'd lost you," he rasps, the words so sincere I almost choke on their potency.

"Can't get rid of me that easily. Besides, I couldn't leave you down here"—I notice a small pile of bones heaped in the corner and gag—"*eating rats.*"

"They're better than the shit we were being served," Aero mumbles, stealing a cautionary glance down the hall while picking the lock on Drake's cell.

I clear my throat and press the back of my hand against my lips. "Sorry, I never used to be so"—*gag*—"vomit-y."

Sol nuzzles my neck and draws a deep whiff, and I'm half tempted to repay the fucking favour so he knows just how it feels.

My ears twitch when he starts to make this low, threatening rumble, his grip tightening—bad news for my poor, crushed boobies. "*Adas tel afen! Heis tame ada druca teis?*"

His voice is something ... *more.* Something fierce and virulent.

I stab an imploring look in Aero's direction. "*Help* ... I think?"

He shakes his head and shoots me a glance as Drake's lock

cracks open. *"Hal gleit hass, vaj aden feit la tame. Druca teis nie —dos navi meh!"*

Sol makes this sharp, scathing sound, scoops me up like a motherfucking infant, and carries me into Drake's cell.

No, no, *nope*.

I pinch the bastard on the arm, but he just grunts. It's not until he lowers me next to Drake that I manage to glance into Sol's sable eyes and realise I'm no longer dealing with my Day God ...

I'm dealing with his beast.

His face has honed into a weapon; the statuesque man even more striking.

He looks ready to dive into battle.

"What the hell is wrong with him?" I ask, flinging myself over Drake's clammy body. I check his injuries, bathed in the overbearing shadow of Sol's alpha presence while Aero works at the cuff around Drake's ankle.

"Just ... try to ignore him."

Easier said than done.

Drake's wings have a dull, metallic ring piercing them together—the torn flesh oozing a putrid stench. They're filthy, probably affecting his ability to heal.

"He's not good," Aero mutters, giving a sweeping assessment I hate to agree with. I've seen enough dying people to know Drake's on a slippery slope to Death's door.

"His link," I whisper, gesturing to my heart. "It seemed to improve for a bit before weakening again."

Aero manoeuvres Drake's dense wings so we can better inspect the damage. "Edom smeared something on them. It slowed the infection caused by all the shit his wounds are trying to heal around. He'd probably be dead if it weren't for that."

I rear back. "Why the fuck would *he* care?"

Sol spits a warning growl that makes me want to curl into

myself, and my hormones cut him a seething glare.

"One of his games," Aero huffs out as I reach for Drake's wing piercing, but my oppressive Day God swats my hand away.

"No," he rumbles, his voice a sinister echo. "It will take from you."

I watch Sol pry the ring apart and toss it to the ground, leaving raw welts on his hand. "Take from me?"

"Iron siphons power," Aero explains as I dig the shit vial out of my pocket. I uncork the lid and gag, blocking my nose, trying not to vomit half-digested cockies everywhere.

"You okay?"

Aero's studying me so thoroughly that I envy my beast's ability to throw a fucking shadow over her head.

"My pre-heat hormones are making me extra sensitive towards things that smell like rotten arsehole." I paint some goo around the most pressing areas of both wings. "I thought you'd know that already? I sure bitch about it plenty."

Sol and Aero share a *look*, before the former ducks out to check the corridor while Aero motions for me to stand. "Dell, I can't hear you anymore."

I cork the vial and shuffle back with a frown. "But you can always hear me ..."

"Yes, but I haven't been able to hear your thoughts since I was bound," he admits, hoisting Drake. "After all the iron exposure ..."

My eyes widen.

No.

"Your tanks are *empty?*"

Sol and Aero both nod.

Shiiiiit.

Who's the big, swinging dick now, huh?

Me. Well ... my psychotic, colon-slicing beast.

What a disaster.

Sol gets under Drake's other arm and I study the lot of them. This is not ideal. Neither Sol nor Aero are in form to be flying with the added weight of an unconscious Dusk God; which probably stands for Kal, too. And we can't use the Bright for risk of being tracked by my homicidal father ...

Drake needs to heal before we leave the city, or we might as well end ourselves now on our own terms.

"We need to get out of here," I mumble, casting my vision down the ominous hall. "Kal's holding the fort. Follow me."

Aero huffs something about hormones making me bossy, but I ignore him and my snarling vagina, keeping to the shade as we shuffle past empty cells.

We reach the fork in the road and the sound of someone whistling makes my ears flick ...

I pause, listening.

I know that tune.

I know that tune very fucking well.

"Dell, what are y—"

"Wait here, I'll only be a minute." I toss Aero the vial of shit and earn myself some rabid rumbles from my two Sun Gods—both desperately trying to find somewhere to prop Drake.

I sprint down the hall, picking up a familiar mix of scents my Sun-God-starved mind must have overlooked earlier—unease churning my organs.

The tune continues, a melody that shattered my mind and plagued my every waking moment since I was tossed in my own pit of darkness all those years ago.

Breathless, I reach a cell tainted with the smell of blood and piss and vomit, seeing a distorted shadow curled in the corner ...

My wings flare.

The tune ceases.

"Hello, Cupcake."

CHAPTER TWENTY-THREE
DELL

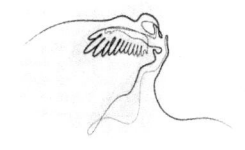

"*Take a look at you ...*"

The voice fills the entire cell then spits out to meet me. I swallow, my tongue a lump of lead in my mouth.

"Kroe."

The word tastes rotten. A festering piece of meat that was palatable when I was starving, but now it just makes me want to gag.

The twisted shape shuffles forward, moving into a shaft of light.

I gasp.

Gone is the pretty face that's hovered in my nightmares; the skin now mottled purple, yellow, and brown. His perfect nose is crooked, hair an oily mess that tickles the grotesque, swollen lid of his left eye—smudged black and matching the darkness he kept me in.

"I always knew you were special," he croaks, regarding my wings with a starved scrutiny. He hacks out a groan and shifts, exposing a bare chest riddled with angry welts. "No wonder you were such a good fuck."

A dominant growl almost carves up my composure.

Sol emerges from the cloak of black, tucked away from Kroe's sight but close enough that I can see the threat in his obsidian eyes ...

I raise a hand, signalling that I'll only be a minute. I don't know what those wards are capable of here in Sterling, and I won't gamble Sol's life for this ... washed up piece of shit.

Kroe rocks his head to the side. "Who's that, huh? Has my Cupcake found herself another keeper?" He slides forward until his chain goes rigid. "Another cock to sink your plush little pussy onto?"

Sol snarls and Kroe hocks a wad of bloody spit at the ground, trying to ooze the bravado we both know he's lacking right now.

It's like a mask—one he doesn't know how to dislodge.

I know that feeling.

"Tell me, Cupcake, does he know you like to be fucked so hard your knees bleed? That you like a finger up your arse when you're about to *cum?* Don't forget, you grew up clenching *my* cock with that sweet little cunt ..."

I hiss at my approaching Day God; his wings splayed as wide as they can manage without scalding themselves on the bars. His face is a midday thunder storm, the intent in his inky eyes clear as fucking crystal.

If I don't walk away soon, he'll drag me out of here himself ... damn the consequences.

I turn back to the broken man before me.

The messy, fucked up part of my heart—the part he stole from a child who just wanted to be loved—is screaming that this is not right. That he *can't die.*

Because that's what will happen if he stays here.

He'll die.

The rest of my heart is telling me he doesn't deserve such a simple death. That he needs to die at the hands of the many women he's tortured and marred. Broken and used ...

Profited from.

That leaving Kroe to rot in this cell is exactly what he deserves, considering he showed me the same courtesy for years.

"Dell. We're going. *Now!*"

Yes, we are.

I clear my throat and turn from the man who poured darkness into my veins; who twisted my mind and my perception of love.

"You're just going to leave me here?" Kroe pleads, his words suddenly soft and beseeching—a delicate spear shot at my fleshy underbelly. "You know I care about you, Adeline. You know I fucking *love* you!"

I wince.

Kroe doesn't understand the true meaning of love, but I do ...

I can feel the sizzle of Sol's savage gaze like a brand on my face, and I'm suddenly drowning in guilt. This is so much worse than the time my Sun Gods summoned their favourite blowjobs to save me from my father ... I basically fed them their own cocks for that stunt. And here I am, chasing the tune of a man who spent nineteen years fucking me; who sold me, broke me, tortured me, and hacked away at me piece by piece.

My mate game needs some work.

I take a step towards Sol with my chin held high. "Goodbye, Kroe."

"What about *them?*" he sneers in a raw voice that hooks my attention. I follow the line of his pointy finger to the cell across the hall tucked in a pocket of shadow—the one I hadn't thought to glance in because I was so distracted by my own fucking woes.

My breath catches.

Hanging on the wall inside the obscure crypt are twelve

women draped in red, teetering on their tippy toes.

Bloody.

Broken.

Gagged.

The ones I left behind ...

"Did you love them at all, or are you just like him, content to watch them *rot?*"

I throw myself against the bars, drinking the ardent sting as iron melts my flesh. Sol hisses, the wild sound like a whip, and I hear Kroe scramble deep into his cell like an exposed crab seeking shelter.

"No, no, no ..." My knees hit the ground and my wings wilt, marinating in the filth while I watch the women, watching me, *hating myself* ...

One of them whimpers.

Even if Aero didn't have my pick, I couldn't let them out. They'd see the Sun Gods helping. They'd taunt those fucking wards.

That precious black link tugs on my heart and my hand flies to my chest ...

My Night God is in trouble.

Fuck.

I make a silent promise to myself, to *them*, before I smack the iron and push away—feeling the weight of the world on my shoulders.

I turn and sprint towards my hostile Day God with bunched fists and a twitching upper lip. Once I'm out of Kroe's line of sight, I'm swooped up and tossed over Sol's shoulder like a sack of grain.

He bolts down the hall so fast I can barely draw breath, and it's only once we reach a crumpled Drake that I'm flipped onto my feet with a snarl.

"Das ve Dell, marush!" Aero snaps, inspecting my hand while Sol cusses at fresh welts on the other.

I throw them both a poisonous glare and snatch my limbs back. "They're already healing!"

"*Vail de na vi! Druca teis me ardeti va!*" Sol declares before hoisting Drake who seems to have a little more colour in his cheeks.

"Kal's in trouble. Try to keep up." I take off down the sinister tunnel, drawing further away from the women I shared a rotten life with.

Women still suffering because of *me*.

I reach the man still passed out on the ground and cringe, leaping over him ...

"Well ... shit," Aero mumbles, followed by the sound of something scuffing the stone. I glance over my shoulder in time to see half a wooden cock ricochet off Aero's boot.

If he still wants to have sex with me after seeing more evidence of my penis-severing skills, it'll be a miracle.

Metal clashes in a shrill symphony, the sound intensifying as I draw further up the stairs. When I finally reach the landing, I see Kal moving like a swift bolt of black lightning, swinging his sword with expert precision—slicing through men, weapons, armour ... painting the ground red.

I lift my hand to my mouth.

Bodies are piling up; all twisted limbs and exposed intestines, vacant gazes and red, severed wings.

He's not even panting. And his eyes ... they're a moonless night sky.

He's a lethal shadow; death incarnate.

Slice, kill.

Stab, kill.

Hack, kill.

It's a savage dance of demise until he's standing alone amongst the carnage—back to me and his body chillingly still.

I step out of the stairwell, watching his ears twitch as he pivots ...

Fuck.

His glare is *devastating*. There's a world of pain behind those ebony eyes.

"Kal ..." I take a step forward but a battered hand grips my arm, halting me in place.

Kal's lips peel back from his teeth, his eyes narrowing on Aero's hand as he starts to snarl ...

"Did you mate with him?"

I nod.

Aero grunts, dropping his grip. "Just ... give him a moment. He needs to calm down or he's going to fuck you right now in that pool of blood."

I glance down and sure enough, Kal's cock is rock solid; the severe outline pointing across his thigh when it should be bruising my ovaries. That cold mask shatters and he shakes his head, stalking towards me. "You never fucking listen, do you?"

Really? He signalled for me to flee, yet there must be over seventy legionnaires scattered all over the ground in *pieces*.

He inspects the welts on my hands while I lift my chin and shrug. "I thought you would have learnt that giving me instructions tends to get you nowhere. Besides, you overreacted. Obviously."

Kal's glower is nothing short of murderous; another God added to the Pissed Off with Our Shared Vagina club. They can plan a little slumber party, gorge on cockies, and bitch about me together.

"*Geil te gleit. Adas tel afen druca teis?*" Aero snaps, his voice so full of venom that I leap sideways and almost trip over a severed head.

Kal sighs, tosses his sword to the side, and shakes his head.

Sol and Aero share a look, and I watch them heap Drake's groaning body against the wall ...

What are they *doing?* We don't have time for this shi—

Aero strides forward and winds his arm back on Kal. *"Glut!"* Blood and spit arc through the air as knuckles and teeth and flesh collide with a cringeworthy *thwack*, and I'm about ready to skin a dawn-dick.

I leap at Aero with my teeth bared, but Sol snatches both my arms and tugs me back against his hard chest. "Uh-uh, you stay right here."

"Let me go, ass-hat!" I whisper-scream, thrashing in Sol's powerful grip. "What the hell was that for?"

I know how fast Kal can move, but he just stood there and took that hit like a *corpse*.

Aero spins, cracking his knuckles, paralysing me with a glare. *"He* knows." I'm jostled into his awaiting hands, allowing Sol the freedom to step forward ...

My Day God almost knocks me out with a dazzling wing as he winds his fist back on a wobbly Kal. *"Glut!"* The collision sends my Night God tumbling to the ground with a spray of red.

These ungrateful arseholes.

I kick Aero in the kneecap, his grip loosening enough that I launch forward and hiss at Sol. He pivots, turning all that ferocity on *me*, and I'm reminded that I'm less than half his size.

Gulp.

He herds me against the wall, pins powerful arms either side of my head, and releases a sharp snarl—his wings stretching to their full, imposing width ...

Holy wingspan.

My own wings do a quivering half stretch because they're traitorous whores, and I glance down, seeing Sol's cock straining against his tattered trousers ...

Sweet, merciful God. That's one hungry dick.

I glance up, breasts rising with each sharp breath. Sol's gaze drops and a rusty grunt swirls in his throat. "Expect one from Drake when he comes around, too," he says in a dark, scathing voice without breaking my eye contact. "Either that or he'll spend the rest of eternity making you feel like your cock's on fire. Now, let's get the fuck out of this shithole."

He pushes off, leaving me slumped against the wall with a wing boner and a puddle in my panties. He and Aero lift Drake off the ground, and my wings go flaccid as I scan them all ...

I'm missing something.

I offer Kal a hand but he opts to push himself up, swaying from Sol's hard hit to the temple.

"You just stood there and let that happen ..."

"Yes." He flicks a piece of innards off his jacket while I drag his sword out of a puddle of death and hand it to him.

"Why?"

"It's complicated," he says, sheathing the weapon. He unbuckles my baldric, repositions it across his chest, and jerks his chin. "Let's go. I thought I sensed Edom's nearness earlier."

I frown, doing a scan of the hall while Kal relieves Sol from his Drake-hauling duties, helping to carry my golden God away from this bloody show of carnage. I narrow my eyes on my feral Day God now blocking the hallway with his flared wings ...

"Fuck off."

"Come here. Now."

"I have two feet that work perfectly fin—"

He dives forward, snatches me up, and tosses me over his shoulder.

"Who are you right now?"

"Shhh," he hisses, slapping my arse and rushing down the hall.

Someone's cruisin' for a ball bruisin'.

"Dell, just roll with it," Aero whispers, fisting his hand into Drake's golden locks to keep his head from flopping around too much as we amble down the long, obscure hall. "He just needs to get it out of his system."

"The only thing he's going to be getting out of his *system* is my foot lodged all the way up his arsehole." I dig my fingers into the long muscle down the side of Sol's abdomen and his grip loosens in a sporadic jolt of limbs. "Hah!"

Victory.

Sol is fucking *ticklish*.

I somehow land on my feet, sprinting forward a few steps before I'm swept up by a storm of stony arms.

God-fucking-dammit.

I slap the sunshiny bastard clean across his cheek, but that just seems to make the bulge in his pants grow. He makes this basely sexual sound and my vagina lifts a brow ...

Hmmm. If we just drop his slacks a little, then ... like ... tear my pants straight down the crotch and push my undies to the side, I could slide right onto him while we're walki—

Dammit, vagina. You almost fell right onto that one, you daft wench!

Growling, I kick him in the cock and leap out of his arms while he coils into a standing version of the fetal position.

Bullseye. I really should have tried that earlier.

He straightens—teeth gritted, wings perched, eyes wild like a predator who just caught the scent of blood. My gaze travels to the bulge still straining against his pants and I almost fucking faint.

"I just kicked you right in the cock!" I whisper-scream. "How is that thing still shucking off its foreskin?"

He scoops me up and pins me in the prison of his

unyielding embrace. I huff my displeasure, at least until I recognise the big rock that's hiding a lump of dead legionnaires ...

It seems Karma likes me again. Perhaps her vagina finally got a cuddle?

"There's no way you're dragging me through that hole, Daydream. Put me down. Now."

His grip tightens. *"Hei de na vi sel?"*

"De nai se la vesh, hast venti ma!" Kal retorts, and even my vagina goes cross-eyed. The exotic lilt is sexy until you realise they're hiding shit from you.

The blackness recedes all the way to Sol's pupils and I sigh, thankful to have my Alpha Arsehole back. He lowers me to the ground and nudges me towards the hole cleared of bodies by an attentive Aero.

"There are spiders through there," I say, pointing at it. "Huge ones. And Kal can't put them to sleep anymore ..."

Sol goes deadly still, his powder blue gaze sliding to Kal. "You out?"

Kal nods once. "Dry as a bone."

"Fuck."

"Is there another way out?" I have zero interest in chewing on another piece of root. Just thinking about it makes me want to hurl all over my Night God.

"Not unless we want to go through the bowels of the castle," Kal points down the ghoulish tunnel we just travelled along, "which is a three hour walk in *that* direct—"

"No. We'll go down the spidery *fucking* cave." I step forward, but Kal wedges in front of me.

"Age before beauty, *jasta*."

Sol snatches my wrist before I even have a chance to open my mouth and argue, and I roll my eyes, watching my Night God squeeze between the rocks like a fucking magician.

"What about Drake?" I ask, brushing a hand across his forehead. I'm gifted with a soft moan that gives me *life*.

"We'll have to wedge him through," Aero announces, and I frown.

My poor Dusk God. He's going to wake up feeling like he's been put through the wringer.

Seeing Kal's feet disappear, I draw some grit straight from my vagina and drop low, wriggling across the ground. Kal tugs me the last couple of metres and props me on my arse between his strong thighs, shielding me while Aero shucks through.

I glance up at gossamer webs doing little to hide all those writhing, black bodies, and my teeth begin to chatter. "Kal-l-l-l..."

"I know," he warns. "Deep breaths and try to stay calm. They're attracted to the scent of fear."

I almost choke.

Great. Pretty sure I *reek* of it.

I watch Aero yank on Drake's burnished locks, trying to tug his hefty frame through the tight space. It's like the stone is giving birth to a bulky man-baby.

"*Heigh!*" Aero snaps. "Kal, I need a hand!"

"What about me? Can't I help?"

Kal kisses the tip of my ear. "Someone with muscles, Little Dove."

Jerk. I have muscles. *Pelvic floor* muscles. I'll remind him of that next time his cock is kissing my cervix.

Kal darts to the rescue and I close my eyes, trying to concentrate on the sound of Drake being guided through the rocky birth canal and ignore all the scuttling...

Easier said than done.

I press my palms to my ears as my wings wrap me in a tight, feathery bundle.

Think happy thoughts.

Think happy thoughts.

Think happ—

Something fuzzy brushes my shoulder and my eyes pop open though I instantly regret it.

They're everywhere; hanging from cloudy strings, perched on walls, creeping across the ground ... Aero and Kal none the wiser to the extended family of arachnids swarming at their backs.

My Sun Gods will *not* be killed by these Fae Fury fucks spurred on by the scent of *my* fear.

I reach into my beast's shadow lair, fish around until I get a grip on her twitchy tail, and tug. She slides out much easier than I anticipated, and I can hardly contain my smirk.

No muscles, my arse!

The moment she sees all the beady eyes and fuzzy legs, a storm gathers inside me. She rips to the surface, dragging that roiling cauldron of lava along for the ride.

What a good girl. Good girls get rewarded.

A smile hooks our lips, the tips of our canines dimpling our chin while we sit deadly still, collecting heat in the palm of our hands. The power scalds our veins and a shrill squeal muddies the sound of all that scuttling ...

And then we pump our fists.

We create a shield wall to segregate our Gods from the writhing mass of arachnids and send a wave of misting energy barrelling through the cave—a symphony of popping spiders following the tide of power that paints the walls with gooey guts.

Our smile turns wicked sharp.

My beast's sadistic predispositions aside, I don't like killing things. Even deadly things with eight hairy legs and long, drippy fangs. But *nothing* will hurt my vulnerable Sun Gods.

Beasty slinks back and I promise her some Godly cock

for her stellar performance. I slip back in control and wipe a bit of goo off my shoulder just as my shield drops ...

Drake finally slides free and my disgruntled Day God follows, his face looking like a cat's arsehole—all puckered and ready to shoot some shit at us.

He snarls, wiping filth off his cheek. "I should have gone first." He points to Drake's flaccid body lumped against the grimy wall, covered in rocky afterbirth. "Because you two pussies have no idea how to handle a big dickhead."

Kal turns, thrusts his wings forth, and wraps me in a feathery embrace. "Are you okay? No spiders on you?"

I shake my head while he scans me from head to toe, and a string of thick, wine-red mucus drips between us.

He frowns, gaze rolling up. "What the ... *fuck?* Where are all the spiders?"

Huh. Seems my wee shield also acted as a sound barrier this time. Interesting.

"Well, would you look at that ..." I muse, studying the walls, the ceiling, and finally ... the three sets of eyes speared at me. "A nice, clear run to get the fuck out of here."

Kal shakes his head and retracts his wings, leaving me free to emerge from my own wing cocoon like a smug, arachnid-killing *wasp*. I've just begun to prance down the tunnel when a hand slides around my middle and splays across my belly button, halting me in place ...

"*Fine.*" I lift my arms and tug my wings flat against my back. "But only because you run faster than me. Just don't ruffle my feathers or I'll kick you in the dick again."

I'm carried back towards the outside world as dread wraps around my neck like a noose ...

I left those girls rotting in my father's dungeon—their only hope for survival relying on some serious Sun God deception.

I'm a terrible mate.

As the light of dawn reaches for us from the entrance, highlighting the coarse cave littered with stretchy slime and vacant cobwebs, a fearsome thought whispers in my ear ...

From all accounts of my father, I expected ... more.

I can't shake the feeling that this was all just a little too easy.

CHAPTER TWENTY-FOUR
DELL

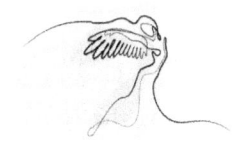

*I*t's freezing.

White flakes spew from low-hanging clouds, creating a light sheen across the city like flour dusting a scone.

"Is that snow?"

Aero nods, scuffing some with his boot. "It is ..."

"I didn't think it snowed in this part of the world?"

"It doesn't," Sol grinds out over the top of my head.

I twist and look into eyes full of frigid, welling frustration. He squints up at the blushing clouds, his silver wings rustling around me.

"Can you"—how do I say this—"erect the sun?"

He shakes his head.

Damn.

Nobody hates losing control more than my big alpha fun-sponge.

"We need to find shelter; somewhere with a tub for this dense fucker to soak," Aero grits out, letting his chagrin bleed into his words.

We stick to the shade and scurry through the city, leaving a trail that's quickly masked by more settling snow. I curl against Sol's hot skin and study my mate bite now girdled by a fucking whore mark ...

My father claimed metaphorical ownership over not just Sol, but also our mateship. Like this is all some messed up game to him.

I swallow bile and turn my attention to our surroundings, peeping through the frame of silver feathers. "It's so quiet ..."

Kal leads us through the labyrinth, testing doors pressed into narrow buildings lining the streets. He finds one that budges and swings it open, sword drawn, motioning for us to hold back while he slips inside.

There's a sharp tug on Drake's tether and I pry Sol's wing back, ignoring his soft rumble. I do a quick scan of my Dusk God who's hanging off Aero like a tumour ...

It's like whatever progress he made has been sapped by the chill. His lips are blue, skin no longer tawny, and my gaze flicks to his legs smothered in Fae Fury guts ...

Fuck.

"Does he have any cuts on his legs?" I ask, wriggling in Sol's arms. He lowers me next to Drake, crouching around me—still shielding my abdomen with his hands. I slap them a few times before conceding they're there to fucking stay.

Scouring Drake's legs, I notice a rancid graze and rip his pant leg further up the thigh—seeing a thick, black line scrawling towards his dick ...

I hiss, spearing my gaze at Aero. "There's spider goo in his cut."

His lips thin. "Meaning ..."

"Shit, sorry. You missed the entire discussion I just had with myself." I tap my temple and hear his teeth grind. "Those were Fae Fury ..."

His eyes widen.

"*Heigh!*" Sol snarls behind me.

I think I just learned my first swear word in the language of the arsehole.

"Yeah ... *heigh!* We need to get him in a tub. Now." Before that line fucks Drake right in the heart.

Thankfully, Kal emerges and motions for us to follow. I'm carried into the narrow stone house that smells of dust mites and stagnant air, and I sneeze all over pretty Day wings.

Gushing water sings from somewhere on the second floor, and Kal shuts the door as Sol sets me down. Aero tries to lug Drake up the narrow stairway while Sol roots around —tossing throws, opening cupboards, and just generally being a messy motherfucker.

"Kal—" I sneeze while my hormones picture Sol's cock in a vice. "He's making a mess!"

With one foot up the stairs, Kal glances sidelong at my disruptive Day God. "*Hai de na ve leis? Geis Dell feis da vi ha ... vailest.*"

"*Dell de na ve! Leis alet hein.*" Sol sniffs a jacket and snarls, then tosses it on the ground with so much force I'm instantly sneezing again. "*Vailest de las! Tat nah.*"

Kal shrugs. "You do you, brother, but she might get a little bitey."

Sol glances at me, grunts, and continues tossing shit around. "I can handle her."

He thinks he can ... *handle me?* Wow. Nobody in their right mind would make such a rash assumption.

Oh, *Sol* ...

My heavy heart sinks into the pit of my stomach as realisation dawns. I've been so, so blind.

I should have known—should have seen the signs. Looking back, I'm not sure how I missed them.

My Alpha Arsehole has gone mad.

He growls at a cushion, tossing it straight into the belly of an unlit hearth, only confirming my suspicions. My wings wilt and I glance at Kal with destitute eyes. "Kal—"

"Stay here," he instructs, then starts up the stairs.

"Hang on just a moment! You're going to leave me down here with ... with *that?*" I whisper-yell, jerking my thumb at my disorderly Day God who's waist-deep in a chest of dusty garments.

Kal sighs, dagger clenched in his fist while I rub my arms in an effort to ward off the bitter chill. "It's just until we get Drake settled in the bath. It's a small room and your wings might get in the way ..."

My feathery fools give me a cuddle, protecting me from the verbal blow I doubt they realise was directed at them. "Look, I know my wings are ..." I drop my voice to a low whisper, *"annoying.* But ... like ... I'm practising this positive wing-reinforcement thing, and I think you should do the same. Just so we're on the same page, you know?"

He blinks at me.

Drake groans from the second floor and I'm just about to storm the staircase when Kal flashes his teeth. "I'm going to help. Stay the fuck here, Dell, or so help me ..."

"Or so help you, what?"

"I'll ... I'll toss rice all over the house."

I wilt. *"You wouldn't ..."*

He takes a menacing step down the stairs and cocks a brow. "Oh, wouldn't I?"

I digress. He totally would, and it's like he just poured black tar all over my compulsion to jump to the rescue.

He nods and continues up the stairs, glancing back every two steps while I stand here simmering. "You have three minutes, Nightcap!"

Bastard. I know what he's doing. He's being a giant *heigh*, grouping the crazies together so we don't get in the way.

I storm into the small, cramped kitchen, trying to ignore the sound of Sol tossing shit around.

Easier said than done.

"What the hell are you doing?" I hiss, rifling through the cabinets for *anything* to eat. I'm hungry, and I'm pretty sure Drake will be when he wakes up, too.

Sol makes a deep, grunting sound and hauls a long, black coat from a basket. He gives it a sniff, then starts beating it like he's trying to convince the thing to breathe again. "This one will do." He walks over and shoves the coat right in my face. "It belonged to a female. I won't have you caped in the scent of another man."

I stare at him, hand in the cupboard, eyebrow raised.

I was preparing the straitjacket, and it appears Sol was just hunting for something warm for me to wear.

He shakes the coat in my face. "I'm not asking."

"What about you?" I ask, seeing goosebumps on his skin—noting those burn marks are looking a bit better.

Unlike the scar on his neck.

He shakes the jacket again. "It won't even fit over my arm. Put it on."

I sigh, take the coat, and wrap it around my shoulders. Sol helps me work the slits over my wings and makes an appreciative grunt when I'm adequately wrapped in the spoils of his looting.

"Thank you ..." I mutter, my feathery friends curling around him, stroking his glossy wings.

They're laying it on far too thick.

Sol nods, nostrils flaring. He jerks his chin at the cupboard I was just elbow deep in. "Most of the food in there is rotten."

My stomach howls and Sol's gaze whips straight to it. I click my fingers, drawing his attention back to my fucking face. "Look. Why don't you root around and find us some food, yeah? Seeing as you're so good at ..." I sweep my hand down the length of my jacket, *"rooting.* I'll be upstairs with Drake."

I tuck my wings behind my back and turn, breathing a small sigh of relief when he doesn't actually follow, although I can tell by the slant of his ears that he's listening to every move I make while he forages through the dusty pantries with vigour ...

I'm not sure what's wrong with Sol, but he'll have to wait until I've patched up my Dusk God with some shit-paste.

A shaded landing has steam billowing from a cracked door to the right, which I shove open to reveal the small room beyond ... and freeze.

"Dell, you said three minutes!" Kal's hands are full of Drake's shredded clothing and he jerks his chin at the door. "You don't need to see this."

"I'm not going anywhere."

He and Aero share a glance while I survey my Dusk God who's lumped next to the bath.

His skin is shredded—hanging off him in places—as if he'd been dragged along the ground for miles. Bits of dirt, rock, and debris litter the grey, festering wounds that are seeping rancid fluid.

The stone floor is stained red.

Aero has Kal's dagger and he's slicing dead pieces of flesh from Drake's wings that are preventing them from healing properly ...

My heart tries to leap out of my throat, my nails gouging half-moon crescents in my palms as my beast sharpens her talons along my insides.

He did this.

"Dell ..." Kal implores, and it registers that I'm banging my fist against my temple. Now I understand why he wanted me to stay downstairs.

Is this how he felt when he found me in that tree hut? Because seeing this damage on my mate—seeing Aero slice off a chunk of wan, feathery flesh and toss it in the corner with a heavy thud—I'm starting to understand his severe reaction.

"I'm fine," I bite out, fumbling with the buttons down my lapel while I force myself to watch Aero slice through golden feathers. I wrangle my wings through the holes as they lower Drake into the steaming pool of water.

Aero digs into his pocket and pulls out the vial of shit I pegged at his face earlier. He hands it to Kal who uncorks it, glancing at me ...

I nod. "Toss the whole thing in."

Plop.

Kal offers me a consolation smile as a thick, pungent waft starts to fill the room. I feel like the past is slipping through my fingers ... but I think my mother would be happy the vial of arse was put to such good use.

Blocking my nose, I strip to my panties and climb in right behind my Dusk God, making sure his wings are submerged between us. I rest his head on my naked breasts and trickle boggy water over his face, shoulders, and chest.

His brow is scathing, and I know it has nothing to do with the temperature of the water ... but I refuse to accept we're too late.

So, we sit—marinating in shit while my stomach gnaws on itself.

Every now and then Aero peers out the window, and eventually, we have to pour more hot water in the bath to stop it from chilling.

"It's taking too long," I complain, running my fingers over half-healed lesions on Drake's chest.

Kal sighs from his spot against the wall. "He had Fae Fury venom in his system, Dell. You and I both know it takes a while for that to siphon out."

Aero's attention snaps to me and Sol pauses on the threshold, jarring me with a bone-creaking scowl.

"Goddammit, Kal." I rest my head against the edge of the bath. "Talk about landing me in shit when I'm already swimming in it."

I know what he's up to. He's got his squad back and I'm outnumbered. But if he thinks cornering me is going to make me crack, he's sorely mistaken.

"What the fuck does that mean?" Sol barks from the door, a hessian sack hanging from each hand. From my initial sniff test, I'd say one is full of aged meat, and the other smells precisely like *air dried beans*...

I gag, and he moves further into the room with that fucking bag.

"The beans." I vomit, then swallow it back. "If you come any further into this room with that bag, I'll throw up all over your pretty wings."

Sol frowns at the sack hanging from his right hand...

I gag again.

He tosses it down the stairs and I breathe a sigh of relief, nestling further into my comatose Dusk God.

Strange. Beans used to be my favourite. I think that bite really messed with my tastebuds.

"She got stung by a Fae Fury."

I narrow my eyes on Kal while Aero and Sol growl like savage animals.

"Don't get your testicles in a twist! If you want to get pissy, I get full disclosure of your time in that dungeon so I get to be equally pissy." I glare at my alpha cock who's found sudden interest in a spot on the floor. "Why were you slashed across the chest, Sol?"

No answer, not that I was expecting one.

"And Aero?" I ask, transferring my attention to my oddly quiet Dawn God. "Want to tell me why it looks like you tried to shuck your foot from its skin?"

He slides back a step, stuffing his hands so deep in his pockets that I think he might lose them.

"I didn't think so. Lose the attitude and let's focus on what's really important." My hormones give me a round of applause and scream for a fucking encore before my stomach rumbles loud enough to wake a hibernating drako ...

Kal, Aero, and Sol all share a *look* before the latter slips a big piece of dried meat between my lips. It may be hard to chew, but I've never been more determined, grinding through the leathery meat like a woman possessed ...

This is *delicious*. It tastes like the flesh of a three-hundred-year-old corpse with a sprinkling of garlic, chili, and disintegrating hessian sack, and I couldn't be happier.

"You sure this isn't just the heel of a well-worn boo—" Aero starts to choke, bashing his chest with a closed fist.

I can't believe he's hacking over such a small piece of meat. My pretty Dawn God wouldn't last a day in the whore house.

"More for me!"

Kal slips his bit into my wide-open mouth, and I almost take his fingers off when I gobble it back like a fucking street dog.

"Is it just meat?" Sol asks, and Kal shakes his head while he watches me chew.

"It's ... *everything*. Well, except beans."

I pick bits of sinew from my teeth and peer up at Sol. "You need to get in here, Daytime. You'd heal a lot faster if you soaked in some shitty water."

He retracts his wings and slides down the wall into a low crouch. "No."

My eyes narrow.

Aero excuses himself to eat some dried beans ... downstairs. Kal quickly follows.

Wise boys.

"What's going on? You're acting weird."

He glances at the ceiling like he's looking for some sort of answer carved in the wooden beams. I spent years looking at a ceiling, a floor, and four dimly lit walls, and I found no answers there.

Just more heartbreak.

"Whatever," I huff, dribbling some shit water over Drake's grazed cheekbone. "Let's just push it under the rug like we always do."

"It's my fault," he spits out, and I almost choke as every cell in my entire body turns its head in his direction.

Is Sol actually ... *talking?*

"*What's* your fault?"

He sighs, slumping further down the wall. "The whole lot. You were taken because I didn't protect you. I was sleeping while you were, what ... *stolen? What the fuck happened?*"

The last four words are a storm in the room.

I close my eyes and groan, flopping my head against the edge of the bath. I'm not sure how he managed to turn this conversation around so quickly. "I don't want to go back there, Sol. I'm sick of living in the past, okay? I've tucked it away; you should do the same."

"I can't."

"Then at least get in the bath. It could heal that scar on your nec—"

His lips peel back from his canines. "I don't want to *heal* it."

I open my mouth ... close it ... open it again ... "You want to wear a whore mark on your neck? Are you kidding me?"

"You wore one for years. I'll wear mine for the rest of eternity. It's my fucking *penance*."

Wow. Turns out I was right. He *is* mad.

"Get in the water. The bath's big enough for three, even with your swelling insanity. Get in the fucking water."

He stands in a torrent of hard, bulky muscle and towers over me with all the might of his crushing alpha presence. "I'm your *mate!*" he roars, and I flinch from the thunderous whiplash. "It's my *privilege* to keep you safe! I failed! And *you* —" he gestures towards me with an outstretched hand ...

Kal and Aero crest over the top of the staircase and cram into the room, smelling like fucking *beans*.

"And I *what?*" I snap, but he just shakes his head and starts to pace—the breadth of his shoulders bunched around his ears.

"I see Sol's just as charming as ever."

Drake's deep, husky voice chews on my heart then spits it out whole.

I choke on a startled yelp while I scramble around and straddle him, mushing my breasts into his face as he tries to sit up. "You're awake!"

It's not until Drake's potent hand sweeps a tear from my cheek that I realise I'm crying. "Don't waste these on me, babe. I'm not going anywhere, and I'm certainly not complaining about waking up with my face buried in your tits." He heaves a little. "Despite the fact that I'm in a pool of shit ..."

I croak out an awkward sound that almost resembles a laugh. "You got off light, Goldicock. I didn't get a dick pillow when I was hauled out of the bog. And this is diluted."

His eyes twinkle and that thick, aurelian link on my heart pulses. "You climbed in a pool of shit for me," he says through a crooked, heart-shattering smile that makes his dimple pucker, and I press our foreheads together.

"If you smell like shit, I smell like shit."

Drake weaves his hand around the back of my neck, and it feels like the world holds its breath as he looks past my eyes and into my fucking soul. But in that burnished gaze I see so much more ...

"Babe, I—"

"I know, Drake. You don't need to say it."

Please don't say it. Not when I'm pretending to be in one piece.

Then his lips are on mine—crushing and possessive and entirely unleashed. He groans into my mouth, but the sound isn't a spike of pleasure ...

It's a spike of *agony. Fear.*

Suffering.

It's a kiss that says I missed you, I need you ...

I moan into his mouth, rolling my hips, his hand cupping my naked breast. His thumb sweeps over my nipple before he gives it a soft, gentle squeeze, and I swear to fuck, it feels like he just knifed me in the tit.

"*Ouch!*" I shove his face, trying to hustle my boobs from his nipply-gripply hands. "Do that again, Twilight, and I'll pinch your fucking foreskin!"

Drake sits up, unveiling smooth, sun-kissed flesh—as well as the upper clefts of dense, tawny wings all sparkly and new again. "That hurt?"

"Are you questioning my *pain tolerance?*"

He clears his throat and scans the others. "I, ahh ... have no power left. I can't feel shit. So ..." he gives me another crooked smile, "kind of?"

Fuck. Now I feel bad.

"Yes ..." I sigh. "That hurt. I have pre-heat boobs. And I'm sorry about your waning power. Everyone else is out, if it makes you feel any better."

Something tells me it won't.

"*Heigh!*" he snarls, glancing at the others who all nod in unison.

"Yeah," I agree. "*Heigh!*"

Drake's nostrils flare, his keen perusal skating over me like a shaving blade. He leans close, nuzzles right into the crook of my neck, and *sniffs.*

"Here we go again ..."

At this point, I'm getting more sniff action than a dog's hairy arsehole.

Drake leans back, his eyes like huge, golden tokens. His throat bobs before he turns his attention to the others; all watching on with three matching winces ... and three matching erections.

Holy huge dicks.

"You know what?" I rasp, barely hearing myself over the sound of my squealing vagina. "I'm sure there's room for five in this bath if you all park your cocks inside me to conserve space ..."

I'm not sure why I'm brimming with good ideas when I *should* be brimming with Sun God cock.

Drake cuts off my excitement with his deep, husky voice. "*Geil te gleit. Adas tel afen ... druca teis?*"

Sol, Aero, and Kal shake their heads in unison, all three of those dicks deflating.

Penis party pooper.

"*Glis aden?*" Drake snarls, the question speared at Kal ... who squares his shoulders, lifts his chin, and tenses those strong thigh muscles.

"Someone really needs to teach me how to speak arsehole ..."

Drake stands in nothing but tight underwear which doubles as a dick tent. He uses his healthy wings to propel himself out of the water, then drives his fist straight into

Kal's jaw—sending him flying back into the door and knocking it straight off its hinges.

"*What the fu—*"

Sol and Drake collide, forehead to forehead, thundering ancient words like a couple of manticores scrapping over a piece of meat.

I slap the water, my inflated boobs wobbling. "Would someone tell me what the hell is going on?"

The lovely moment is diffused by a distant roar that makes the walls shudder ...

The room chills.

"What ... what was that?"

I'm plucked out of the water and my wings get fluffy as I'm dried with a towel that makes me sneeze—the sense of urgency thickening as if Death itself is hovering in the hallway.

"*What the fuck was that?*"

"That was Kyro," Aero growls, buttoning the back of my blouse around my wings. "We need to get out of here. I wouldn't put it past him to burn the city."

My heart spears itself on a rib.

"That was ... my father's *drako?*"

Aero ducks my wing, steps around me, and begins to button the front of my blouse. "Yes. He's responsible for the near extinction of his own kind. He hunted them one by one and tore them all to shreds."

Realisation bleeds into my lungs and tries to choke me. "Was ... was he the one who burnt my mother?"

There's a long, pregnant pause.

"*Dell—*"

I latch onto Kal as my knees crumble ...

Fuck.

Drake takes my face in his hands, forcing me to focus on

his steady, auric gaze. "We'll protect you, babe. Nothing's going to happen to you, okay?"

I nod.

I don't have the heart to remind him that he's powerless right now ...

I also don't have the heart to tell him that it's not my life I'm worried about.

CHAPTER TWENTY-FIVE
DELL

"You're going to have to let me go ..."

Drake pries his gaze from the falling snow and glances down at me, my back pressed flat against his chest like a feathery pancake.

"What?" he retorts. "My wings are fine. I'm fucking carrying you!"

Oh, boy.

I can feel the searing attention of the others—no longer scanning the sky from our place perched behind a large, obscure rock on the edge of the city.

My cheeks burn as I peel Drake's hands off me finger by finger and drop into the powdery snow. "I can do it myself now, Sunset."

His eyes widen. "You're fucking with me, right?"

"I made sure she knew how before we started the rescue mission," Kal says, scanning me from wingtip to wingtip. "Cost me my wish ... and almost my balls."

The last part is said under his breath and I certainly don't argue.

Aero starts to chuckle, Sol makes a surprised grunting sound, and Drake straight up slaps Kal on the shoulder—beaming from ear to ear, telling Kal he 'redeemed himself' ... whatever the hell that means.

"So," I say, flexing my wings, "can we get out of here or what?"

Silence ensues as we survey the sky for a long, tense moment before Aero nods. "I think we're safe. I'll go firs—"

I'm already shooting through the air like bait for a hunting hawk ... or so I tell myself. I may be scared of the beast that melted my mother's skin, but I'm *petrified* of what it'll do to my four helpless Sun Gods.

And I'm not helpless. Not anymore.

I couldn't save my mother. I will not let my Sun Gods suffer the same fate.

Sol converges on my airspace—his massive, shiny wings slicing through the sky like blades, big globs of snow trying to soften his sharpening features. *"What the fuck was that?"*

Oops.

Sol's path curls with mine as I catch a draft and bank. There's another beat behind me and I glance over my shoulder to see Drake's golden wings making the sky their bitch.

Healthy.

Whole.

I could cry with relief. But then my Dusk God *snarls* at me, and I register his deadly glower. He looks about ready to bury a hoe—those molten eyes overflowing with scalding disappointment.

I'm in the middle of an angry alpha sandwich, and if we weren't mid-flight and running from a vicious, fire-breathing drako, I'd suggest they find more productive ways to expel all that angry energy.

"One more stunt like that and I swear to *fuck*, I'll be chaining you to my chest."

I roll my eyes at my melodramatic Dusk God. "Calm down, Golden Hour. I blend with the scenery at the moment." I gesture to my hair and wings, and somehow manage to knock myself off balance. "Oops!"

Sol cuts the air *and* my confidence with a sharp sound while he carves beneath me, acting like a safety net.

"You two are distracting! Go find someone else to flank!"

"You're too unsteady for my liking," Sol grouses, and I frown. Apparently he didn't get the memo about positive wing-reinforcement.

"My wings are doing a *magnificent* job, thank you very much! They've come leaps and bounds from their first efforts. They used to go flaccid mid-flight, but now look at them go ..." I point my thumb over my shoulder and puff my chest with pride. "They're basically pros."

"*Flaccid?* What's that supposed to mean?" Drake asks, and I wave a dismissive hand.

"They just used to get a little tired and retreat for a nap." I shoot a poignant glare over my shoulder. "Let's not make a *thing* out of it."

And put ideas in their feathery heads.

I shrug, re-capturing Sol's wide, unblinking gaze—like he can't bear to miss a single *beat* of my glorious wings.

So sweet.

"All part of the learning process, I'm sure. Did yours ever do that when you were a little baby Day God learning to fly?"

My womb does a cartwheel and my boobs get a bit tingly. I can just picture it; wide, powder blue eyes and pint-sized wings that are too big for his roly-poly baby body ...

Sigh.

Sol doesn't answer—just continues to stare at me. I glance

over my shoulder and Drake's doing the same, apparently speechless for the first time in his entire life.

Strange.

Sol shakes his head as if he's trying to dislodge his automatic compulsion to throw me a verbal turd. "Are you telling me your wings were giving up *mid-fucking-flight?* What terrain were you flying over?"

A shrill siren takes mental jabs at me, screaming for me to abort the fucking mission ...

I open my mouth, then snap it shut. I tend to choke on lies these days and that's no fun for anyone. Besides, I'm forgetting my sparkly new weapon: attack them with the truth.

"Look, the important thing is I survived, okay? Kal only had to save my life *once* throughout the entire learning process. Yes, I got a tad close to a baby lava monster, but how was I supposed to know the crater lake that softened my landing was its fucking lair! Believe it or not, they don't teach you that sorta shit at the whore hou—"

Kal chooses that exact moment to veer into our airspace.

Sol and Drake *explode*, both barrelling into my Night God in a mash of muscle and feather and fangs and ...

Poor Kal.

"*Stop!*" I shriek, watching them plummet then rise, plummet then rise.

"What did I miss?" Aero asks from behind, his voice all breathy.

I shake my head and sigh. "Just the regular bullshit spurred on by my thoughtless garble."

"Dell, this is regular behaviour for a freshly mated pair, and you have more than one mate. There's bound to be the odd ..." he clears his throat as Kal lands a knee dangerously close to Drake's dick, "bump in the road."

"This is more than just a *bump*, Aero." I glance over my shoulder, trying not to get distracted by all the pretty pastel blades of his sunrise wings. "We're supposed to be leaving Sterling inconspicuously, yet they're clashing together like a thunderstorm while they compare the size of their cocks."

"Kal and I were scouting until we were well past the borders ..."

I gesture to the three Gods trying to rip each other to shreds less than twenty metres away.

"But you have a good point."

Yes, I fucking do.

"I'll be right back." He shoots past me, spearing towards the skirmish.

They all return a little worse for wear and slot around me —creating a tight, snarling cocoon.

"Are you all going to behave yourselves now?"

Nobody answers, tension crackles, and I frown at this wee formation we have here ...

So much for me protecting *them*.

We fall into a comfortable beat while dollops of snow lash our faces. Sol, Drake, and Aero end up with ice beards, courtesy of their break in the capital's weepy arsehole without a razor blade.

Fuck, it's cold.

Really, I should just summon my beast and let her warm me, but last time I let her control my wings, she dove into a storm and made my Night God all huffy. Kal's dealt with enough of my shit. He deserves a break.

Drake drifts close to my back, and in one swift motion I'm tugged against his body, my wings tucked around my middle. "H-h-e-e-y-y."

"You've proven yourself, babe. Nuzzle in and let me warm you."

Guess I'm no help to anyone if I'm an ice cube.

The others press closer and the flight becomes smooth, only muddied by the howling wind and a constant pitter-patter of snow battering the protective clothing my Gods looted.

"We need to gain altitude," Kal grates out with a face full of snow, and the other three grunt in agreeance.

We pierce a heavy cloud and Drake tugs me closer, pitching us higher and higher until we emerge—bathed in the soft, serene light of dawn.

The chill is more bone jarring, but that *view* ...

"It's p-p-pretty up h—"

My words catch as the bulging cloud ahead becomes something *more*. Something shaded and ...

Moving.

Massive, black wings *whuff* out of the fluffy clouds, stirring up the sea of pink while lethal claws make blind grabs for my scattering Sun Gods.

"*Dive!*" Kal roars, and I don't even have the chance to scream before we're plummeting.

A swell of fire chases our feet, our destination unknown as eddying mist and snow obscure our view. The fog suddenly dissolves, revealing the unforgiving ground only metres away ...

Drake roars, bringing us to an abrupt, flapping halt. He spins, falling backwards to the acute symphony of bones snapping, and I watch the other three crash around us with the same shattering blows ...

"*Hide!*" Drake snarls, rolling over and digging his arm into the ground like a spade. I'm tucked in the hole and smothered by his burly body as he hauls crunching, crumbling debris atop us both—a tandem grave of his own creation.

The air becomes dense with the musk of death; a scent I know all too well.

I gag.

Drake presses his nose into the crook of my neck, flattens his hand across my mouth, and stops moving. "*Shhhh ...*"

I nod, my tongue marinating in bile.

A thunderous roar makes the ground shudder before it quakes with a *thump* that's too loud to be anything other than a giant drako. Flames marry moisture with a hiss and a roar, then an ancient groan makes my bones ache as I hear the distinct sound of a tree snapping.

I crunch my eyes shut, willing myself into a place of calm —hoping, *pleading* that our hiding spots are overlooked and under smelt.

I hear a breathy *whoosh* ... then another, and another. The sound grows louder, more frenzied, as if the beast is scenting the ground like a fucking bloodhound.

Not here.

Not now.

Not like this ...

I stop breathing. Even my heart stops beating.

There's a sharp snarl that sounds like frustration and ... *agony*. An airy throb gathers in momentum then fades away ...

Drake huffs into my neck, pressing his lips against a tender spot beneath my ear. "Fucking ... *fuck.*"

I brace as he hauls me up; the debris that was covering us clanking away like the sound of jewellery, armour, and ...

Bones.

I spit vomit everywhere, seeing exposed knuckles and sallow, rotten flesh trying to cling to a wrist. There's a skull wearing partially preserved lips trapped in a perpetual scream.

Amongst the remains are spindly feathers bent against the grain; burnt orange, buttercup yellow, the colour of dirty wool ...

I wipe my face with the back of my arm. "This is ... This is ..."

"A mass grave," Sol hisses, tossing a skull to the side. "Get her out of here! *Now!*"

Drake propels us into the air with a fierce pump of his wings—the ground smudged by a sheet of mist as we rise above sheer crevice walls.

"Who were those people?"

"It's best not to think about it." Drake's rusty voice bites harder than the bitter chill as he drops us into a clearing sheltered by a frame of ghostly trees.

"Is that where all Sterling's residents are? In that fucking *crevice?*"

He spins me around, his fingers digging into my shoulders. "Stop, Dell. Just ... *not now.*"

His words are a snap, a groan, a plea ...

Did he know some of the people rotting in that mass grave?

I reach out but he sits on his heels, splaying his hands across his face like a mask. The others land, and it's only when Kal tucks me against his chest that I register just how much I'm trembling. "Shh, it's okay ..." he whispers, almost begging me to believe him.

It's not okay.

Are those twelve girls—the ones I left behind—going to become part of the jungle of bones that represents nobody and *everybody* all at once? Will my mates end up there if someone doesn't put an end to my father?

I already know the answer.

"We need to seek shelter," Sol sneers, stalking through the trees.

I trail Aero, weaving between long, stagnant shadows with Drake following up the rear, and I peep back at him ...

It's easy to forget they're suffering, too. They look so strong—seem so sure of themselves. But their world is falling apart; their people on the verge of extinction due to the fault of a man they once trusted ...

Even Gods have a breaking point.

CHAPTER TWENTY-SIX
DELL

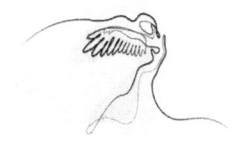

"We have to stay under the radar," Aero states as we pause near a clearing, brush off our jackets, and shake our filthy wings out.

We're literally smeared in death.

"Agreed, but we need to find somewhere to bunker down." Sol's gaze practically scours me. "She can't be out in the cold much longer. And she looks like she needs a nap ... and she's probably due a feed soon."

My eyes widen.

Did he just—

"What's all this talk about me 'looking like I need a nap'? If I look tired, it's because I just crawled out of a *grave*. You should see yourself!"

Kal and Aero wince while Drake tries to block my view of Sol with his bulky shoulders. He reaches forward and strokes the chilly rounds of my cheeks. "It's okay, babe. I know the stick Sol keeps up his arse makes him act a bit cunty sometimes, but he didn't mean any harm b—"

I mush my hand into Drake's face and palm him off, then

close in on my Day God, choosing to ignore the amused hook of his lips. "And you need to *feed me? Seriously?* What am I, a fucking house cat that conveniently warms your dick?"

He cocks a brow, taking a menacing step into the fucking red zone. "Feeling a little feisty, are we?"

I hiss at him.

He rolls his sleeves, revealing thick, powerful forearms, then steps wide and spreads his colossal wings.

He's preparing for battle.

I'll give him a fucking battle.

I splay my own wings though my span is half the width of his, which only adds to my roiling well of irrational anger. My beast stirs, inspects the unfolding situation, looks at me like I'm *daft*, then settles down and falls straight back to sleep.

Bitch.

Looks like I'm waging unreasonable war alone.

Sol drags his gaze from white wingtip to white fucking wingtip and, although his bulge seems to swell, he gives me a soft, condescending grunt. "Come on then. Show me what you've got."

This dick.

I strike—all flailing limbs and snappy teeth—but I might as well be tossing myself against a stone wall. Sol snatches my thrashing wrists, spins us around, and nails me to a tree with a spear of his hips—his hard cock nuzzled between my thighs ...

He leans in, grating his abrasive stubble along the sharp of my jawline. "Cute. But you're forgetting who you're dealing with, *Sparrow.*"

The way that name rolls off his tongue ...

"I'm your *mate*. If I say you need to be fed, then you need to be fucking *fed*. If I say you need to be *fucked* ..." he jerks his hips and I fight the urge to moan, "then prepare to fucking *mewl.*"

Holy daydream. My vagina opens her mouth like a little baby bird.

I roll my hips, rubbing against his stiff, twitching cock. Only a moment ago, I was ready to string him up by his ball sack, but this seems like a more valuable use of time.

My stomach rumbles and I stop grinding, sniffing the air …

Damn, I'm hungry.

Sol arcs a brow and I frown, trying to jiggle out of his unforgiving hold. "Can you … just …" I wiggle a bit more. "I want to grab your meat."

He instantly drops my wrists and slides back a step. I reach into his pocket and fish around while I chew my tongue, certain I can smell some cured meat stashed in here somewhere.

Sol groans, thrusting when I swipe against his dick by accident. "Just a little more to the left …"

I roll my eyes and snag a piece of jerky, sneer at my slack-faced Sun Gods, then skulk towards the clearing to eat my bounty in peace. I've got a mouth full of meat when the ground trembles, dislodging chunks of snow from laden branches …

My attention is drawn to the massive, imposing shadow stalking towards me from the middle of the clearing, and my heart catapults into my throat …

Time seems to stretch.

Kyro.

His boxy head is armoured with spikes, those billowy wings stretching—making my gaze sway from side to side while I admire their full majesty. But it's not his imposing stature that I can't look away from; not even those reflective scales or the way his talons tear up the ground.

It's the scars circling his neck and mottling his wings. It's the cuff around his hind leg that's oozing blood and the stench of crushed embers.

It's the way his eyes meet mine; calling to me like one tortured soul to another, both twisted and shaded on the inside ...

He shakes his head, loosening a roar that's loud enough to make my bones quiver—those keen, ruddy eyes seeming to regard me.

Beasty snarls, dragging sharp claws across my internal gloom ...

Firm hands haul me back, sending me tumbling into soft snow behind four sets of imposing wings. An impenetrable God shield.

That won't do at all.

Guess it's time to flex my vagina.

I set my beast free, letting her toss me into a pool of blackness. We throw up a shield that snares all four of our mates in a tight, convenient cluster, then sashay around them, hips swinging like a pendulum. "Thank me later! A little bit of cock-coin never goes astray."

She doesn't even look over our shoulder to gauge their reactions, but unfortunately, we do hear their disapproving ruckus once they register they're trapped ...

Should have used the soundproof one.

We swagger into the clearing towards the mountain-sized drako. His cavernous maw yawns wide, and we see the bud of fire swelling in his throat a split second before the boisterous flames hit ... but we anticipated that.

We watch the firestorm lick around our shield while we slosh through water and mud, hearing distant hollers for us to *lower the fucking shield*.

My beast rolls our eyes and I'm inclined to agree. Can't

they see there's a vicious, fire-breathing drako at large? Honestly, sometimes I think I'm the only one with any common sense.

The fire subsides and Kyro huffs when he sees we're left standing here, unharmed. He roars, the corruptive sound making our bones shake, but we just spread our wings—trying to look a lot bigger than we actually are.

He drops flat to the ground, masks his face with an enormous claw, and lets out a tortured, pleading *whine*.

Our breath catches at the fraught sound.

Is he ... afraid?

Stepping into his toasty aura, we reach a small hand towards his quivering nose. He peers down at us between splayed talons, studying our white wings the same way I used to study the bastard wielding the whip before I was lashed to ribbons ...

He thinks we're going to hurt him.

The revelation hits so hard that even my callous beast falters. It's hard to believe something once grand and mighty has been beaten down to nothing more than a fierce, tormented shadow.

"I'm so sorry ..."

The compassionate words ride a murderous tone, and his entire body shudders; like he expected them to land with the slice of a blade or a powerful blow. The milky plume of Kyro's breath thickens as we slide a hand through our shield and flatten it against a warm scale ...

Skin to brimstone. Both products of my father's wrath.

His claw peels away, revealing a large, round eye steeped in equal parts fear and intrigue. "I'm not going to hurt you ..."

I only have a brief moment to question my beast's sanity before we drop our shield entirely. We clamber onto Kyro's nose, curl into the small well between his eyes, and press our ear to his scales—listening to the swift, steady *whoosh* of his heart.

Then we start to hum.

It's a simple tune, one mummy used to sing when I was sick, tired, or grumpy. It's a song about a woman who pieced her baby together with bits of the earth, the stars, the sun ... *herself*.

It sings of sacrifice and freedom, but above all, it sings of harbouring a love despite knowing it cannot last forever.

Kyro's pulse slows to a soft, steady beat, his claw sweeping over us to create a talon-cave that's surprisingly cosy.

Sometimes, you just need a good cuddle.

Time slips by and eventually the bitter taste of guilt starts to override our comfort ...

We left our Sun Gods in a snare.

I wince. This is far worse than the time I sin-binned most of their asses.

We wiggle out, slide down Kyro's snout onto the sludgy earth, then sneer at the metal ring chewing on his hind leg. We step towards it, and Kyro's heart starts to gallop.

The latch keeping the cuff in place doesn't appear to require a key—just a small, malleable hand. Glancing over our shoulder, we see him watching us with round eyes that look nowhere near as fearsome as they did earlier. "This is going to hurt ..."

He blinks.

We probe the latch, fish around for the trigger, hook our finger into the hidden loop, and pull. The lock pops open and Kyro snarls as we pry the thick pins out of his flesh, leaving a ring of shredded tissue that's oozing burnt blood.

The cuff clanks to the ground.

It's nothing life changing, but my beast has been in chains

enough times to know how good it feels to have them removed.

So have I.

Kyro sniffs the damage, drenching us in hot breath that smells of charred cow. He picks the cuff up in his giant maw and flings it away, then glances at our God pen, letting out a rolling rumble that seems to go on and on and—

Is he laughing?

He spreads his enormous wings and launches skyward, disappearing into the low-hanging clouds ...

Now for the whiplash.

Beasty wipes messy hands on our coat before I haul her back into the shadows and slip into control, dropping the shield. I only have to wait three point two seconds before I'm surrounded by a riot of growling Gods lifting my arms and scouring my body, and I wince at all the bloody knuckles, stormy eyes, and sharp teeth ...

Oh, boy.

Drake crams into my personal space and roars, *"What the fuck, Adeline?"*

Wow. I knew they'd be pissed, but *full name* pissed is hardly warranted. I just eliminated a deadly threat and freed a leaden soul from his torture device. The real question is, why am I not being rewarded with multiple orgasms?

"He didn't eat me. Calm down, Five O'*Cock* Shadow." I waggle my brows to insinuate that my thirsty love nest is ready to receive his big, golden D.

Unfortunately, it seems to fall on deaf ears.

I glance down.

Hmm. Even his dick isn't paying attention. Perhaps I should get down on my knees? Who can turn down an award-winning blowjob?

Sol storms off into the clearing, pacing back and forth

with his hands threaded behind his head. "She needs to fucking know!"

"Who ... me? Know what?"

"*Don't* ..." Kal warns in a fierce tone that puts nails in my chest, but Drake shoves him off and gets all up in my face, condemning me with an overbearing glower.

"You have to stop this selfless shit! Fuck, babe!" I'm herded back until I'm pressed against an Aero wall—his unstable fingers digging into my shoulders. "You're risking more than just your *own stubborn self* when you do stupid shit like that!"

"I ..." *Huh?*

The black in Kal's eyes whittles away and he crowds Drake, grabbing his burly shoulders. "Brother ... *don't*. Not like this. You don't know what you're doi—"

Drake shucks him off.

"What are you talking about?"

"*Don't!*" Kal berates, but Drake's face is all hard lines and static resolve.

He cups my cheek, tilting my head so I have no choice but to hold his molten gaze. "You're pregnant."

Pffft.

"Bullshit."

Kal sighs and spins, stalking off through the mud.

Drake pinches my chin and drops low until he's fanning hot breath all over me. "We can scent the changes in your body, Dell. You're carrying a cub."

"Impossible. I'm about to go into hea—" My wings create a defensive shield around my body, and I realise with a gasp that they aren't protecting *me* ... they're protecting my fucking *womb*.

It feels like my chest collapses—broken bits using my heart as a pin cushion while I try to remember how to breathe.

The compulsive nesting ...

The nausea ...

The aching boobs ...

The insatiable hunger ...

The desire to skin a God one minute, ride his face the next ...

No.

Fuck no.

My vision starts to smudge and I draw a sharp gasp into my starving lungs—but once I start, *I can't stop.*

My breaths come hard and short—seizing my lungs, making my head spin and spin and ...

Not real. This is not real. *This can't be fucking real.*

I jerk my chin out of Drake's biting grip, pull away from Aero's scalding hands, and stumble out of my Sun God sandwich before colliding with something hard and unyielding.

"Dell ..."

Tender hands paw my back and try to halt me in place. They're barbs through my heart.

"No ... *no-no-no* ..." I mutter, extracting myself, moving far from Sol's deep, salted musk—the smell an acrid mix of hope and confusion.

A writhing ache roars to life inside me as I walk in abstract lines that leave me knee-deep in snow and shaking my head—trying to dislodge the violent wariness that just flayed me from the inside.

He probably thinks this child is his. Perhaps Drake does, too.

Dark room.

Smells like piss.

Probing things that claimed my insides ...

The thought knocks the breath right out of my lungs. My emotions bubble and bulge until my skin starts to split, and I fall to my knees with a guttural groan.

I throw my face into my hands, crack myself open, and let all the ugly darkness spill right out in a shrill scream that cleaves the air in two ...

It's only when I feel warm water leech through my clothes that I realise I'm on fire.

CHAPTER TWENTY-SEVEN
KAL

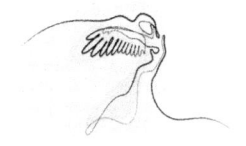

She's a storm—finally unleashing the tempestuous well of anguish she's tried so hard to hide.

Her flaming corona flickers a bright, iridescent blue that scorches the snow, turning the entire field to mush.

Drake's wings stretch, hand shielding his face while he advances on the calamity he uncorked.

"*Don't!*" I roar, flexing my own fucking wings. "I told you to leave it!"

His face is slapped with confusion ... which makes sense. She kept her walls up and Drake didn't see the evidence of rape engraved on her body.

Branded on her arse.

I bunch my fists, wishing I could carve that memory from my mind with a rusty blade—give myself a different hurt to focus on.

Perhaps I finally understand Aero's obsession with pain.

"We can't fucking leave her like that!" Drake thunders over the boisterous flame stirring his hair.

He's right.

We can't.

I look at the rabid inferno; at the girl huddled in its heart like a small, frightened child. Her wings are twisted around her ... always protecting her.

I meet Sol's hardened gaze through the flames—see his wings perched to strike—and realise he's about to dive in like he's got something to prove.

"No, you daft idiot! I've got this!"

"That's not your child in there!" he thunders, eyes blazing on par with her firestorm.

It's probably not his, either.

I shake my head, drag my sword out and unleash my beast. *"Back off!"*

Our attention flicks to Aero creeping up our flank and our body twists, arm snapping out. "I mean it."

He pivots on the point of *Requiem's* tip now kissing his carotid, then swallows, purposely making the ball of his throat roll against the merciless edge. A fat bulb of blood dribbles down his neck. "Hurry the fuck up."

I leash my darkness, sheathe my sword, and advance—halting only when my skin feels like it's about to bubble. "Dell ..."

She peeps over her wings, grey eyes like shattered diamonds threatening to crumble down her cheeks.

No swarthy eyes.

No beast ...

She's doing this herself.

Shit.

It took me a decade to harness my power without assistance.

"Little Dove?" Her face twists and she nuzzles behind her wings again. "*Jasta*, don't hide from me."

She starts to rock and I raise my hand, protecting my face from the swaying inferno—the flame transforming to a stark, glowing white.

"Dell, you can do this."

"I can't, Kal ... *I can't.*"

"Why?" I ask, tugging my wings into my back as I take a step closer despite the scalding heat.

She lifts her head and peers at me through a wealth of lashes, her gaze as heavy as my aching heart. "You know why."

"Say it."

She studies me for a long beat before spitting the words that have been bruising her heart for far too long. "They raped me. A lot."

The verbal confirmation is a bolt straight through my fucking chest. My beast bludgeons my insides and I draw a deep, uneven breath; tempted to hold it until my lungs burst. My fists clench, release, clench, release ... crushing seeds of murderous rage. Trying to cultivate my anger into something less explosive.

I hear bodies clash, and I know my brothers are digesting this the only way they know how ... *fist to flesh.*

Perhaps I should have warned them—told them about the damage I saw on her body rather than letting her come to that in her own time.

I take a step forward, then another, our gazes locked as I draw closer to the furnace that will undoubtedly kill me.

I've never seen Edom conjure fire. Not even the woman who bore my son could render this sort of heat. It leads me to consider the possibility that Dell might be more powerful than the lot of us. Untamed strength bundled up inside my beautifully broken Queen.

It's almost frightening ...

Almost.

I draw close enough that my senses are screaming to retreat. But I won't. I'd go to hell and back for this woman.

I'd die for her.

"You gonna let me burn, baby?"

Just when I think that's exactly what's about to fucking happen, the blazing wall parts like a curtain, creating an entry point for me to slip through before licking shut behind me.

I sit cross-legged in the muddy muck, her eyes following my every movement. If my wings were out they'd be fried by now. "Can I hold you?"

The question hangs between us and I hold my breath until she gifts me a slow nod.

I shift her onto my lap, tucking her head beneath my chin. She's rigid—a puzzle piece that refuses to sink into the spot it fucking belongs. So, I rock back and forth and hum into her nest of hair, just like coaxing a rabbit from a hole. You need a lot of *patience*.

Well, I have eternity.

"I feel trapped," she rasps and a tear drips on my arm, then another ...

It feels like a lifetime before her body moulds into me—my sleeve damp when she finally speaks again. "The baby probably belongs to one of them."

Her voice is flat.

Resigned.

Even my heart holds its breath at the dull baritone that sounds nothing like my girl.

I wasn't frightened by her show of raw, untamed power ... but this? *This* frightens me.

"We'll love the child just as much either way." The words flow like silk because they're the truth. Any child of hers is a fucking gift.

I hear her swallow, feel the weight of her next words before they leave her lips. "But what if *I* can't?"

My wings escape and arc around us, carving uncomfortably close to a fiery demise. "You will ..."

The words are haunted by the strangled beat of my heart. By my own fucking shadows.

"You don't know that, Kal. You can't know that."

I can, baby.

I tuck her further closer, running a finger through her feathers. The last thing I want is to lay this on her ... I'd hoped to go eternity without it. But it seems I have no choice.

"I do know that, Dell. Because I love Cassian, despite the act in which he was conceived."

I hear her breath catch and hold her tighter, but she twists and catches my gaze like a midnight owl.

Shocked.

Unbelieving.

Pleading.

I twist a curl behind her ear. "Don't ask, Little Dove. It can be easy to dwell on the past and forget to feel the sun on your face."

She studies me, her eyes searching mine. Just when I think she's about to call me out on my façade, she nods and nuzzles back into my chest.

I release a shuddering breath.

I know I just sounded strong and composed, like someone who's dealt with their past shit, but it's a mask I'm forced to wear.

A flaming shadow will likely always haunt me, the only reprise being the son I never knew I wanted, or needed, until he was pressed against my chest.

But Dell doesn't need to hear that. What she needs right now is strength. Support. Understanding. And that ... *that* is something I can give.

That is something I pour into her until the flames subside and we're left with nothing but the ashy residue of her pain.

CHAPTER TWENTY-EIGHT
DELL

Aero found a cave behind a frozen waterfall—a turquoise sheet of icy rage with a crack down the side big enough for us to fit through. Drake and Sol gathered stray sticks and have since been at work snapping a large log into smaller pieces with their bare, *shredded* hands.

Kal's scouting the area, and Aero's out catching game; probably with his teeth considering he's been stalking around with coals for eyes since I snuffed my flame.

I keep telling myself not to be concerned—that his beast needs space to run off steam ...

Not that it helps.

The last time something like this happened, savage Aero ended up slicing a bunch of legionnaire's wings off at the nub.

There's an air about the place; fleeting, concerned glances that never meet my eye and deep, lingering breaths expelled with gusto. Their silence is deafening, and I want to bunch the awkward tension into a ball and toss it in the snow for the crows to pick at.

I quietly sigh when Drake and Sol abandon their

passion project, relieved I no longer have to watch them beat themselves up against a dead tree. Sol storms off into the belly of the cave and Drake kneels in front of me, stacking wood into a nice, flammable pile while my wings pet his face.

The tarts need to take it down a notch; let him simmer while he digests the womb full of fuckery we just choked on. Besides, I don't know why they're trying to draw attention when they're in such a filthy state.

He clears his throat and his eyes meet mine for the first time since he unveiled the 'no vacancy' sign on my uterus. "Any chance you could ... ahh ..."

He waves his hand at the doomed pile of wood and I glare at him. Surely he doesn't mean what I think he fucking means?

"Any chance I could *what*, Drake?"

He shrugs, looking about as uncomfortable as I feel after being told to lick a stranger's ball sack. "You know ... do your fire thing so we don't freeze our genitals off."

"You want me to unleash my beast right now? You really think that's a good idea?"

He frowns and those grand, golden wings get a little jerky. "Babe, it was *you* who kindled that flame. Not your beast."

I give him the side eye. "Well, I don't know how I did it. Don't you dare expect me to light that fire, Drake."

He makes a coarse sound and stands. "I'll find some rocks to bash together."

Wise decision.

I hold my breath hostage until he disappears around the corner. I've just reconvened my chilly brooding when I hear Sol and Drake start to toss words at each other in that ancient dialect ...

Groaning, I drag my feet towards their bickering—the

sickening thud of fist against flesh and bone making my legs churn faster.

"*Goddammit,*" I mutter, rounding on their fray. A crack in the cave roof allows light and snow to filter down, dusting the idiots while they tear each other apart.

They're wasting energy fighting each other when the real enemy is out *there*.

"Guys, stop!"

My words achieve absolutely nothing. The beefcakes don't even look at me.

My poor, invaded uterus has actually made me invisible.

"Dell?" Kal's voice hits me at the same time as the smell of burning wood does.

At least someone has their priorities in order.

"Down here," I yell, trying to amplify my voice enough that it overthrows the sound of Drake slinging Sol against the ground like a corpse.

I jolt when Kal's hands fold my wings into a tight parcel, then snake around my sides and settle on my midriff, right atop my ... *womb.* "You don't need to see this."

Though his voice is soft, it's also the exact fucking opposite.

It's a command.

I swallow bile, watching Sol flip Drake onto his back and pin him down, his canines hovering dangerously close to Drake's neck. "We should split them up ..."

"It wouldn't help," Kal mutters, turning me around, steering me towards the promising crackle of flames. "They're not fighting each other. Not really."

I glance over my shoulder, pressing the back of my hand against my lips.

Doesn't look that way ...

"Are you feeling sick again?"

I nod, letting Kal lead me while I watch Sol spit a wad of red at the dirt.

"You'll need to start retaining everything you eat, Little Dove ..."

"Wouldn't that be nice."

Sol roars, tackles Drake, and propels them both around a sharp bend with a deafening crunch that shakes the fucking walls. "If they're not careful, they're going to collapse the cave, Kal."

"C'mon, *jasta*. You know I won't let it get that far."

We reach the fire and Kal tugs me down onto his lap. He wraps me in his body, tilts us both onto our sides, and settles my head on his outstretched arm—his bulging bicep making a surprisingly comfortable pillow.

My eyes zero in on his knuckles—to the fresh blood dribbling from ghastly abrasions ...

They're new.

"What did you mean when you said they're not really fighting each other?" I whisper, watching orange and blue flames lick up the side of a log while I bask in the comfort of Kal's body. It would almost be romantic if it weren't for the shadows staining my mind, the foreign weight anchoring my womb, and the sound of my mates trying to kill each other.

Kal traces invisible patterns over my temple, lulling my eyes closed and turning my coiled mind to liquid. "Go to sleep, Little Dove."

But I'm already halfway there—my mind so pathetically desperate for the promise of escape.

I toss my head from side to side while someone chases my brow with a cloth. "Why is it not crying?" I plead, trying to rise onto my elbows.

Firm hands nail my shoulders to the bed—hands I don't have the energy to fight—accompanied by hushed whispers in a foreign language I don't understand.

One I *should* understand.

"Why is it not crying?" I scream, finding some inner strength to raise my voice.

"Shh, honey. You're okay ..." a soft, feminine voice coos.

Lies.

I'm not okay. I feel like I've been ripped in half.

I feel wrecked.

Void.

More murmuring and shuffling steps. Someone pushes on my stomach and warm liquid gushes out of me.

It hurts. *It hurts so much.* But it's nothing compared to the pain I feel in my heart. A pain that's blaring at me ...

Something's not right.

"Where's my baby? Let me hold my baby!"

I'm met with the null of contemplation. More hollow silence lacking *life*.

A shadow eclipses the light and I glance up, seeing a man who takes up too much space in the room. Massive wings curled around his body seem to hold him together, his full-moon eyes lined with a thread of silver.

In them, I see oblivion.

I see my worst fears reflecting back at me.

His wings fold back to reveal the fortress of his chest and arms protecting a small, naked baby. He's cradling the child like it's the most precious thing he's ever touched ...

Little white wings sponged with red lay limp over his strong, corded arm. I can't tell if it's blood that coats them or if the feathers sprouted that way.

The man steps forward and rests the baby across the swell of my naked breasts while warm liquid continues to drain from the ache between my legs. "A boy," he rasps as I trace the child's spine with the tip of an unsteady finger. "Ziorn ..."

My heart beats a rickety rhythm as I taste the word myself, repeating it back. "Ziorn ..."

His tiny wings are fanned across my chest like armour for the hopeless, staggering organ inside it. His ears are small and dainty—the pointed tip so delicate. He has fine, white curls pressed flat against the side of his perfectly round head —plastered there by all the muck he just swam through to get here.

His eyes are closed, hiding their colour from me. I lean forward and plant the seed of a kiss on each, urging them open ...

They don't.

"Is he ... sleeping?" I rasp, willing those lids to flicker.

Willing him to move for me.

Breathe for me.

Live for me.

"Please, tell me he's sleeping ..."

A large hand cups the side of my face, warm fingers sweeping tears from my cheek that I didn't feel drop. "He's not sleeping, love ..."

I choke on my breath, a ball of bile welling in my throat as reality grips me.

Tugs me.

Rips me.

Calls to me ...

I'm pulled from the velvet depths of my nightmare by a warm hand tucked under my many layers of clothing, rubbing small circles on my lower back. "Shh, babe ... shhh ..."

The dream floats away like stray petals on a brisk wind until there's nothing left but a cold spectre hanging over me. I draw a deep, shuddering breath and open my eyes, trying to ignore the fat tear that rolls down my cheek and collects on the tawny chest beneath me.

The tawny, *naked* chest ...

I blink away the haze of sleep and lift my head, seeing Drake peering at me, his eyes shaded by lack of sleep and the dark stain of concern. "You okay?"

"Bad dream," I say, wiping my face. "Where's Kal?"

"Scouting. What was it about?" he murmurs, his voice hoarse. Probably from all the screaming he and Sol did earlier while they were ripping each other to shreds.

"I ..." I shake my head, trying to catch the petals and piece them back together, but they keep slipping through my fingers. "I can't really remember."

His frown deepens.

I know, it's not like me to forget shit.

"Sorry," I murmur, then glance around the cave, finding it empty. I try to arch off him but end up barking out a startled yelp when Drake folds his arm around my back, pins my unruly wings down, and locks me in place. "*Oomph.*"

"Sorry for what? For having a nightmare?" His voice is liquid lustre. It's the light that spills across the land at dusk, making you feel warm and radiant and full of life.

"No." I make myself comfortable, watching the flames dance across the fresh log. "I'm sorry for *everything*."

I ploughed my way into their lives and they've barely had a chance to catch their breaths. And now ... *this*.

Unexpected, unidentified womb-fruit.

"What's *that* supposed to mean?"

"You want me to spell it out?" I drawl, rubbing my face, tired and hollow despite the fact that I just woke up from a nap.

"Yes. I want you to spell it out. Very. Fucking. Clearly."

Pushy Dusk God has his balls in a twist. Actually, I'm not sure why I'm so surprised; nothing gets past my cocky rooster. But right now, I barely have the energy to keep my eyes open, let alone autopsy my cleaved chest cavity. "Can't we just—"

"*No*," he growls, gripping my hair, tugging until I'm forced to meet his punishing stare. "We are not going to ignore this, babe. Don't ask me to do that. Not after ... *everything*."

Goddammit, Drake. Why won't you just let me cuddle you in peace?

"Fine," I snap, going from zero to one hundred like a hormonal *bolt*. I shake my hair out of his grip and push up until I'm straddling his waist with my legs curled either side. "Let's talk about it, then."

His brows lift and I try to ignore the hands that park on the rounds of my hips, taunting the pregnancy hormones I'm pretending don't exist.

"No matter what, we'll always be anchored by a reminder of what happened." I gesture towards my uterus—the one I've had for two fucking seconds and is already inhabited. "I don't know how we move past this. I just ... don't." My next words choke me, and when I finally manage to force them out, they sound damaged from the journey up my throat. "I ... I understand if you want to break our bond."

Drake's eyes narrow as he starts to snarl.

I look to the roof for its stony, non-responsive stare. "I know I've spent my life being used, but this was different. Every time they invaded my body, I felt like our links became just a little more ... *tarnished*."

I swallow thickly, trying to stoke my piddly well of courage.

"I've never felt more violated. And I couldn't hide—couldn't numb my mind. It's like the deeper I fall into you all, the more clearly I see. It's like ripping off the happy web I've been relying on for longer than I care to admit."

Glancing sidelong at the crackling fire, I think back to the moment my beast crawled out of her hole; the moment she blew those men to shreds and took enjoyment out of making them shit themselves. "I lost a part of myself in that dungeon, Drake."

His grip tightens. "Dell, yo—"

"And *now?*" I continue, not wanting to hear his pity. I don't need it. I just need him to know I won't chain him to the catastrophe that is *me*, even if the thought of losing him makes me want to scoop out my own heart and toss it to the ground at his feet. "Now, I'm stained. Spoiled. Likely carrying a child conceived from that torture, who'll be brought into a world that *feeds* off fucking torture. How can I love *me* enough so I'm capable of loving this *child* the way it deserves?"

Drake grips my cheeks and I nail my gaze to his chin while his thumb sweeps the tears I'm choosing to ignore. "Dell, look at me."

I shake my head but his grip tightens.

"*Look at me!*" he roars, peddling all the power of his alpha authority.

Sigh.

My lungs seize the moment I catch his disarming stare.

"I fucking *love* you, Adeline. I'll always love you. And I'm talking for us all when I say that our love extends to every part of you." He drops a hand and rests it over my belly button. "Every single *fucking* part of you."

Heat explodes all through my chest and I press the back of my hand over my lips to stifle the sob that tries to slip out.

Drake just said he loves me ...

Me.

The messy tangle they plucked off the edge of a cliff.

I have no idea what I did to deserve these men. I feared at least one of them was going to use this situation as a convenient excuse to escape my smack talking.

"Do you believe me?"

"You love me?" My voice cracks on the last word and he nods.

"Say it," he commands. "Say that you believe me. That you fucking *hear* me."

I wipe my face and stare at him. "I believe you, Drake. And I love you, too." They're probably the easiest words I've ever said—a decompression I never knew I needed.

He lets out a deep sigh, that golden gaze going from simmering to *scalding* with a different heat entirely. "Good," he mumbles, then wraps his hands around the swell of my arse, settling me on his rock-solid cock so I'm tilted forward with hair curtaining my face ...

My wings fluff into a frenzy and he rolls his hips, stoking a flame between my legs that instantly ruins my underwear. I'm so much more sensitive than I usually am, and I know, I just know he's found my weakness ...

Fucking pregnancy hormones.

"I think this ... *situation* is going to work in your favour," I groan, and Drake chuckles.

"Or in yours," he says, unbuttoning my pants, wedging my trousers and panties down a single leg, leaving the one farthest from the flame still covered ...

Something so simple.

So thoughtful.

He weaves his hand under my top and brushes my pebbled nipple, sending a zing all the way to my clit.

I toss my hair over a shoulder and tip my head to the side as Drake's palm coasts up my bare leg, his lips skimming my throat. "This neck," he drags me down and licks a long, hot line towards my ear, "so long and elegant."

"Make the most of it. I'm on a long road to three chins."

He chuckles, then sinks his teeth into the needy flesh and I cry out, trying to curl into him as he reclaims his territory.

Me.

He licks the hurt, then takes my lips in a brawling kiss that tastes like lust and blood. We riot against his pants, edging them down narrow hips until his solid dick slaps against his stomach, and we both moan.

I straddle strong upper thighs and spit on his cock—making a slick sound when I pump the hard, velvet length.

Drake watches me while his chest battles for breath. "Fuck babe, you're good at that ..."

I'm about to tell him it's because I've had a lot of practise but my voyeur beast sneers at me from her spot reclining in a shadow.

I get the sense she thinks the comment will ruin his mood.

Drake tilts me back until he has a direct line of sight to my naked core throbbing its own hot beat, spread for him and oh so fucking vulnerable.

He growls—a deep, possessive sound that melts my bones. "You're so ready ..." A finger slides in, catching me with a hook of pleasure. "I'm going to lay you next to the fire, spread these pretty thighs, and make a fucking meal out of you before I finally stake my claim on this pussy again." He winds his finger deeper as I dive into his dirty words and almost forget how to breathe. "My seed's going to be dribbling down your thighs for the next twenty-four *fucking* hours. Every time you take a step, you're going to be reminded that this pussy is *mine*."

"Really, Drake?" Sol roars, tossing a pile of wood by the entry.

His wings snap out and I can't help but shriek like I've done something wrong.

"So much for giving her time to come out of her *fucking* shell. Two seconds alone with her and you've already got your cock out."

Drake sits up, crushing me against his chest and spreading his own wings. "I don't answer to you. Now, turn around and flutter off before I dislocate your other shoulder, you big, silver nipple."

Sweet, merciful lord ... he just called Sol a nipple.

My Day God stalks towards us with a puffed-up chest and war in his eyes. "Put your dick away and come say that to my face."

My vagina pouts around Drake's retreating finger as we both get the gist she's no longer at the top of his priority list.

Why do bad things happen to good vaginas?

Drake goes to shift me off as I drag my beast to the surface, our thighs clamping down around him. I sit back in my shadows while she sneers in his face and gives his dick the good ol' five-finger-choker-squeeze.

Drake's muscles lock up and his mouth pops open—his eyes widening so much I can see more white than gold.

The feral bitch seems to have that effect on others. No idea why.

She glares between the two of them, seeming to take some sense of pride from the colour that drains from their faces. "If you cockblock Dell's pregnancy hormones and destroy my viewing pleasure because you're too interested in measuring your dicks, I swear to *fuck* ... I will strip you both naked and lasso you with a rope of power. *Together*. Dick to fucking *dick*." She arcs our back, making our arse cheeks spread as she leans forward and flicks Drake's lobe with the tip of our tongue.

His hips buck and a deep, guttural moan makes our breasts feel even more swollen.

"You can sit with your faces to the wall and listen to me scream as my pussy creams all over my *own* fucking fingers again and again."

I almost choke on a shadow.

We swivel our gaze between the two of them, unbuttoning our jacket and blouse, freeing our aching breasts and tossing the garments aside. "So, make your choice, boys. Either learn to play nice ..." she swirls her fingers around our pebbled nipples, "or get used to your wanking hands and pray for a good imagination."

I'm not sure where this bitch got her gall from.

Beasty throws our head back with an animalistic moan, and I wrangle her down before she gets any ideas about stuffing me under a veil.

Drake's wings disappear.

"You heard our girl," he rasps, jerking his chin at Sol whose low, abrasive rumble makes my skin prickle. "She wants us to play nice *together*."

I blink at him.

The way he said those words ... it's like he was *taming* them. Fitting them with a bridle and making them his bitch.

I glance sideways at Sol smirking like he's just won a lifetime supply of gold vagina stars. He tugs his wings into his back and advances.

Warning bells scream shrill in my ears ...

"Wh—what's happening?" I ask, watching Sol shuck off his snow-dusted jacket and toss it on the ground.

I gulp.

"You've gone and done it now, babe," Drake rumbles, dragging my chin back, stealing a kiss that punishes my lips. His flavour—a burnt summer's day—dances across my tongue, making my pulse beat through my pussy.

When he breaks away, I'm fucking liquid.

Drake chuckles and I sway my half-lidded gaze from one to the other, seeing Sol loosening the tie on his slacks, looking at me like he's going to devour me ...

I find my spine again, and every other bone in my body.

"What ... exactly have I gone and done?" I squeak,

watching Sol's thick, angry cock spring free. My wings pat the air like they're trying to draw his attention to their semi-wide span.

Drake tugs me forward so my knees are almost meeting my armpits. "You want us to play nice? Fine. But you're going to be our buffer."

"Your ... *buffer?*"

"Yes. You're going to take us both at the same time. Here ..." he swirls his dick around the crown of my wet, swollen entrance, then stamps a finger on my puckered rosebud. "And *here.*"

Oh ... *heigh*.

It's happening.

My wings go soft and limp, as if they've just achieved their one fucking goal in life—to get me double dicked by my two Alpha Arseholes.

They obviously haven't contemplated the repercussions of having two Sun God cocks inside my body, battling for territory.

My beast smirks from her viewing platform. What a cunt. I'm half tempted to throw the bitch out here so *she* can deal with the consequences. I know I exude sexual confidence but now that we're here ... I'm not entirely sure I have the lady balls to follow through.

"Can't we just ... *tag team?*"

That sounds safer.

Sol reaches around and cups my face, twisting the upper half of my body and luring me into a searing kiss. His brutal tongue probes and commands, leaving my lips puffy and bruised when he finally breaks away. "Don't forget your safe word. Okay?"

I nod, anchored to his grip.

Clay in his fucking hands.

Drake lifts my hips and my mouth pops open when he

lowers me onto his hard, girthy cock—inch by glorious, stretching inch. "That's it, babe ... right where you belong." He grabs me by the back of the neck and takes my mouth while I settle onto him like a lock clicking into place.

I grip his shoulders and roll my hips—my body reacquainting with Drake's feel; his scent; his intrusive cock. Molten heat pools in my core; the sort that threatens to turn your insides to ash and numb your mind of anything but erotic pleasure.

And I want it. I want it so fucking bad.

I hold my breath, grinding, pressing my arse out to open and take more of him while my climax starts to crest ...

Sol grips my throat from behind and my mouth pops open, breasts thrusting up. "Uh-uh-uh," he warns, his voice grating past my ear, thumb dragging across my lower lip. "Not yet, Sparrow."

My beast purrs so loud my entire body vibrates as Drake flicks his tongue over my vulnerable nipple ...

I whimper.

Sol's hand splays between the buds of my wings and I'm tipped forward, hips pawed, rough fingers almost puncturing flesh that's too hot, too sensitive. I glance over my shoulder and watch him pull two fingers from his mouth with a suggestive 'pop'.

"Stay right there," he commands, painting my arse with a gentle brush of his fingers, and I'm so desperate for that orgasm that I stretch to expose myself entirely ...

Until he dips a finger in my arsehole and I almost buck off Drake's dick.

"You okay?"

Yes.

No.

Fuck ...

I nod. "I'm fine."

It's not like I haven't done this before—obviously—but I'm a wee bit twitchy seeing as their cocks are a lot bigger than anything I've ever experienced.

"I'm just warming you up. I don't want it to hurt."

Well ... that's a whole lot of words I've never heard crammed into one sentence before.

"Okay ... sure. Warm her up," I chime. "Do your thing."

My tender, achy walls clench around Drake's cock and he groans, rolling his hips, stoking the flame low in my belly. Sol spits on his fingers and does probing circles around my entrance, getting my nerves well acquainted with the impending sensation ...

This time when it slides in, I'm ready—even a bit *hungry* for it.

I rock back, moaning into Drake's mouth when that digit dips past the second knuckle. "That's it," Sol rasps, moving his hand to the pulse of Drake's thrusts.

We find a smooth, sensual rhythm before I hear the wet sound of more spit being slapped around. Sol's finger retreats and I feel the gentle prod of something *much larger*.

Drake pauses, cups the globes of my arse, and presents me like a sacrificial arse offering.

Holy fucking—

"Sol ..." I plead, as he applies more pressure, creating a soft, sensual burn.

"That's it, Sparrow. Push back onto me when you're ready ..."

When I'm ... *ready?*

Another first for my arsehole—he deserves a gold vagina star for his chivalry.

My wings do a flirtatious flap as I ease back, feeling the familiar *pop* when the head of his cock finally slips past my tight ring.

Sol releases a sharp slice of breath and I deflate against Drake's chest ...

"You okay?" they both ask in unison.

I did it.

Well, sort of ... we got the tip in. The battle's half won.

"I'm fine," I say, trying to sound super chill—not at all the victory holler I want to screech.

I breathe through the tight, consuming feel of them both and tilt my hips, easing myself further onto Sol's wide girth as Drake takes my lips in a devastating kiss. They start to rock; sliding in unison while I whimper into Drake's mouth ...

"That's it, Sparrow. Now lick your hand and play with yourself."

I do as he says—sucking a sharp breath every time my fingers slide over my swollen bud.

Sol grips my hair, using it as leverage to steal my mouth. His tongue sweeps in and makes itself at home—unabashedly exploring while filling my lungs with raw, greedy sounds.

"Fucking hell," Drake groans, digging his nails into my thighs. "You're a goddess of creation. Look at you—playing with yourself, riding us both like a fucking *queen*."

Queen of the Dual Cock.

I'll tell him my new title later.

"*Cum*," Sol growls, taking my bottom lip between his teeth and biting down hard enough to draw blood. My entire body convulses and I curve forward while Drake roars his own release—his cock throbbing as I drain him of every last drop of dusky seed ...

My wings retreat and Sol pulls out, thundering while hot ropes scribble across my back. If he did that just a *split* second earlier, my poor feathers would have been smothered in sticky jizz ...

"I did it ..." I croon and receive one rusty chuckle and a proud grunt from Sol that makes me go all gooey inside.

"I'll grab some snow," he announces, walking his fine, naked arse towards the mouth of the cave.

Drake pushes my hair back from my face. "You okay?"

I nod, yawning so wide my face almost splits.

He laughs and pulls out with a pained groan, then lowers me back down. I'm half asleep, still using Drake as a chaise, when Sol returns and swipes at my tender core with something *frozen*.

I rear back, screaming, and end up sprawled across the ground with two wide-eyed Gods staring down at me. *"What the fuck was that?"*

Sol glances at his handful of snow, then back at me, his cock hanging heavy between his legs. "Clean-up? I thought it would be soothing after all that dick ..."

I huff and wobble to a stand. "Well, you thought wrong, Daymare! You're banned from post coital 'clean-up' for the foreseeable future. I'll be surprised if my vagina doesn't have frostbite after all that." I spread my legs and give the poor girl a prod, inspecting her from all angles. "Lucky for you, she's a tough twat."

"Babe, you can't go back to sleep like that ..."

I glare at Drake who's *apparently* taking Sol's side after their dual-dick bonding session. "You've obviously never spent a day working in a whore house," I state, chin in the air as I snatch my blouse off the ground, put it to my teeth, and tear off a strip. "I'll have you know, there's more than one way to clean a vagina."

I finish mopping my back and happy valley, toss the rag in the fire, then go about reapplying my many layers of clothing. I glare at Sol watching me, still naked. "I know you're in the post-coital sin bin, but it's your turn to be my snuggle slut. Unless you want to know how it feels to have your genitals frozen, I suggest you put some pants on."

He arcs a brow, releases a rumbling sound that's more animal than man, and follows my instructions—not taking his eyes off me the entire time.

Drake plants a kiss on my nose. "I'll go help find some food."

"Be careful. And keep your wings in! If I never see another damaged Sun God wing, it'll be too soon."

He throws me a wink and contorts through the crack in the angry ice.

Sol pulls me down and fits us together—furling his wings around me and creating a safe, sheltered space where only he and I exist. I nuzzle into his neck, drawing on his deep, salted musk.

"Go to sleep. We have a long flight when you wake."

I try to ask more but all that comes out is garble as I'm lost to a delayed orgasmic coma.

CHAPTER TWENTY-NINE
DELL

The men are working around a makeshift spitroast, kindly ignoring the overwhelming smell of sex while cooking the haul of animals Aero and Drake collected. We're all perched on large rocks dotted around the fire, watching the constant drip of sizzling meat juice.

Though my vagina's still wearing her sleepy-eye, my wings have popped out and are bartering for an encore—draped around the shoulders of my busy Sun Gods and reaching for their cocks. It's embarrassing, but I'm too busy trying not to pee myself and salivating over the scent of roasted game to do anything about it.

"That smells really, *really* good," I tell Aero, who's mysteriously battered and bruised.

He nods but doesn't look at me—just continues turning rabbits and chickens with sticks shoved up their arses.

Hmm.

"How much longer?" I flap a hand towards our impending meal, bouncing up and down while Drake watches me with a raised brow.

"Ten minutes," Aero mumbles with the enthusiasm of a corpse ...

Did one of those sticks work their way up his own arse?

I stand up, drag my wings away from Kal's cock, then stride towards the exit.

"Where are you going?" Sol snaps, and I roll my eyes, turning ...

My hormones do the same.

"Who ... *me?*"

He tosses Kal the oversized camel scrotum he just took a swig from. "Yes, Dell. *You.* Where are you going?"

The man claims my arsehole and he's still acting like he missed his midday nap every day for the past century.

"I need to pee. And I'm not squatting in here with an audience, soooo ..." I point to the crack in the ice door, then frown as Sol tucks his wings into his back and stalks towards me. "What are you doing?"

"Escorting you." He gestures for me to continue walking, but I just fold my arms over my chest and stand my fucking ground.

His eyes narrow.

"I'm not a dog that needs to be taken for a walk so it can relieve itself. Unless you want me to shove one of those rabbit sticks up your arse, I suggest you back the fuck up and set that fine tush back down like a good boy."

I'm all talk—I'd never shove a stick up his arse. Certainly not for his inability to grant me personal space after some of the shit we've been through recently.

By the look on his face, I'd say he knows it, too.

He glances over his shoulder. *"Hein da ve, juis van denalia te mein."*

"Veil de ma?" Drake yells and Sol regards me with a raised brow, then tosses me over his shoulder.

Sigh.

I bat a defeated wave at the others, taking the opportunity to perv at Sol's arse from upside down while he carries me outside. My only chance to preserve the dwindling scraps of my dignity is to find a sheltered spot to piddle away from Sol's prying eyes.

He jumps over a log and I almost wet myself. "Don't jostle me!"

"Well, stop wiggling." He slaps my arse and I yelp, then pinch the thin skin at the back of his arm ... and get zero response. I'm about to jab him right in his tickle spot when he drops me next to a small cluster of tall shrubs. "There," he says, gesturing towards the sparse thicket. *"Toilet."*

I stare at the ... *offering*. "You better be joking, Daydick."

"Not at all. You pee there or you pee right here in front of me. It's your choice."

Well then.

My pregnancy hormones are about to pat his nose with my fist when he tugs me forward and starts unbuttoning my pants.

"You know what, Sol? You're being a real *heigh*."

He cocks a brow. *"Excuse me?"*

"You heard me." I slap him away and snarl at the handsy motherfucker, finishing the job myself while I stalk behind the shrubs. "You really need to work on your communication skills," I grumble, trying to wriggle my pants down. "And turn around!"

He makes a raspy sound, then spins, and I keep my eyes pinned to the back of his head while I attempt a squat. Easier said than done when you have wayward wings that like to fluff about and play in the snow. They render me unbalanced and I topple forward, landing face first with my wee tuna fish sniffing the air. *"Oomph!"*

"What's wrong?"

"I'm fine! Don't look!" I squeal, fumbling to regain my

composure, then check that Sol's not watching me fold over myself in a knot of filthy limbs.

He is.

"Spin around!"

He rolls his eyes, crosses his arms over his chest, and turns. "You're pregnant, Dell. I don't know how much you know about High Fae pregnancy traditions or pregnancy in *general*, but your dignity is about to go out the fucking window."

Well, that ship already sailed.

And sunk.

Then smashed against the ocean floor.

God, it's hard to wee with an audience. I make the egg-laying face, trying to force my bladder into compliance. "Thanks for the pep talk, you're making me feel so much better."

"I'm just preparing you," he sighs, widening his stance. "Like how I primed that little arsehole before you backed yourself onto me."

My vagina chokes mid-pee. "Stop distracting me!" I close my eyes and hum to try and clear my mind of penis.

Once I'm done, I wander towards my Day God while buttoning my pants. "You're a terrible toilet buddy, you know that?"

He quirks a brow and opens his mouth, before stumbling back a step. His features pinch into something unrecognisable on his generally stoic face ...

Confusion.

His hand flicks to his chest as I feel something thin and fragile curl around our link; a fine weave of silver and white that's so beautiful—so *precious*—I instantly know I'd give my life to make sure it never loses its lustre.

I'm reaching for it with my trembling internal hand when I notice another hair twisting around Drake's mate tether; a delicate twist of gold and white so perfect, so *breath-taking*, that my tears barely have a chance to well before they're falling down my cheeks.

I'm unblinking. Unseeing. Unfunctional. All I want to do is to wrap them both in sunlight ...

But that's not enough.

I want to twist my very *essence* around them, smother them with my soul, just to be certain they'll *always* be safe. That nothing will ever damage them for as long as I'm breathing ... and even when I'm not? I'll make sure my body remains a relic that'll continue to buffer them.

Forever.

My breath catches and I gasp, my hand flying to my chest as if it could form another layer of protection. My wings fold around me and I fall to my knees. Sol does the same—some form of hopeless recognition crossing his face while his boneless wings blanket the snow.

"Sol—"

Drake bursts out of the cave and shoots into the air faster than I can trace. He lands with an explosion of snow like icy confetti. His twisted face is stained with tears, fist knotted in the fabric of his shirt ...

He, too, appears to be lost for fucking words.

Whatever these are—these *things* inside my chest that I'd give my life to preserve—they're *important*.

"What's happening?" I manage to shriek, wondering if it's some sort of prolonged reaction to our DP session. My purring beast gives the new additions long, doting licks with her strangely tender tongue ...

What is she *doing*?

"Dell ..." Drake chokes out, stepping past Sol who seems to be frozen. "Babe, can you feel it?" His voice is heartbreakingly hopeful, and I have no idea what to make of that.

"Can I feel wh—"

Oh.

Fuck.

"The—" I clear my throat, my thoughts battling each other for airtime. "The little twisty-goldy-whitey thread wrapped around our tether ... you can feel it too?"

I watch in a strange mix of astonishment and relief as he nods his fucking head, his wide smile beaming brighter than any sunset I've ever seen.

I open my mouth to speak, close it. Repeat.

Not. Fucking. Possible.

"Is that ..." I shake my head and continue. "Is that tiny tether our ... our *child?*"

Drake nods and falls to his knees, his face so bunched with happiness that I whimper. It feels like a barb rips out of my chest—a soul splinter that was a constant reminder of things I wish I could forget. The initial flood of relief that follows is so consuming I have to fight the urge to vomit everywhere.

This baby wasn't spawned from darkness. It was spawned from sunshine and *love* and ...

Wait a fucking minute.

I bat away the tear ripping down my cheek and turn my attention to Sol. "If Drake got me pregnant ... then what the hell is that little thread clinging to *our* link?"

Please tell me it's an arse claiming thread. Pleeease ...

Sol doesn't answer, he doesn't even move. Drake, however, straight up gapes at him. "*You have a baby tether, too?*"

Fuck my life.

Sol nods, his eyes round like the midday sun. Drake looks at me, then the bastard has the nerve to *laugh*.

I'm looking around for something to gag him with when I notice Kal and Aero watching from a few metres away, trying—and failing—to blend in with the shrubbery.

"So, what we're getting at here," I yell, shaking my head, "is that I've been inseminated not once but *twice*, by two separate Sun Gods?"

My uterus pumps her ovaries while my vagina hides beneath a little flap of shame.

Drake shrugs, wiping stray tears from his face. "That's my theory. Superfecundation is rare but it's not unprecedented."

I have no idea what that word means but it sounds uncomfortable. And ... *big*.

"Anyone else want to put their two tokens in?" he asks, glancing back at Kal and Aero.

They wince, perhaps sensing that Drake's about to be strung up by his fertile ball sack.

Two babies spawned from love, destined for a *rotting* world ...

I think of Cassian—always hiding.

Two.

Babies.

I stand and storm toward the cave—needing space before I say something I might regret.

"Dell!" Kal hollers, but I wave my hand in the air.

"I just need a moment. Or, like ... a century."

A century sounds good.

Fucking hell.

I snag a piece of wood off the dwindling pile and toss it on the campfire, causing an explosion of sparks. My uterus might as well have leaped out of my body, donned a colossal sized strap-on, and made me her bitch. Unfortunately, she failed to consider the consequences of her actions, and now she's harbouring *two* children who both deserve so much more than the shit they're set to inherit.

So irresponsible.

I shake my head, feeling the space cram with the static of sun-fed Godliness.

Bastards gave me two point three seconds of alone time.

"I didn't want to bring *one* child into this hostile world. Bringing *two* into it is just plain stupid."

"I agree," Sol says, shocking me with his brutal honesty.

I turn to him. "Then, what? What do we do? Because there's no taking *this* back." I gesture to my womb and they all glance down at once.

Godammit. I can barely juggle four mates ... how am I going to manage twins *and* a broken world?

Drake steps forward, his cock straining against his slacks and making my fanny flutter.

Fucking vagina, she's had her fill. Now I'm stuck cradling the bittersweet aftertaste of her desire to please my cum-calling womb.

"We make the world a better place, babe. That's what we do."

I step away from that pumped erection in case my touchy wings cause a mess in his pants, and think very hard on that statement ...

Resolve hardens my heart as I realise what it is I have to do. Soon. Before I have my own centre of gravity.

Fuck me, how did I get here?

CHAPTER THIRTY
DELL

"I'm surprised you haven't cleared every rock out of this cave already," Kal says, trying to contain a smirk.

Unsuccessfully.

I give him the side-eye.

"What do you mean?" Drake asks from his place seated on my right, picking gristle from between his teeth with a stick. Across the fire, Sol and Aero give our conversation their full, undivided attention—which I don't appreciate.

I know where this is going.

"We almost lost our little mate in an old drako den," Kal declares, ignoring the way I'm snarling around the bottom half of a roasted rabbit.

"Why?" Drake pats my wings which earns him a nostril full of over appreciative feathers.

"She was *nesting*." Kal tosses his sharpened stick in the flames and plants a swift kiss on the tip of my screwed-up nose. "She thought she could sort an entire hoard into *piles*."

Brave, brave man.

"I'w nesk on yur pase iph yu'r gnot carephul," I manage to slog out around my mouthful of rabbit arse.

Kal takes a suggestive swig from his camel scrotum, leaving a wet smear across his lips. "Sounds delightful to me," he purrs with a silky smile that's all teeth.

I'm surprised he even understood me.

"Count me in, too," Drake says, his husky voice promising hot, wet sex. He leans back against the wall, looking *way* too comfortable with his dimple on display ...

Did he know that was an insult? Because my vagina doesn't.

I suck the marrow from a little drumstick, making a loud slurping sound. "So ... when do we leave?"

Kal looks sidelong at me while I lick fat off my fingers. "I doubt you'll make it more than two metres off the ground by yourself after all that."

I glance at the carcasses piled at my feet, entirely stripped of everything except sharp chicken claws and little furry feet. "What? I was hungry." I follow Drake's lead and use a sharpened stick-skewer to pick sinew from between my teeth.

"She's eating for three, remember," Sol croons, crossing his arms over his chest, appraising me like he wants to pin a star to my lapel for eating all my giblets ... and then some.

I stand and dust myself off, flicking some stray pin bones to the ground. "Yes, well, thanks for the reminder. I'll probably just hack it up in half an hour. Are we going to get a move on? My wings are getting bored." I jerk my pointy stick towards the fluffy fools waving their feathers in the air like they just don't care.

Now that we're defrosted, fed, *pregnant*, and smelling like sex, I'm pretty eager to find somewhere safe to bunker down properly—preferably with some warm water and an abundance of cockies.

Though I don't personally intend on doing much bunkering down.

The way I see it, my window of opportunity is small before I'm ... the exact opposite. I have zero interest in putting these babies in more danger than necessary. I may not have wanted this, and I may not be ready for this, but we're fucking here now ... and there's something that needs to be done before I ride my Sun Gods into the sunset.

"Why are you in such a rush?" Kal asks, peering at me from between slitted eyes.

"We've been in one place for too long. It's not safe."

For them.

I feel Aero's eyes on me, but when I glance his way, he's already averted his gaze—though I can still see the shadow of a frown on his face.

His mood is deteriorating by the hour.

I'm about to ask what his problem is when he stands and stalks toward the exit—his wings unfurling in a dramatic sweep of peach, burgundy, and orange. "I'll make sure it's all clear."

I'm about to follow when Sol flings a robust, silver wing in my path. "Stay," he brays with a warning growl that fills the cave and makes my hackles rise. "We need to be sure the way is clear."

My eyes narrow. "I think you're forgetting I'm the only one with any power right now, Daymare. He'll be in the air where there's a high chance of being seen from a distance. What if something happens to him?"

"What if something happens to *you?*"

This Alpha Arsehole should know better than to take that angle with me.

I shove past his wing, making a beeline for that big crack in the ice. "Don't spin that shit with me, Sol. Surely I demonstrated I'm no fragile finch when I summoned flames hot enough to melt a field of snow."

"*Dell*," Drake warns though I ignore him entirely.

Team Alpha is getting on my nerves.

Sol shoves in front of me, cramming the space full of himself. "You could set the fucking world on fire and I *still* wouldn't let you go out there. Learn some fucking *patience*, Adeline. I know you're not defenceless but you're carrying two cubs, and I will not take any chances."

"That's *Aero* out there!" I bellow, forcing my pitiful, quivering wings to spread to their full span. Now's your time to shine, bitches! "He's scouting the area, completely powerless, when I'm the only one with access to a fucking shield!"

Sol's suddenly all up in my face, his big hands wrapped around my shoulders. "For fuck sake, Dell! We're talking about your *father*! He's powerful, unpredictable, manipulative. If he got hold of you, there's no telling what he might do. What he might be *after*."

You don't speak that way unless you've looked the devil in the eye and seen your own oblivion. What horrors did Sol face in those dungeons? What's pinching him so ruthlessly that he's clinging to me like I'm the sum of his salvation?

"Then what about Aero, huh? You're happy to sacrifice *him* for the cause?" I prod his chest with my pointy finger ... and instantly regret it.

"*Ouch!*"

It's like he's made of stone.

"You underestimate him. Aero's beast is formidable; more than capable of holding off your father long enough for us to take you somewhere safe."

Rewind.

Re-fucking-wind.

Kal clears his throat and tries to steer me away, but I shuck him off. "I did *not* plunge you out of Sterling's arsehole just so I could whittle you all away as sacrificial offerings for my deranged father!" I sneer, pitching my pointy stick at the ground.

Except it doesn't land on the ground.

Sol lets out a surprised grunt and we both glance down at the skewer that was previously stuck up a rabbit's backside now protruding from his foot.

Whelp. It seems I'm yet to understand the true extent of my immortal reflexes.

"Ahhh ... *balls*. I wasn't ... that wasn't meant to ..." I peek up, shrinking at the red cheeks, gritted teeth, and chilling gaze speared at little ol' me.

My vagina puckers like an arsehole.

He's not blinking. He's not even breathing. And I swear the temperature has dropped.

"My bad. I'll just ... you know ..." I kneel and gesture to his foot, but receive no answer, probably indication that he wants me to proceed. I grip the stick and tug—certainly not expecting a thick stream of blood to come shooting out at me.

"*Fuck!*" I bung it with my finger and glance up through my lashes. "It seems you have a weepy hole in your foot. Never mind though! I'm plugging it with my unsanitary finger."

There's a loud thud and our collective attention whips to Aero slipping through the crack in the ice. "All clear," he says before appraising me perched on the ground at Sol's feet with my finger plugged in his bleedy hole.

"What the hell happened here? I was only gone for two minutes ..."

"Sol pissed off her hormones," Drake stage whispers, and I'm half tempted to stab him in the foot, too. He plucks me off the ground and plonks me on my feet. "You're probably doing more harm than good, babe. He's a fast healer." He gestures to Sol's foot, now only trickling blood ...

307

"Oh yeah ..."

"All good out there?" Kal asks, and Aero nods while Sol hobbles off towards the fire.

"But there's another storm closing in. We need to move if we're going to make it across the eastern ocean without freezing to death."

I stare at him.

Across the ... *ocean?*

"East will lead us straight past Grueling," Sol snaps from his place on a rock, lacing the boot he probably wishes he was wearing a few minutes ago.

Aero shakes his feathers out. "It's our only option, unless we want to fly for days along the coast in the other direction. Or fly straight past the capital again."

The other three nod and I'm stuck here, stewing.

Fuck.

I was hoping to find a nice, cosy house nearby ... not *on a different continent.*

"What's that face for?" Sol asks, and I lift a shoulder idly; a sweet, deceptive ruse that tastes like guilt and Sun God preservation.

"Risking the storm sounds like a terrible idea. Perhaps we just ... stay here after all? It's quite snug. We can have a cave orgy," I offer, hoping they'll take my vagina bait and gorge on it.

"No," Aero snaps, finally meeting my gaze for the first time in hours though it's with a cunning glare I'd rather not be on the receiving end of. "We can't. Want to tell me why you want to stay here, Dell? Because you have that look in your eyes that suggests you're *hiding* shit."

Gulp.

"You're in fine form today, aren't you?"

He spits out this dark, corrosive sound that makes me flinch, and stalks towards the entrance of the cave, nearly knocking Drake out with his twitchy wing in the process. "You coming or not?"

It feels like the equivalent of a smacked bottom.

I bristle.

Kal mumbles something under his breath, Drake dishes me a sympathetic look, and Sol narrows his eyes on me.

I guess we're flying across the fucking ocean.

CHAPTER THIRTY-ONE
DELL

*D*ense, purple clouds rumble in the distance, chewing up the sky and spearing the messy ocean with luminous forks.

That thing looks lethal. I've never seen anything like it before ...

We're running out of time.

"Dell? Did you hear me?"

I peer sidelong at Drake, my hair a tangle of messy knots whipping across my face. "Huh?"

"I said we need to move *faster* if we're going to make landfall before that thing hits!"

Oh, right. His way of kindly telling me to focus ... and hurry the fuck up.

Fair call.

I've been distracted by other things—like my vulnerable Sun Gods, the two baby threads I'm compulsively cradling, and the fact that we're flying in the *opposite* direction of Sterling. But he's right. Unless I put my game face on, we're going to get swallowed up by that storm and regurgitated into the ocean where we'll probably become penis serpent chow.

"Told you we should have stayed in that cave and had an orgy!" I yell, gaining a few curse words slung in my direction.

I mean it though; I'm aching all over. I can only imagine how Drake's feeling, considering his wings looked like a fishnet less than twenty-four hours ago.

A fierce draft strikes me sideways, making my wings flounder.

I squeal like a stuck pig.

Sol slides under me—cutting through the tremulous air like a hot blade through butter ...

I ignore him and his impeccable flying skills, churning my wings, focusing on Kal's boots.

Nobody likes a show off.

"*Dell ...*" Drake warns from his place at my flank.

"*I'll be fine.*"

"We can carry you, babe."

I find my balance and thunder forward, chased by Drake's murmurings about stubborn hormonal females and traits he hopes will skip the next generation.

He doesn't get it.

I *can't* rely on them; otherwise, what will I do when they aren't around? I need to be a self-sufficient flying machine.

But as that angry mass of death draws near and the smudge of land expands much slower than I wish it would, I'm haunted by an uneasiness that makes my stomach feel like a fish out of water. "I don't think we're going to make it ..."

"We will," Kal barks from ahead of our pack. "But we're way the fuck off trajectory. Hopefully we can find somewhere to bunker down when we hit land, or else the Bright may be our only choice."

That's not an option.

Not for them.

I push my wings to their limit while sleet lashes my side, the wind growing bolder by the second. Eventually, I make out the serrated line of a cliff, barren trees, scarce piles of rubble ...

A bolt of lightning cleaves our view and momentarily blinds me. I lose all sense of self—screaming, tumbling out of the sky before I slam against a hard body of muscle.

Strong arms lock around me.

"I've got you," Sol mumbles close to my ear while we spiral at a sickening speed, and all I can think is I just failed my own goddamn flight exam. He throws his wings out, cuts the air with enviable finesse, and floats us to the ground like a fucking feather.

"You made that look far too easy," I heave, squinting at the low-hanging clouds for any sign of the others.

Sol's grip tightens, like he doesn't trust me sliding down his body without suffering a mortal injury. "I've had a lot more practise than you, Sparrow."

"Only because you're *thousands* of years older than me. I should be mortified."

"And I should be *inside* you," he rumbles, making me squirm as Kal, Drake, and Aero pepper around us—the latter doing a quick scan of my body before taking in our surroundings.

Following his line of sight, my lungs collapse with a *whoosh*.

Shit.

I wiggle in Sol's choking grip. "Put me down. *Please* ..."

He makes a gruff, disapproving sound as I'm released the same way I imagine one might part with a child in a crowd; reluctantly, like he has to physically force himself to unstick his hands from my body.

The ground is frozen beneath my boots, crunching when

I take tentative steps towards the remnants of a dismantled home once made from those red stones now littering the ground. The house's innards are held in by a skeletal fence that still has a chain attached to one of the rotten pickets.

A chain which used to belong to a dog with a sharp, yapping bark.

My heart chokes on its next beat.

"Wh—where are we?"

"South West of Grueling," Kal remarks from behind me. "I'd say this is the village of Moft. Or what's left of it."

"Moft," I repeat, feeling the name on my tongue—tasting it. "Moft ..."

Flakes of snow dust the ground, our hair, and the sleek feathers of our icy wings as I scan the dismantled settlement. Another bolt of lightning cracks the sky open.

Everyone flinches but me.

That storm pales in comparison to the one surging beneath my skin.

"Dell? We need to find shelter ..."

I shake off Drake's well-meaning brush of a hand and turn, casting my gaze over another spineless building before I set my sight on a small, decrepit house. Air becomes acid in my lungs, my heart a stone in my chest as I take in the home where I spent the first four years of my life.

It's small with two windows and a door painted eggshell blue, chipped and faded with age. The surrounding fence smiles at us; teeth jagged and broken with rogue vines choking the life out of them.

The front gate jerks in the volatile breeze ...

Squeak.

Squeak.

Squeeeak.

"Dell?" Kal's fingers brush my cheek and I spin, jolting at

his close proximity. He scans my face, frowning, and I feel as if I've just been flayed.

Exposed.

There's a rustle and a snap and I glance over my shoulder. Sol's ripping luscious red apples from an overgrown tree just outside the fence of my childhood home—gathering them in the scalloped hem of his coat.

Mummy and I used to do the same thing.

"I need you to get inside that house, Little Dove. We only have a few moments before the storm hits ..."

I tilt my head back, seeing heavy clouds sponging the light, threatening to batter us with their contents ...

Right. Okay.

I nod and my feet begin to move.

Perhaps this is a nightmare. Perhaps I'll wake soon—find us still in the cave, nesting around a fire and smelling like sex warmed up ...

Perhaps I just have to watch my mother die first. That's usually how they go.

I push the gate open while my heart tries to escape its bony cage. Five more steps and I'm at the front door, tall grass brushing my kneecaps.

I wonder if I'll be met by the chair I shoved against the door so I could climb up and open it. Back when I was smothered from head to toe in my mother's blood—when hunger, the thick stench of death, and the choking circle of rats finally forced me to find a way out of the house.

After all these years, I can finally reach the doorknob ...

Snow settles on my hand while I draw a pregnant breath. It's not really the chair I'm worried about ... it's the pile of bones I'll likely find scattered on the floor. The remnants of a woman who gave her life so that I could live.

The sky darkens.

We have no choice.

I twist the handle, herded by the laden presence of my mates speaking quietly between each other in the language of the arsehole. They can probably scent the unease peeling off me like old layers of skin.

The door creaks and I'm struck with dense, dusty air and the musky scent of rotting flowers. I sneeze as I step into the shadows, the memories, the haunting well of sentiment.

The floor groans beneath my feet and I cast my gaze like a net to the big, black stain on the wooden floorboards weathered with age ...

The residue of death, but no bones.

No bones.

She's not here anymore.

I don't realise my legs have given out until I'm caught, wrapped up in Aero's scent, and lowered to the ground. "I'm here, baby. I've got you ..."

I shake my head as he protects my bunched body and barks out words I don't understand. My gaze staggers across the square of space that was our kitchen, our living room, our bedroom ...

Our life together.

It's missing a few pieces of broken furniture, and the mess that littered the place has been tidied, but otherwise my childhood home appears the same as it does in the living beat of my memories.

"Fucking hell."

Drake's sharp words seize my attention—his feet surrounded by a blanket of river rocks, pieces of moss, and bundles of dead flowers ...

But he's not looking at the debris.

He's looking at the wall directly in front of him—a spot obscured from my view by his broad silhouette.

"Move, Drake."

My voice is cold, hollow, somehow penetrating ancient words being thrown around like boulders.

Drake looks back at me, his eyes churning pits of concern.

"*Now.*"

Kal steps between us. "No, Dell. *No.*"

Beasty snarls, tugging on her restraints. She wants to know what's behind the pretty God wall, too.

"I need to see it," I try to growl, but my voice comes out in a pathetic rasp of barely contained emotion.

Aero's arms tighten. "Is there somewhere else we can go?"

His voice is strained; desperate. I can hear the brittle undertones, the edgy rawness aggravating his words.

He's fighting his beast, too.

There's a near-blinding flash, the instant assault of thunder.

The walls shake.

"We're not going anywhere." My wings cleave the nest of Aero's grip and curl around my body, seeming to know something I'm also beginning to suspect. I narrow my eyes on Kal, loosening my internal shackles and allowing my beast to peer at him through my eyes. "*Move out of the way.*"

He doesn't even flinch. "Little Dove, trust me. You don't want to see this."

She flashes our teeth, showing him she means business. He knows what happens when she means fucking business.

We blow shit up.

"If you don't move, I'll *make* you move."

He makes a low, abrasive sound as we reach forward and shove him out of the way, then pin Drake with the same condemning glare.

"Fuck," he rasps and shifts to the side.

Our eyes widen ...

High on the wall are two tiny puffs of white, fanned out like splayed hands, tacked in place with rusty nails.

Our wings.

Beasty takes one look at the display, coils inside me, and wraps herself in my internal shadows—leaving me cold, weary, and bitterly empty.

Old blood muddies the otherwise pristine feathers, and my back burns with phantom pain—the grate of unforgiving teeth that bite and bite and bite. A grinding sound hacks through my memory, making bile rise in my throat while the ghost of warm blood pools under my belly.

My nostrils flare, seeking the briny scent of my mother's tears.

I study the graffiti someone's carved in the wooden wall below the morbid display; the words *Little Dove* and *she walks among us* casting my tiny wings in a permanent spotlight of expectation ...

The room becomes too small, too dark. My shoulders fold forward and even my lungs feel like they lack the space to move inside my body.

I shuck out of Aero's tight grip and stand on unsteady legs—drawn to my severed wings like a moth to flame.

That's my innocence on the wall.

Dead.

My boot nudges the offerings as I stroke dainty, delicate feathers that will never know what it's like to cut through clouds. My *living* wings constrict—vibrating around me ...

"Dell?" Aero's voice slices through my reverie. "Look at me."

I glance over my shoulder and catch his astute gaze—like twin suns peeking over the horizon, attempting to chase away the darkness.

I can tell he wants to gut the subject open and spill its

contents everywhere. Problem is, I don't think I have the energy to clean up all the mess it'll make.

Nor do I want to.

"What do you need?"

I shake my head and he nods once. A wordless truce.

Later.

He's the only one who'll truly understand, the only one who walked that memory with me. The last thing I want is for the others to have to bear the same burden on top of everything else.

Wind howls at the window panes, making them quiver. I gesture to the sink, folding my emotions deep inside and refusing to look at those tiny wings pinned to the wall like a dead butterfly. "I wonder if the water still works ..."

Sol looks at me like he has a million words clogged in his throat and no tongue to speak them, and Kal makes a low, grating sound before heavy bodies start to shift.

Drake sighs, massages the bridge of his nose, then steps forward and twists the faucet. It groans, producing a slow dribble of water. "The pipes are probably freezing over. Best we wash now. Find some containers to fill for drinking while we still can."

And just like that, there's a flurry of movement—the clanking of drawers, cupboards, and pots while my mates jostle around in an effort to fill the deafening silence.

Someone tries to warm this tomb by lighting the freestanding stove as part of me slips away—goes somewhere dark in the corner of my mind.

Somewhere familiar.

Strong hands peel away my physical layers while I stare out the window at the broken view; imprisoned in a home riddled with ghosts from my past. Water is brushed over my skin, through my hair, over my wings; the filthy remnants rung out, draining away like my fluid thoughts.

I'm re-dressed and handed a familiar metal cup I used to drink warm milk and honey from. I sip from it while lightning scuttles across the sky and debris batters the house, that gate squeak-squeak-squeaking away.

An apple is rolled into my hand and although I'm ravenous, I barely register eating the sour thing—core and all.

I'm led to the bed I once shared with someone else I loved. Although I need to pee again, I avoid even glancing at the backdoor ...

It may lead to the toilet stall out back, but that path will take me straight past a trapdoor that drops down into the haunted basement tucked below the house.

It's safer to be down there during a storm, but I can't bring myself to suggest it.

Thankfully, neither does Aero.

Kal, Drake, and I curl into a mess of limbs and wings on the bed. Aero takes the couch and Sol ends up folded on the deteriorating recliner by the door. Hours of insomnia drip by while Kal and Drake slumber around me, and I know Sol's not asleep. I'm almost certain Aero isn't, either. I can feel turmoil washing off them—hear it in their deep sighs and shallow breathing.

Lightning crackles and I sneak peeks at the tiny wings pinned to the wall, accentuated by the menacing scene unravelling outside ...

The world's angry at the ones who were supposed to protect it, and she's got a score to settle.

I don't blame the bitch.

Resolve settles deep in my heart and when I finally fall asleep, it's to an internal mantra on repeat ...

My mother's sacrifice will not be in vain.

Neither will my own.

CHAPTER THIRTY-TWO
DELL

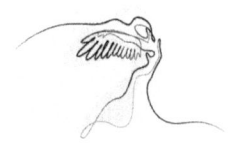

I'm jerked awake by a flash so bright it has me curling away from the windows. Drake's heavy arm is draped over the dip of my waist, his hand stamped against my lower abdomen. He tugs me closer while Kal sleeps soundly with his wing folded over my legs.

This could almost be happily ever after, were it not for my amputated baby wings pinned to the wall not five metres away or the fact that the world is shredding itself to pieces outside.

I shiver despite being surrounded by warm-blooded Gods.

Another flash illuminates a dark figure standing by the motherfucking window. I suck a sharp breath as my heart attempts to gag me, trying to focus on the shadowy mass ...

Another bolt scatters the darkness—highlighting high cheekbones and unruly hair that looks like muted flames.

Fucking hell.

Aero. Not a monster with black eyes and big, white wings.

Apparently my pelvic floor muscles aren't so fantastic after all.

I watch Aero cross his arms over his bare chest; looking out through the small peek-a-boo window. His wings stretch, shake, then settle flat against his back again.

Perhaps he needs help expelling some of that tension? I happen to be particularly ... *handy* to have around in such circumstances.

I wiggle beneath Kal's wing and slide off the bed, the floorboards cold beneath my feet. Aero doesn't move; not even when I slip in front of him and press my folded wings against the window skirting.

Another flash illuminates his stormy eyes in the stark light—his severe, *drawn* gaze honed on me.

"You look tired ..."

"Exhausted."

"Can't sleep?"

Another bolt and he shakes his head, jerking his chin at the two tiny wings pinned to the wall.

I nod.

I get it. Fuck, do I get it.

I ran from that memory for most of my life; hid behind a veil, started talking to myself ... all to escape the bitter reality of my past. Now it's staring me right in the face.

The wings.

The blackened bloodstain on the floorboards.

That door that leads to a room where my innocence died a vile, brutal death.

"I'm sorry you have to see that," I whisper, jerking my chin towards the morose shrine on the wall.

Aero's jaw ticks in the winking light, his eyes becoming molten rocks. "You're *apologising* to me?"

"Well, I wasn't the only one forced into that memory ..."

and I know just what it's like to have that splinter in your mind.

Really fucking uncomfortable. I wouldn't be surprised if Aero starts having deep and meaningful conversations with his cock.

His wings flair and his eyes close, his sharp breath distilling the air and lacing it with traces of raw, primal *rage* ...

His canines stretch and my beast snarls from her hole in my shadows. "Aero ..." I brush his chiselled jawline, but he snatches my wrist and holds it hostage.

When he finally opens his eyes, I see the man staring back at me, not the beast. "This isn't about that, Dell. This is about you closing off from me. This is about you *hiding shit* from me."

Ahh, *heigh*. I know where this is going.

He lets my wrist fall to my side and I glance away. "I don't know what you want me to say ..."

"You filtered your thoughts. You cut me off through most of what you went through in that dungeon." He glides forward and nails me to the wall with his hips, hooking his finger under my chin. The next flash illuminates his head tilted to the side; his eyes entirely shaded. "You're a logical girl, I know that. I know you would have kept that line of communication open at all costs if it meant a possibility of us finding you, save for *one reason*."

Fuck.

I close my eyes and breathe.

Breathe ...

"You were protecting me."

Dammit, Aero. He's not even in my head, yet he's *in my fucking head.*

I open my eyes and glower at him, saying nothing. I certainly can't deny it ... I'll fucking choke.

If he knew who the men were, what their incentive to torture me was, it would destroy him. He'd probably never forgive himself.

"Were you protecting me?" he probes, jerking his hips, and I slide my canine through my tongue in an effort to stop myself from moaning.

"*Answer me.*"

Sweet, unmerciful Dawn God ... he won't give up. Not until I give him some semblance of an answer.

A piece of my truth.

I widen my eyes, fuelling them with all the conviction in my heavy heart. "I'll always protect you, Aero. Until my last breath."

"Don't." He grips my chin and squeezes until it hurts, flashing his canines at my face. "Don't *fucking* say that."

"It's true."

"You're not your mother, Adeline. I know Mare gave her life to protect you, giving you some twisted perception that you need to do the same to protect the ones you care about, but I'll follow you to Death's *fucking* door if you throw your life away."

He jerks his hips again and this time, I can't contain the moan that slides out while his cock throbs between my thighs.

"You don't have to prove yourself. Not to us. Not to *anyone*." He takes a step back, leaving me hanging against the windowsill with a wet patch between my legs.

He's using his dick to bait me into talking.

Well, unlucky for him, I'm nowhere near as silly as the twat between my legs. Perhaps I thought this conversation would end up with me getting pegged by his morning glory, maybe even his teeth, but it seems angry sex isn't on the cards.

Not unless I break his heart first.

Time to abort mission.

I try to shuffle away, but he slams his hand on the wall and blocks me, making me jump. "You haven't answered me," he growls, and my beast starts to prowl beneath my skin, testing her restraints ...

How dare he take so much interest in my emotional well-being.

"What's done is done," I sneer, feeling his chest heave against the swell of my breasts. "I'm not going back to that. I won't. You want specifics? You want to *feel* that pain, Aero? You aren't going to siphon your hit from me. *Let it go.*"

He whips his hand back, then lands his fist in the stone right beside my head, narrowly missing the window. Another flash of light turns Sol's eyes iridescent, revealing the fact that he's very much awake on that seater ... his balled fists resting on his knees.

Aero pushes off the wall and swings the front door open, flurries blasting through the house as I watch the idiot stalk into the apocalypse before slamming the door shut.

Motherfucker.

I storm across the room and am reaching for the handle when Kal and Drake pounce at the same time, hauling me to the bed as my flapping wings kick up as much snow as the open door just did.

Kal groans when I spear his guts with an elbow, narrowly missing his balls on purpose to prove my loyalty to them.

"Stop, babe." Drake tries to wrestle my flailing limbs back under the covers. "Aero just needs to blow off steam."

"He'll freeze to death." I try to pinch the tawny fucker, but his tight skin is barely holding all his muscle in and I have virtually nothing to grip hold of. I'm not against kicking some golden testicles considering Drake's already shot me full of his baby gravy.

It's not like he needs them anymore.

"He's made from the Sun; he'll survive," he grumbles as he

and Kal grip two limbs apiece and pin me to the bed. "You and the babies *will not.*"

Low. Fucking. Blow.

I hiss, going immediately floppy.

Drake suffocates me in a dusty blanket and I sneeze again. "You bastard, pulling out the baby card," I grouse, checking those two tiny filaments for the millionth time for any damage or loss of lustre.

"It's an easy one to play."

Sigh. It really is.

He tucks me in, making sure I'm a secure parcel of warmth and allergies. "Now, go back to fucking sleep."

"It's hard. I keep sneezing."

"I know," all three of them groan in unison.

Kal tugs me against his body, nuzzles his nose into my neck, wraps me in the weight of his wing, and swiftly nods off. A few moments later, Drake's breathing becomes heavy, too.

If only it were that easy for me.

Despite the fact that I'm the meat in a sleeping Sun God sandwich again, I can't drift off because somewhere outside my Dawn God is running a riot, 'blowing off steam'.

Such a shame when he could have been doing that between my thighs.

It's not until he steps back into the house a few hours later that my chest finally loosens its hold on my heart. By the erratic light of the electrical storm, I watch him dust off in the kitchen, rinse his bloody fists in a pot of water, and settle back on the sofa before falling into a heavy breathing pattern.

I release a deep breath, content with having all my cocks under one roof again, safe and sound and sleepi—

"Go to sleep, Dell," Sol orders from his spot on the seater by the door.

Hmm.

Seems I have a babysitter. Bastard's been sitting there awake, playing sentry this entire time.

I get it. He's probably a bit damaged after I was stolen from his bathtub while he slept soundly in the room next door ...

Slipping away on my own is going to be a lot harder than I thought.

A sneeze rips out of me, dissolving a nightmare riddled with black eyes and tiny, white wings that wouldn't move. "Fucking dust," I groan, rubbing my swollen eyes.

The first thing I notice is the empty bed, chair, and couch —though my collection of heart tethers are healthy and whole.

I clamber towards the window, seeing a new world iced with fluffy snow ...

Seems the storm finally passed.

There are several sets of footsteps embossed in the white powder, leading a trail away from the house. Hopefully they've gone to search for supplies ... supplies I'll need access to.

I sniff out two apples on the kitchen bench and crack a drawer open, hunting for a sharp knife. I rummage through old baking utensils, trying not to think about the vision of my mother standing at this kitchen bench covered in flour.

I'm just about to give up when I spot a blade at the back of the drawer.

One I recognise.

I hook it out by the small wooden handle and study it.

Mummy always told me I wasn't allowed to touch this blade, but she always kept it close ...

Always.

Except for that day.

If my memory serves me correctly, she left it on the bedside table, probably too distracted by my wayward wings. I sniff the handle, wondering how it found a home in this drawer, and come up short ...

Hmm.

I run my finger along the blunt edge, and it draws a line of fire. *"Ouch,"* I hiss, whipping my hand away.

Iron.

Mum kept an *iron* blade next to her at all times, and I doubt it was to slice my fucking apples up. It was probably all she had left to protect me with ...

Suddenly, I'm not so hungry anymore.

I press my palm flat against the metal and listen to the whispered sizzle of burning flesh, absorbing the sting that torments my skin.

It hurts, but it certainly doesn't feel like the blade's *taking* from me ... not that I really know what to look for.

"Maybe I'm broken," I mutter, tossing it at the bench, strumming the tips of my fingers on the wooden surface while I glare daggers at the dagger ... trying not to pee myself.

Guess it's time to see if the old toilet still exists.

The storage room door is slightly ajar, as always. If I use my imagination, I can picture a pair of grey eyes staring back at me through the long sliver of black ...

Fuck.

I snap the door open, pick up my lady balls, and weave through empty, wide-open barrels without even glancing in the direction of the trapdoor. I'm all too happy to step into the toilet stall, and I don't shy away from my dramatic sigh as I lock myself in.

I was holding my breath that entire time, hoping I wouldn't vomit my anxiety everywhere.

The wooden toilet seat feels like a brand on my poor arse, my vagina losing all sensation when she gets exposed to the chilly air. I shake my hips, then pull my pants up, trying to fasten them with frozen fingers. "Goddamn ... buttons," I mumble, pushing back into the storage room while wrestling the knobbly fuckers. For the sake of this unseasonal winter and my needy hormones, I need to go back to drawstrings immediately.

I weave through the barrels until my foot scuffs against something abrasive and I stop cold, staring down at the trapdoor ...

A large lump works its way up my throat—one that could very well be my withering heart.

My wings twist around me, trembling.

Something tells me the gesture isn't to protect me. Not this time. For once, they are the ones who need this cuddle.

This comfort.

To be reminded they didn't go through that horror alone.

I'm not sure how much time passes while I study the flat wooden door that haunts my nightmares just as much as the man with black eyes and a sharp smile ... but eventually I step to the side, hoist it up, and descend into the shadows of my past.

CHAPTER THIRTY-THREE
AERO

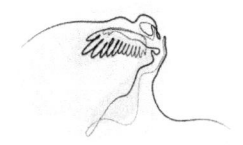

I stalk towards the house, clenching my hands—relishing the sting of torn flesh tugged taut over tender knuckles.

My mind's a prisoner, clawing at bars of iron while rotten flesh peels off its bones.

It's not used to being so *fucking* lonely.

I've always hated my gift. I can't share someone's company without their thoughts stabbing me in the head like an incessant bane. But then Dell stumbled into my life with the unique shape of her mind, and I was instantly captivated; *compelled* even.

Placed under her fucking spell.

Her thoughts shone like the sun peeking over the horizon at first light, and suddenly this gift didn't seem like such a curse.

She's a balm I've come to rely on—tamping my need to distract myself with mind-numbing pain.

And now she's gone.

It's a twisted case of irony—one that feels like fucking

brain rot. I can tell she's putting on a show while planning something behind those smoke screen eyes, but I can't get in there. I'm forced to *guess*.

Such bullshit.

My beast is in an uproar; driving me to unleash him for long bursts while he wrecks us against trees, rocks—anything without a pulse. I can't give her the berth she thinks she needs. Not when he's wanting to crack her open, spill her secrets, then examine them piece by piece while we put her back together again.

A perfect mosaic of our beautiful, broken goddess; the woman we fell in love with when she was teetering on the crest of dawn, ready to throw it all away.

We knew then we'd kill for her.

Die for her.

I open the front door, expecting to see her fast asleep in the bed. But she's not.

Don't panic.

I haven't been gone long. Enough time for my beast to bash my fist against a tree before he realised bleeding was only getting us so far.

"Dell?" I scan the small square of space, avoiding her tiny wings pinned to the wall like a crude taxidermy display, and notice the door to the storage room has shifted position. "*Fuck.*"

I dash through it, spotting the trapdoor I saw in her memory.

It's wide open.

My wings jerk their impatience and I drag my palm down my face, weighing the merits of letting her have a small moment of peace ...

I lean closer, scenting the sharp tang of anxiety. Fear. Sorrow.

Fuck her fucking peace.

I'm halfway down, my head just dipping below the floorboards when I spot her; curled on the ground before the wooden table that's stained with her aged blood ...

My little Queen. She's spent her life bleeding for a world that's done nothing but tear her mind and body to shreds, leaving the remnants to be picked apart by the vultures.

We don't deserve her. We'll never fucking deserve her.

"Dell?"

The void of silence swallows my voice as I study her small, huddled form caped in a quivering coat of white wings. Like they know this place, too.

Like they're afraid of it.

I climb off the last rung and take a step towards her. "Baby ..."

It's all too familiar.

Too raw.

I can feel the shadows threatening to choke me.

"Out of sight, out of mind," a voice whispers, but it's not Dell's ...

It's her inner darkness. Her turmoil.

Her *beast*.

She unravels in a fluid flash of wings and white hair, and my heart chokes at the crude sight of her ...

A desolate creature stares back; haunted eyes framed by the wild lope of curls that brush her hips. A sharp, angular face so exquisite it could bring the entire world to its knees.

I lift my hands—an attempt to tame the fierce, beautiful creature I'm beginning to believe is just as unpredictable as my own inner beast.

Her eyes flick to the movement and full lips stretch back from sharp canines that almost brush her chin. She squares her shoulders, splays her palms, then pumps her hands into synchronised fists.

The entire room explodes.

My beast tries to rip me down the middle as a fine dust is pitched into the air, creating a dense, churning cloud I can't see *shit* through.

"*Dell!*" I roar, smashing my fists against an invisible force penning me in. *Protecting* me. "*Drop the fucking shield!*"

I bash and bash and bash, littering myself with blood, choking on the smell of my own desperation.

"*Dell!*" A stiff breeze siphons the dust away, and I pause mid-strike, watching a small, curvy silhouette emerge from the cloud of anguish—wings stretched as she finally comes into full, exquisite focus ...

There's my Queen; untouched, pristine, coated in the sharp glamour of her beast. Bits of snow cling to her curls and I glance up, squinting, trying to hide my shock ...

We're standing at the base of a *crater*.

She blew up the entire house.

Fuck.

She walks forward with a sway in her step, and I do my best to wipe my face clean of disbelief.

Kal told us what she did to that table, but this ... this is something else. Something cataclysmic.

She's a bomb, just waiting to detonate.

She's a weapon.

If her father got hold of her, he'd paint his wards with her blood and bind her to his will.

Or he'd kill her.

I fall to my knees as snow begins to collect on my shoulders, float my wings to the ground, and drop my gaze in respect for the raw power that just exploded from a woman who grew up doubting the value of her own worth.

"Bring him out." Her obscure voice makes my skin prickle as she tilts my chin so I'm meeting her black-velvet gaze. "Now."

I shake my head, purposely beseeching, trying to tame her into something less wild. "He's not in a good way."

"Neither are we," she purrs, twisting her hand into my hair before she tugs. *Hard.*

I groan against the sting.

"She needs a distraction. We need him to make us *feel*."

I almost crumble as her lips accentuate the last word. Finally, some progress. Some admission of her agony.

A crack in her fucking armour.

"He's not gentle, baby ..."

"Do I look like I need *gentle* right now?"

The darkness inside me roils like an ocean crammed into a tiny jar.

"No."

"*Bring him out.*"

Her guttural cadence darts straight to my dick, causing my concentration to waver for a fraction of a second ...

The key to his freedom.

He shreds my waning walls, tossing me into the backseat of my own body like the ruthless cunt he is.

No manners.

No fucking *respect*.

But still he kneels before our woman, on his knees in the grime of her nightmare. "You summoned me, Mistress?"

You summ—

I shake my head, feeling the vague beat of his sadistic amusement.

Fucking suck-up.

He drags a hand through the silt while we listen to her growl, scenting her churning well of emotions.

Her desire to mate.

He watches her pierce that lower lip with an unforgiving canine—the scent of her blood making our muscles tense, our nostrils flare, and our balls tighten.

We smear the silt down our sharp cheeks, showing that we accept every broken part of her. Every single *fucking* particle.

She starts to speak, but we snatch her up and tear at her waistband, leaving her pants and underwear in tatters, humming when we find her pussy lips glistening ... suddenly fucking *famished*.

He flicks her leg over our shoulder and opens her up, diving into our meal like a starved animal.

He's not delicate. Not with the taste of her finally on our tongue.

Our blood boils as we palp her clit, driving our tongue around the crown of her tight hole before starting the main course. We pulse and probe and fucking *consume*, grounding her by our fingers clawed into the flesh of her arse.

Her body tides, answering every flick and plunge like an angry ocean. We worship it all looking up at her from between her grappling thighs, wishing we could hear her thoughts as her pleasure forms its own heartbeat around our tongue.

Our wings spread when she tips over that crest, screaming—a sharp, shadowy sound that's so at odds with the softness of her body. My beast gorges on her cream, refusing to blink or breathe for fear he'll waste a single fucking drop.

"You've been holding out," she pants, kneading the last of her orgasm from our face. It's not until she bends back that we notice her wings are gone ...

Done.

But we've only just begun.

We stand, feathers reaching for the edge of the crater while she wavers—white hair askew, pussy blushing, blood trailing down her chin ...

Fucking perfection.

We're on her in a heartbeat—like stars colliding—and we spread her across the ground, crushing her space with our presence.

Her back arches, hair dragging through the mess like a brush being drawn through paint. We bunch the loose blouse around her breasts and roll a puckered nipple, her raw, wanton sounds luring us to squeeze the soft peak.

Hard.

She jerks her hips ... *presenting.*

"You're mine," we rumble, lubing our fingers with hot swipes of our tongue. "Mine to protect. Mine to devour. Mine *forever*." We sink three digits inside her and spread them out—stretching her, making every muscle in her body contract as her eyes roll back. "Do you understand? If you want out, you're going to have to send me back to the Sun and pray I fucking stay there."

"Prove it." She shreds our pants, like she needs this claiming just as much as we do. "Prove that I'm yours."

We split her legs, grip our cock, and swirl the head around her entrance—a coarse, unfamiliar sound erupting from deep inside our chest. "*Look at me.*"

She does; her eyes widen at whatever it is she sees on our face. Then her body surges as we push into her with one long drive of our hips.

It's not tender.

She screams, a smile splitting her angular face while our hips slap against the soft flesh of her inner-thighs. We drive her along the ground with each declaring thrust, sinking greedy fingers into her waist and shoulder.

My beast doesn't do ... gentle.

He's claiming her hard. He's claiming her fast. Yet she's screaming for *more*.

She drags her nails down our torso—drawing long lines of pain we *devour*. If she dug a little deeper, she might even skim the flesh of our heart so she can feel how hard it's beating for her.

My beast stuffs himself full of her bleeding rage, smudging our blood across her skin, creating a pretty portrait we hope she'll like ...

Instead she growls and snatches our hand, guiding it around her neck. She drags us down, trying to make us tighten our grip, like she doesn't know how to separate love from pain.

Fuck.

We nuzzle into her neck and nudge her head to the side, finding the spot behind her ear that's potent with her unique perfume. "No. You're hurting enough."

His words.

Not mine.

He's treating her like a delicate flower—sniffing and cradling her after he just drove into her so hard we practically dug a ditch in the ground.

I'm not opposed, I'm just ... *shocked*.

"If you want to see pain, you give it to me."

She sneers, flicking our hand away, and we only have a split second to tug our wings in before she rolls us over, nailing us to the dirt while her filthy hair drags across our face.

It's the first time we've been under a woman. Our first time being in such a compromised position.

The pulse of our fucking eases, our dick still heavy inside her as we watch her face hone. She lashes out, drawing nails through our skin and cutting deep, malicious gouges—beating our chest with frantic blows while her black eyes become cold, hollow pits ...

We let her.

We let her beast bruise us; shred us with the fuel of her torment.

Pain, we enjoy. We'll gladly bathe in *hers*. Anything so that she won't feel it herself.

"Is that all you've got?" we roar, threading our hands around her tiny waist, dragging her so close our lips brush when we hiss in her face. Dell's proven she could turn us to dust with a single errant thought, but we'll happily break if it makes her feel just a little more whole.

She jerks against our hold, her eyes widening, the black fading to a soft, stormy grey ...

Her canines shorten. Features soften.

My beast coils up on his own accord; backing away from a fight for the first time in eternity. I'm stumbling over my thoughts while my girl holds my gaze, heaving breath, shivering against the snow fall.

Her face contorts. Breaks.

Shatters.

Tears begin to streak through the filth as deep, ravaged sobs spill all over me—jerking her chest and stripping her bare.

"Baby ..." I move to pull out and lift her off, but she drags herself back onto me.

"No." Her voice is like a lute string stretched too taut, tearing a hole in my heart and bleeding it dry. "Make me forget."

I watch her for a long moment—watch a hot tear drip onto my chest.

"Please."

My cock's no magic wand, but hell ... I'm willing to give it a go.

I band my arms around her and flip on top, setting her down like she's made of fucking crystal. My blood dribbles onto her skin, and I smear my hand through the fresh trail, smudging her in my scent while she watches me through wide, glassy eyes.

I grip the side of her face, holding her stone-still so she couldn't look away even if she tried. And then gently, too fucking gently, I move—savouring the feel of her clenching around me as I drive with purpose, collecting her tears with my tongue and tasting her complex emotions in every brilliant bead.

Her muscles grow greedy and drag me deeper, *squeezing* me, making my thighs quiver—every cell screaming to drive inside the chalice of her body.

I may like pain but this ... this is *salvation*.

This is home. Right here, buried inside her, stirring her to fucking *spill* around me.

My arms lock up, my wings whisk the air, and her entire back curves as I match the beat of her climax; pump her full of *me*.

She'll never be able to scrape my scent from her body. Not after that.

She's *mine*.

Forever.

I laugh low and shake my head—feeding on the feel of her pussy dragging pleasure from my cock—when her pearly skin starts to ... *glow*.

My fucking breath catches.

"De—"

Beams of light begin to shaft from her eyes, her ears, her wide-open mouth—flooding the crater with a stark luminescent glow that's raw as untarnished sunshine; the essence of *life itself*.

Like a moth to flame I latch on, diving into her mouth, tasting crispy brightness on her lips and gorging on her in a different way. I can feel it filling me up, like warm static under my skin, and then she slides her canine through the flesh of my fucking lip ...

My entire body vibrates with a pure spike of ecstasy.

This beautiful, exquisite creature is choosing *me*.

Body.

Soul.

Fucking *all* of it.

I thread her a moan as her venom ignites a blistering trail, making my tongue tingle for a taste of her life force. My canines become a force of nature, drilling down from my gums, preparing to pierce her flesh.

I deepen the kiss, burning to do just that, when a swish of her thoughts kiss my mind—a whorl of smoke that keeps slipping through my fingers: *'Perhaps he thinks that was an accident? Maybe I should nip him again, but ... like ... really hard, just to make sure he knows that he's mine.'*

My lungs are hit with their first full breath since I was shackled in iron. I savour the shape of her thoughts like the addict I am, curling them around my heart where they tame my beast.

The light winks out just as quickly as it started, along with her internal whispers.

Cold nips my skin.

I open my eyes, break our kiss, and gape—snared in the net of Dell's unguarded gaze. Floored by the fucking *vision* of her.

She's no longer covered in filth, nor smeared in my blood, because I'm no longer *bleeding*—my knuckles, chest, and entire body now buttered with perfectly smooth skin. Instead, she's drenched in the soft glow of a flickering lantern flame, a hard-packed dirt floor stretched beneath her ...

I take in our surroundings and something inside me goes very, very still.

She put it all back together again. Every single fucking *speck*.

I cast my gaze over the woman sprawled beneath me, studying every dip and curve of her face like I'm seeing her for the first time ...

"*Impossible.*"

CHAPTER THIRTY-FOUR
DELL

*A*ero hovers over me like a storm cloud while I scan the room, recovering from the flux of heat that just played puppet with my body.

Holy ... *shit.*

Gnarled tree roots jut from hard-packed walls and cobwebs dust the roof in gossamer white. The lantern oozes its creamy light, illuminating the table that haunts my nightmares.

A bottle of oily, green liquid lies discarded next to a spoon face down in the dirt.

Everything appears exactly as it was before my beast obliterated my childhood home in a blind effort to ease my pain.

"Did I just ..."

No. I must be dreaming or ... something. Perhaps hallucination is a by-product of my withering mental state?

Fuck. I've actually gone mad.

"*Remake* the house?" Aero rasps, his breath hot on the side of my face. "Yes, Dell. You did."

Huh ... go fucking figure. My scant sanity lives to fight another day.

"Well," I say, trying to keep my voice steady. "That saves me having to explain the crater to the others when they return."

I can't imagine that conversation would have gone very well. Something a little like *'you're going to be a mother, Dell. You can't go around blowing houses up or skewering your mates in the foot just because you're struggling with some pent-up emotions'*.

I hear Aero swallow.

"Dell?" he bites out, like my name's nailed to his tongue. "What just happened?"

He's studying me with voracious eyes that keep flicking to my neck, and I sense the ardour of his beast hovering just beneath those shields of glazed amber.

Watching me.

I feel more naked than I ever have before, like I'm being dismantled; scattered all over the floor.

"I have no idea," I say, avoiding Aero's scouring gaze. I brush his chest with the tips of my fingers; creating a coarse path on his perfect complexion—no longer tarnished by the damage my beast inflicted during her efforts to purge my bottled emotions.

Strange ...

"Have you done that before?"

"Lit up like a Fae orb?"

He gives me a sharp nod.

"My beast has," I whisper, scribing the swell of his shoulders, convinced his skin is softer than it was before. "Twice. But we didn't fix anything either of those times. Just blew shit up."

"After the Fae Fury bite Kal told us about? Or before?"

I practically knife him with a glare.

The last thing I want to think about while marinating in

the aftermath of our sex is a spider the size of a small dog. Is he purposely trying to dehydrate my vagina?

The corner of his mouth twitches. "Well?"

"*After*. Now can we jus—"

He makes a grating sound and scoops me off the ground so fast I lose all sense of bearing until my arse connects with a cold, unforgiving surface.

Every cell in my body becomes terribly aware and deadly still.

There's a black stain under my bum—old blood fused with the grain much like the way it lingers on the whipping dais no matter how much it's scrubbed.

Aero steps between my thighs and his hands bracket my ribcage. "Breathe, baby. *Breathe* ..."

Not possible.

My skin's too tight. I think it'll split if I attempt to draw a single breath.

"It's okay, Dell. You're here with me. You're safe now."

I'm not.

I'm a child again, sitting on *the* table, looking up at someone I love.

Preparing to be wrecked.

Grind.

Grind.

Grind.

Why is she hurting me? I thought I was her world ...

I squeeze my eyes shut and scream my thoughts—telling Aero I have wounds on my back and a hole in my heart.

That fire is melting my skin.

No matter how loud my mind roars, I don't think he hears me.

He's powerless. Helpless.

So am I.

I hear a rustle and a swish, see a flash of peach and pink

as Aero's wings shroud me but fail to stop the phantom blade from chewing feather and bone.

I'm trapped in this tiny body. Can he see how small I am? Can he see the blood I can feel on my skin?

My head feels light and airy, my limbs begin to tingle ...

He nuzzles my neck, rests his lips against my skin and collects my hair—tucking it between us. His fingers dent my back then slide up the muscles cushioning my spine, kneading the knot of my nightmares.

My entire back volutes as I suck a sharp breath on impulse. It strikes my throat like a blade and makes me taste blood.

"That's it," Aero whispers, repeating the motion—this time dragging down until he hits the dip of my waist. "And another. Come on, Dell. Work with me here."

I try, but my lungs are set in stone. If I draw another breath I'll smell her tears.

I'll choke on them.

Grind.

Grind.

Splayed fingers dig into the tight muscles between my shoulder blades, dragging out across twin stamps of phantom pain, and my wings quiver inside my body as my head tips forward into the scoop of Aero's shoulder.

He nips my neck; a gentle command. *"Breathe,* baby. Or I'll breathe for you."

Fingers brace my spine and traverse down, easing the taut muscles into something less haunted ...

I inhale, expecting the smell of heartbreak, and instead I'm smacked with the scent of citrus and sage and the perfume of our sex.

It's a fucking gift for my starved lungs.

I gulp and gulp until I'm drunk and floating. Until the phantom pain is gone and that cauldron bubbles in my belly.

I'm here, with Aero.

Safe.

Powerful.

I'm okay.

I feel him smile against my neck, the gentle scrape of his canines almost vibrating against my skin. "There you are ..."

His voice is stretched too thin ...

I mould into him, feeling his tendons pop to the surface as I flatten my palms against his back, letting the rhythm of his breathing teach my lungs how to work again. By the time we're synchronised, every muscle in my back is tension free.

"Dell ..."

"Mmm."

"I don't think you were glowing gratuitously when it happened the first two times, and I think it was entirely unrelated to you 'blowing shit up' ... as you put it."

I barely trust myself to speak just yet, but this opportunity is just too good to pass up. "Big word for a ... *big boy*."

He tips his head back, revealing an arched brow and eyes that harbour a heartbeat in their pupils, making me feel like I'm being hunted by some prehistoric predator. I can even sense his beast's tail swishing back and forth, as if it's preparing to pounce ...

My venom's doing a dirty on him, and I'm a bit disappointed he's not gnawing on me already.

I lean forward and nuzzle Aero's chest, petting his skin like I do my inner bitch when she starts flashing her fangs. "Why do you think I got my glow on the first two times?"

Aero digs his face into my hair, skates his nose up the side of my neck, and inhales, pressing his hand flat against my lower stomach. "I think you were sending that light to your womb—protecting these tiny beads of life from the Fae Fury venom."

My breathing stops.

My fucking heart stops.

"And that makes you so much *more* ..."

I put my hands on his pecs and shove him back so I can look him square in the eye. His cheekbones are blades, the rest of him soft—like neither he nor his beast want to step back and let the other have the reins.

"What do you mean?"

My voice is weak. His, the opposite.

"That I know you doubt your capacity to give these children the love they deserve ... however, I have a theory, and I want you to hear me out."

I open my mouth, but he tamps my words by sliding his hand around the side of my neck and gripping hard.

"Something inside you defended these little seeds of life before you even knew they existed; saved *them* despite the fact you were in desperate need of the same energy to heal your wounds." He shakes me a little, probably trying to kick-start my heart. "Don't you see, Dell? You're already more than these children will ever need because there isn't a single part of you that wouldn't give *everything* to see them thrive."

I let my hands slide down his chest and fall into my lap.

The air between us thickens and he gives me a warm, lopsided smile that looks so out of place coupled with his sharpness.

I don't smile back.

I can't even bring myself to blink, knowing my thoughts will spill down my cheeks the moment I do.

Aero just gave me a gift far more precious than he could rightly comprehend. I thought my twisted alter-ego did nothing but wreak bloody carnage ... but perhaps I'm not all that broken after all.

Aero's smile fades, his eyes dipping to my neck again.

Every muscle in my body goes taut as I watch those canines dribble a pearly bead of venom down his chin. I barely register my head lolling towards my shoulder—exposing my thundering carotid—until he starts to snarl ...

My eyes flick to his.

Fuck.

We collide in a clash of teeth and tongue, his feathers rustling while we cram full of each other. My fingers dig into trembling muscle, tug unruly hair, and brush wings that quiver in the wake of my touch ...

Aero tips his head back, dragging my bottom lip. "I love you," he groans around his mouthful of flesh, and my eyes widen.

Hearing him say it with his physical self makes me feel so ... seen. Especially for him to say it here—in the room my mother uttered those exact words when I was sprawled on this table with raw wounds and a broken heart. When I realised the world wasn't a safe place filled with buttery scones and icy swims in the lake; that perhaps my mother's love was so fierce because she knew it couldn't last forever.

When I realised those three little words actually meant goodbye.

But I don't get the chance to make my thoughts tangible as he drops my lip, tugs my head to the side, and strikes.

It's not a gentle claim; it's all hunger and compulsion. The sort of impact that shows he's been wrestling my venom since my teeth slid out of his lip.

He claws my back, that auburn link solidifying, his muscles battling beneath my fingers ...

I whimper with every draw of his thirsty tongue, but it's not enough.

I push until the rest of his teeth gouge my flesh and he's forced to gulp at the gushing wound, picturing myself curled inside his chest—safe and secure—not about to abandon my mates in a house where I spent the most treasured and painful moments of my life.

His canines lengthen and I feel the desperate ferocity of his beast take hold as he gathers me in a crushing embrace, *devouring* me.

Cutting deep, making me *feel*.

He laps and sucks and growls—gorging on my life force, spiking me with venom. It sears my veins, turning me wanton in his arms, lacing me with a lethal dose of desire.

It occurs to me that I'm bleeding on this table again, but Aero's not letting a single drop fall to the wood ...

The frame of my vision begins to blur and I feel the ghost of a smile touch my lips as I dive headfirst into the beckoning darkness.

CHAPTER THIRTY-FIVE
DELL

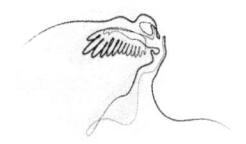

"I can smell her all over you, dick! What did you do, fuck her until she *fainted?*"

Aero's arms tighten around me.

My eyes pop open and I see we're no longer in the suffocating basement ... but on the bed with three cold, angry shadows bending over us.

Freshly shaven shadows.

Nice.

Drake brushes my fresh mating bite, earning himself a sack tap from my Dawn God that makes him curl into a ball of guttural groans.

Aero shifts me on his lap, putting a metal cup to my lips. He tilts it up and I drink the cool water in big, greedy gulps. "You okay?"

I yawn, push the cup away, and nod, waving at the overbearing bastards who are all up in my jam, smelling like concern with an aftershave of ... *Grueling*.

They went to that shithole? I'm so glad they left me out of the family outing.

"I'm fine. The babies are fine. Calm your canines," I mutter, watching Drake massage his balls.

I assess my attire ...

Seems Aero cleaned and dressed me while I was unconscious. What a good man, giving my vagina the privacy to sleep off his probing in peace. I sit up, swing my legs over the side, and catch the waft of an unsavoury scent that has me narrowing my gaze on the sack strung over Drake's shoulder ...

"Get rid of it. Now."

His face blanches, eyes becoming large, metallic orbs. "Are you kidding me? I triple wrapped them, just as Sol instructed!"

"Did he also instruct that beans are on my current hit list?" I enquire, feeling oddly suspicious.

Drake flashes a sideways glance at Sol, his upper lip curling back from his teeth. "That wasn't *quite* how he put it, no ... he just said you're a bit sensitive to smell at the moment."

Sol brushes snow out of his hair and the corner of his mouth twitches. He almost looks ... *amused*.

Fuck my life. How am I going to handle mini versions of these two petty arseholes?

"I was going to bake them into a nutritious pie," Drake continues, pulling a roll of pastry from his sack, giving me a lopsided smile that punctuates his dimple. "It'll be really good for the babies ..."

Well ... damn. That's adorable. And I *really* hate to break his bean-baking heart, but I have to do it.

"Babies say no. Just the smell of them makes me want to hurl my intestines at you. I'm sorry. Maybe an apple pie?"

Drake sighs and charters the sack outside, coming back a few moments later smelling significantly less repulsive.

I watch Sol rummage through his own sack, hauling out clothing and a small bag of—

"Jerky!" Four sets of wings flare as I snatch the bag and tow out a piece the size of my foot, then grind through the desaturated flesh like a woman possessed. "Gold vagina star for you!"

Drake's eyes narrow.

Kal is elbows deep in his own pack, watching me with hooded eyes, his lips curled in a sexy smirk that makes me want to ride his face.

I sniff the air ...

"Please tell me that's what I think it is. Please, for the love of my vagina and her impending doom, please tell me you have cockies in that bag."

"What's a fucking *cockie?*" Drake rumbles, earning himself a rib jab from Kal.

My Night God kneels before me like a chivalrous knight and places a bulging sack of freshly baked cockies in my lap —an offering to his hormonal Blowjob Queen.

I stare at it, too stunned to speak.

A tear slips down my cheek.

"You," I sniff, pulling him up and patting him on the dick, "are a good man. A really, really good man."

Kal chuckles, his penis swelling to half-mast as he throws me a vagina-eating smirk. "There's a small bag of dried flowers in there, too. Chew one whenever you're feeling sick. Took me hours to find someone who grew them in that rancid town."

My eyes widen.

Not only did he bring me cockies, but he also ensured I'm not going to vomit them everywhere.

"And your efforts will not go unrewarded," I say around a mouthful of crumbling goodness, prying open the gauzy bag of potpourri. Three pink buds add to the mess in my mouth while Drake glares at the half-eaten treat in my hand.

"Are you shitting me? Those things have piss all nutritional value. I brought you some prime baby-baking fuel and I didn't get a pat on the dick!"

"Let her eat her snacks," Sol grumbles from his spot on the recliner, rifling through the contents of a bag. "I think our mate has had enough dick for the time being."

Drake grunts and saunters off to help the others assess their supplies now sprawled across the floor.

"Shouldn't I be the judge of that?" I protest before stuffing my mouth full, scanning the ground, doing a mental inventory of the supplies ...

Five packs of jerky, a few bags of dried fruit, three testicles filled with water, a little teardrop vial of ... no idea, and seven blades—three of which appear to be dappled with blood.

More than enough for me to scrape some supplies off the top and they'll still be left with plenty.

They blatantly ignore my question, talking amongst themselves in the language of the arsehole—no doubt categorising their inventory, preparing to store everything somewhere safe and out of the way.

I can't have that. Not yet.

I set my snacks on the bedside table, roll my sleeves, and stand. "Look, I need to be honest with you all. I met another penis on my journey to the East."

Four pairs of eyes flick to my face and Sol stumbles the step he was taking, his hand stretched out towards a toothy blade. "*Gevin mi?*" He shakes his head. "*Excuse me?*"

"It's okay, it's okay," I say, patting the air with both hands and dropping onto the couch. I heel kick a small bag of jerky and a camel scrotum beneath it while their attentions are fixed on my face. "He was a needy little fucker. I had to set him free." They start to snarl and I tap the swell of my lip. "Though, I wouldn't mind being reacquainted with him when he grows up to be a really big Willy, even if he did like to get stiff and choke me."

"Dell," Drake thunders, casting me in his golden umbra while his wings get greedy with the limited space. "Let's get *one* thing straight. You will nurture no cock, big or fucking *small*, aside from ours. Do you understand?" He even has his pointy finger out, ramming it in my face when he should be shoving it up my arse while his dick kisses my cervix.

"That's not very fair," I pout, nudging a small blade beneath the couch—hopefully the clean one. "He was really cute!"

"*Cute?* Are you kidding with me?" He throws his hands in the air and turns to Kal who's glowering at me like I just committed a mortal sin. "Take over before I fuck some sense into her."

Bullseye.

"*Dell ...*" Kal warns, and I bat my lashes.

"Wait," I say, raising a hand, sending a bag of dried fruit sliding beneath the couch with my toe. "I want to go back to the part where Drake fucks some sense into me."

"No, you need to tame that wee womb and *listen*."

I quirk a brow, giving him my full attention, and only because he didn't call my ill-fated womb 'big'.

"Yes, Kal?"

"Look," he says, stalking closer, ducking Drake's outstretched wing. "We're happy to share you between each other, but that's where we draw the line. The hard, non-fucking-negotiable line. And by that, I mean my beast will castrate any cunt who points his cock at you." He tilts his head to the side and I can almost *feel* the wicked sharpness of his beast peering at me through Kal's eyes. "Do you understand, Little Dove, or would you like an example? Because we'd be more than happy to oblige."

I gulp.

I think he's serious. It leads me to wonder what they were doing in Grueling that involved bloody daggers ...

Best I don't ask.

"No ... no example required," I hurry to say. "I don't want anything bad happening to Willy. He's a good dick, and I was only trying to keep him lubricated."

Cue hissing, growling, and a myriad of feathers all up in my face while I spot a flash of Kal buckling his sword down his spine. I can hardly see past all this wing.

I take the opportunity to kick a small sack of ... actually, I don't know what that was—hopefully something helpful.

"I think you all need to show me more empathy," I yell over all their foreign grousing. "Do you know how hard it is to keep a baby penis serpent constantly wet?" I don't bother telling them dry penis serpents are just as healthy as wet ones. I don't want them picturing dry dicks right now.

I stand and plough through a flurry of feathers on my journey towards the bed.

"Wait ... wait a fucking minute," Drake bellows, grabbing my elbow and spinning me to face him. "Did you just say *penis serpent?*"

"Yes ..." I bat some black feathers out of my face. It's a wing orgy in here. "Why, what did you think I was talking about?"

"So ... hang on, let me get this straight. You were caring for a baby *sea serpent?*"

"Penis serpent," I correct. "And I was a really good penis mother, thank you very much." Even if I did haul him halfway across the desert and almost starve the poor dick.

Drake's face softens and he takes another step towards me while the others fold their wings. "I bet you fucking were," he rasps, cupping my face with a hand that almost swallows it whole.

"Screw it," Sol snaps, tossing a blade on the ground. "Inventory can wait."

Four sets of eyes are suddenly on me—four sets of wings disappearing entirely, as if they're trying to make more ... room.

"Do you mean ..."

Group gangbang with my four sexy Sun Gods?

I don't say it aloud for fear it will dissolve, and I can't have that. I *need* this right now ...

To be smothered in their scents and drown them in my own—making sure that any female within a two-mile radius knows that these four men belong to *me*.

To be nobody. Be only *their* somebody.

To be weak. Greedy. Selfish ... even if it's just for one fucking moment.

Sol slides forward and grips the back of my neck, stealing me from Drake and jerking me against himself. "I mean," he growls, his eyes chips of ice, "that it's time you learn exactly what it means to be mated to all four of us, *Sparrow*."

I can hear blood whooshing in my ears as my heart storms into action ...

Hear that, vagina?

Did.

You.

Hear.

That?

An immense presence commands the hair on the back of my neck to stand—Kal's verbena and jasmine scent plumping my breasts full of hot lust. His hands snake around my ribs, canines dragging up the side of my neck and almost drawing blood. "Are you going to be good for us, Kitty?"

The name spurs straight to my pussy, and I nod, tilting my head into the crook under his chin ...

He makes a turbulent sound that riles my nerves.

"Lift your arms." Sol's voice is hoarse as he grips the hem of my shirt. He shucks the layers over my head and my hair gushes out, my bare nipples turning into tight little points.

Drake produces a rough, hearty sound and twists my hips, digging his hand into my trousers—the intrusion making my pussy throb to be touched and flicked and spread. "She's so fucking ready," he rumbles, making me gasp when two fingers glide up into me ...

Probing.

Stretching.

Sol paces like a caged feline, his cerulean gaze *skewering*.

His fists are balled. Chest puffed.

"Pull down her pants, Dawn. I want to see her pleasure dripping down her thighs."

Aero obliges, the strangled material still clinging to one ankle when he nips my arse ...

I whimper.

That auburn tether throbs and I dip my back, glancing back as Aero kneads the hurt with the pad of his thumb.

"She likes that," Sol growls, and a hungry sound spills from my lips. "Do it again."

Aero gives me a sharp smirk and bites into the other globe.

My knees wobble, Sol's gaze like a fucking lure commanding me to keep my feet firmly rooted to the ground.

Drake drops to a kneel, guiding my hand towards my clit before his hot tongue spears into me on a snarl ...

I almost topple over—seizing his hair, crying out, stroking my swollen nub, and *opening* myself.

He's rough and hungry, like I'm the first meal he's had in

weeks. His tongue twists and digs while Aero nips a delicate trail of pain down the back of my thigh—spiking me with his venom over and over again.

I almost back up onto his face just to alleviate this violent urge to be filled.

A hand fists my hair and tugs, Kal's lips skimming my jaw. "Your arse is *mine*," he growls, and I hear a cork pop before warm liquid dribbles down my crack ...

"*What—the fu—is that?*"

I peek over my shoulder at Aero smearing it around, massaging big, circular motions over each cheek.

Stretching me ...

Presenting me ...

While Drake fucking *devours* me.

A thumb grazes my star and I buck.

"A group gift," Kal mumbles, threading his hand around my throat and dragging his thumb across my puffy lower lip. "Lube."

My. Gods.

I'm the luckiest girl in the world.

"*Gold vagi—stars fo—e'ryon'!*" I holler, gaining three chuckles and one appreciative grunt.

Sol stalks towards the bed and I watch him strip through half-lidded eyes, seeing strong slabs of muscle twist against tapered lines. He unbuttons his pants, his dick lurches free, and my mouth drops open ...

He looks about ready to carve me down the middle with his cock.

He stretches out on the corner of the bed, his legs hanging off the edge while he fists himself, giving me a flash of teeth that's all predator. "Get over here. Now. I need to fuck you."

I'm nudged towards the bed on shaky legs, snatched around the waist, and planted on Sol—stretched out and straddling him, sketching his hot skin with the tips of my fingers.

"You're going to let me ... ride you?" I ask, knowing he prefers me on my hands and knees with my arse in the air ... *submitting*.

He twists my hair around his wrist and guides my head until the shell of my ear is brushing his lips ...

"I want our baby between us."

A weak sound slips out of me; those low, raspy words flattening my lungs and making my heart flip.

He tugs my hair until my neck is stretched—scalp stinging from his dominance. "Now, spread that pussy for me."

Fuck ...

I reach between us, back arched and tits poking forward, and part my wet flesh before he pushes up into me—his muscles hard and bulging with each stroke of his hips. His abs tighten as he crunches up and digs his teeth into my neck, leaving me corrupted by lust ... stuffed full and losing my fucking mind.

Someone grips an arse cheek, opens me up, and a slippery finger pushes into my tight, little star ...

Again.

And *again*.

I hear Kal *purr*—feel it vibrate up my arse through his fucking *finger*—and it stirs a hunger that loosens my hips and has sweat gathering down my spine.

Drake crouches next to me and smears lube over my breasts, swirling it around the hard peaks of my nipples. Aero slides onto the bed, that hungry Dawn cock staring me in the face, and I peek at him through my lashes as he fists it with a white-knuckled grip ...

Sol tugs on my hair and my mouth pops open.

Oh ... *god*.

This is it. The moment of truth.

Aero guides the big, round tip past my lips, and I'm silently proud of myself for taking his girth without dislocating my jaw.

"More?" he asks, and I nod, pushing onto him until he's nudging the back of my throat ...

I'm suddenly fucking *starving*.

I rock back and forth, jerking the base while I lather him with spit. Sol grips my hips and spikes me with asserting hits of *rapture* while Kal matches him with the stretching pleasure of his finger ...

Drake continues to massage my bouncing breasts with slick, precise sweeps, and from my peripheral, I see his dick sliding through his tight grip—oiled and hard and *ready* for me.

A bead of pre-cum rolls down the tip and the lower half of my body constricts ...

I pull off Aero with a *pop* and catch that pearly drop with the tip of my tongue, humming when his saltiness smacks my buds.

Mine.

Kal spreads the rounds of my arse while I glide my tongue around Drake's tip, teasing him, taking his length until he's so deep I can't even catch breath through my nose.

I hear him hiss and it gets me all sorts of riled—choking on his cock while excitement bubbles in my tight chest. He jerks back and I look up, that oily sheen coating my lips while he melts me with a galvanised stare ...

"Harder," I whisper.

Please ...

His eyes widen and he nods, then digs his hand into my hair and sinks back in—my fingers gouging his tensed arse cheek while he gives me what I want.

What I fucking *need*.

Something very large stamps against my tight ring and locks my spine, gagging pleasure streaking down my cheeks ...

"*Relax,*" Kal coos, his voice black velvet and midnight sex under the stars. "And dip your back ... just like that. You're so wet and ready, you'll barely feel me sliding in."

I almost laugh at my arsehole's expense, certain his giant penis is about to prove that theory well and truly wrong.

Sol pinches my clit and I almost break apart—feeling myself grow plump around his brutish strikes.

He does it again and again, only stopping when I'm riding that fucking edge and panting around Drake's heavy girth powering into my mouth ...

"You want it?" Sol asks, and I nod as he drives into me so hard my entire body tides. He swirls his finger around my aching nub, skating that bundle of nerves *screaming* for friction ... then pulls his hand away.

"*Soon.*"

I whimper ...

Bastard.

Someone grips the back of my neck, and I'm tugged back, mouth still hanging open, staring up at Aero's eager length again ...

I salivate.

As he eases it past my lips, I watch all the tendons in his strong arms and neck strain against the confines of his skin. I cup his balls and he hisses, digging deeper, making me gag ...

The sound has me producing a deep belly groan—my muscles clamping around Sol's girth while the rest of my body becomes soft and malleable ...

Kal takes the opportunity to sink his hard, claiming cock into my arse, which is ... *holy fuck.* Where has this lube been all my life? They must have been dishing us the cheap stuff at Kroe's because this ... *this* is the nectar of the Anal Gods.

My hips loosen, my body poised to receive the slow fill of his dick pushing into me, until he's sheathed to the hilt—my every nerve taut and tingly.

I've never been so full.

Fucking *brimming*.

They start to move again, Sol and Kal finding their rhythm, and it's like my body can't catch a single breath between the delicious blows of pleasure.

I reach out, gripping Drake's thick, lubricated cock, and a zap of excitement travels down into my lower belly. I glide my hand up, down, up ... then swirl my thumb around the head ...

Aero's fingers thread into my hair and he jerks his hips, branding his tip against the back of my throat for a long, drawn out second. My cheeks hollow and I gag, stirring that heat deep in my belly—making my pussy tighten.

I feel his dick begin to pulse and I thrive on his ravenous grunts. He pulls back, then drives back in before he tips his head and starts to pour into me ...

I gulp him back like a cum-starved courtesan.

The more of them on me—in me—the more I'll smell like *them*.

Drake's hot, velvet length grows larger in my sliding hand ... his pleasure pulsing through him. I suck the last of Aero off his cock and toss my hair over my shoulder, pushing my tits out ...

"I want your cum all over me."

Drake swears, hot ropes of creamy seed shoot across my neck and breasts, and a deep, satisfied purr makes my entire chest vibrate as it trails down past my navel. He smears it across my lower abdomen, fuelling a tortured heat that sizzles all the way to my toes and kindles a fire in my belly ...

Kal's fingers dig into the rolling flesh of my arse—his

deep-seated throb making me clutch onto Sol's sliding cock. "Fuck yes ..."

Every muscle in my body knots and my spine tries to curl; twin strikes of pleasure driving me higher.

Higher.

Kal digs in deep and *holds*, emptying himself, causing my muscles to grip down ...

"That's it, Kitty. *Cum.*"

The command shatters any remaining composure and my climax bundles me up, then throws me to oblivion.

Kal eases out as Sol paws my waist, my orgasm still rippling around him while he thunders into me ...

It's hard. Affirming. His staking hips a relentless storm; his eyes pulsing with their own swarthy heartbeat.

I tip forward, holding his gaze while I take his lower lip—biting down hard enough to spike him with my venom ... staring past his eyes and into his fucking soul.

He shudders, his skin turns febrile, and he *grows* inside me. Ancient words erupt on a voice that's threatening to become something so much *more*—his wetness filling me up and sliding down the inside of my thigh ...

My bones melt.

I drop his lip and lose all rigidity, folding onto his tiding chest, wanting to disappear inside him ...

I want to stay right here forever.

Bodies shuffle and someone guzzles water. My hair is swept off my back and braided to the side while Sol traces little circles between my shoulder blades that have me wishing I could fall into a deep, sex-induced sleep ...

My spine tingles, my wings burst out with a dramatic

swish, and Sol releases a deep, gravely rumble that makes his chest vibrate.

"*There* they are."

I mumble something incoherent and nuzzle his chest while my feathery tarts pat the air.

Firm fingers knead the bud of a wing. "Don't get too comfortable, Sparrow ..."

"What do you mean?" I murmur, fighting a post-orgasm yawn, vaguely aware that Drake's stacking pillows on the middle of the bed.

"You think we're done with you?"

Ahh ...

I tip my head back and study the cunning glint in his eyes.

Honestly, I did. I just took four dicks at once ... surely they need a half hour cool-down period before I lure them into my vagina flaptrap again?

Kal chuckles and Sol bucks his hips, making my eyelids flutter as every nerve in my body stirs to life ...

He's hard and heavy inside me again.

"If you're not careful, you're going to screw me into a coma ..."

"That's the fucking point," Aero growls with a sharp edge that's a promise of dark, delicious things. "Now, give me those pretty lips."

I almost sob.

That *is* the point, except I'm not going to be the one in a sex-induced stupor ...

They are.

It's a bitter tonic I'll probably choke on later, but that's fine. Just so long as they're safe. Because without them?

There is no world for anyone.

CHAPTER THIRTY-SIX
DELL

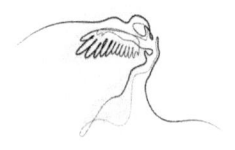

"Why didn't you tell them?"

Aero swipes a curl off my cheek and cocks a brow. "Didn't feel the time was right to casually mention you blew up the house ... then rebuilt it."

I clear my throat, listening to the others slumber through their sex-induced exhaustion. "Fair enough ..."

A yawn splits his face and he throws his head back into a pillow, closing his eyes. "I'll tell them after they're rested."

Glad I'm not going to be around for that conversation.

I climb out of bed and pluck a cloth from one of the drawers in the kitchen. "Just going to the toilet," I mumble, stepping into the storage room.

"Don't take long."

I skulk between the barrels and find my way to the small bathroom. Getting another cold arse branding, I expand my lungs to full capacity ...

My Gods won't forgive me for what I'm about to do, but I refuse to bring our children into this rancid world I grew up in, and I'm the only one with any power. The means to protect myself.

My options are limited.

I clean myself up, then tiptoe back to the room and ransack the clothing strewn across the floor until I find my pants, top, and underwear; purposely making a mess of the supplies so they don't notice things are missing straight away.

Every second is going to count.

"What are you doing?" Aero asks, watching with heavy eyes while I step into my underwear.

"Unlike you, I don't have sunshine pumping through my veins. I need to layer up."

It's just a happy convenience I'm getting a head start on my plan—getting all my base layers on *now* rather than later.

I drag my pants up before buttoning them at the waist ... though the top button doesn't quite reach the fucking hole.

Rude.

"I'll warm you up," Aero says, barely hiding the smirk in his voice as he no doubt witnesses me waging war against my waistband. I throw my hands up and sigh.

"Come back to bed, Dell."

I do, moving like molasses, scanning the room and trying to locate my coat so I don't have to rustle about later. I finally spot it hanging over a seat while I nuzzle against Aero's bareness. He locks me in place with his arms and I marinate in his scent—the rhythmic beat of his chest lulling me into a false sense of security ...

I fit so perfectly.

For the first time since my mother lured me into that basement, I feel such a strong sense of belonging. Like my heart is finally safe again—because I know my men will take good care of it. They've worked too hard piecing it back together to let it go to waste.

And here I am about to leave them, just like *she* left me ...

The thought slaps me so hard my eyes pop open. I know

what it's like to be haunted by the dull ache of abandonment; it follows you around, takes gentle sips of your sanity, and makes you feel like you're untethered—floating without direction.

I wouldn't wish it on my worst enemy, let alone the people I love ...

I don't *want* to deceive them, I just thought it was my only option. But perhaps I've been looking at this from the wrong angle ...

From the angle of someone who's used to fighting from her place on her back—pegged down by a society governed by lawless ass-hats.

Thanks to these men, I'm not on my back anymore, but I've still been looking at this like I'm on my own.

I'm not.

What if there's a way to rescue the girls without taunting those wards, then take care of my father as a unit? Surely that's better than sailing in there on my own and hoping for the best? I mean, if things get prickly, I can trap them in a little God cage. I'm getting pretty good at those.

Fuck. I think I was about to make the biggest mistake of my life.

I draw a deep, unguarded breath, melting into my Dawn God. He's going to be so proud of me for acting like a team player for the first time in my entire existence. I hope.

When we wake, I'm calling a family meeting. Let's pray the others are in a listening mood.

"Dell?" Aero's voice whips at my attention.

I was so deep in my thinking hole that I hadn't noticed his heart pounding against me ...

It kicks up the dust of my anxiety.

"Yes?"

"If your father ever gets hold of you, he can't see inside," he says, the words slow and punctuated. Like this is the most important thing he's ever told me. "He can't see your beast."

An oily feeling, thick and heavy, settles in the pit of my stomach.

Something's going on. Something I don't know.

I close my eyes.

Breathe ...

"What if that's the only option?"

It's *my* only option. It's what my little plan was relying on. If that bitch can blow up a house, she might just have the power to stand against my father.

I feel him shake his head, his fingers deftly untangling the knots in my hair. "No. Not even then. He likes to play with his food, but only if he knows he's got the upper hand. He'll either use you as a weapon or kill you for being a threat, depending on his mood. I know our options seem scant, but you need to know we have a plan."

God-fucking-dammit.

Of course they do. A plan they've been leaving me out of.

I sit up and stare daggers at him. "What *plan?*"

He etches the angles of my face with the tips of his fingers, seemingly unperturbed by the death glare condemning him to the vaginaless pit of my sin bin. "Put an end to him, plain and simple. Take the bastard out."

"But you're warded against killing him," I hiss, trying to keep my rage contained so I don't wake my other Gods. "Whatever this plan is, it's a *suicide* mission."

He rolls his eyes. "You underestimate us, Dell. We now know exactly where that ward is, and it seems the shield he wears isn't immune to iron. We wouldn't even be considering this otherwise."

"But none of you have any power!"

"And he's *outnumbered*," he responds, averting his gaze.

Apparently, the view out the window is very fucking interesting all of a sudden.

I know avoidance tactics when I see them. I practically invented them.

He's not anticipating being powerless. Meaning they're likely planning to use the last two wishes before they leave; hoping they'll siphon a power boost from me.

I *really* need to learn to speak arsehole.

"And the sun cycle? What about that?" Surely my generous vagina hasn't tempted them to forget about their meaning for *existence*.

His hands clamp around my waist and he spears me with a hard look. "Something's gotta give, Dell. You know it, so do I. It's a necessary gamble."

A gamble.

They're going all in with their lives, and everyone else's, on a *gamble*.

My vagina really did a dirty on their common sense.

"Well ... where do I fit into this 'plan'?" I grate out, trying to hide the fact that my hands are shaking—praying he's about to tell me I'm hitching along for the ride so I don't have to peel someone's cock like a banana.

Thunder rumbles in the distance.

He yawns again and tugs me against his chest, unravelling my braid, flattening my hair down my back with long strokes of his hand while I stare off to the side. Waiting. Listening to the unsaid words in the rise and fall of his lungs. "Sol collected a lifetime supply of jerky to keep those teeth occupied while we're out."

I close my eyes and exhale a shuddering breath.

I've learnt to have entire conversations with my fellow whores without uttering a single sound, so I know exactly what Aero's saying right now ...

They're going to tether me to said 'lifetime supply of jerky' with the fucking *wishes*.

They're leaving me here so there's no trail back to me, probably thinking I'll be pliable because I'm laden with Sun spawn.

They should know better.

Aero, specifically, should know better.

There's a chance they won't come back—a big chance I'll be left in this house to raise these children on my own.

I refuse to sit idly by, waiting for the day my father hunts me down and I'm forced to make the decision between carving off my children's wings or exposing them to the wrath of a monster.

I refuse.

Because I know what it feels like to float through Grueling, looking up at everyone from their kneecaps, searching for something to fill the gaping wound in my heart left by an absent mother link.

I stare at that bloodstain on the ground, then at my baby wings nailed to the wall, finally understanding why my mother refused to look back that day she left me on the table smothered in her own life force.

She was ashamed.

She felt like she'd failed me—loved me too fucking much to face what she just did to the child who trusted and loved her mummy with her entire heart.

Who still does.

But she didn't fail me. Not at all. Even from the grave she's showing me the way.

Sitting here is a death sentence, no matter how pretty you paint it. Not just for myself, but for the ones who really matter.

I don't want my children to end up on the edge of a cliff one day, ready to throw it all away.

I nuzzle against Aero's chest and force my muscles to relax—pretending I'm not wound in a knot and bubbling with courage.

It's time for my mates to learn that I can take care of myself.

That I can take care of them.

That I can take care of our children.

And above all ... that I can take care of this messed up world we live in.

A storm rages outside, cracking the sky open and battering the house with more snow.

I shiver.

I'd originally planned to fly into Sterling's arsehole unnoticed. I certainly hadn't planned to risk the Bright. But now this mission is time sensitive, and I doubt I'll be any match for the wild elements if I make a mad flap across the ocean with my unruly beast at the helm.

I remind myself that I have no choice.

Once I go, there will only be a small slice of time before one of my guys wakes up, and then they'll be on my tail like a shadow. Knowing them, they'll probably risk the Bright in an attempt to drag the attention away from me.

But it's a risk I have to take.

Drawing strength from Aero's scent, I allow myself another moment to feel the rise and fall of his chest ...

I can't fail.

"I love you," I murmur before sliding off the bed onto unsteady legs.

Goodbye.

My footsteps feel a lot heavier than they usually are as I pad across the wooden floorboards. I snatch my jacket off the chair, shuck it on, then drop down and slide my hand under the couch—retrieving the blade, jerky, and the swollen camel scrotum. Everything but the dagger gets stuffed in the small bag before I sling it over my head and pocket my pouch of dried flowers.

I retrieve my lock-pick from Aero's pants, then pluck my boots off the ground and clutch them in my resolved grip—blade in the other.

My composure is barely leashed as I watch my mates, praying they sleep long and deep.

Please don't hate me ...

God, who am I kidding? They're going to be so pissed with me when this is over. But they pieced together my shattered heart, so they can't complain about it beating for them.

The backdoor is already open, and I'm thankful for its shitty, unreliable doorknob for the first time in my life.

I steal a final peep at my men, then tear myself away.

Once I'm sitting on the toilet with the door closed, I pull my socks and boots on, tying the laces with unsteady fingers.

Ignoring the tear darting my cheek.

If one of them snaps this door open, I'm screwed. They'd probably chain me to a post somewhere, and I'd only have myself to blame.

I go to stuff the blade into my boot and hiss when its sharp face brushes against the pad of my thumb ...

Iron. That might come in handy ...

Thank you, Karma!

I slide it down the side of my boot and dive into my dark place, finding my beast perched nice and high. She's watching me with wide eyes, her tail flicking back and forth like a whip.

She starts to snarl.

Crap.

It looks like she's in a particularly cunty mood. I hadn't banked on battling Beasty for safe passage ...

"Look, bitch. We can either do this the easy way or the hard way. The ball's in your ... paw."

She lowers herself, wobbling on her haunches, readying to pounce.

Sigh.

The moment she launches forward I fling myself sideways, tumbling low, barely missing a slash of her talons. I crawl towards that tiny bead of light and almost have my hand on it when I get the odd sense that I'm about to be mauled.

I roll over just in time to see her hurtling through the air —paws stretched and lethal talons gleaming. I kick out a split second before we collide, sending her rolling across the ground with a myriad of shadowy thuds.

I snap restraints around her limbs, making her *yelp*.

She makes this odd sort of keening sound from her place pinned to the ground, and I shake my head, trying to ignore the rock weighing down my insides as I sweep the little bead of light into the palm of my hand. It swells until I'm standing in front of that familiar luminescent skin webbed with thick, pulsing veins ...

My beast starts to wail this dreadful sound I've never heard before, but I tune her out, concentrating on the Bright's waxy, radiant skin I'm about to mangle. "Sorry about this ..."

I plunge my fingers into a bulging vein, using my semi-sharp nails to make a messy, fleshy hole. I'm assaulted by a flood of white light as the storm rips apart the sky outside ...

A timely disguise.

Before I can second guess myself, I relax into my fate and step through the rip.

CHAPTER THIRTY-SEVEN
DELL

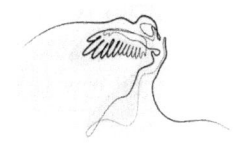

The halls are long and dark ... damp.
Unfamiliar.

So, I overshot my landing zone, and I have no idea where I am ...

Minor inconvenience.

I'm not risking the Bright this close to the castle, so I guess I'll be searching these empty halls on foot until I find something familiar.

I anticipated needing to *poof* some fuckers, and I've been pep talking myself to do just that. Alas, the place is barren of everything but the odd scuttling rat.

I come to a damp intersection sketched with shade and scent both ways. To the left, all I'm getting is more stagnant air, but to the right ...

Blood.

"I'm a real sucker for punishment," I mutter, chewing on a flower so I don't spray vomit everywhere.

I carve towards the source of the thick, metallic scent, down a narrow hallway cast in abrupt pockets of shadow. A particularly dark section has me quickening my steps as my heart rate ratchets up a notch. When I emerge, the walls are no longer paved in stone ... but *bones*.

Little rib bones. Rows and rows of them lined up and stacked atop each other, threatening to topple down and bury me.

I keep walking, almost compelled by this morose pathway to vagina knows where as ribs become skulls with secrets forever trapped behind the forced grit of their teeth ...

I don't think this is the right way. In fact, I think I'm a *long* way off.

The distant sound of chains jingling has my heart leaping into my throat.

What if someone's *trapped* down here? And I'm the idiot considering diving to the rescue, armed with nothing reliable except my iron blade and a camel testicle.

What if it's a trap ...

But what if it's not.

"Goddammit," I hiss, stalking deeper into the halls of death.

Skulls become vertebra, then pelvises—the ground powdered with a bleached dust littered with shards of bone that crunch beneath my heavy boots.

I come to a plain door that's slightly ajar, stepping into a shard of lantern light spilling through the crack ...

No lock.

No guards.

Whoever's in here, the captor believes them to be well enough contained.

I push the door open, step inside the cell, and fall to my knees as my hands flutter to my mouth.

I can't breathe. Can't think. Can't move. All I can do is stare at the woman strung on the wall by the shackles circumnavigating her wrists, her toes barely kissing the floor ...

Her hair is a river of ink flowing over naked breasts, tickling curvaceous hips.

Cleaned.

Groomed.

Cared for.

Her skin is the same colour as the pallid bones heaped around her, like it hasn't seen the sun in far too long. Thick lashes rest on the upper arch of her cheeks—her face appearing to be hewn from a piece of marble.

Her modesty is only mildly protected by the sheet of hair ... and her wing.

Her *one* red wing making a feeble attempt to cloak her skin.

She's the most beautiful woman I've ever seen.

She makes a soft whimpering sound and I lurch forward, digging through my pocket for the metal pin. Iron bites my fingers as I work the shackle around her wrist, trying to pick its brains apart, wondering what happened to this woman for her to end up buried alive in a catacomb.

Perhaps all the bones are parts of people she once knew? Perhaps she's the only one left and she's had to watch everyone she cares about rot away in this cell?

What an existence ...

I feel the moment she wakes up; feel her gaze hot on my face.

"I'm helping," I whisper, jiggling the pick. "Don't scream."

"I won't," the woman replies in a voice that's liquid fire—all sex and sin. It paints my skin and makes my cheeks flush.

The shackle clanks open and I stare at the exposed wrist ringed with savage scars and deep, red welts that dig all the way to the bone.

This woman has been here a very long time.

"What's your name?" I ask in an effort to keep her conscious while I fumble with the other cuff. I have no idea what I'm going to do with her once she's free, but I'll think of something ...

"Sel ..."

I nod, battling the lock, chewing my tongue.

This one's all rusted ...

"Well, I'm going to get you out of here," I say, breathing a sharp sigh when it finally falls away from her tortured wrist.

I half expect her to collapse in a heap at my boots.

She doesn't.

I drop my gaze to her bare feet flat on the ground, then slowly trace the lines of her body until I reach her eyes.

Black eyes.

I stumble back a step.

She inspects her wrists, then stretches her wing and pumps it, sending bone dust gusting through the air. I sneeze as she cracks her neck from side to side before nailing her predatory glower on *me*.

Fuck my fucking life. How do I get myself into these situations?

"Thank you," she purrs, sliding forward like she's floating on air.

I take another step back, Beasty watching from my internal shadows with narrow slits for eyes. The lock-pick slips from my fingers and gets lost somewhere in all that bone dust.

"Don't mention it. We women have to look out for each other, right?"

Right?

Please agree with me. Please don't make me *poof* you.

"What can I call you?" she asks in a voice that's glassy calm but flickers with its own hidden threat.

I try to lie ... I guess old habits die hard. Predictably, it comes out as a strangled choke.

Fucking honesty wings.

"Tssst ... an immortal, then." She cocks her head to the side, exposing a perfectly round breast with a pebbled, pink nipple. "Tell me, doll, what colour are the wings you're hiding?"

Don't tell her.

My conscience *screams* it at me.

She glides forward a step, her sensual hips swaying like a dance.

Something's not right.

Perhaps she's been down here too long? Perhaps she's lost her mind?

Whatever it is, it feels like she's looking at me like I'm a snack. And not a tasty vagina snack. A fucking *meal* snack.

I step back ... into a wall.

Shit.

"I'm—I'm sorry you've been through this ..."

"You're *sorry?*" she snaps, like the crackle of embers. "My darling, I've been either pegged to the ground or strung up like curing meat for hundreds of years. You just freed me. You have nothing to be *sorry* about."

My relief is so consuming that I nearly hug the frightening, beautiful creature. "Oh, good. Well ... in that case, I'll just be goi—"

She dips her nose into the crook of my neck, drawing a deep breath and making my spine lock. "Under the musk of all that cum, you smell *good.*" My cheeks heat as her lips brush my throat, canines dimpling my flesh, nipples skimming my jacket. "Very, *very* good ..."

Surely, she's not going to try and take a bite out of me ...

Surely.

Her ears flick and she stabs her gaze to the door for a

swift moment. When she glances back at me, I can almost see a spark of fear in her eyes. She twists her finger through the strap between my breasts, snaps it, then swings my bag into her hand while narrowing her eyes on my coat. "Take it off. Now."

I get right to work on the buttons. Not because I'm intimidated ... even though I *am* intimidated ... but because she has her labia out for everyone to see.

Every girl deserves a bit of modesty.

She snatches the coat and shucks it on, manoeuvring her lonely wing through one of the slits in the back. After the last button is secure and her tits are no longer in my face, she flicks her hair over her shoulder and pulls my bag to her chest. "Good luck with the pregnancy." She tucks a rivulet of hair behind her ear, her almond eyes seeming to darken further. "Pray for a boy. None of my females survived."

My mind empties. Did she just say what I think she said?

No. The words came out too smooth, too unblemished.

Maybe I misheard ...

She takes three steps back before she lopes to the doorway and slips through, leaving me brewing in total silence. I've never been more thankful for it in my entire life.

My breath whooshes out of me as I drag my back down the wall ...

She just took my camel scrotum. And my jerky. And the flowers Kal worked so hard to find.

Who the hell does that?

I'm so glad I had the foresight to stuff the blade in my boot. Small mercies.

I don't know what just happened, but I hope that woman finds the help she needs and learns it isn't kosher to steal a pregnant woman's jerky.

I come to the easy conclusion there's no way I'm running back down those halls again ...

No fucking way. Who knows what else I might inevitably stumble upon?

I need to use the Bright one more time if I want to avoid getting eaten by that black-haired woman who may or may not have a taste for Fae flesh.

CHAPTER THIRTY-EIGHT
KAL

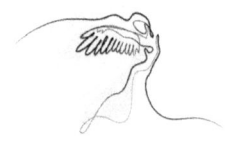

I nuzzle against the soft skin pillowing my face, wind my arm and leg around Dell's curvy body, and let out a long, lustful hum.

This ... this is *bliss*. Waking up tucked around my girl, feeling her chest rise and fall beneath me.

I dance the tips of my fingers over her pebbling skin, making her nipple pucker into a tight little nub ...

My dick hardens against her thigh.

She likes that.

A low, hungry rumble builds in the back of my throat as I cup her breast, expecting to hold the weight of a soft, handful of tit ... but I don't. All I feel is hard, unyielding muscle.

Strange. Perhaps it's the position she's lying in?

Yawning, I brush my hand down the lean lines of her stomach, ready to sink my fingers between her lips and wake her up in just the right way. She's going to be cumming all over my hand before she even realises she's awake. Then I'll lick her clean—make a fucking breakfast out of her.

I cup her crotch, expecting to find Dell's warm, supple pussy ...

But I don't.

I feel a rock-solid cock, raring to fucking rumble.

My eyes pop open and I notice Drake's chest is cushioning my head. He's looking at me with wide eyes that swing down to my hand wrapped around his cock ...

We both scream, swinging arms only getting more tangled, before we fall backwards off the bed and land in a twisted heap on the ground ... soft, hairy balls damn near pillowing my landing and one big, golden dick staring straight at me.

We scream again, shove off each other, and end up on separate sides of the room—both curled in the fetal position.

I know he's not my blood brother but fuck me, close *e-fucking-nough*.

"What the hell!" Sol grumbles from his spot lounged on the recliner.

Sleeping separately to avoid the early morning penis grab ...

Smart man.

He leans forward and musses his hair, his face sliced with a disapproving frown. "What was all that about?"

"Kal touched my dick," Drake grumbles, bunched on the floor, rocking back and forth. "And I didn't like it."

Sol cocks a brow, pinches the bridge of his nose, and then he actually fucking *chuckles*.

Well, I'll be damned.

I feel something trying to strangle my dick, and I glance down, seeing a long, white hair coiled around the base—literally choking my cock.

Despite the fact that my knob is turning blue, I can't help but smile.

I unravel the noose and hold up the hair, glancing at the bed, seeking out my little Goddess so I can give her shit about trying to decapitate another penis.

All I see is Aero, somehow still sleeping despite the fact that I almost put a finger up Drake's arsehole.

"Where is Dell?" I ask, and that wakes him right the fuck up.

Drake instantly uncurls from his tortured ball of limbs and muscle and spears a glance at the bed.

Sol scans the room as he launches out of the recliner. "Must have gone to the bathroom." He snatches his pants off the ground and pulls them on. "I'll go check."

He disappears through the backdoor while Aero prowls towards the edge of the bed where he sits deadly still, listening to Sol make his way to the back of the tiny house.

I can hear Aero's heart pounding, scent his rising anxiety ... or maybe that's mine.

Or Drake's.

We don't need heightened senses to hear Sol curse when he finds the stall empty. I've never seen Aero move so fast—heading straight for the trapdoor. I listen to him descend into the basement as Drake and I pull our own clothes on, reassembling ourselves while I try not to lose my cool.

For her sake, I hope she's down there, otherwise she's going to have four fucked-off Sun Gods on her arse like a third-degree sunburn.

Aero returns in a blur of bristling anger—no longer in charge of his body.

His beast dresses and straps weapons to his chest and hip, his agile movements laced with a lethal sense of urgency. "I *knew* she was up to something."

"Brother, slow the fuck down. We need to think this through. There's a storm out, so she couldn't have gone far."

... *Shit.*

"*Unless ...*"

"What?" Aero booms, his gaze fucking flaying me.

No less than I deserve.

"I taught her to use the Bright. For emergencies."

His eyes widen. "And I was the idiot who told her we had a plan in motion."

"*You what?*" Drake roars, but Aero just snarls at him then rips through the Bright while the rest of us scream at him to stop.

He's already gone.

Drake's pupils have their own pulse as he tosses shit around, searching for his other boot. "We only have ourselves to blame. We should have spent that time talking with her about our plans rather than getting our dicks wet."

He's not wrong.

"My guess is Sterling," Sol snaps, his wings unfurling in a flash of silver. He whips his coat off the side of the couch and tries to manoeuvre it on, but his wings aren't cooperating. He tosses it, searching through the weapons scattered across the floor, each movement a strike of muscle.

Powerful.

Erratic.

I've never seen him look so rattled.

"That doesn't make sense," I counter, saddling my sword. "She wouldn't risk it ..."

"*Gas heighin tev!*" Sol bellows, buckling a baldric over his chest, and I frown.

"*Elaborate.*"

"There were girls in the dungeon," he says, pushing the hair out of his eyes and knifing me with a glare. "Girls she knew from that cesspit she used to live in. We all know she feels some sense of responsibility for their lives."

My blood chills.

Always one step ahead ...

"And you didn't think to tether her to this side of the continent with *that* fucking knowledge?" Drake roars, making the windows shake, his eyes more black than gold.

Sol's wings spread, stuffing the room full as he pins Drake with a glower. "I have other plans for my wish that don't involve having my cock flayed for penning her in like an animal!"

"Like trying to regenerate your balls? I never thought I'd see the day Sol grew a fucking clitoris!"

I drown them out, searching for the iron blade I scored in Grueling. I didn't see Aero take it ...

No.

"She planned this. She took the iron blade ..."

A hollow silence fills the room before we all explode into action.

I stuff my feet in my boots and knot the laces with unsteady hands, my concentration split as I strain to keep my beast contained.

"We have to fly," Drake snaps, layering up—taking what's left of our small armoury and buckling shit around his waist.

Sol nods, sharp and final. "Agreed. We can't risk the Bright. If Aero makes it without getting caught, fucking swell. But we can't rely on that."

I stand, my wings unfurling like restless shadows. Drake swings the front door open and we pour out—shooting into the sky, getting lashed with snow and wind and the bitter reality that we might be too late.

CHAPTER THIRTY-NINE
DELL

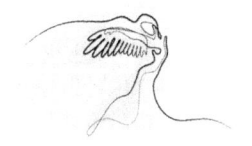

By some twist of fate, I emerge from the Bright right outside Kroe's cell—my gaze swinging to the adjacent one as hollow as the ensuing sensation in my chest.

A pathetic, whimpering sound slips out of me as I latch onto the bars, taking my punishment from the icy burn ...

They're gone.

I'm too late.

I turn to the sleeping shadow curled in the corner of Kroe's cage; his ankle cuffed in iron that doesn't burn his Lesser flesh.

"Where are they?" I roar, slapping my hand against his cell bars and making him jerk into the light. His face has somewhat healed since I saw him last—looking more like the Kroe who taught me how to fuck when I was too young to understand what it really meant.

His eyes widen, drinking me in—taking large gulps.

"Cupcake ..." he slurs with a sleepy voice I wish I wasn't so familiar with. He unravels, the heavy chain that anchors him clanking with the motion.

"Don't call me that."

He swaggers towards the bars, slicking his hair. "Really? But you love it when I whisper it close to your ear." He shoves his face between the bars and paints me with an oily assessment. "When you're pulsing around my cock, giving me all that sweet, creamy filling ..."

"I'm not here for a trip down memory *fucking* lane, Kroe."

"I know," he groans, the ball of his throat bobbing as he reaches down and fists his junk through filthy pants. "You forget how well I know you, Adeline. You're here because you came back for us."

I rear back, watching him screw his own hand ...

I'm not the one turning him on right now.

He thinks he's in control.

There's a nagging twist of my guts telling me something's ... off.

"I came back for *them*," I snarl, pointing to the empty cell across from him, dragging my gaze away from his jerking hand. "So, either you tell me whe—"

"Now, now, Cupcake, put those teeth away," he says with a blatant tint of ownership—as if he's standing centre stage, divvying up his bounty, telling me who to screw. "Your efforts would be better spent on your knees with my cock in your mouth, showing daddy what an obedient little slut you are."

Daddy ...

I take a step back.

Kroe flashes a sharp smile that makes my skin crawl, then starts whistling a tune ... the song he whistles when he's just dished me a decent fucking.

I turn, ready to run the halls and find the girls myself, and realise I'm standing in the shadow of a monster.

The monster who's haunted my nightmares since I was

four years old; since I watched him slice my mother's throat with that blade hanging from the hilt at his hip.

Even though I'd expected this moment, anticipated it, it still knocks the breath right out of me.

Not now.

Not yet.

I'm not ready ...

I drag my gaze up the King's immaculate clothing; black leather pants and a white linen top stretched across his muscular frame. The buttons are undone to his sternum, revealing a peek of his wide, hairless chest with strange markings carved into his pearly skin.

When I finally meet his eyes, my lungs forget how to work.

The blackness in those inky pits bleeds down his face and over bladed cheekbones sharp enough to slice. But it's not the harshness of his appearance that has me withering ...

It's the way he's looking at me—looking down *into* me. Like he's just sat down to feast for the first time in his very long life.

I lean forward, barely enough for him to notice, and draw a little breath through my nose—curious about his scent for my own morose, selfish reasons.

Nothing penetrates that shimmering shield clinging to him like a second skin, and I get this crushing sensation in my chest.

Turns out, my daddy issues are far more deeply rooted than I thought they were.

The corner of his lips quirk. "Daughter. I've been waiting for you."

I shiver—the motion starting at my toes and ending with me clenching my teeth to stop them from chittering. It's as if all the warmth has been sponged out of the chilling melody of his voice.

Looking inside myself, I find Beasty coiled in her shadow den—wound so tightly I can hardly make heads or tails of the bitch.

I prod her, but her only reaction is to quiver like a castrated nympho at an orgy as she tugs a veil of shadow over her head.

Shit.

Is she afraid of him? I mean, I understand, but she's going to have to get over that pretty fucking quickly unless she wants to give up an eternity of Sun God cock.

"Where are they?" I ask with a steady voice that somehow masks the storm thrumming through my veins.

His eyes narrow. "Is that any way to greet your father?"

"Wouldn't know. I've never done it before."

"Well. We'll work on that," he says, splaying his hands. He dangles a pair of shackles made from a shiny metal the same colour and lustre as Kal's sword, but I can see a dull iron band lining the inside of each cuff ...

Manacles that don't pose a threat to *him*.

Smart.

I jerk my chin towards the vile looking things. "Those for me?"

"They are."

I nod.

I'd expected as much. Planned for it.

"You're awfully calm," he states, taking a smooth step forward while he assesses me like a market whore.

I'm not calm.

I'm clinging to my baby tethers with a white-knuckled grip; frightened that if I let go, he'll rip them right out of my heart. My hormones are *screaming* at me to tear through the Bright and take my sun buns somewhere safe ... but there is nowhere safe. Not while this man still has breath in his lungs.

"So are you."

Even the air seems to shift around him as he takes another step, nostrils flaring. "And ..." his brow pinches, "you're *pregnant*."

It sounds like a curse coming from his mouth.

"Yes," I reply, sickly sweet. I even flash him a smile that feels like a lie branded across my face. "You're going to be a grandfather. Congratulations."

He makes a gruff sound and sets his features back in their steely mould.

"*Impossible*," Kroe breathes from his place in the cell, the scent of his shock permeating the air.

I swallow the bile creeping up my throat.

The King prowls towards the cell and looks down on the man who tore my uterus from my body, casting him in a bigger-than-life shadow. "Tell me, Kroe. How many times did you fuck my daughter?"

My heart squeezes itself into a tight ball. The question almost sounds ... *accusatory*.

Kroe blanches and I take a step back, looking from monster to monster, seeing Kroe's flippant confusion and my father's unyielding resolve.

"Ahh ... many times, milord." Kroe dips his head, perhaps in a sign of appreciation for the 'gift' of pruning his daughter's pert little flower in all the wrong ways. He lifts his chin and squares his shoulders with swelling pride. "I had her in my care since she was no taller than my kneecaps."

"In your ... care?"

Something in Edom's voice makes my brows dig towards each other, and I study the side of his face, trying to put my finger on exactly what's throwing me.

"Yes, milord."

"I see." He turns his attention to me, etching me with his stare. "And did you enjoy it, Daughter?"

My cheeks burn.

Well, this is awkward. I tell you what, I never anticipated having *this* conversation with my murdering, psychopathic daddy. I prod my beast extra hard in an effort to absolve myself before I die of fucking shame.

"Answer me, Daughter."

Fucking hell.

I open my mouth to tell him I didn't, that I hated every moment of it; that I *despise* the man in that cell ...

I choke on my words.

My father frowns, his eyes blazing over me with a disapproving smoulder. "I see."

I feel like I've just been sent to bed without dinner for being a bad little hoe.

He takes a step towards me, then another, and then he's standing so close I have to tilt my head back only to be crushed by his heavy gaze. "And tell me, *Daughter*, did you come here today to rescue the man in this cell?"

Easy answer.

I open my mouth to tell him 'no,' but all that comes out is a gargle.

My eyes widen as I choke on the utter shock that I wasn't going to leave here without the man who chained me to his dick for nineteen fucking years.

My father grunts on a long, suffering sigh ... like he's *disappointed* with me.

I definitely just got put in the corner to think about what I've done, and I have to say, it's damn lonely in here.

I hear footsteps and my gaze snaps at the red-winged guards emerging behind my father like bloody silhouettes. Feeling the brand of Edom's stare, I clear my throat, ripping my attention from the crimson puffs poised at their backs while I have a one-sided conversation with my beast about performance anxiety.

I don't have time for this limp dick bullshit.

"Take him to the throne room, along with the new prisoner. Nail them to the stands and assemble a crowd."

"Yes, Lord."

"And fetch the inmates from cell 7,063 and 304; set up separately on the field," he says, his gaze still pinned to the side of my face. "My daughter and I have some catching up to do."

I lift a brow, meeting his cunning eyes.

Am I going to get told off because I spread my legs for the wrong man? Because that's what it feels like. We could be here for a while having our daddy-daughter chitchat about all the men who've dicked me over the years, and I'm on a tight schedule.

I have four unpredictable mates who'll probably be waking up soon, and unfortunately, two of them still have *wishes*.

Drake or Sol could wish me to leave Sterling and I'd be powerless to stop them from going against my father with their limited resources.

"*But, sire!*" Kroe pleads, flinging himself to the ground, peering up through the bars like he's hoping my father will reconsider, unbutton his trousers, and flop his cock into his mouth instead.

I've seen girls look at Kroe the same way—begging for the lesser of two evils—right before he ordered their heads to roll.

"You—you told me you'd free me once she returned ..."

"I did, didn't I?" my father agrees, then swivels his stare back to me, scouring me like a dirty pan. "Well, I changed my mind."

Kroe wilts like a dying flower.

I take a step back, watching the guards unshackle his ankle, then lug him into the hall while my fists bunch and release. Bunch and release ...

I shouldn't care this much.

I don't *want* to care this much.

I want to tear him to shreds. I want to break him apart, bit by bit, until there's nothing left of the man that won't drip between the gaps in my closed fists.

But I also want none of those things.

My father snatches Kroe's elbow as he passes, drawing him so close they almost look like they're embracing. "You really fucked with her, didn't you."

It's not a question. And I'm officially baffled.

"Sire, *please*," Kroe begs, his wild gaze darting to me then back to my father. The smell of urine permeates the air as a damp spot blooms from his crotch.

I thought it would feel vindicating to see Kroe in such a compromised position, especially considering all the times I pissed myself on that whipping dais.

But it just makes me want to vomit.

Edom shoves him at a legionnaire and waves a flippant hand, like ordering a maid to take out the trash.

We watch each other, unmoving, listening to them retreat while my heart bruises my chest cavity. Just when I'm beginning to think I can't stand the silence any longer, he speaks. "Love makes you weak, Adeline. That man broke you in like a prized mare, yet you love him."

I turn my head, preferring to stare in the empty cell than at the monster judging me when he has no right to do so.

"But you also want him dead ..."

I growl as he steps closer, casting me in the overbearing aura of his presence while I take the shackles off my beast altogether—hoping it will entice her to slip into control. "You think you know me?"

"Oh, I do." He plucks one of my curls and pulls, making me grit my teeth against the sharp sting. "I also know how it feels to wish for someone you love to die, if only to put an end to all the *suffering*. We're the same, you and I."

"We're nothing alike."

He threads a cold finger under my chin, tilting my head, studying me so intently I feel like I'm standing in the middle of a crowded room with no clothes on. "And I see you have your mother's eyes ..."

I hiss, the calamity inside me overflowing as I reach the conclusion my beast is a no show ...

I'm on my own.

The thought sits like lead in my stomach.

"But not her temperament," he says, tightening his grip on my chin. "That will have to change. I can't have you setting a bad example of our family. You need to know your place, Little Dove."

"Don't call me that."

"What?" he asks, feigning indifference. "Little Dove?"

His voice taints the name again, and I release a shuddering breath, trying to ignore the tears threatening to spill down my cheeks.

"Did your mummy used to call you that?"

"Fuck you." I jerk my chin from his grip and look away, feeling a tear pave a path down my cheek.

I swat it away.

"Well, isn't that just *precious*."

"You've seen my wings ..."

He doesn't strike me as someone to act on hearsay. He knows for certain they're pure, cursed *white*.

He grabs my hands with a surprising tenderness—a vast contrast to the bite of iron that he clamps around my wrists. "I have."

There's a sharpness to his tone I certainly don't miss as I repress the urge to hiss through the pain.

"You were watching me that day."

"What makes you say that?" he asks, lifting his gaze, leaving a prickly trail in the wake of his path.

"I could feel your eyes on me while I was rescuing them."

Just as I can feel them now.

He makes a small grunting sound, like he's actually impressed.

I hate that pleasing my deranged father somehow makes me feel validated.

"Very good," he murmurs, wrapping a cold hand around my elbow and steering me down the hall, past cell after cell of empty, sullen tombs.

"And the drako?"

He shrugs. "I like games. The surly thing was supposed to come back with a dead Sun God. I even weakened them for him. I peeled some scales for his insolence."

The admission has my entire body vibrating with unspent rage.

He not only planned to kill one of my mates, but also wounded that poor, frightened animal ... because of *me*.

"I noticed you like to torture him," I lash with the bitter whip of my tongue, fisting my hands and making the cuffs bite—the manacles like flaming teeth circumnavigating my wrists.

I have no idea how Sel lasted without chewing her own arms off.

"It was *you* who removed the cuff?" he asks, assessing me with a sidelong glance. "Curious ... I replaced it, by the way."

My lips pull back.

"That pains you?"

I don't answer—just grit my teeth, train my face into something less wild, and try to concentrate on my footing.

"Interesting ..."

He shifts his hand to my lower back, making my spine crawl while he directs me around a corner and up a shaded pair of steps with cobwebs hanging everywhere, like this place hasn't been cleaned in forever.

I sneeze.

Fucking dust.

"I used to be like you, you know. So caring. So *weak*."

"I call bullshit," I murmur before I gather the sense to catch myself.

"And why is that?" he asks as we crest the top of the stairs and start down a long, hollow hall paved with a marble floor.

"All five of us were right here, yet you let me cut them loose. That doesn't sound like a person who's lost their heart entirely." Even though I hate to admit it.

He chuckles, but the sound is curdled poison. "You have me all wrong, child. I was more interested in watching you, weighing your worth. You think I care about four weak Gods who are already bound to me?" he asks, his voice flat and monotone as I stab a glance at the side of his face. "You mated yourself to *puppets*. You'll do well to remember that."

"I don't give a fuck what you think."

He grinds to a halt.

In the blink of an eye, my back is slammed against the wall, his forearm pressed across my throat. Caged in his overpowering dominance, I gasp for air while I study his smooth, pearlescent skin from close proximity ...

It's strange to be sired by a man who looks only five years older than me.

Seriously. Fucking weird.

His upper lip is trembling, his arm hard like the branch of a tree. "Careful, Daughter. My patience can only be spread so thin."

He's trying to intimidate me, but he hasn't tried to *kill* me yet, contradicting the rumour I heard about my father killing his female spawn.

Perhaps he wants to watch me suffer? To rip off a wing and chain me in a dungeon somewhere?

Beasty may have gone all limp dick on me, but I'm not easily bruised.

"I've seen many monsters, *Father*. All of which you've created. You think I'm afraid of you?"

He steps closer until all that's separating us is a thin slice of air and my fragile composure. "You should be. I can take everything from you." He threads his other hand between us and splays it across my abdomen, making my breath hitch. "*Everything*."

I hold his punishing stare, fighting the reflexive instinct to dive into my shadows, dig under my beast, find the seed of the Bright, and flee.

Not my little sun buns.

I may not be able to lie, but one thing Kal's taught me is how to twist the truth to save your children.

I drop my voice and harden my features, picturing them just as sharp and punishing as his own. "What makes you think I give a shit? What makes you think I want to bring children into a world that's so utterly *fucked up?*"

The questions flow like honey, even if the aftertaste makes me want to vomit all over him.

His brow pinches. "Do you, Daughter? Do you want to bring them into this world?"

"No," I say honestly, holding his gaze.

I watch his features drop, turn sour, and twist.

It's the truth.

I don't want to bring my children into this world. *Not as it is now.*

They deserve so much more than that.

Just when I think he's about to put more pressure on his arm and choke me to death, he un-nails me from the wall.

I fall forward, grasping my tender neck as he runs a cold

finger up my cheek. He threads his hand into my hair and tugs, *hard*, making my mouth drop open in a soundless scream.

Just when I thought we were bonding, too.

"I guess we'll see about that."

CHAPTER FORTY
DELL

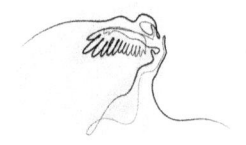

"Now might be a good time to tell you I hate walking," I murmur, as we round another corner in this endless maze of corridors. Perhaps it's my raging hormones, or the fact we've been touring this dusty castle for so long my feet are aching, but I'm channelling my terrible twos. "Not to ruin this iconic family reunion or anything."

He makes this dark, grating sound, and I smirk, giving Beasty another blind prod.

My Sun Gods would be mortified if they knew I was taunting my father, but I know things they don't.

At least, I think I do.

I just have to get my beast to respond, and the bitch does that best under extreme, life threatening duress.

I give her another jab and make a little extra effort to drag my feet.

I'm tugged sideways, towards a large set of double doors embossed in a wall of smooth, white marble—the raven wood engraved with deep filigree.

They're exquisite. But I want nothing to do with them and the sharp scent that leaks through the crack down the centre because they're staring down at me like they want to cleave their jaw open and swallow me whole.

Every bone in my body screams for me to *flee* ...

All the blood drains from my face and I attempt to pull back, about to suggest another fifty laps of the corridors.

Edom shoves me forward. "What's the matter, Daughter? Don't like the *smell?*"

"I—I don't like this place ..."

The words sound like they were cut with a serrated knife.

My father splays his hand on the door. "I'd be surprised if you did," he murmurs, the obscure cadence of his voice making every muscle in my body tremor. "You see, this world is fickle. One minute it loves you, the next ..."

The door swings open and I flounder forward into bitter darkness, hollow of any sound other than the thudding roar of my heart. I suck a sharp breath and gag on a conglomeration of scents so utterly *wrong* together ...

An ancient stillness.

The subtle but distinct tang of the world's boggy arsehole ...

Death.

The back of my eyes burn, threatening to split my composure straight down the middle.

"Let there be light." My father's voice rumbles through the room, and hundreds of Fae orbs flare to life.

I choke on a scream, knees cracking on the marble floor, but all I can feel is the acute ache of my heart splitting open —spilling icy realisation through my chest.

Rows and rows of sterling pedestals line the room, and atop each is a single glass jar.

Within each halcyon vase, suspended in a steeped liquid that looks painfully familiar, is the fragile remains of a small, sleeping baby with tiny white wings ...

Some are no bigger than my palm.

Some the size of a full-term baby.

Each jar is stamped with a little stone plaque engraved with a name.

Roe.

Orien.

Prium.

Haviar.

Van.

Ziorn.

Countless more.

Edom gestures to the mass grave with a wide sweep of his hand. "All of your siblings."

My nausea becomes a living, breathing thing—worming its way up my throat. I want to walk back out those doors and never come back. I want this to be some sort of illusion; a trick fuelled by the man I've spent the past nineteen years hating with every beat of my fucked up heart.

Please don't be real.

The world can't really be this cruel.

I study the sleeping faces with tiny rosebud lips perpetually pouting ...

Peaceful. Like they could wake any moment and cry for their mother.

Our mother.

She'd already lost so much before she gave her life to save mine.

The devastation slams a whoosh of breath from my lungs that spills out in the shape of a raw, twisted sound.

My strong, fearless mummy. She loved me like I was the sun itself. Like her life *depended* on my existence.

After so much loss, perhaps it did ...

My beast digs herself a hole while I fold forward and heave—my body working to expel the meagre contents of my stomach.

"Oh, she never told you?" Edom asks, his feet a smudge in

my peripheral. "The world *created* Mare for me. She was supposed to be the one woman to love me unconditionally." His voice is hollow. Void of a soul; like it dripped out of him, leaving nothing but a cold, empty shell. "And then *this* happened." He spears his arms out and does a slow spin.

The entire place is crammed with my mother's grief.

With *their* grief.

I vomit again, the cuffs gnawing on my wrists while I retch and retch. My father sucks a whistling breath as my wings pierce the slits in my clothes and scoop around my body, like they're trying to protect me from the heartbreaking truth laid out before me ...

Because be it one or a thousand, the ravenous pain of losing someone—that all-consuming emotion that bites into your heart every time you take a breath *without* them ... there is no coming back from that.

No absolving it.

There's only coping ... or not.

My father's not an evil man. He's a broken one.

Tears blaze down my cheeks while I try to avoid looking at all those stony plaques; names I'll never forget for as long as I live.

Fable.

Xies.

Sian.

No females.

There are no females.

Sitting on his heels, he tilts my chin with fingers that bite, forcing me to look up into his velvet eyes. "So tell me, Daughter. Why did you deserve to live when the rest of them died?"

The words are a pike through my already battered heart; I've asked myself the same question so many times, never realising just how painfully accurate it is.

I crunch my eyes shut, fall back, and curl myself into a ball—a pathetic, useless attempt to protect my unborn children from the poisonous pain I can't escape. "*I don't know ...*"

He laughs, the sound dark and bitter.

Dead.

"Well, I guess that makes two of us. And this life growing inside you?" he asks, swiping a tear from the swell of my cheek with the pad of his thumb. "What makes you think your child's fate will be any different to *theirs?*"

I wither under the weight of his words, my wings tightening their hold as if they're trying to dig past my skin and coil around those little glowing filaments.

Vail.

Loui.

Ochras.

Thatcher.

Bron.

Did my mother choose these names when her baby tethers still shone with life?

... Did my father?

"You see, Edom learnt the world doesn't give a fuck. Eventually, he let me wrap him in shadows and shield him from ... *this.*" He waves at the room and I crunch my eyes shut, rocking back and forth, smacking my temples—my cuffs shucking flesh down my wrists.

"Do you think you could handle having hundreds of tiny holes in your heart left by absent tethers? Will you judge him for seeking me out?"

"Shut up," I groan, smacking myself harder; pleading for my flaccid beast to take over and protect me from this pain I don't want to shoulder ...

Does that cast me in the same shadow as him? The fact that I want to curl up in the cosy blackness and *hide* while my beast rides this bitter wave?

I open my eyes to see him studying me with heartless conduct, his gaze almost offering some sick token of compassion. "The world sliced away at you, too. It's obvious if you know where to look." He stands, circles me like a shark, and uses my wings like handles to uncoil my body. I'm tugged back against his chest, his grip tightening around the sensitive bud of my wing—right where it spawns from my shoulder blade ...

He slips an arctic hand under my chin, forcing me to face the calamity before us. "Can you *feel it*, Daughter? The weight of all this loss?"

More tears spill down my cheeks, and I can't help but nod.

His words brush my ear and every nerve in my body knots. "They're innocent. Born of a man, not a beast. But you ... you represent everything I've unleashed on this world. You're the darkness I've nourished. The spawn of a monster." His voice drops to a chilling whisper. "*I* made you, Adeline."

He snaps my wing at the bud.

I release a blood-curdling scream, frigid pain lancing down my spine. My entire body trembles and I'm dropped to the ground like a lump of stone—my limp wing following with a sickening, lifeless thud that rips another scream from my throat.

"That hurts, doesn't it?" His voice is almost sympathetic as he swipes another tear from my cheek—the touch slow and tender.

I hate that my starved soul is screaming for me to lean into him. She's such a sucker for punishment.

"I'm no stranger to pain," I grind, jerking from his touch. My father could break every bone in my body, and it wouldn't come close to the agony I felt when my mother—someone who *loved* me—carved my wings from my back just so she could throw her life away in a blind effort to save me.

He uses the broken wing to lure me to my feet again.

I try not to scream.

I fail.

"Your mother used to say the same thing," he whispers as I'm forced to use him as a crutch, scanning the room, seeing things so much more *clearly* now.

He may think he doesn't care, that he's immune to the hurt ... but I see the truth.

I see brown fluid preserving tiny, fragile bodies; smell putrid traces of the bog.

I see a room clear of dust, debris, cobwebs ...

He visits regularly.

"You're hurting," I rasp, my words a splinter in the silence, and I wipe the remaining tears from my face with the ball of my shoulder.

He spins me around and tucks coiled hair behind my ear —his eyes black stains of ... *pity*. "I'm not hurting. Not anymore."

"Why else would you bring me here?"

His lips curl into the cruel smile I'm starting to believe doesn't suit him one bit. "To call you on your bluff. Show you everything you've got to lose." He nods to my hands and my one functional wing idly protecting my womb. "Mare wasn't the only Goddess to struggle with fertility. I doubt you'll be spared."

The woman who stole my scrotum.

The one who said none of her daughters survived ...

He shrugs. "You're destined to fail. There is no happily ever after for those of us born into divinity ... though I'm sure you've already worked that one out. There's just an endless trail of solitary servitude that takes everything and gives *nothing* in return."

His words no longer sound like the words of a monster. All I can hear is the world of loss stashed behind them.

Not just my father's, but my mother's, too.

And I'm well aware I likely won't get a happily ever after, not that I ever expected one given my muddy track record. But the rest of his statement is so very, very wrong ...

My mother didn't fail anybody. She certainly didn't fail me.

If only I could go back to that day and say it to her face—recreate our final moment so I didn't flinch from her touch right before she kissed me goodbye.

"I don't look around this room and see a woman's failure. I see her heartbreak—her yearning to make a family with a man she must have loved. But that man hid from her pain, from his own, then *you* tore off her wings and tried to feed her to a fucking *drako*." I shake my head, watching his eyes ignite. "She didn't fail you. She *destroyed* herself for you."

The very air seems to still—becoming charged with an energy that lifts the delicate hairs off my arms. His canines pierce his chin, condemning a bead of blood to the ground. "No, Daughter. She destroyed *us*. She broke our bond and almost killed us both because she couldn't stomach my dark side. Because she blamed *herself*."

She broke their bond.

Damn ...

Suddenly, it all makes such terrible sense. Every single fucked up part of it.

"A real man would have picked up the pieces before it came to that." I think of my men and how they protected me, loved me ... *chose* me well before I had a fucking uterus. Back when I was being sold for the meagre price of a token. "*You* failed *her*, not the other way around. And then you turned the world's men into monsters and made every woman suffer because in some messed up way, it made you feel better about yourself."

His eyes glaze over—as if the man just coiled further into

the beast. "You're just a child," he snips, shoving me in the chest, making me stumble and groan from the bolt of pain that lashes my spine.

There's a swishing sound; a flash of white.

When I look up, I see him standing over me with frosty hate smeared across his face and massive motherfucking wings reaching for the walls. *"You know nothing."*

I can't stop the airy gasp that slips out of me.

Divinity incarnate.

His wings have to be twice the width of mine—the feathers long and perfectly tapered. Where mine are fluffy and feminine, his are strong and so white they appear to glow with their own light source.

He's trying to ascertain his dominance, but I won't be intimidated by him ... no matter how big and pretty his wings are. What mine lack in size and brain cells, they make up for in *heart*.

I jut my chin and flare my left wing, gritting my teeth against the pain that punches me between the shoulder blades. "I may seem like a child to you, but I've spent my life in the dirt with a gag in my mouth, trying to pick up the pieces of the mess you made. A woman's worth is not defined by what she can give you ... it's defined by the way she makes you *feel*." My voice breaks on the last word as I crack open, exposing the deep gouge in my own heart—the tombstone of a wilted link I've been nursing for the past nineteen years. "I *felt* my mother's love. I fucking *felt* it. Even in the wake of all this ... this loss."

A muscle pops along his jaw and for just a second, the strong stance of his wings crimp.

I hit a nerve.

Good.

I slide forward, dragging my poor, limp wing behind me

while the other stands strong. "And *you?* You were too *weak* to be the man she needed you to be."

His eyes narrow, his upper lip twitching. "You talk too much."

It's the only warning I get before the back of his hand collides with my face.

My head snaps to the side, my brain rattling inside my skull, blood spraying across the perfectly polished ground.

My beast doesn't lift a paw.

We're trapped in some sort of messed up suspension where his won't fuck off and mine refuses to show her feral face.

"That's because I spent the majority of my life *silenced*," I rasp before spitting a wad of red on the ground.

His sigh is almost palpable.

"You're a difficult thing, aren't you?" he says, producing a white cloth he uses to blot my cheek. It would be a caring gesture if it was coming from the man, not the monster; if we lived in some different reality where he loved me just as much as my mother did.

In a reality where he wasn't the one to put the blood on my face in the first place.

He pinches my chin, guiding me, chasing the residue of my pain. "I bet you grind Sol's nerves. Aero probably finds you amusing, though it's only a matter of time before he's bashing his head against a wall to escape the incessant garble. Drake likely sees you as a convenient vessel to carry his spawn, and Kal's assumedly enjoying a temporary balm for the slashed-up heart he tries to hide by pretending his cock is constantly wet."

I swat his hand away. *"Don't talk about them."*

He frowns as if he actually thought he was giving his daughter some good, fatherly advice.

"Bossy, too," he mumbles as he studies my lips, chin, and

cheek like the bruise that's probably blooming there *bugs* him. "If you were born with a cock, you would have made a worthy heir."

"Funny that. Because ninety-nine point nine percent of the men in this world spend most of their time being *cunts*."

I almost fist bop myself though he doesn't seem anywhere near as impressed with my little observation—shaking his head, folding the cloth into a bloody square he pockets. "You, Daughter, have a foul mouth."

"And you're a big *heigh*."

He lifts a brow. "Oh really?"

Fucking nailed it.

"Yes. You are. And before you reach for the soap, remember I was raised in a whore house, not a palace."

I swear the air chills as I watch him unbutton his top further, exposing broad, rolling muscles and deeply marred flesh.

Strange words I don't understand stain his pearly skin, and I'm oddly drawn to the swirls, jagged lines, and sporadic dots ...

Must be the language of the arsehole.

I don't notice I'm tracing the markings, his flesh *warm* beneath all ten of my fingers, until he snatches both my hands and halts their feathering journey. *"That's enough."*

The harsh words are almost whispered, like they weren't meant for me to hear.

My gaze snaps to his face—to his gritted teeth and narrowed eyes—then down to the pebbled flesh stretched across his chest ...

Oh.

His sparkly shell knits back together as I watch in stunned silence.

He let me past his shield ...

Don't dwell on that, you desperate, fatherless whore.

I clear my throat and jerk my chin at the unique markings stained claret. "Does that blood belong to my ... my mates?"

I glance up in time to see my father's sharp features turn into a weapon of their own right. "Yes," he sneers, tossing my hands at my chest and making the cuffs chew. "And once I've drawn you onto my skin, the bond we have will be *limitless*."

My heart stops beating.

Aero was right.

And if I'm bound by my father's wards, he could force me to do *anything*.

I stop myself from taking that thought any further and square my shoulders—trying to mask the splits in my seams. "What makes you think you'd have anything to gain from putting a leash on me?" I ask, hoping the scent of my pain veils the smell of my terror.

He pops a brow, the white flop of his hair doing nothing to hide his curiosity. "You didn't mist two of my men?"

My lungs seize.

"You didn't gut Drue after he raped, branded, and tortured you, then hacked at your wings?"

He knows what they did to me ... what I did to them.

My wing kinks from the verbal trip down memory lane ...

He rolls back on his heels, looking down on me.

Judging me.

"I'll take your silence as a yes."

My legs give way, but his fingers dig into my shoulders so I'm hanging limp—remembering a dark room that smelt like piss.

Blood on my hands.

"I saw the establishment you *grew up* in." His grip tightens, voice hardens. "What do you owe anyone? All they've done is *take*."

He's been there.

Seen it.

The hammer of shame smacks my lungs and I try to look away—look at anything but him.

I'm hoisted like a puppet, steadied with a hand around my lower back while he pinches my chin, forcing me to hold his harrowing gaze. "Don't hide from me, Daughter. I'm offering you a *gift*." He tugs me so close I can almost feel his breath on my face. "Imagine being judge *and* executioner. Letting the blood of our people slick your skin without feeling an ounce of guilt—making them pay for *everything* they've taken from us ..."

Realisation kicks me in the guts, my beast vibrating as I choke on the breath I finally heave.

He wants to use me as a weapon—wants to sit back while I blow this world to pieces like some grand, symbolic *fuck you*.

Perhaps that's why my beast is so subdued? She doesn't want us to end up chained to my father's monster if she shows him what's in her arsenal but fucks up the kill shot.

She's protecting me by being a limp dick, and I've been over here calling the poor thing a cunt.

"Show me your darkness," he whispers. "Let me bleed you both so we can bond. Isn't that what you want? Something to fill that hole in your heart?"

The question knifes me.

Not like that.

Never like that.

"Think I'll pass," I rasp, shoving away. I dig into my beast's burrow and give the floppy thing a tender pat on her feral head. She deserves a bit of recognition for showing such foresight.

"No?" he scoffs, looking genuinely surprised I just turned down his offer to start a massacre.

"No. Hard no."

Besides, he's proven he's capable of screwing this world

up all on his own. The fact that he used his sleeping sons as a ploy to coerce me ... well, that proves how far gone he really is.

Sol was right; there's nothing left of the man.

There's only the monster.

But Beasty and I, we finally understand each other ...

It's time to initiate plan B and the shield-slashing iron blade stashed down my boot. I just have to take a page right out of Willy's book and wait for the perfect opportunity to strike.

My father's eyes glaze over. "This world's a bitter poison to an unshielded heart, Daughter ..."

Preaching to the choir, daddy-douche.

"I'm well aware of just how bitter this world can be—I've spent the last nineteen years asphyxiating on it. But mass genocide is not the answer. So, unless you want to step back and let me have a conversation with the man who helped *make* this world, you can kindly go fuck yourself, *Lord*."

Boom.

That's what happens when you rile a pregnant whore with a fractured wing, mates to protect, and a broken world to nurse.

"Well," he sneers, looking at me the same way I once looked at a piece of shit on the bottom of my shoe, "I guess we're doing this the hard way."

CHAPTER FORTY-ONE
DELL

"You always sneeze this much?" my father asks, trailing me up the stairs.

I roll my eyes at the ease of which he speaks. He's not even *breathing* hard.

"Yes," I huff, wiping my sweaty face, wincing when the cuffs find more flesh to sink their sizzling teeth into. "I'm allergic to dust, and your *home* happens to be riddled with it. You should take more pride in your housekeeping."

He's let this beautiful, ancient palace go to waste; just as he has the rest of the world.

"I have no reason to keep the place clean," he mutters as we crest over the top of this endless staircase, onto a large landing with another pair of judgmental doors far bigger than the last set.

No more stairs.

I hack a sigh of relief.

"It might be a good idea to tug your wings in," Edom drawls, shoving me towards the doors. "You're only causing the broken one more damage by dragging it around."

Coming from the man who snapped it in the first place? I can't keep up with all this emotional whiplash.

"Plus, they smell ..." I glance over my shoulder to see him scrunching his nose, "*unsavoury.*"

I clear my throat.

They smell like sex. That's what he really means.

I thought he hadn't noticed.

More blood rushes to my cheeks and I officially want to bury myself under a shadow rock.

"I can't pull them in." At least not without an orgasm, but that is not a topic I want to discuss with my sadistic father while I'm plotting to put an iron blade through his heart.

I can feel his gaze branding the side of my face. "And why not?"

Oh look, Karma's a cunt again.

"You don't want to know. Please, don't make me say it."

Please.

We come to a halt before the doors and he taps his foot on the marble ground. "I have all eternity, Daughter. And I'm a *very* patient man."

Fuck my life.

Fuck my fucking life.

"*Because-my-wings-don't-work-properly-and-the-only-way-to-get-them-back-in-is-with-a-wingasm,*" I yell, at the top of my mortified lungs.

I look sideways to see him peering sightlessly at an empty space between us. He opens his mouth, closes it, then shakes his head. "I ... don't want to know what that is."

And here I was thinking my nightmares couldn't get any worse. I'm sure to relive this moment over and over until the end of fucking time.

Ground swallow me whole.

He clears his throat, waves a stiff hand, and the colossal

doors begin to yawn open. He grabs the chain scalloped between my cuffs and drags me into a monolithic chamber while my beast coils further at the vision expanding before us ...

I swallow the lump that works its way up my throat.

Bleached marble walls with tall, peek-a-boo windows offer sips of the pink clouds outside. I arch my neck to see flaming pendants hanging from dainty chains, spilling teardrops of white fire that wither and die before they reach the ground.

It would almost be impressive if it weren't for the rows and rows of armoured legionnaires stuffed in the room—a sea of red pulsing with its own vile heartbeat.

I can smell their twisted desire to *own* me. It perfumes the air and awakens the memory of phantom hands on my skin —of my body crammed with hateful organs that take and take and take.

My wings tremble and pain lances my spine.

Looks like the King's death is going to have a very large audience.

Not fucking ideal.

His immaculate wings are perched high on his proud shoulders as he drags me through a cleft in the crowd, towards the sterling throne lording over us—its backdrop a stretched view of the sky. Men spit at my dragging feet with poisonous tongues and lips that cut straight slashes across their vicious faces.

"Filthy cunt!"

"Whore!"

Really, they should get more creative with their slut shaming.

Their jabbering curses become background noise to my rising anxiety—my skin crawling as a thousand eyes sweep every curve of my body. I'm so busy trying to focus on everything *but* their scouring attention that I let out an indignant squeal when a rogue hand snakes up my inner thigh ...

There's a swift whirring sound before I hear the sickening crack of bone splitting.

The crowd goes silent.

I glance sideways, seeing a black-haired man with a very familiar blade buried hilt deep in his skull, right between his wide-open eyes ...

"Did I say you could touch her?" the King asks, and something inside me stills at his tone.

The legionnaire answers with a bubbling groan, his ruby wings pooling to the ground before he falls forward.

I jerk sideways, right into the unyielding wall of my father—his fingers blunt blades against my shoulder. "Found your dagger, by the way."

"Yeah, I can see that."

Always one step ahead.

I'm still choking on my thoughts—on the knowledge that my plan B just cleaved a legionnaire's skull in two—when I'm dragged forward and flung across the ground.

He just protected me, yet here I am sliding across the marble like a filthy cum rag.

I come to a bone-crunching halt, mashed up against the base of the dais, leaving a smear of crimson in my wake. Stifling a whimper, I shift my body so I'm not crimping my broken wing.

I don't want to show any weakness here. The legionnaires feed off that shit.

"Last chance to show me what's under that skin, Daughter."

With hands that feel like they're bound with fire, I manage to clamber up onto unsteady feet, meeting his imperious gaze. "I can't," I snap as I prod my beast's shaded hole.

It's the truth.

The bitch is comatose. And I'm out of fucking options.

He steps closer, standing over me like a small mountain. "Well. Time to draw the cat out of her cave, I guess."

He has no idea how accurate that statement really is right now.

He waves his hand and the sound of churning chains makes my bones ache. I look up to see two cages dropping from large, black holes in the roof ...

My blood chills.

The King sheathes his hand in a mesh glove while stalking up the dais, snatching something off the throne that jingles.

He tosses it through the air.

A heavy set of keys skim across the ground, coming to a stop at my boots. I stare at them for a long moment before I hear the roaring lick of a small, unthreatening flame that expels from one of the lowering cages ...

No.

Oh, god. *Please, no* ...

Time crawls as I watch them descend with my heart in my throat. They land with twin clanks and I look from one to the other, clutching my chest.

In the cage on my left are the girls from the dungeon— huddled together in a messy pile of limbs and red fabric ... the sound of chattering teeth trying to pull me down.

Their scents are sharp with terror though their features soften when they take in the crooked cape of my white wings —a look of relief that fucking crushes me.

One of the girls is the redhead I wished for Kal to screw. The one with the broken gaze who wouldn't have survived that legionnaire fucking her the way he fucked me ...

Perhaps it would have been a mercy for her to die then? Because part of me is screaming that this can only end in heartbreak.

Sap is in the one on my right; back arched, tossing fire towards the roiling crowd and not doing a single lick of damage. She keeps going until all she's spitting is sparks and smoke and her desperate, frightened roar ... then she sees me, and all the wrath slides off her face.

She flutters close, ramming herself against the bars and crying out with sharp, sorrowful pleas that cleave me down the middle.

Ohh ... god.

"It's okay, baby girl. It's alright ... I'll get you out and back to your daddy."

"Will you though?" my father drawls, leaning against the throne with his arms knotted across his chest, looking down at me with piqued interest.

"Let them go."

Kyro lands atop the balcony outside—a bolt of black lightning scattering the snow.

Sap's little yelps intensify.

His ruddy eyes narrow on my golden firefly, and I slide between them, cutting off his lethal stare.

He releases a short, huffy rumble and extends his wings, showcasing fresh gouges in the stretched canvas of his inky scales ...

I taste bile.

"You want to be the hero, *Little Dove?* Well, now's your chance." The King settles on his throne and gives me a smile that's all teeth. "You have three minutes to free them."

I stare, wide-eyed, an icky feeling settling over me like a second skin. "Or *what?*"

He reaches under his arse with his gloved hand, hauls out a sister set of keys, and tosses them to the floor next to the first lot. "Anyone still locked in their cage will be killed. Good luck."

He can't be serious.

I gape at the keys lumped on the ground like dead, metallic spiders, trying to wrap my mind around this monumental pile of shit I've just been heaped in. I look from cell to cell ...

Surely, he's not serious.

"You're wasting precious time, Princess."

I spring into action, seize the keys, and groan when they sizzle my skin.

Iron.

My heart calcifies in my chest as I turn my back on Sap, throwing myself towards the closest cage ...

Nobody's going to die today. It doesn't matter who I start with.

My fingers are littered with welts by the time I begin plugging the biting fuckers in the stubborn hole. I don't feel any pain over the adrenaline screaming through my body, making my teeth chatter while I fail to contain my whimpers.

The first ring yields no success, and I scream a symphony of swear words I pray will roll my father into a deep, deep grave.

"One minute down!"

I toss the useless set towards Sap's cage and begin working through the second. "Come on, come on ..."

The keys slide away from my fumbling grip and clatter against the marble. *"Heigh!"*

I snatch them back up to the vile melody of my father's chuckle.

Arsehole.

"Costly mistake, Princess," he yells over the swelling roar of the crowd.

Not for me.

If he knew me, he'd know I have an impeccable memory.

I recognise every key I've already tried based on the unique shape of their iron teeth ...

The first one I jam into the hole makes the lock clank open, and the girls breathe a symphony of sighs.

"One minute to go," Edom rumbles, his voice not quite holding the same excited lustre it was before.

I fling myself towards Sap, howling when my broken wing snags on the cage and makes me stumble over my steps. Precious time slips away as I fall face-first into the bars and receive a big, wet tongue to the mouth, dousing me in the smell of fried sheep.

Moaning, I snatch the second set and start to work my way through them. "It's okay, baby. Mumma's gonna get you out of there ..."

Sap rubs her hot body against the bars, trying to get closer, lapping at my fumbling fingers.

She probably thinks she's helping, but there are *twelve keys* left. That's one for every four seconds ...

I can't afford any more mistakes.

One by one, I work my way through them despite all the drako saliva.

Key—hole—twist.

Flick to the next.

Key—hole—twist.

Flick to the next.

Key—hole—twist ...

"Thirty seconds!"

I drop the keys again.

The crowd roars and I almost vomit on the spot. "*No!*" I flounder to pick them up, searching for my place.

"*Ten seconds ...*"

I jam a key in the slot, my heart twisting in my chest when the lock *doesn't clank open.*

There's only one more on this ring ...

I shove it in the hole, turn, and my heart stops pounding when I'm *still met with resistance.*

That twisted, conniving ... *"Fuck you!"*

"Five seconds!"

A sob bubbles out of me, melding with the raw scream that follows as I snatch the other set, my hands shaking too much for me to study the keys properly.

I pick one at random, jam it in, and *twist*.

"One!"

The lock clicks open.

The crowd falls silent.

My heart dive-bombs into my stomach.

I saved Drake's baby ...

My bones seem to fold and I fall back, absorbing the pain of my wings spreading beneath me, my face twisting as silent sobs spill into my hands.

The door creaks and a round body flops onto my convulsing chest; that warm, abrasive tongue lapping all the salt off my face.

She's okay.

So are the girls.

"How sweet," Edom snips, his heavy footsteps thudding down the dais. I hear the other cage door groan. "Out you come, girls. My daughter has set you free."

Dragging my hands down my face, I see the King herding the line of broken women. The limping redhead glances at me—her wide eyes spilling emotion ...

Fear.

"Right this way," the monster drones, directing them past the throne and towards the roofless balcony.

Something isn't right.

I force myself up, bringing the pint sized fire-breather with me as I follow the girls past the massive, black drako, feeling his gaze smoulder my skin. I make a mental note to remove that metal cuff from his hind leg the first chance I get.

Sap's tiny limbs are clinging to me, her head resting in the crook of my neck while I trail the girls onto the colossal ledge dusted with a wealth of snow. When I can no longer feel Kyro's fervid breath on my skin, Edom turns his inky gaze on me.

An uneasiness sours my stomach.

He studies the line of women, then waves his hand towards the edge of the platform that blends with the sky. "Well, *be free.*"

Huh?

What does he expect them to do? Flap to freedom with their *arms?* We're over a thousand feet in the air. I should know. My arse counted every one of those steps and will surely punish me for it.

I can smell the sour tang of confusion though the girls keep their lips sealed. We've seen too many women lose limbs from back talking entitled arseholes.

Edom claps his hands and we all jolt. "*Chop-chop!*"

They start to run in the direction he's pointing, their red skirts billowing like tortured, bloody ghosts—some dragging the more injured ones along.

My father flays me with his stare, a wicked smile accentuating his sharp chin as they pass him by.

The girls reach the edge and spin, eyes wide and so very animated ...

There's nowhere to go.

Nowhere but down.

Edom whistles and Kyro releases a barrelling roar.

Sap nuzzles against my chest as I pivot, seeing black, leathery wings half splayed—his jaw cranking open to reveal a hoard of sharp, pearly teeth ...

Then he starts to charge.

My legs move before my mind catches up, and I stumble out of the way just before he rips by. He gallops past my father with smoke streaming from his mouth, and a couple of the girls make a futile leap of faith ...

"*Noooo!*" I stagger forward, reaching inside, ordering my beast to *do something*.

Kyro releases a torrent of flames and I fall, skidding to my knees at the caustic sound of sizzling screams.

Then ... *silence.*

I heave a shuddering breath, seeing but not seeing.

Feeling but not feeling.

Numb.

That was likely the first sound those women made in years ... and it was their dying screams.

He burned them, just like he burned my mother.

"Go on, Adeline." The words snag my attention, and I roll my gaze to the black-eyed monster who haunts my nightmares.

What did he just say?

My good wing locks around Sap.

"That *thing* you're holding will have better luck surviving the fall than those girls did. But you're going to have to hurry ..."

I blink at him, then peer down at the bundle of gold wrapped in my arms ...

Realisation slaps me in the heart.

No ...

"*You said they'd be set free!*"

Edom's eyes narrow. "But I did set them free. Free from this cruel, twisted world. You're welcome, by the way."

That. Manipulative. Fuck.

I look to the drako perched behind him, prowling towards us; eyes of ember pinned to me.

No ...

Pinned to Sap.

"No ... no!" I scream, holding her tighter. "You can go fuck yourself! I'm not letting her go!"

"Then you'll both get fried, as well as your child. Unless, of course, you show me your beast." He brushes snow off his wide shoulders. "You have thirty seconds to decide."

I'm running before he's even finished his sentence, prodding my beast, trying to get her to *make a fucking move*.

Don't let this happen ...

Please, please don't let this happen!

Sap deserves so much better than this; better than me. So does Drake.

This is his baby.

I'm down on my knees in my internal shadows, shamelessly *begging*. If we fail, we do it with the knowledge that we *tried*.

My cheeks are sodden with tears by the time I reach the edge.

Shackles shuck my skin, my wing peeling back as I kiss Sap on the nose—prying her off my body limb by quaking limb.

She starts to whine like a dying dog, watching me with wide, glassy eyes while I toil with her persistent wings—pushing her away despite every inch of my body wanting to do the exact opposite.

Does she understand what's happening? Perhaps she's only absorbing pieces and her last thoughts will be that I abandoned her ...

I know how that feels.

"I need you to fly, okay?" I force myself to give her a reassuring smile that feels like a lie branding my face. "I need you to fly really, *really* fast!" I press my lips to her wet nose and throw her over the side ...

She makes a keening sound as she plummets, but I hold her gaze until she disappears through a pillow of clouds.

My eyes close, and I tune in to the eventual flutter of her wings ...

Edom whistles.

The landing trembles beneath my feet.

Thump.

Thump.

Thud-ump.

I open my eyes in time to see Kyro dive down the side of the stark, white building, disappearing through the same cloud that swallowed Sap.

The world is silent for a second, like the interlude of a street play. A false sense of peace while I hold my breath ... waiting ...

It's shattered by a roaring lick of flames.

"He likes to fry his meal before he eats it."

The words crack my reverie and I buckle, my chest rattling with barely contained rage as I dip inside to unleash my fury on my beast ...

I fucking hate her.

I.

Hate.

Her.

I hate myself more.

A cold finger swipes my cheek and I gasp but allow my father to wipe away the tears he created. "Don't cry, Little Dove. There's a certain beauty in death ..."

His voice is almost soothing, and I look sidelong at the man who just executed thirteen innocent souls without blinking an eye.

He tilts his head to the side. "I just want to see your darkness. Then this all stops."

"Why?" I rasp, and he frowns, catching another tear before it has a chance to make it far past my lashes.

He doesn't need me to help him burn, destroy, *kill* ...

His face softens ever so slightly. "Even a monster needs company in the shadows ..."

There's almost a glimmer of sincerity in his eyes.

Always one step ahead.

I swat his hand, straighten my shoulders, and stand, looking down into the soulless pits of his eyes with a raging well of hate in my heart. "Look elsewhere. I'd rather go back to the fucking whore house."

Any trace of sincerity melts right off his face, and if I didn't know any better, I'd say he almost looks ... hurt.

Black veins swell beneath the thin, translucent skin around his eyes, and he jerks his head to the side—features whetting into sharp, unforgiving edges as he rises over me.

He snatches the chains linking my wrists, pulling me so close I can feel the aura of pure, unrestrained wrath pressing against my skin. "I'm going to make your pretty heart *bleed*."

CHAPTER FORTY-TWO

DELL

I'm tossed to the ground, the scoop of my shackles bolted to a small length of chain embedded in the marble. I give it a tug, making metal grate against my wrist bones ...

I do it again.

And again.

And again.

The King clicks his fingers, silencing the erratic howls of the crowd. Stone grinds against stone and a previously concealed podium rises from the ground just left of the throne ...

My breath snags.

There, hanging between twin wooden poles, is Kroe—blood dribbling from the gnarly spikes nailed through his palms.

Sliding forward on impulse, I almost trip sideways when the taut chain makes my cuffs bite.

I'm caught in the crossfire of my father's unwavering stare. He clicks his fingers again, smirking like a shark.

More stone shifts, a second podium rising from the ground on the right side of the throne ...

No.

I fall into a boneless heap, my wing reaching ...

Tawny skin I know the taste of ...

Big, wide shoulders.

Auburn hair.

No, no, no ...

Nailed between iron polls with thick spikes through his tender hands is Aero. *My Aero.*

I tug that auburn tether, screaming his name, trying to get him to *look at me.*

A damp, leathery nose nudges out of my beast's shadow den, whiskers twitching ...

Aero lifts his head, wild eyes peeking through the fall of rusty hair, every muscle in his body seeming to swell. Even his hands try to ball into fists while he studies me with black eyes framed by broken, swollen flesh.

In the depth of that anguished gaze, I see something shatter.

His head flops forward, like he can't bear to watch this show unfold.

"Let him go!" The words rip my throat raw as I try and try and *try* to slip my hands from my cuffs.

Perhaps it will peel the skin right off like a glove.

Perhaps the pain will distract me from the haunting sensation of my heart choking on its own beats.

"Maybe ..." My father pulls something from his pocket and gives me a smoky grin—his eyes pots of coal. "I'm partial to a game of chance, and I'm interested to see how many tethers I have to sever to drag your beast out."

Aero's features hone further, and my father slides forward, dark eyes mocking, looking down on me lumped at his feet. "I shouldn't be surprised she's holding back. After all,

I heard my men spent three whole days slicing you up. Raping you. That they even nailed your fingers to a chair before she finally showed her face."

The legionnaires thunder their sick satisfaction at the picture he's painting though Aero's deep, tortured groan is somehow *louder*.

I die a little inside.

"How about an encore?" he asks, and I feel an icy static sweep across the room. Feel Aero's gaze stabbing my skin as I ponder the words ...

Encore?

Edom gestures behind me, and I turn ...

My beast starts to snarl.

A contingent of wingless men with sunken cheeks are being led through the doors at the back of the hall, the skin under their eyes bruised with sleeplessness.

The fuckers from the dungeon.

We should have locked that door and let them *rot*.

They see me and a frigid sort of regard settles over their hollow gazes while Beasty stalks into the open and starts to pace ...

I don't comment on it, don't dare attempt to pull her towards the surface. She might not come if I force her paw.

"Behold!" my father declares with a bite in his tone. "The men responsible for your torture. The ones your *beast* let slip through the cracks. Perhaps you'll bring her out for *them?*"

I hear a choking sound and dare a glance at Aero—seeing all the colour drain from his face.

He recognises them.

My eyes squeeze shut and I breathe through my nose ...

Breathe.

Why didn't I tell him?

I open my eyes and see him shaking his stubborn head, his eyes *imploring* me.

I glance away.

He tugs on our mate tether, but I ignore it.

He starts to snarl—a deep, threatening sound that prickles my skin. If only he could hear my thoughts, I'd tell him to put a muzzle on it. If he wanted an obedient mate, he barked up the wrong whore.

"Let's see if we can find your snapping point, shall we?" my father asks, pacing before the throne in long, lazy strides like we have all the time in the world.

I don't.

Aero's found his way here, it's only a matter of time before the others do, too.

"Griffin for Kroe, claw for Aero."

I suck a sharp breath as he flicks a token into the air. Morning sun glints off its spinning faces before it plummets—landing flat in his awaiting palm. He slaps the coin onto the back of his hand, revealing the fate of whatever fucked up game he has in mind.

He glances down and I hold my breath, my beast's tail flicking back and forth ...

"Hmm, griffin."

Kroe.

The majority of my body softens while a tear streaks down my cheek, and I watch my father stalk towards the man who dominated my body for nineteen years.

The broken King draws his blade, and my beast backs into shadow ...

No.

Please don't leave me.

She's trembling. I've never seen her look so frightened.

I think she hates that blade just as much as I do.

"Tell me, Adeline," my father purrs, placing the sharp, pointy end to Kroe's sternum.

Kroe lifts his head, rousing to full consciousness with a gasp.

"Tell me ... does your heart belong to this man?"

What the f—

Kroe looks at me—*into* me—and I can almost see his soul reaching through his eyes. The vision twists that tiny, shaded part of my heart that belongs to him.

"You really want me to answer that?" I scream, trying to hide the desperation in my voice.

"I do." He presses some weight onto the blade, sending a ribbon of blood trickling down the muscle, tarnishing Kroe's olive flesh ...

The deep, rusty howl that ensues blisters the fucked up organ in my chest.

Kroe makes the same sound when he's climaxing—a sound that signifies the pain is just about to stop.

"And quickly, too," my father throws over his shoulder while Kroe roars my name, making my skin crawl. "This man's a Lesser. They bleed out rather quickly."

My beast makes a meek, mewling sound and I can feel Aero's gaze scalding the side of my face ...

Thud-ump.

Thud-ump.

Thud-ump ...

My heart sounds like the beat of a distant drum.

"Not my whole heart!" I yell while I stroke Beasty, trying to subdue the sick sound spilling out of her. "But yes, part of me loves him ..."

The crowd murmurs and I can't look Aero in the eye.

Yes, I feel filthy. But you can't just heal from a lifetime of torment after a few short months of Sun God petting. I wish it worked that easily—that I was stronger, that I could *forget*. But once upon a time I felt some sense of safety in that dark little room Kroe built for me. Felt companionship in my rotten mattress and hessian blanket; in the rock painted with bloody love hearts which hid all my most painful secrets.

I felt safe from a bigger evil than the man who visited me daily—safe from my father and the bitter reality of my past.

I taught myself to love my chains.

"Then prove it," Edom sneers, dragging the blade down, down, *down* ... slicing Kroe's chest and abdomen clean open.

His intestines spill onto the floor and I stand, pulling my chains taut.

It should be *my* choice if Kroe lives or dies. I did the time, I should get to do the fucking crime, and he damn well knows it!

Edom smirks over his shoulder, slicing Kroe nipple to nipple while I scream at him to stop ...

While Kroe begs me to *make it stop.*

My father's taking my hard-earned revenge, crushing that piece of my heart that should have been *mine* to crush when I was ready.

Mine.

He sheathes his gory blade and peels back the layers of skin doing little to hold Kroe together. Hooking grisly fingers around each rib, he cracks them away like snapping branches, tossing them onto the marble in a small, messy heap while Kroe continues to scream.

I can feel Aero's gaze branding the side of my face while I watch through the hazy cloud of shock. Watch my father shove his hand into Kroe's chest cavity and rip out his heart.

Kroe's tortured sounds fade out, his head flopping forward, and my beast goes stone silent ...

I wilt into a messy knot on the ground.

Limp.

Hollow.

My father strides towards me—crimson death dribbling from his fingers while he carries my revenge like a trophy.

"Hold out your hand," he orders, his voice a dark, judgmental whisper.

I do as he says, a puppet on his string.

The lump of convulsing muscle is flopped into my palm—the organ slimy, wet, and warm. "There, you finally have his heart. Tell me, Daughter. How does it feel?"

I pry my gaze from the red, vascular thing, my teeth chattering as he drops to a kneel—studying me like you would a strange, exotic animal. "Did part of you just die with him?"

My hand begins to tremble.

I lower my gaze ... a thousand words clogged in the back of my throat.

After years of being silenced, I finally have a chance to say anything I want to the monster who let this world rot, but all I can do is look at the bloody heart in my hand as I watch it pump its final beat.

Dead.

He's dead.

I've imagined Kroe's death so many times ... but never as some sick, sacrificial offering from the man who spawned me.

"What an anti-climax," my father tuts, using the front of his shirt to clean the blood off his hands, jerking his chin at someone behind me.

Five guards herd the sullen, wingless shadows until they're crammed in my personal space, reeking of hate and a touch of ...

Fear.

Probably because my beast made them shit themselves last time we saw them.

I notice a long, toothy blade hanging from a white-knuckled fist, and a phantom chill hacks at my spine ...

It's much like the one my mother used on me.

I trail my gaze up the man's familiar arm, all the way to ember eyes half hidden by a fall of red hair.

He winks.

"Daughter?"

I jump at the snap of my father's voice, peeking sideways. He's sitting on his heels, depravity glazing his sooty eyes.

"Please, don't do this ..."

I can't go through this again. Parents are supposed to keep their babies whole, not carve them to pieces.

"Now, you're going to be a good girl and let these men clip your wings."

Kroe's heart rolls out of my hand and thumps against the marble as a warning growl crackles from Aero—his obsidian gaze darting from rapist to rapist.

No, no, no ...

"Is this what you really want?" I rasp, finally finding my voice, jerking against my iron leash again, and again, and again. Blind to the pain. "To *mutilate* me?"

"Yes," he answers, seeming entranced by the sight of my blood dribbling to the ground. "I want *you*, Daughter. Loyal to nobody but *me*." The ball of his throat bobs, and he looks to the man with vengeance in his eyes and a wing-hacking saw in the palm of his hand.

"Slice off the tips, I want her flightless but not ruined." His gaze skims back to me. "One less way for her to *leave*."

They converge and my pure, undiluted fear perfumes the air.

'Don't watch, Aero. Please don't watch.' I know he can't hear me, but my mind screams it anyway.

Someone kneels on my broken wing, pinning it to the ground. I scream loud enough to battle the howling crowd.

Aero roars; the ground shakes. Metal kisses feather and bone. I hold my father's gaze, staring sightlessly into his darkness as that vicious, toothy blade starts to chew ...

The familiar burn lacerates me over, and over, and over.

Grind.

Grind.

Grind.

Don't break, Dell.

Let him see what he's doing to you.

My eyelids flicker with every long drag of the saw, but I hold them open, carving my father up in my own spiteful way.

Grind.

Grind ...

His wide, inky eyes start to blur and I'm forced to blink, sending twin tears darting down my cheeks. His left eyelid twitches and he casts his gaze on the vacant space between us ...

I feel the feathery tip fall away—hear it slap against the ground.

My name cracks from Aero like thunder.

He clipped me.

All I ever wanted was to fly and *he clipped me.*

"Set your beast free and the other one stays intact!"

There's a tremble in my father's voice that I try to ignore.

I suck a sharp gasp, and when he finally looks back to me, I swear I see him flinch.

He's weak. Selfish.

Couldn't even do it himself.

"Fuck. You."

Something hard falls over his face and he looks down his nose at me. "Then it's time to up the stakes," he sneers with a lilt that sounds like disappointment. "I can't wait to see just how hard Aero's heart beats for you, Daughter."

... No.

CHAPTER FORTY-THREE
DELL

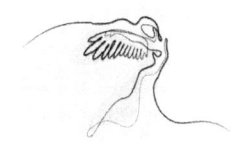

Aero's features soften, like he's already accepted his fate as the King prowls towards him.

I start to snarl and his heart-rate ratchets up a notch.

Thud-thud, thud-thud, thud-thud ...

Beasty stalks out of the shadows with her ears pinned back while I jerk against my bindings, feeling my canines bore down from my gums.

Aero's gaze morphs from resignation to *desperation*.

"Don't, Dell," he begs, his voice strangled. "It's okay, baby ... I've got this one. *I've got you.*"

Too-tight cuffs peel skin down my wrists as I watch my father press the tip of his blade into Aero's sternum ...

A bead of blood paves a path between his abdominals.

We stop thrashing.

The wingless men fall back—that bloody saw clattering to the marble.

"*No ...*" Aero pleads, a tear rolling down his cheek.

We stand, drawing Father's attention from the blade about to gut the man we love straight down the middle.

This chain ...

These cuffs ...

They're too constricting.

We tug, testing the resistance, our fingertips pooling with liquid fire.

Relief crumbles me into a pile of internal shadows.

Father's mouth curls and we sneer at his sick satisfaction. *"There* she is ..."

Yes. Here we fucking are.

He won't be smiling soon.

"You harm my mate; I'll eat your heart."

His smile is all predator. "I don't doubt you'll try. But that's what the cuffs are for."

We tug at them, our hands blazing with a delicious throb of heat.

"I'll remove them once you're *here,*" he smacks the left side of his chest with a closed fist, "once you've shown your loyalty by slaughtering the rest of your *mates;* weeding that pretty heart until you're nothing but an empty, broken husk ... *just like me."* He digs his blade deep, sending a ribbon of red twirling down Aero's torso. "Perhaps then, *Daughter,* you'll realise this world deserves to rot."

"You don't get it," we purr in a voice that's liquid death. "We're already broken."

Our hands curl into tight fists and power explodes, crumbling our fortified iron shackles. Nothing but ash falls away, leaving meaty scars that feed our wrath.

The wingless mortals churn, trying to escape, but that won't be happening again.

They're *ours* now.

We shatter their kneecaps with another bolt of power, watching them crumble in a halo of fleshy heaps.

Screams follow as tendons snap, hands twist, teeth shatter, and we take a moment to scan our victims—wishing these rapists still had wings to shred ...

Pity.

Instead, we *pop* their testicles and watch blood seep from their crotches. Then we mist their dicks—weapons that were used to break us now liquid filling their pants.

We smile, their panicked pleas music to our fucking ears.

When their voices run dry, we *pop* the heads hanging limp between their shoulders—dousing us in red, liquid *death*.

My beast stands a little straighter because it's her favourite *fucking* colour.

We roll our neck and stretch our fingers, listening to the screams of a thousand men who came to watch the fall of a woman they underestimated.

"*That was iron!*" Father roars. He sheathes the blade and stumbles towards us—his eyes threatening to pop out of their sockets.

Yes. It *was* iron.

Seems my dip in the bog didn't rid me of my Lesser immunity to it—something I probably banked on just a *little* too much.

Karma is my best buddy again.

Father clambers to a halt and we watch that glittery shield lift off his skin and expand, rushing towards us. We splay our hands and catch the force, sliding back a step, channelling heat into the thin, glassy barrier.

Our powers collide with a loud *crack*.

His cheeks redden and he grits his teeth as we pour and pour and *pour*. "Knock, knock, *Daddy Dearest*."

Knock.

Fucking.

Knock.

"*That was fucking iron!*" he bellows again, and we roll our eyes—vaguely aware that Aero's ripped his hands from his spikes like a psychopath. He's now lumped on the ground in a pool of his own blood, kicking the shield wrapped around *him*.

Good luck getting through that thing, Morning Glory.

No Sun God is dying today. Not on our watch.

"What are you?"

Father's sputtering puts a little extra pep in our poise, and we give him a sinister smile that's all teeth. "I represent everything you've unleashed on this world. I'm the darkness you've nourished; the spawn of a monster." We narrow our eyes, hitting him with another bolt of power. "*You made me*, Father."

He blanches, edging back a step, his hand glimmering as a luminous spear takes shape in his white-knuckled grip. He drags his arm back, then pitches the sharp weapon, sending it bolting towards our body.

He's aimed it straight at our *uterus*.

What a cunt.

We retreat our attack, moulding our power into a protective dome, when a large shadow drops from the sky ...

Sol lands in a crouch.

We have milliseconds to study his round eyes before a soft grunt puffs out of him and something *tings* against our shield.

"*Sol?*"

He lets out a gargled breath and drops to his knees, spitting blood down his chin. We scan the slice of air between us, seeing scarlet ribbons rippling around his sweat-slicked muscles, the bloody tip of Father's spear protruding from his chest ...

We're only vaguely aware of the pandemonium breaking out, each second crawling by slower than the last.

Beasty coils up and I step into control, feeling her shield dissolve. I wrap my hands around Sol's face and open my mouth to scream.

Nothing comes out.

Like one of those dreams where I'm running from something dark and threatening, but my legs refuse to work properly.

That's how this feels.

Slow.

Painful.

A nightmare.

"No, no, no ..." I rasp, and his hands rise, smearing my cheeks with warm liquid. "No, Sol. No!"

"Shhhh ..." he coos, both thumbs brushing my lips like he's worshiping them. The ball of his throat rolls and I drag my gaze up, seeing amnesty in his powdery eyes. "I love you, Adeline Sterling."

The words strike me.

"Don't say that. We're *not* saying goodbye!" I grip the spear, preparing to push it out of his body, but his hand snags my partially healed wrist like a shackle.

He hacks out a cough and more blood spills from his lips, painting his teeth red. "It will take me quicker if you push it out. Put your shield back up. *Now.*"

I shake my head.

This isn't happening ...

Just another horrible nightmare.

Sol's wings scoop me up, creating a silver shell. I look down at his wealth of white hair while he rolls the hem of my shredded blouse, dips his head, and presses damp lips to my abdomen ...

When he looks up at me through a fringe of lashes, his face is split with the sincerest smile, exposing a dimple on his right cheek that I haven't seen before. "I wish for our child to live a long and happy life."

A rope of warmth twists around my body.

My soul.

Our little sun bun's tether ...

Something mangled squeezes up my throat and my hand flutters to his face. "*Sol—*"

He crumbles sideways, landing in a heavy heap of muscle and long, silver feathers. I watch in muted horror while the father of my unborn child continues to bleed out on the floor, eyes wide and glassy ...

Unseeing.

Lifeless.

Sol's silver link wrenches from my heart, the lancing pain dragging me to my knees while I clutch my chest and *scream* ...

I grip the tether, try to stab its roots back in place. It disintegrates in the palm of my internal hand, leaving a raw, fleshy wound and our lonely baby thread trying to find an anchor to curl around.

An unrelenting vice clamps onto my heart and squeezes so hard I'm afraid it might burst—a suffocating, all-consuming pressure that's too familiar ...

No.

I stagger forward through blood and teeth and bits of bone, wrap my hands around the smooth spear, and slide it out of his body.

Of course he couldn't heal with that thing stuck through his chest.

Now he can—now he'll come back.

Heaving for breath, I roll him onto his back, grab his wing, and peel it off his chest.

It's so much heavier than mine. I love it when I wake up and it's hanging over me like a shield, trying to protect me from all the bad things.

The massive thing finally gives way and slaps into a pool of blood. I throw my leg over his hips and nuzzle into the warm flesh of his neck, cramming myself full of his deep, salty scent. "Don't leave me ... *I love you.*"

The words taste like oceanside kisses stolen under a midday sun, yet they're laced with icy regret.

He can't hear me.

He doesn't know I love him, too.

Warm blood gushes against my chest, my good wing mirroring the large silver one stretched across the floor while I picture myself donning his body like armour ...

Protecting him.

Strengthening him.

My beast coils into a quivering ball, watching me push all my weight against the wound. If I press hard enough, he'll stop bleeding and the flesh will have a chance to knit together.

The world continues to fall apart, but I close my eyes and murmur the song my mummy used to sing when I was sick or sad or hurt.

It made me feel better every single time.

My bleeding always dried up by the time she finished and the pain wouldn't feel so bad anymore.

> *She made her daughter's hair from moss,*
> *Plucked her eyes from a riverbed.*
> *She wove her skin from water's fall,*
> *Then painted her lips an apple red.*
> *She formed her curls with coiled vines,*
> *But forgot to ask them to be tame.*
> *She smeared them with soft clouds instead,*
> *Then prayed she'd love them just the same.*
> *She plucked a star from the sky above,*
> *Then set it in her daughter's soul.*
> *She asked it to watch over her*
> *And keep her daughter whole.*

But the Faeling did not weep or stir
Or breathe upon the lips that kissed.
So, she rolled her up in sunshine,
Then stole a smile from the sun's eclipse.
But still the child did not move,
And so she fell upon her knees.
The mother reached inside herself,
And gave her heart to sow the seed.
And though her daughter was made whole
With pieces of the world's bouquet,
The mother knew deep down inside
She was never meant to stay.
Her eyes would sink to the riverbed,
Her lips would bleed their hue.
Her skin would fall back to the lake,
The moss would take its due.
But perhaps the sun would be so kind
To love her daughter anyway.
And it would piece her back together
In her own mosaic way.

The last word leaves my lips, and I notice his wound is no longer pushing blood against me.

It worked.

Smiling, I peel off his chest and see a steaming, red puddle stretched beneath him—soaking through silver feathers, reflecting in his idle eyes.

My smile falls ...

He has no blood left to bleed.

Another spear cleaves the ground beside me, and I flinch, nudging against Sol's neck, digging fingers into his hair ...

"Wake up. Please wake up."

Beasty steps forward, confusion marring her sweet, feral face as she brushes against the wound in my heart, scenting the damage and licking the lonely baby tether with long, tender laps ...

She nudges the limping organ and I drop the reins, allowing her to slip into control.

It's so easy—a seamless transition as simple as drawing breath. Because I don't want to feel this pain.

Ever.

My beast releases a small wash of power from the tips of our fingers, smothering us with a shield, protecting our mate from the chaos exploding around us. She nudges his cheek, making a soft, mewling sound when his head flops to the other side ...

She snarls, then burrows into his neck and nips the soft skin below his ear, gaining no response.

She sinks our teeth into his pulseless flesh, growling. When she withdraws, she kisses the hurt and scans his tarnished chest; the deep gash not even the slightest bit healed ...

Dead.

Our fingers curl into merciless claws, features whetted by the stone of our wrathful heart. Vicious, bubbling heat begins to flood as reality strikes—cleaving our cauldron in two ...

We failed.

I dig myself into a dark, obscure corner inside my beast—hiding from the truth.

He's gone.

I close my eyes, close my heart.

I tug a shadow over my face and pretend I don't exist, relinquishing control to the feral part of me that does not feel.

I've had enough.

CHAPTER FORTY-FOUR
BEASTY

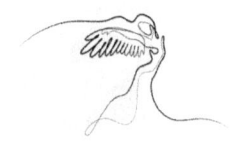

I dip blazing fingers into the gaping wound in his chest, lift them to my nose, and sniff—absorbing the coppery tang that lacks the sweet scent of life.

Searing wrath clouds my vision, honing it into something sharp as I take cunning sips of my surroundings. A churning pit of living, breathing monsters who need to *suffer*.

Free rein, that's what she's given me. Permission to do whatever it takes to protect my most precious.

I can't feel her. Can't see her. She's tucked herself somewhere deep.

Hiding.

I'm not angry about it—she won't cope with what I'm about to do. She cares too much. Too fragile to take a life herself without feeling the whiplash.

I'm not.

They all need to pay for the sick and twisted things they've done to her. To everyone.

They need to pay for taking my mate.

I smear his liquid down my cheeks, acutely aware of the

presence of my other mates. The raging battle that can't touch us through my shield.

I hear Drake scream *her* name over the sound of my thrumming pulse—the destructive throb of blazing heat shooting through my veins, igniting my skin.

Static wisps of power ebb from my pores, creating ripples through the pool of blood stretched beneath me ...

My mate's blood.

I double check my fingers don't end in pointy talons before twisting them through Sol's hair, tipping my head so our foreheads meet—releasing a frothy, poisonous sound of admittance.

Final.

Deadly.

Kal lands outside my shield and I snap my head to the side, hissing, seeing the devastation on his bruised, sweaty face while I defend Sol with my body.

His eyes widen and he stumbles back a step, wings crimping ...

Perhaps he sees the truth in my eyes.

She's gone.

"Fuck ... Drake! Aero! Back the fuck up. *Now!*"

I won't hurt him. I won't hurt my other mates, either.

He should know that.

I draw myself closer to Sol's body, returning my attention to his sightless gaze, the pressure building in the frigid dark of my insides.

The pool of his blood is now cool and sticky.

I taste death on his lips.

My eyes squeeze shut, my lids aflame with *heat*. My fingers dig through his hair while molten pressure contends with my ribs, saturates my organs, and turns my bleeding heart black.

Every hair stands on end as I near capacity; body peeling back, chest dragging to the sky ...

I spawned from the shadows they created—the ones they etched with strokes of their brutality.

They were wrong to disregard me.

They were wrong to hurt her.

They were wrong to take my mate ...

I have no fucking mercy.

I throw my head back and scream for the world that lost its heart a long time ago.

CHAPTER FORTY-FIVE
DRAKE

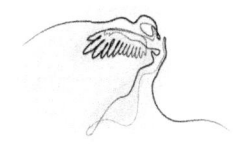

A hollow pulse drums through the room, as if some sort of ocean is pulling back into itself.

I toss a dead legionnaire to the ground—heart going one way, body another.

A sea of heads turn while we stand, float, or perch in a messy cluster of gore and tattered feathers, transfixed by the woman huddled over my fallen brother ...

That dull, dead link in our solar-chain feels like a piece of iron wedged in my heart, and I dare a peek at Sol's unseeing gaze ...

Bad choice. I almost vomit.

Fuck, Sol.

Kal screams for us to run, his eyes wild and so fucking serious.

I won't leave her here, fraying at the edges.

Lost.

I refuse to be any less than the man lying beneath her.

Edom's watching from across the ocean of soldiers, white wings pounding, shimmering with the shield he's probably stacking his energy into. His brows are knotted, dark eyes heaped with calculating intelligence, as if Dell's a puzzle he needs to solve ...

Good luck, fucker. You don't know our girl. You'll *never* know her. Though something tells me he's about to be slapped with some heavy insight.

She tosses her head back, her bloody curls snapping through the air, the exquisite movement laced with lethal power. Chest pointed to the sky; she releases a guttural wail that bites with teeth sharpened by sorrow ...

The sound tries to smudge my brain into a pulp.

Fuck.

I cover my ears, struck with potent, crushing panic. "*Aero! Kal!* You need to get the fuck ou—"

Her hands curl into claws that grip nothing but air, and a wreath of black mist swells then *explodes* from the wild twist of her body. A riot of darkness ploughs through the chamber —crushing bones and popping heads, pulverising legionnaire after legionnaire to a fine, cherry mist.

They don't even have time to scream.

I'm assaulted by the wild storm of death, the haze swarming my body and wings without touching ... without *harming.*

I thrash the protective fucking shield she's gloved me with until ribbons of flesh are peeling off my hands. Nobody could expel that sort of power and survive entirely intact.

Nobody.

When I'm sweaty and spent—when the crimson veil slides off her shield and reveals a flat, empty void with no roof, no walls, and no fucking legionnaires—I see Dell standing over Sol with her wing flared.

Whole.

Doused in the blood of those she just slaughtered, black eyes peering at me through glossy, red skin she wears like armour.

Fucking impossible.

She looks like a Goddess of Death, awash with the texture of her enemies.

My throat turns acrid as she does a tight spin, wearing a sharp smirk while she inspects the carnage ...

"De—"

The Bright splits and her hollow eyes stare boldly at Edom emerging through the spill of light; solid, ancient, untarnished—his face unnaturally pale.

He must have stepped out to avoid his daughter's mass slaughter.

"Chicken shit!"

Edom's eyes flick to me, Dell snarls at us both, and his stare quickly diverts while mine fucking holds.

I watch him take in the claret slab—what was a throne room now just a flat piece of marble perched high in the sky; the cursed throne gone.

She wiped the slate clean.

Dell takes a step towards the King and every muscle in my body knots. A beat rages between them and I start to roar, trying to make myself bigger, digging my dagger into this fucking *shield* ...

The tendons in Edom's forearms become long, sweat-slicked tracks as he drops to the ground, and it takes me too long to realise she's hacking through his defences.

But Edom always has a backup plan.

Always.

He's trying to bait her.

She takes a step forward, then another, and Edom's mouth curls into a wicked smirk before he rips a hole in the Bright and slides backwards through it with lupine poise ...

I know my girl. He might as well have put a fucking leash around her neck.

"Dell, no! Don't you *dare!*"

She doesn't listen. She doesn't even *look* at me—like I'm a random arse mute, not her mate and the father of her unborn child.

She waits two purposeful beats, then dashes directly into the pointy tail of the rip and disappears entirely.

Her shield dissolves and the stench of carrion rams down my throat.

Oh, no you fucking didn't.

I dive forward, sliding through warm wetness as I dip inside myself, desperate to tear into the wispy end of their rip ... make it big enough for me to fit through.

It seals shut, disappears.

I missed it.

She made damn *sure* I would.

I punch the ground so hard a crack forms in the marble. "*Fuuuuck!*"

Aero slashes through the Bright and fucks off without a single word of parting while Kal thunders so loud the hairs on the back of my neck lift.

She's gone.

Edom is the epitome of violence. And Dell? She's *unleashed*. Together, they could turn this world to dust ...

And they could be fucking anywhere.

CHAPTER FORTY-SIX
BEASTY

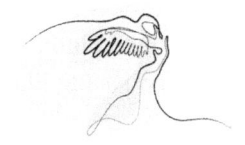

Shards of colour and light slice past, assaulting me as if I'm some sort of cancer muddying the Bright's atmosphere.

Ungrateful bitch.

It's hard not to be offended when I've spent my entire existence protecting that seed of shiny shit like Dell's life depended on it.

My eyes are fixed on what's really important—the man declaring war against *my* world.

My mates.

My children.

He shouldn't have taunted me. He should have let the sleeping beast lie. Now ... *now* I know what I'm capable of. I'm going to feast on his flesh and bathe in the blood of every man who ever hurt her.

He makes an exit wound and pours out with a spill of light. I follow ... but not very well.

My new body grates across punishing, weather-beaten slate, tearing ribbons of skin off my arms and legs.

I inspect the damage, and it's not pretty.

"You made a bit of a mess back there," Father huffs, slipping his hands into his pockets.

I roll my eyes, leaping up, watching him through snow-littered air.

Of course he landed perfectly; he's had time to mould with his pretty skin.

Not me.

I feel like a square beast shoved in a round hoe. And I'm still coming to terms with these blunt, fragile fingers. Talons would be mighty helpful for slicing his heart straight from his chest ...

I'll improvise. My teeth are sharp, I just have to crack through that shield first.

He staggers back as I hone some power into his sparkly wall. "You killed my mate; I killed your men. Tit for twat."

I'm sure that's how the saying goes.

Glancing past him, I see a round table and those tiny chairs brushed in a thick layer of white ...

Neutral Rock.

Not a bad place for him to die, I guess. Unfortunately no audience, but I'm sure I can swallow my pride for the sake of convenience.

"You killed over a thousand men. Your charge was rather ... *steep*."

My lips curl and I stab another bolt of energy at his protective shell. "I'm not done collecting payment yet."

"I can see that," he grits out, and my smirk sharpens as I stalk forward, an extra *I'm-going-to-pop-your-head-then-gut-you-like-a-pig* sway in my step.

"You know," Father gestures to the big, triangular fins jutting through austere waves, "ancient lore suggests that if you kill one of the guardians of this rock, its hungry soul will feed on yours for half a century."

He's stalling. Perhaps he values his head ...

"Learned that one the hard way, did you?"

His nostrils flare and his gaze darts around the table. "Someone I know did, yes." He steps toward the seat I once occupied and grazes his finger across the surface. "You've come here before ..."

I tap my lips, thinking back. My memory's muddy since I'm generally half asleep unless something interesting is happening ... but I certainly don't remember Dell *cumming* on this island. I would have woken up for that. I'm quite partial to voyeurism.

"No ... unfortunately not. They had a chastity belt on us at the time. Bit of a cock block, though I think that was the point."

Father's face slackens. "That's ... not what I meant."

"Oh ..."

"So, *they* brought you here?"

How dare he talk about my mates.

"Yes," I scorn, threading more energy into his shield, watching the vein in his temple pulse. "That surprises you?"

His upper lip twitches, and a force begins to press against my *own* shield.

Oh, I do love a good challenge.

I strengthen my silent attack, feeding on the vision of the tendons in his neck fighting against the confounds of his skin, hoping to see them *snap*.

I'm salivating.

"It does," he says, pointing to a chair—the one I know is black and charred beneath the cap of snow. "Did your precious *mates* tell you who that seat belongs to?"

No, they did not. And Dell rolled over like a severed cock when they refused to answer.

I hiss, stalking forward.

"I'll take that as a no," he murmurs, arching a perfect brow, feigning a casual ease we both know is a fucking smoke screen. He points to my broken wing and the trail of red staining the snow in my wake. "You're not the first red-winged Goddess to break ..."

"My wings are *white*." I pour more heat into my attack, making him grunt.

Sol made the same sound right after Father put a spear through his back ...

My blood boils.

"No," he etches out, then hacks a crow's laugh. "The gore may wash off, but they'll always be stained by the lives you've taken. There is no coming back from that." He takes a step towards me, brushing snow off his wide shoulders, perhaps trying to hide the fact that his hands are shaking. "You think anyone could love a monster? If Adeline slides back into the mould, she'll find that pretty skin hardly fits anymore."

"*Leave her out of this*," I sneer, my nails biting the fleshy part of my palms. "I did this. Not her. She's never taken a life. Not once."

He smacks his broad, muscular chest with a closed fist and flares his wings. "Neither has *he*, Daughter."

I snort. One of those pretty wards must allow him to lie.

"What ... you think you're any different to me? You think you can look in the mirror and not see a monster staring back at you?"

He almost looks sincere.

So fucking manipulative. I have no taste for it. And *she* doesn't need to hear this.

"Is that why you've decided you want me dead?" I ask, splaying my functioning wing. "Because you can't stand to look at my sharp face? Because you see *yourself?*"

His responding snarl is damning.

Dell pushes the shadow off her lily-white face; her hollow eyes curious.

"I want you dead because you're not worthy. You'll never

be worthy." His head jerks to the side like some sort of feral twitch. "I want you dead because you're a fucking *monster*."

Dell places a pearly hand on my heart, suggesting she'd like to take the reins ...

Not fucking likely.

She growls at me, then she starts to *battle* me ...

"I think ..." I clear my throat and pry her hand away, storing her in a pile of shadows like an old pair of boots—screaming for her to *stay down*, because it's not safe ...

She's not safe.

She needs to be where I can protect her from things that might make her hurt. Even if she thinks she's ready to face the world again, I know she's not.

She's exactly where she needs to be.

Forever.

"You think?" he asks, in a voice that's somewhat softer, his tone almost ... *hopeful.*

Dell laps up the sound, scrambling through her shadows, trying to make it to the surface.

No.

Down, hoe.

My feet become anchors, my shoulders square, and I shackle Adeline to a shadow rock then stuff a velvet gag in her mouth, muting her piercing screams.

I'll keep you safe.

I'll never let you hurt again.

I meet his insidious gaze that's not quite as obscure as it usually is.

I'm sick of his games.

"I think you're a dead man."

I release another wave of energy, but this time I don't aim it at his shield. I aim it at this fucking *island*. It explodes into a cloud of grey mist that swallows me whole, and I fall into the chilling embrace of tremulous waves.

Bye-bye, poisoned, ancient relic.

Unfortunately, it's not until I'm submerged, beating my single wing against the angry current that I realise I've made a grave mistake ...

Watery hands drag me down, constricting my airway and shocking my lungs into a semi-state of stasis. The island silt is pulled away by a heaving wave, and I see dark, monstrous beasts lurking—cutting smooth paths through the drab water.

I did not think this through.

Big, glossy eyes lock on to *me*, and I realise I just led myself straight to the dinner table.

Oops.

Adeline's going to be so pissed if I land us inside a megalodon's gut not five minutes after taking the reins.

The creature flicks its tail, slicing towards me, cranking open its cavernous maw.

My hands begin to smoulder with eager power ...

Screw Father's stupid *lore*. This gluttonous creature can have my soul. It's already fucked.

A flash of light illuminates all those shiny teeth as large hands tug me through the Bright like a fish on a line. I land in a feathery, sodden heap on some wooden floorboards— my lungs wrestling with half the ocean I just inhaled.

I hack and wheeze, seeing an aged bloodstain I recognise all too well, and scan the room ... expecting to see one of my mates hanging over me like a feral, pissy shadow.

I don't.

I cock my head to the side, striking my chest—half choking on the ocean, half choking on this strange image.

There, kneeling by the shrine lain at the base of the morbid display of my tiny wings, is Father.

I toss up a shield, then take note of his odd posture.

His shoulders are slumped, his palms up at his sides, and

he's drenched—massive wings lain out behind him, rich with the scent of brine ...

Father was the one who saved me?

It's enough to make me pause for a moment.

Observe.

He lifts his hand, tracing the shape of my tiny wings through the air like he's re-enacting a finger painting.

No.

As if he's *worshiping* them.

"Adeline ..." he rasps like a wish, and my breath catches on the snag of it.

That's a voice I've never heard before.

It's deep and gravely. Weak.

Tortured.

"I'm so sorry," he says, and I watch him reach an unsteady hand deep into the pit of his pocket; the movement slow and awkward, like his body is confused by his command.

When he pulls his hand out again, he's clutching a small, folded cloth that's blotted with blood.

Our blood.

He cradles it the same way I've seen Dell handle that river stone she keeps in her box of special things—like it's the most precious thing he's ever held. He lowers it into the scoop of a soft pink seashell, and I frown, noticing an unconventional pattern ...

Perhaps it's because I'm shaped from unbridled logic, but I can see each piece has some sort of chaotic sense to its placement.

A bundle of vines sits beside a pile of pearly stones, each as big as the pad of my thumb with either a chip or a stain on their otherwise untarnished faces.

Perfectly imperfect.

There's a black stone the size of my fist that glimmers in places—secrets trapped beneath its gnarly surface. It's set in the palm of a white clam that's lost half its structure, leaving only calcified fingers that could pass as the cage of someone's ribs.

Right in the centre of all the chaos is an old birds' nest which cups nineteen perfectly preserved rosebuds. One of them still looks crisp and white at the base, and I think they must have *all* been that colour when they still held moisture ...

Nineteen years since she died.

Dell begs to talk to him herself, and I don't hesitate; not even for a second.

I take a step back into the gloom and set her free.

I may be a monster, but I'm not heartless. Just like Dell, I spawned in the darkness ... so I'm also starved for *light*.

And this moment is not for me.

This moment is for her.

CHAPTER FORTY-SEVEN
DELL

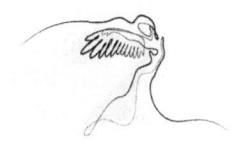

"I failed you," he croaks, his voice no more than a shredded whisper. He pivots and my shoulders fall, all the breath whooshing out of me. "I failed everyone."

His features are no longer sharp like a blade, but smooth and soft—his eyes dull, grey orbs of regret.

I recognise this man. Somehow. From somewhere. But his gaze holds an ancient sort of exhaustion—irises throbbing as if they have their own mournful heartbeat.

His face contorts, like he's fighting an internal battle. One I now understand ...

His beast wants to protect him from the pain.

I push off the ground and stand, looking down on my *father* and not the monster who destroyed this world.

He studies me, the breadth of his shoulders yielding to an invisible force. "You were still here when he came ..."

He.

His beast.

I pass a glance over the stain on the ground and nod.

He closes his eyes and draws a deep, vulnerable breath. When he opens them again, they're flat and hopeless.

"You saw what he did."

It's not a question.

I feel a tear break free, slide down, and marry with the brine on my cheek. His face twists and I brace, watching his eyes pulse with that inky sheen ...

What's left of my heart feels like it flops out of my chest and lands with a sodden *thud* in his lap.

This man is my father.

The one bowing before the shrine of dead flowers and my morbid, splayed wings, tentative to touch them lest he damage the child they once belonged to.

The damage is already done, but I don't say that aloud. I barely allow myself to think it because at this moment, I'm speaking to someone just as broken as I am.

My fingers knead the skin stretched over my collarbone, trying to loosen grief's hold on my heart, wondering if the pain in his chest feels just like *this* ...

Deadly.

Like I'll never know what it's like to draw a full breath again.

His face softens and I try to ignore the warm wash of relief that makes the lump in my throat swell. "You're not like me at all."

I'm ...

"What?"

He shakes his head, features buttering further, almost unrecognisable to the monster my beast wants to disembowel with a rusty spoon. "I broke and it made me weak. What I gained in power, I lost in every other aspect." I open my mouth to speak, but he cuts me off. "You broke, Adeline, and it made you *stronger*."

"I'm not strong." I shake my head, feeling another tear add to the ocean on my face. "I just blew up an entire hall of men because I was too fucked up to care. And the worst thing ...

part of me wants to do it again, and again, and *again*, hoping it will numb this hollow *ache*." I bang my chest and watch his lids flutter.

I certainly wasn't expecting to have a deep, meaningful conversation with my messed-up father today, but here he is ... and here I am, desperately pouring my emotional turmoil onto the floorboards between us.

"It won't," he says, shaking his head, his voice less fragile than before. Almost berating. "But you know those men deserved to die. They're abominations who feed on brutality, bred from a monster who's lost just as much as I have over the years. Maybe more. Hunt every last one down, give them a quick death, and consider it a kindness."

"I don't understand. You're telling me to kill your entire Legion?" Well, the ones who aren't already dripping off his marble slab.

"I'm telling you to make the world *right!*" he hollers, the words clutching me like a frenzied grip. "Because *I can't!* I can't ..."

He's giving me a to-do list. Is this some sort of rewards chart he intends to nail to the cooler box and tick off every night before dishing me my pocket tokens?

Unless ...

I study the shrine at his knees and reality dawns—a brutal slap to the heart that sends me stumbling back a step, dragging the raw stub of my wing along the wooden grain of the floorboards ...

He's familiar with this ... *reliquary*. Not shocked by it.

He made it.

"You knew. This entire time, *you knew* I existed."

I watch him draw a deep, unguarded breath; as if it's the first he's drawn in decades.

"Part of me knew you were no longer a threat; was content with that." He gestures to my wings on the wall.

"The other part ... *hoped* no child of mine could stay silent forever."

My lungs twist into a knot, making it hard for me to breathe.

He planned for me.

Fucking *anticipated* me.

"Why?" I croak, like the crack of a whip. "Why did you *hope?*"

But even as I ask the question, I already know the answer.

It's in the snow dusting the windows, and in the memory of a scar that was once carved across my stomach.

It's in the bloodstain at my feet and those tiny wings that belonged to a girl who was untarnished ... unaware she was the seed of a monster. That she was a monster *herself*, capable of terrible, frightening things.

It's staring back at me, tortured and ruined—a man worshiping my baby wings as if he believes they'll magically fix the world.

Like they're the sum of his salvation.

His head spasms, features honing. "My sword is made from darnium, but it's laced with *iron*," he whispers, his gaze cast on the ground at my feet. "It won't immobilise my powers, but it will weaken me. Don't hesitate, Adeline. *Please.*"

"What—"

"*Don't hesitate*," he thunders, and the voice is no longer just his. It's threatening to become something so much ... *more.*

Something deadly.

He brings his hand up to his chest, curls his fingertips, then drags sharp nails down the beautifully tailored symbols, right over his heart. And I know ... I just *know* he's destroyed the ward which prevented the Sun Gods from landing that fateful blow without killing themselves.

I'm still stumbling over my thoughts, grasping at the fraying edges of my composure when I realise my father's gone. The beast uncurls, rising from the ground like a hungry shadow, every movement laced with lethal power.

He looks down at me with a murderous gaze, his features sculpted by the blade of loss.

Here is the monster who killed my mate, my mother, and threatened my unborn children. Inside him is a broken man who's lost the strength to fight ...

Perhaps that's what he just did.

I stumble back, *screaming* for my beast to take over. Because I know what he just asked me to do, and I can't ...

I can't.

But she's a lump of fluff lying lifeless in my internal shade, as if she's playing *dead*. As if she, too, is *conflicted*.

He stalks me, wings rising—his strong, sleek feathers like glassy blades in the low light. I'm herded against the kitchen bench, pinned to it with his hard body. "So easy to bait," he purrs, coiling one of my curls around his finger like a cat taunting a mouse. "Your conscience makes you weak, Daughter."

Always one step ahead.

My father didn't overthrow his beast; the beast *allowed* him to speak with me because I was gaining the upper hand.

"You knew he'd draw me out ..."

He answers with a lopsided smirk that cuts his face into something even more punishing. "Are you going to run, Little Dove?"

I shake my head, square my shoulders, and slip my hand through the curtain of my wings, searching the bench for my mother's iron blade—hoping one of my mates didn't move the fucking thing. "That's not really my style."

Not unless I'm running from Sun Gods to save my fellow hoes.

"Pity," he scalds, dropping his lips close to my ear, "I rather enjoy a chase."

A blinding flash spits out a bloody, heaving tower of muscle, and I look straight into the wide, ochre eyes of my turbulent Dawn God ...

Fuck.

How is he still in control right now? I thought his beast would be riding him like a pony.

His hands look somewhat healed, which is about the only source of relief I feel from seeing him right now.

His whisky gaze traces the ruined skin on my father's chest, and he sucks a sharp breath through clenched teeth, making my lungs constrict.

My hand brushes against the familiar slice of iron ...

Thank the Vagina Gods.

I snatch the object as I feel the tell-tale ebb of my father's powers ... coiling just the way Willy does right before he strikes.

I take a moment to stroke Aero's link while coaxing my beast off that tiny seed of Bright, then tear into the waxy, iridescent skin and tug my father through the hole ...

And though I know better, I hope to hell Aero's not following our tail.

CHAPTER FORTY-EIGHT
DELL

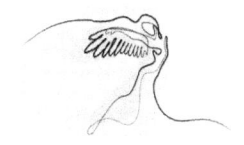

Colour and light zip past while I pitch my mother's blade directly into my father's gut, feeling warm blood rush out to meet me.

His responding roar is almost deafening.

I prod it deeper with a finger, shoving until I'm knuckle deep in flesh and barely fighting off the urge to vomit all over him.

"You little *bitch!*"

It's no killing blow but if he wants to get that iron fuck out, he's going to have to dig deep and pray for a strong gag reflex.

I just evened the playing field. By the murderous look in his eyes, I'd say he knows it, too.

He reaches for my throat as I slice an exit though I quickly realise his grabby hand is the least of my problems.

I intended to plant us on the ruins of the throne room, but I was a little distracted and somehow landed us about ... five hundred vertical metres above that fabled destination.

We plummet like lumps of lead.

He howls while I cling to his oozing body, then throws

his wings out. We come to a jarring halt, and I scream as my grip on his arm slips ...

I'm dangling, suspended above the patio that once held the Sterling relic of his sovereignty.

His expression twists into a victorious leer—eyes darting to my mangled wing hanging off me like a weight.

"White! White!"

His expression fractures. *"What?"*

"It's my safe word! You know, the word I use when I'm gett—"

"I know what it means!" he snaps. "It doesn't apply here."

"Oh ..."

Worth a shot.

His head spasms and his eyes go from pitch black to a soft, molten grey before his pupils expand again. He curls an icy hand around my wrist, and I can almost picture sharp talons digging into my skin ...

I'm forced to loosen my grip, trying to buff the fear from my face.

"He's screaming for me to show you *mercy*."

It takes me a second to realise he means my father—his personal prisoner from the war of his own grief.

A small sound slips out, making the harsh cut of his lips curl. He pries my hand off his arm, holding me aloft ...

"I have no fucking mercy."

He releases his hold and I fall, tumbling towards the ground like a rock; too fast for my scattered thoughts to latch onto that bead and rip into the Bright. My one useful wing tries to catch the air with desperate, irrational swoops that send us into a sickening spiral ...

I release a tortured sound that bleeds straight from my heart.

I scream for Sol, and for my unborn children. I scream for the world that's doomed to meet a cold, bitter demise ...

Most of all, I scream for my father.

For the man trapped in the shadows, about to watch another child die.

The ground swells and I'm struck by a hard body—arms sweeping around me, gripping my waist and the back of my neck. "I've got you baby. I'm not letting go."

Aero.

I glance up, wrapping my shield around us both, seeing his attention locked on the man hovering high above us ...

He's likely pinging the others, alerting them that they now have the freedom to strike that killing blow.

Auburn wings deliver us to the deserted throne room floor varnished with half-frozen blood. He latches onto my arms with unyielding force, shackling me, and I frown, peering up at him through a tangle of curls. "Aero, *no* ..."

There's a flash of teeth and he snaps his wild gaze to me, his hands tightening. "Now is not the time to test my fucking limits, Dell. You're staying right here with me. Kal and Drake will finish him off. This will all be over soon."

He doesn't get it, none of that is an option.

My gaze swivels to Sol splayed on the ground. Lifeless.

So much death.

I open my mouth to have a mature conversation about responsibility, but Aero *hisses* at me.

Whelp. Looks like we're doing this the painful way. Can't say I didn't try.

I whisper to my beast ... calling her. She prowls towards me, no doubt picturing all the gory ways she wants to shred my father for tossing me to the ground like a piece of trash.

I wait until she's so close I can smell her lust for blood, then I snatch her by the scruff, pin her to my shadows, and scream at her to give me the *fucking* power.

She cocks her head to the side, licks her lips, and nods.

Huh?

'Really? That's it? I thought you'd demand a severed testicle as payment ... or something.'

I swear those oily eyes roll as I drop the tart and watch her skulk back to her perch ...

What an anti-climax.

I start to feel a flood of heat and my attention shifts to the man holding me hostage, perhaps thinking he can trap me in the cage of his love.

He can't.

The heat pools in my fingertips, then it paints long strokes up my arms and swirls in my stomach.

"No, Aero." I jerk against his unyielding grip and his eyes narrow. "That's not how this is going to go."

"What the fuck is *that* supposed to mean?"

I give him a soft, reassuring smile. "I've got *you*, and I *am* letting go."

His eyes widen.

I release a flood of energy, spawning a new shield straight from my centre. It segregates me from Aero, prying his hands from my arms, sliding him backwards across the marble while his lips scream for me to stop.

But he's powerless right now.

I'm not.

My shield expands like a bubble, catching my father like a giant fish in a net. I watch anger twist Aero's face, and I shake the memory of his grip off my arms so I can focus on my task ...

Two flashes careen with the edge of my defence, making the entire dome shudder. My gaze swivels between Drake and Kal, both beating against the shield separating us ...

Kal starts winding around the edge, attacking at regular intervals, trying to find a weakness. Drake takes off in the opposite direction doing the same.

Aero knows better.

He's seen my power in full force; knows I've left no holes.

His forehead kisses the shield as his lips shape the word *please*.

"I'm sorry ... no."

Any remaining hope melts off his face, our mate bond going taut. His gaze lifts, the colour draining from his cheeks, and I turn, following his line of sight to my father hovering not too far away.

That generally stony face is twisted, his bloody hand clutching Mother's bloody blade. It's tossed to the side, clattering against the marble.

Someone's pissed. Can't imagine why.

"You dare to use iron on *me?*" he bellows, dropping to the ground with a boisterous thud.

"Oh, don't be such a kitten. It was just a little prickle."

He snarls, eyes narrowing as he studies the new perimeter of our battlefield. "This shield was foolish, Daughter. Edom, for once, agrees with me."

Of course he does. He has no idea what's good for him anymore.

I shrug, trying to hide a wince when I feel Kal start to hack at my shimmery dome with his big-boy sword. "I don't want us getting distracted. This is between you and me."

His lips curl at the corner. "As you wish."

I only have a moment to brace—to throw a secondary shield around *me* before a spear begins to form in his hand. He pitches it, sending it slicing through the air much faster than I can trace.

It shatters against my defence like stardust, and I let out a laboured breath.

Fuck, he's got a good arm. I should have practiced tossing something other than pointy sticks in preparation for ... this.

Then another one hits.

And another.

And *another* ...

My mates dig at my shield while my father advances, hammering my only wall of defence with persistent prongs of power.

Sweat trickles down my spine, my attention flicking to Drake whose beast is beating the edge of my sparkly barrier like a psychotic animal.

"*Stop!*" I scream though I doubt they can hear me. They probably think I need their help ...

I don't.

All they're doing is distracting me. Forcing me to fortify the shield I'm using to keep them safe, leaving small cracks in my *own* protection that I pray my father doesn't notice.

"Getting tired, Daughter?"

I groan, my entire body twisting into a knot of tension. My lips curl back when Aero decides to join in and thrash against my barrier with his full feral force ...

It's too much.

Kal's sword makes a hairline fracture that I scramble to fill just as my father throws another spear. It flies straight through a flaw in my protective shell, embedding deep in the vulnerable flesh of my shoulder ...

I shudder back.

"*Motherfu—ouch!*"

Everyone seems to hold their breath for an extended beat while I rip the spear out and watch a gush of glossy red pour down my breast ...

My Gods *triple* their efforts. So does my father—his eyes lit with the flame of impending victory.

I toss the bloody weapon to the ground and accelerate the trickle of power not refilling me *fast enough.*

If only I'd thought to refill as I go ...

I whimper, digging my nails into the fleshy part of my palms, crunching my eyes shut ...

Not like this.

If I die, they'll tear each other to shreds and the world will quickly yield to the same doom.

I need ... *more*. More than what I've got.

Dipping inside myself, I stalk deep into my belly of blackness, screaming for my beast to stay the fuck down.

When I reach a corner crammed with shadow, I toss shaded memories aside—rooting about like a paternal Day God hunting for a jacket for his chilly mate. Until I'm no longer digging through darkness ... but shards of colourful *light*.

These are the memories I've stashed away, protected in the deepest corners of my mind.

Somewhere I knew nobody would ever be able to find them.

Picking the luminous panes up one at a time, I gently pile them to the side until I locate what I'm looking for.

I snap a piece of selflessness from the moment Sol gave his dying words to wish his child a long and happy life, trying to ignore the buckling pain that threatens to make my heart pop.

I take love from the feel of my mother's arms around me.

Resilience—I find that in a basement with a stained wooden table, when Aero kneaded my back and nursed my nightmare into submission.

There's strength in the memory of Drake declaring he'd love my child no matter the conception, and I crack a slither of sacrifice from the knowledge that Kal's been hiding his son since the day he was born.

Finally, I take a long splinter of hope from the second I realised my father's been waiting for me to set him free from his own living nightmare ...

The second I realised he needs a hero, not an executioner.

Once my hands are full, I stab the shards into my chest,

one at a time, until I'm buzzing with the best parts of the people who have had the biggest impact on my life. I dart back to the surface, slide into my body, and throw my head back—releasing a wash of sparkling energy straight from my heart ...

Well, that's new.

Sometimes instinct works in my favour, other times I end up naked on a whipping dais. There really is no in between.

It's not until I straighten and open my eyes that I notice the world is now awash with a stark, blinding *light*. I lift a hand, use it as a visor, and choke on my next breath ...

Shit.

I think I just froze the fucking world.

Drake's stuck mid-growl, wings spread, balled fists about to pound my shield. Aero has his teeth gnashed into it like a starved animal, and Kal has his big-boy sword perched mid-air, mid-hack, his face locked in a perpetual roar.

I shake my head.

They think *I'm* the one who lacks self-preservation?

I think it's about time they learn that when I say I've got them, it means I've fucking *got them*.

Sighing, I stalk towards my father; past one of his fancy spears suspended mid-air. I'm almost at him when my boot hits something ...

Mother's blade.

I pluck it off the ground, study it, then verge on the broken man who broke the world.

His jaw is clenched, teeth bared ... eyes full of hate.

I shake my head, studying the angles of his face. Even though it's distorted by the cut of his beast, I can see we have the same sharp jaw, the same full lips and well-defined cupid's bow, and the same long lashes.

But his eyes are black.

He's lost. Just like *I've* been lost.

"I see you," I whisper, pressing my cheek to the icy palm he just used to wound me. "I know it hurts ... goddamn, I know it hurts. And I know that pain is suffocating. But you don't belong in there. *You don't.*"

He doesn't answer.

Doesn't blink.

Doesn't even breathe.

He just continues to stare at me blindly, and I'm glad my mates are too frozen to see the tear that slips down my cheek.

I finally get some semblance of a father, and he's too tired to fight for me after years of being silenced.

I get it. I once stood on the edge of a cliff for the very same reason.

Because my heart's a pathetic, dried-up thing, I close my eyes and picture a life where we loved each other. I picture his touch unaffected by shadows and wonder if he would have been strict. Or perhaps he would have been the parent I went to because Mummy knew how to draw a hard line ...

I wrap my hand around the back of his, using it as leverage to press my cheek into his palm before opening my eyes ...

I follow the trail of his brutal gaze to the spear halted mid-air, aimed to *kill*.

"No wonder my mates were losing their minds," I mutter to no one but myself.

The monster wants company ... but not enough to risk the life of the one he's protecting. Even if the man within is so desperate to end himself that he lured his own daughter to do the fucking deed.

But I didn't sign up for shit.

Sighing, I unfasten the sheath that holds the sword from my nightmares and tug it from the scabbard ... despising the weight of it.

This is the blade that took my mother's life.

I examine the fierce edge and see a slice of my reflection, barely recognising the woman staring back. I've spent most of my life hating the man who spawned me ... now my entire world has been turned on its tits.

I return the weapon to its holster, buckle it around my hips, then pat my father on his icy cheek. "I'm sorry ..."

My teeth grit, and I try not to gag as I slide Mother's tiny iron dagger into the half-healed hole in his guts.

Closing my eyes, I press my palms against his temples, gather heat in my hands, and aim it directly at his mind—hoping I don't accidentally *poof* his brain in the process.

I managed to communicate with Aero's soul while we were oceans apart, surely I can get into my own father's head at such close range ...

I have to at least try.

He needs to learn that we're not defined by the monsters that haunt us, but by the way we rise from the ashes of our sins.

Too much death. I'm done with all the death.

It's time we all started to *live*.

CHAPTER FORTY-NINE
EDOM

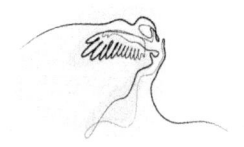

Calcified shadows cling to me like armour, pretending to protect me.

It's comfortable.

Safe.

It's none of those things.

I'm a prisoner in my own body. A prisoner of my own pain and grief and all the vile things my beast has done.

Endless memories. Never changing. Never fading.

I remember every life he's taken with my hands, every instance he's cast darkness over this world we were supposed to tend and nurture.

The deeper I dove, the more disconnected my beast and I became, the more he tried to protect me in the only way he knew how.

Cold, hard brutality.

I'm responsible. I lost the strength to fight him. Lost the resolve to claw into my body and absorb the flood of pain that's built up over the years.

There is no coming back from everything he's done. No washing the blood off my hands. My conscience.

Damien.
Roland.
Darius.
Roe.
Orien.
Haviar.
Ziorn.

I run through their names like a song on repeat, over and over and over again.

So many sons. So many losses.

Each tore a chunk from my heart—now all that's left of the organ is a black, dimpled thing that resents its own beat.

Xies.
Sian.
Arose.
Jal.
Adeline ...

My favourite name for a girl.

Mare was my better half in every way. Even after everything my beast did to her—after he sliced off her wings and ordered Kyro to burn her body to a cinder—she still named our girl Adeline.

I always wanted a daughter, never got one. My beast did, and he fucking *destroyed* her.

I'm trying so hard to make it right because I failed *her* most of all.

Something bright pierces my darkness like a distant star, dribbling light into my hole of dishonour, and I know it's her. I know before her pearly face and those diamond eyes even come into view.

Her hair is a halo of chaos and my hands itch to tuck that rogue curl behind her ear ...

She sits down, folding her legs beneath her as if she's a child and not the grown woman before me. "There you are," she whispers, like she's talking to an injured bird. "You weren't easy to find ..."

No, I can't imagine I was.

I howled, *pleaded* with my beast while he tossed shards of power at her over and over again ... then he struck her.

I couldn't watch any longer. Couldn't watch another child die.

"You shouldn't be down here," I grate, throat raw, studying the streaks of light shooting off her from all angles.

I wonder if she realises.

She reaches out a hand, offering me something I don't deserve. "Neither should you."

I scramble back.

She frowns, but where I expect to see defeat in those big, grey eyes, I see *determination*.

"I want to show you something."

No.

Don't give her anything else to cling to.

"I've seen enough. You know what you need to do."

She shakes her head, the resolve in her gaze only hardening. "Not yet. Not until you've seen ... *this*."

"Why?"

Why won't she just let me go?

Her eyes glitter like marbles. "Because. I want you to see what you missed out on."

Fucking hell.

And just like that, she's dangled the only carrot I'd ever consider following.

Like a dry sponge, I lap at the words until there's nothing left but the silence hanging between us, waiting for me to fill the void with my answer. And because I'm a pathetic excuse for a man, I'm going to break my own rule, just like I've broken everything else.

"And then you'll do it?" I rasp, and she nods once. It

doesn't evade me that she holds back the words she knows she'll choke on.

Nice try, little one.

"*Prove it.*"

She makes a small grunting sound, then lifts her chin regally. I can't deny it's the cutest fucking thing I've ever seen. "I have your sword."

Sigh.

You have a piece of metal you don't want to use anymore, sweetheart. My beast will hone that weakness into something that will gut her like a fish.

"That's not enough," I snarl, bunching my fists so hard I feel the bones in my hands groan.

"I also pierced you with iron ... *again.*"

Huh. That'll do. The cunt really struggled to get it out the first time.

"Good. You learn fast."

"I have too much to lose."

I drop my gaze to her abdomen ...

Fuck.

I hadn't noticed the *two* swirls of light eddying there—now I can barely take my eyes away. "Twins ..."

She nods once.

The tethers must have already formed. I felt them with all my other children ... treasured them. Even knotted myself around them in an effort to keep them in place.

I also felt them rip free and disintegrate—tried to stick them back together, shovelling deep into the graves on my heart so I could give them more of me to cling to.

It never worked, but it didn't stop me from trying again, and again ...

I wish I could forget. Even down here, the pain still haunts me.

Tries to choke me.

A WOMAN'S WORTH

Adeline ... I never felt hers. Something else I missed by burrowing away, driving Mare to break our bond.

"I told you not to hesitate," I snarl, flashing my teeth and pushing away. *"What are you waiting for?"*

"No. Your beast took a father from *them*," she berates, stern eyes narrowing. "You allowed him to take a father from *me*. You owe it to me to at least *try!*"

And suddenly I see more than just the woman—broken yet still so incredibly whole. I see the child, thrown into a rotten world that took and took and took ...

No wonder she's so strong. She learnt to survive on *nothing*.

Perhaps I was selfish to expect she'd use my own brutality against me. I'd hoped she'd make it quick and we wouldn't have to drag each other through all ... *this*.

I certainly wasn't counting on her seeing past the monster.

Somehow, she's developed the ability to see in the dark. That's nothing I can be proud of.

I clear my throat, staring at the blank space between us. "Adeline ... you can paint a nightmare pretty colours, but it's still a fucking nightmare."

She forces her hand into my line of sight. *"You owe it to me."*

I release a deep, tortured breath.

Tenacious little thing.

And because I'm *weak*, I give her exactly what she asked for—not even bothering to dust off the shadows before my hand swallows hers.

She threads her fingers around my palm and I relish the feel, fuelling the fire of my own self-hatred.

Her grip tightens. "Now. Close your eyes ..."

The scent of freshly turned soil and crisp morning dew has the backs of my eyes prickling. A soft breeze tickles my cheek and I curl my toes into the fleshy ground.

I tip my head as sunshine warms my face—something I'd lost hope I'd ever feel again ...

A soft giggle ripples through the air and my heart stops beating. I open my eyes to see a child skipping through the grass towards me—her tiny feet bare, the hem of her simple dress flicking about her knees.

White hair dances around her smooth face, her eyes like river rocks that sparkle when they catch shards of sun cutting through the trees.

Adeline.

She's happy, full of light, and so fucking gorgeous.

Our eyes meet and her smile blooms, making my heart thud one hungry beat ...

It's the most beautiful smile I've ever seen.

That smile could light up the entire world, and I can't help but wonder if she uses it anymore ... or if I took that from her, too.

"Little Dove!"

I turn, seeing Mare approach through the trees, and my heart plunges. She has a bag slung over her shoulder and she's wearing a long-sleeved dress—simple and modest— hiding most of the twisted skin that no doubt covers every part of her.

There's a smile pulling the melted flesh on her face at odd angles, and I let out a deep, shuddering breath ...

I did that to her.

Me.

You're a fucking monster, Edom.

"Slow down, baby! You know I don't like you running so far ahead ..."

Adeline does the most dramatic fucking twirl coupled with a slight groan that makes me raise a brow. She can't be any older than three or four, yet she has the attitude of a teenager.

No wonder she gave my beast such a run for his tokens.

She bounds back to Mare, wearing a little pout that thaws when she digs her heels into the soil and comes to an abrupt halt. Her face blossoms as she plucks a yellow flower then dashes towards her mother, those curls leaving a smoky trail behind her.

"Is that for me?"

Adeline nods, presenting the bloom like it's made of gold. "It was looking up at me from the grass."

Mare takes the gift and tips it to her nose, dusting the tip yellow.

"It's pretty, mummy. Just like you."

A slow blush creeps across Mare's cheeks, turning my guilt into a poisonous thing, but I refuse to look away ...

This is my penance.

"Don't drop it ..." Adeline warns, nailing little fists on her hips.

If only I'd known buttercups held a special place in their hearts.

"I won't, Little Dove."

I can tell Mare is trying to be serious, only because I loved her; shared hopes and dreams and a life with her. Watched her swell with life and obsess over names to paint on the wall of yet *another* nursery because she couldn't bear to open the door of the last one she prepared ...

Held her in my arms time and time again while she tried not to fall apart at the seams.

Before I failed her.

Mare points towards a wiggly path through the trees. "Let's go. I know it's your special birthday swim in the sun, but we still need to get home before it gets too high in the sky."

... Birthday?

"I wish we could swim with the sun *all* the time! I love the sun!"

Mare kneels and plants a chaste kiss on our daughter's pouty lips. "I know, Little Dove. And so you should."

Mare plucks Adeline off the ground, swinging her around, and I swear that little giggle makes the birds sing louder. They walk past me together, into the fleshy forest stained in morning light.

I follow.

My daughter watches me over her mother's shoulder, those wide eyes pervading while I dodge coiled vines and small clusters of purple flowers—tugging my wings close so I don't disturb the perfect stillness.

She slips her thumb into her mouth, leaning into the crook of her mother's neck ...

"You're not sucking your thumb again, are you?"

Mare's voice is sharp with warning, and I watch Adeline pull it out long enough to mumble the word 'no' before threading it back between her lips.

I couldn't stop the smile that splits my face if I tried.

Adeline's own cheeks swell, twin dimples puckering while she keeps her lips wrapped around her thumb.

She's so cheeky and defiant ... it kills me.

She kills me.

I would have snuck her candy at bedtime, hidden with her under the blankets while we ate them together, then laughed when Mare found the wrappers all through the sheets the next morning.

I would have been her hero. Her best friend. Her partner in crime.

I would have taken her side *every fucking time*.

But instead I was none of those things.

You're a fucking monster, Edom.

My smile falls at the thought of what could have been, and hers quickly follows, making those dimples disappear as her mother weaves through a thicket. Adeline arches her neck, lifting up in an effort to see me ... and because I'm *weak*, I quicken my pace simply so I can feel her eyes on me again.

I wish I could live in this moment forever. Right here.

The bush opens up, revealing a silver lake fringed with fluffy trees. I can hear the trickle of a waterfall feeding into it, but the surface reflects the puffy clouds perfectly.

It looks like liquid starlight.

Mare lowers our daughter to the soft, spongy moss that kisses the water's edge, then tugs the shift over Adeline's head. A whitewash of curls gushes around her slight shoulders and tries to swallow her whole.

She's so small. Fragile.

None of those things.

She jiggles on the spot in a tiny homemade bathing suit. "Can I go?"

"Yes. I'll be right behind you. No silly business, please. Hide-and-go-seek isn't as fun for Mummy as you think it is."

Hide-and-go ... *huh?*

"Fiiine," she grumbles but her little dimples are showing.

Adeline dips her toes into the glassy water, and I watch the surface crinkle, unsettling the perfection but replacing it with something far more beautiful.

She giggles again, and I can't help but savour my new favourite sound ... right before she *dives*.

I lurch forward a step before realising there's nothing I can do anyway.

I snap my attention to Mare standing in her own bathing suit, glancing out across the lake and oozing pride. "You're going to let her jump in the water all on her *own?* What if she drowns?"

She doesn't answer me of course, because I'm not really here. I'm just some figment of our daughter's imagination.

And though I know the outcome—know she must make it to the surface if she's alive today—I still hold my breath until she pops up, treading with obvious finesse.

I shake my head, watching her cut through the water towards the other side of the lake ...

Mare taught our baby to swim at such a young age—gave her a skill she might need to fend for herself against the world.

Against *me.*

It's like a spear straight through my fucking heart.

Mare dives and I launch into the air, sailing out across the lake, seeking my reflection in the crumpled surface ...

There is none.

Another bitter reminder that I'm not really here; that Adeline's showing me something that will never truly be mine.

Still, I stalk her like a shark, my hunger stemming from the tarnished organ caught in the shell of my ribs.

When I land on the other side, I fold my wings flat against my back and storm into the water.

I want her swimming towards me, not away from me.

I keep going until I'm chest-deep, watching her slice through the mirror of liquid, listening to the soft pant of her breath. Once we're close enough to touch, she begins to tread, white hair slicked back and those big, glossy eyes peering up at me ...

Fuck.

I so badly want to tell her how beautiful she is. That her

face is like the sun, and that it could bring the world to its knees.

But I don't.

I doubt she wants to hear that from me.

My body moves on its own accord, and I slide forward a step, opening my arms. I've never felt so frightened in my very long life as I stand here, watching her watch me, preparing for the slap of rejection that'll undoubtedly ensue.

But then she kicks at the water, glides against me, and a small, hopeless sound leaks from my throat at the contact, making me hate myself just a little bit more.

I tuck my arms around her, telling myself it's for practical reasons ...

Treading water is tiring—especially for tiny legs.

Her cold hand wiggles between us and she traces my runes, her brows furrowed. She presses her nose to my chest and draws a deep breath, making the hairs on the back of my neck stand on end.

"What are you doing?"

The voice doesn't sound like my own.

It's raspy and weak.

Vulnerable.

"Smelling you. You smell like dirt, but in a nice way." I suck a sharp breath when she turns her head to the side and flattens her cheek against my painted flesh, using me as a pillow. My lungs cease with the fear that if I move at all, I'll scare her away and ruin this moment just like I ruin everything else.

"I'm storing it in here." She taps her temple and the urge to snatch her porcelain hand and hold it tight almost splits me right down the middle.

I tilt my head, looking skyward. Wanting to tuck her inside my hollowness where I can keep her safe for eternity ...

Except I can't, because I don't deserve her.

Because today, tomorrow, or maybe the next day after that, I'll force my way into a home and ruin this child's life. I'll take everything she's ever loved, leaving her to wander the streets of a nearby town in search of someone, anyone, to fill that void in her tiny chest.

She'll stumble upon a man who'll promise to care for her, and instead he'll stash her in a room with two ways in and only one way out—with a rotten mattress and a hessian blanket that'll probably make her sneeze. He'll break my little girl apart until there's nothing left of the child who once swam carelessly across this lake. Until she's scratching her mother's face into the constant companion of her four walls, and she's forced to find pleasure in her own undoing just to survive.

I don't deserve her.

I hear Mare paddle towards us, then silence as I drop my gaze from the destitute sky.

She's standing a small distance away wearing sad eyes and a tortured frown of my own creation. Water beads off her smudged features, dripping to the lake as her lungs count down their final breaths.

Aside from that, she's totally still.

This memory is realising I don't belong here. As if together, Adeline and I are beginning to push the boundaries of time—something that shouldn't be tampered with.

I watch the ripples scatter ...

Perhaps we've already gone too far.

Tucking her close, I weave my hand around the back of her neck.

My time is running out.

"Adeline, baby?" Mare's voice echoes across the lake, and I bite my tongue so hard it bleeds.

"Coming ..." her mumbled words brush my skin and make it pebble.

Just one revelry before she goes.

One.

I press my lips to the top of her head and draw a deep breath—inhaling the smell of teardrops, moss, and sweet apples. I screw my eyes shut, storing the scent, wishing I could spend eternity sipping it.

Savouring it.

She wiggles in my iron grip, and I know it's time for me to let her go before I cause more damage than I already have.

But I don't want to.

Not yet.

This is the happiest moment of my life ... but it's also the exact opposite. Because I know with absolute certainty that my little girl is destined to be exposed to the blunt brutality of this world I turned my back on. That it will pull her apart, piece by piece, until she's barely holding herself together.

Perhaps one day she'll even try to throw it all away.

But this is just a memory, that's all this is. And even if it wasn't, I have nothing left to give.

Except ...

I watch the ripples flutter over the surface of the water, and I squeeze her tighter, nuzzling towards her dainty ear. *"Gleitz adorn, de mel te heist. Sevana ta lein."*

Even though the words should be useless spoken by a reflection-less wisp in the distant memory of a child, the words sear my throat like they're burning to be cast.

Like they still hold *power.*

She pulls back, peering up at me. "Why ...?"

I shake my head, catching a bead of water racing down her cheek with the pad of my thumb. "Because those words stood for something once. Helped people." I tuck a lock of hair behind her ear and swallow the lump of regret clogging my throat. "They're all I have to offer; I just wish I had the power to give you more."

But I don't, and I never will.

My power doesn't belong to me anymore. It belongs to the monster who tried to kill my baby.

She tips her head to the side and stamps her hand against my cheek, looking at me with such wide, earnest eyes that I swear I can see the woman staring back at me ...

The one who's worth more to this world than the tip of my pinky finger.

Her features soften, replaced with that of a happy child who has no idea what horrors lie ahead. She smiles, giggles, then wiggles again ...

This time, I swallow my selfish desires and let her go, watching her paddle a few metres before Mare begins the watery trek towards the opposite shore.

Adeline pivots, treading on the spot. "Come on, Daddy. Come swim with me. The water's so nice!"

Daddy.

The word saturates me ... almost *drowns* me.

It doesn't fit.

I would have given her the world, but I didn't.

I gave her a broken one.

I shake my head though I know it will hurt her—but that's all I'm really good for anymore. Offering the kindness of a clean slice. "You know I can't."

Her face bunches, those tiny hands ball into fists, and I can almost see her stomping her feet beneath the surface. "Just *swim!* All you have to do is swim!"

I'm getting put in my place by a three-year-old.

I'd swim with her forever if I could, but that's not really what she's asking me to do ...

I know that. So does she.

Her face crumbles and it shatters my heart into a thousand tiny pieces—watching a child so small shed tears without uttering a single sound.

When she opens her eyes again, they're large, stormy, and *determined*. She looks at me one final time, then dives beneath the surface ...

The ripples stop.

I frown, scanning the lake, waiting for her to re-emerge. Moments drip by and it takes me far too long to realise she's not coming back.

Hide-and-go-fucking-seek.

Mare was right, there's nothing fun about this game.

I tuck my wings flat against my back, draw a deep breath, and dive, shooting into the sable water. The current caresses my skin much like my shadows do; a reminder of the chilling loneliness I can't escape. It's the sort of solitude that squeezes your heart and never lets go—not even when you're coiled up around the ache, weeping for release.

I spot her pearly feet kicking furiously, driving her further into the gloomy depths, and I use my wings like propellers to catapult me towards her ...

Darkness absorbs us both, and I can no longer see.

Crushing panic tries to strangle me. I lost her ... I lost her in the darkness.

I failed her again.

I scream into the void, emptying my lungs, begging the world to keep her safe.

Alive.

For it to give me this *one parting wish.*

A small hand wraps around my wrist and yanks with unnatural force until I'm no longer drowning in blackness and compounding loss, but staring into round eyes the colour of river rocks, standing on the ruins of a haunted throne room floor.

I draw a gasping breath ...

My girl.

She dove into my darkness and dragged me back to the light.

She's *everything* this world needs.

Her eyes are dripping hope, her hands trembling against my temples, and I can see she's holding her breath. Warm blood dribbles from the wound in my stomach—that small iron blade cauterising me from the inside, threatening to gut me.

She doesn't do anything by half measures.

The thought makes me smile, but the way her face lights up in response guts me in an entirely different way.

She thinks she chased him away forever ... but she doesn't understand.

He's never gone.

He's part of me, fused to my soul, and he's done terrible things. Things I can't bear to live with.

My beast thrashes against my restraints, drowning me with his roaring protests at being confined to the shade where he can't *protect me* ... despite the fact that I don't want to be protected.

I'm too weak to hold him down for much longer.

I hear a creaking groan, an ear-splitting blow, and I glance up to see Kal, Aero, and Drake tearing chunks from a crack in her shield while she screams for them to *stop*—that there's nothing to be afraid of anymore ...

She's wrong.

They know that. They saw me turn, watched me twist into nothing but a parasite that feeds on the relationships I once valued more than my own life.

But even after seeing all her brutal parts, they look at her like she's the sun itself.

Sol fucking *died* for her ...

My baby's in good hands.

There's only one thing left to do. She'll hate me for it, but I'd rather suffer her wrath a million times over than feel her blood on my hands.

I have one final chance to be the father she never had, and this time, I refuse to fail her.

It's time my girl started to *live*.

CHAPTER FIFTY
DELL

*S*hards of my shield rain from the sky, collide with the ground, and shatter like glass.

I shake my head and scream at my boisterous Sun Gods to *stop wrecking shit*. My father's back, nobody else needs to die!

I saved him ...

He followed me into the light.

I turn to my dad, but that warm smile that gave me life is *gone* ...

He's unblinking, tracing the curves of my face with his gaze like this is the last time he'll ever see me.

My heart plummets into the acidic pool of my stomach.

He doesn't want to stay.

"No," I breathe, trying to ignore the sound of my mates roaring my name—their voices dark and savage to the core.

"Adeline ..."

"No. Don't you dare do this to me!"

Something in his flat gaze fragments, all his muscles tensing as he balls his hands into fists at his sides, like he's trying to stop from reaching out. "Put the blade to my throat," he whispers, and I choke on my next breath.

After everything I just showed him, he still wants to leave me. And he wants *me* to do it ...

Well ... fuck that.

I take a step back, shaking my head, ready to dish him a steaming pile of all the teenage tantrums we both missed out on. "No. *Hell* no. The first rule in our new relationship is that you can't make me do *shit*."

He snarls, and I wince as another shard shatters against the marble. I glance over my shoulder, seeing Drake manoeuvring through a God-sized gap; features as sharp as the jagged edges slicing his flesh.

He's going to impale himself on the shield I erected for their own protection. I think my lack of self-preservation is rubbing off on them, and my fragile heart is not okay with that.

"*Stop!*" I scream, backing myself into my father as if I could protect him against the three feral Gods. "I'm fucking safe, goddammit!"

Drake falls through to the ground with a solid, meaty thump, exposing gnarly gashes through the bloody ribbons of his shirt. His wings uncurl while Kal and Aero try to dive through the hole at the same time ...

I hear something skate across the marble and Drake's hands fly to his throat—his face turning a dark shade of purple while he sucks sharp, whistling breaths.

"*Drake?*"

The black and auburn links on my heart *tug*, and I glance up to see Kal and Aero tangled in the web of my ravaged shield, choking on the same unseen force.

Beasty gnaws on her own limbs, trying to break free of her restraints ...

No.

Please no.

I reel around, mentally preparing to see my father black-eyed and feral again ...

He's not.

His eyes are grey, flat, and watery. His brow is dappled with sweat, the veins in his temples pulsing. I note the bitter tang of agony leaching from his pores and the fresh blood dribbling from his right hand—the one he undoubtedly used to pry the dagger from his innards for the second time in less than half an hour.

"What are you doing ..."

He shakes his head and speaks through gritted teeth. "*I said*, put the blade to my throat." His attention slices past me, and I follow his stare to my three immobilised mates, fighting for little drops of breath. "Or I cut their airflow entirely."

I whip back around. "You wouldn't do that to me!" He wouldn't give me everything, then take it away in the very next breath. I may be new at this father-daughter ... *stuff*, but that can't be how this works!

"I would," he says, his voice holding zero remorse, and my heart forgets how to beat.

I believe him.

This isn't the man from the lake.

This isn't the man who nuzzled his nose into my hair and sipped on my scent.

"I can't let you take them from me," I bite out, trying to keep my emotions from bleeding through my words. "I'm hurting too, okay? But we can heal *together*."

He shakes his head as if he's repulsed by the mere *suggestion*. "No. This is the only option. I have no choice."

He might as well gaff me in the chest, because forcing me to be his executioner, knowing what I know, is a form of torture I'm not accustomed to ...

It might just be the key to my undoing.

"Adeline ..." He says my name like a prayer, but I'm starting to think it's more of a curse. "There's very little airflow getting through to your mates' lungs. They won't last forever, and I can't slide that blade across my own throat ..."

I blink at him, dissecting those words.

He can't lie.

He's tried to kill himself before ...

My beast is spitting wrath, her limbs all bloody gore and exposed bone. I try to erect a shield over my Gods—block the force restricting their airflow and buy myself time to think ...

It's impossible.

He's too determined. Too focused.

Me?

I'm cracking open.

I swallow the lump of dread trying to choke me. I can feel the attention of my mates like a brand, and I'm so fucking thankful they can't feel my pain, my emotional angst, or hear my thoughts right now. I don't want them to suffer any more than they already have.

A tear slides down my cheek as I force myself to take a step forward, then another. My father's eyes soften, and it leaves a bitter taste in my mouth because even though I broke him out of his shell, I'm still not enough.

He still wants to leave me.

I break away from his tacky gaze and duck his outstretched wing, dragging his dagger from the hilt at my hip ...

My beast goes stone silent.

I fucking *hate* this blade.

He drops to his knees, wings pooling to the marble, and I force myself to step in close to his heaving body. Drake tries to crawl towards me, grappling for small sips of breath while Kal and Aero continue to writhe in the web of my shield ...

I'll be the monster they need me to be, even if it costs me the father I never knew I had.

The weapon is heavy, hard to balance in my unsteady hand, but I curl it around my father's throat and press the sharp edge against his stretched flesh.

It takes me back to the day I watched him do the same to my mother.

"It's okay, Adeline ..."

"It's not okay."

It's so far from okay.

My hand shakes, the mild scent of sizzling flesh making my nose itch. All I can see is the white-haired man holding me in the lake, thinking about how safe I felt with his big arms wrapped around me.

I can't help but picture his unburdened smile when he saw me sucking my thumb. I just know he would have been on my side growing up—that he would have kept my secrets safe and slipped me treats before dinnertime.

The sound of his deep voice whispering those words in my ear—the ones that summoned my Sun Gods when I needed them the most—is like an echo on my heart ...

Those words saved my life, and now he's refusing to let me repay the favor.

"Do it, Adeline. *Do it.*"

Mummy said the same thing before she died, and I doubt it's a coincidence ...

How much did my father scream for his beast to show her mercy? What carnage was being wrought inside that shaded labyrinth—the one which took me fucking *forever* to crawl through, searching for the man within the beast.

Fat tears roll down my cheeks, and my grip on the blade loosens. "I can't ..."

I can't do this.

I don't *want* to do this.

I want to rip into the Bright, lose myself to the nothingness, and forget my heart even has a broken beat.

A warm hand slides over mine—over the one holding the blade to my father's throat.

His hand.

"Wh—what are you doing ..."

My one responsive wing curls around his body, brushing his coiled, twitching muscles like it's trying to comfort him.

He gives me a gentle squeeze. "I'm helping, sweetheart."

"You're not *helping!*" If I pull away, the blade will slip along his throat and end the tortured man who just wanted a family to share his infinite life with.

Well, I'm here. He fucking has me. Why doesn't he want me? Am I not *good enough* for him?

I realise I've said the words aloud when he makes a soft choking sound. His hold tightens, and the coppery scent of blood permeates the air. "I do want you," he gurgles with a shaded voice that dents my awareness. "But I want to save you *more.*"

Save m—

My chest caves, bitter realisation hitting me so hard a little sound leaks out.

I may have brought him back to the surface, but the gift was only temporary.

His beast is too strong.

And I know as well as he does that his monster has too much misery to feed on. He won't have the same mercy as the broken man who once owned that body. He won't just kill my mates and my children. He'll eventually destroy the world because in his own caustic way, he sees it as a remedy for his own loneliness.

My father's not giving up. He's sacrificing himself so the

rest of us can *live* ... and though it hurts to admit, I feel like we finally understand each other.

Turns out, his beast was right after all. My father and I are the same, right down to our sacrificial, selfless cores ...

There's no changing his mind. One way or another, this is happening. I know he'll find a way, because that's exactly what I'd do.

My next breath tastes like poison that seeps straight into my ill-fated conscience that was doomed the moment I was born. "We're sitting on the edge of a cliff with our bare feet swinging over the side," I whisper, my voice stretched too thin to fit through the swell of my throat.

I don't want to be here right now, so I'm going to take us somewhere else. Somewhere nice and happy, where the sky isn't crying icy tears. A place where the world doesn't feel quite so brutal.

A place where we can pretend our story didn't start and end this way.

"Morning light is cresting over the mountains, and it's warm on our skin," he grates out, trembling in my arms, making my heart twist in my chest as my hand starts to shake. His grip tightens. "And I can't stop looking at the way the sun lights up your beautiful face."

My features crumble. I have to squeeze my lips together to stifle a sob.

My father just called me beautiful.

It's something I didn't know I needed to hear until this very moment.

"My w-wings are out," I stutter, trying to tamp my emotions for the sake of keeping this picture we're painting a happy one, "and you've wanted to teach me to fly since I learnt to crawl because there are so many ledges in that big ol' castle that you think are unsafe for a toddler. But today ... mum *finally* agreed."

I hate that he chokes on his next breath.

I hate that I feel something warm drip onto my arm that smells just like the tears mummy cried as she was sawing off my wings.

"The wind is perfect for learning," he rasps, and I can almost feel it on my face.

I hope he can, too.

I hope he's using his imagination to take him there, to this alternate reality where life doesn't hurt ... but feels *good*.

"Though I'm only small, I'm so determined to make you proud, Dad."

More warm liquid drips onto my arm as the muscles under his painted skin come alive. "I know, my girl. I know you wi—"

I remind myself how it felt to have his arms around me in the lake as I feel him slip away.

He starts to snarl.

My father's gone.

"Are you ready to fall with me?" I squeeze out, tightening my grip on the beast now thrashing in my arms.

He doesn't answer.

"Good," I nod, blinking away the tears muddying my vision as I strengthen my arm with a splint of power, hoping the man below the surface of the feral shell can still hear me. That he's still picturing himself sitting on the edge of a cliff with his daughter, ready to take her on her first flying lesson.

I close my eyes as his wings snap at the air, trying to lift us off the ground, but I have a leash of power holding us down.

Always one step ahead.

"I stretch my wings, noticing mine are so much smaller than yours ... but you tell me they'll grow big and strong as you take my hand, and together, we fall forward into those fluffy, golden clouds ..."

I drag the sword across his throat, feeling the warm spill of blood coat my fingers. His body loses all its rigidity and slides out of my wing's softening embrace.

He thuds against the marble, his wings quickly following, making the same sickening sound mine made after my mother severed them from my back.

Then ... nothing. Only the faint sound of snow pattering and the gasping draws of my mates as they scramble towards me.

I just bought their lives with my father's.

I absorb the shield, open my eyes, and study the side of my father's face—his eyes wide and inky, a puddle of steaming death blooming beneath him. Beasty crawls out of her hole to watch it swell, and where I thought I'd see some sort of satisfied smirk from the merciless part of me ... I don't.

My father's finally free.

I'm an orphan.

No matter which way you flip this token, it still lands in the mud.

I know my mates are crowding me, touching me, checking me over as they whisper blank words that try, and fail, to patch up the crumbling remnants of my conscience ...

I just killed my own father.

I toss the fucking blade and fall to the ground, watching that wretched piece of metal slide over the edge of the marble slab, disappearing out of my life forever.

It doesn't strip the blood off my hands.

I look down and study them while someone checks the raw stump of my broken wing. Someone else has their forehead pressed to my abdomen, stabilising me with large, trembling hands. Someone examines the hole in my shoulder but ignores the gaping wound in my heart.

Someone else is laying on the floor over there, lifeless.

I lift my hands higher, close my eyes, and drag my father's blood down my face while emotion boils to the surface—stretching my skin so thin it rips, cleaving my chest right down the middle.

I swear I can feel all my ribs snapping, one by one, exposing a bruised heart to my remaining mates ...

This was the pain he was hiding from. The compounding impact of *loss*.

The scream that pours out of me is coarse, ripping my throat raw. The sound is a promise to my broken world ...

Enough.

CHAPTER FIFTY-ONE
DELL

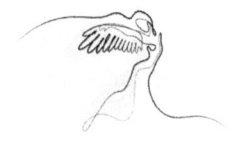

"*D*ell ..."

I open my eyes.

Drake's arms are spread, exposing the carnage of his ravaged chest. The ball of his throat rolls and I can smell the sharp scent of his concern. "Babe ... can I hold you? It's freezing, and you're ..."

Covered in my father's blood, falling apart on the icy ground.

Right.

He wouldn't have wanted this. He didn't do this to hurt me, he did it to *save* me ... trusting I'd piece the world back together in his stead.

But it's hard to fix a world that's permanently cast in dawn, not to mention the lonely baby tether floating around inside my wounded chest.

My attention snaps to Sol.

Aero tries to steady me as I stand, but I peel his hands off and avoid glancing down at my father—pushing those emotions down, down, *down* ...

I wobble around Drake's wing that attempts to herd me in, bump off Kal's sweeping touch, and straighten my spine, dragging my ruined wing across the marble.

Perhaps I'm so unsteady because I'm now carrying the weight of my father's murder on my shoulders.

I'm surprised I can even stand.

I take off, as if I can escape the suffocating press of my new reality, hearing the others flap after me—mumbling words between themselves in that ancient language.

The arctic ground bites my knees as I sweep snow off Sol's cheeks and forehead with gory fingers that only serve to tarnish him in a different way. "You're too cold," I whisper. "You need to warm up, Daydream. Our sun bun needs you, okay?"

He doesn't answer. He's never been much of a talker, but I just don't have the patience for it right now.

"Don't ignore me, Sol. I'm not in the mood for your games." I wrap a hand around his big arm, close my eyes, and try to focus on shifting my beast off that little bead of light ... but the bitch just hisses, looking at me like I'm a broken, crazy hoe.

I'm about to strangle the bitch with some shadow twine when someone cups my jaw, and I open my eyes to see two liquid swirls of amber. It's only when Aero rolls my lower lip with the pad of his thumb that I realise I'm snarling.

"Dell ... baby. What are you doing?"

"My beast is being unreasonable. I need you to take him to the bog." I point to Sol and Aero's eyes widen. "Right now. Before he gets frostbite."

He opens his mouth, but nothing comes out. He certainly doesn't fucking *move* us.

Probably because I forgot to use my manners.

"Please!"

He flinches, his grip on my face tightening, and he shifts his gaze behind me as a lump of shade stems the constant littering of snow.

Still, he doesn't move, the world continues to suffer in its everlasting dawn, and that wispy tether continues to flutter about without the anchor of its daddy.

I refuse to accept this. Sol wished for our child to live a long and happy life—well, he can come back and make sure of that himself or so help me Day God, I'll follow him to his sunny afterlife and drag him back here by his dick.

Unfortunately, it seems Aero's brain has frosted from the chill.

I look over my shoulder to my Dusk God standing guard like a bloody rock that's seen better days, staring down at Sol with blank eyes. *"Drake?"*

His gaze snaps to me, then ... *nothing*.

I'm seriously running out of options here.

"*Kal?*" I look to my Night God, his wings shielding Sol's body from the imposing elements. His starry flecked eyes are so stark against the brutal scene, his hand splayed over the bottom half of his face.

He doesn't shift a feather. Nobody does.

"Why aren't we moving? That smelly shit might be able to fix him! It's worth a shot!"

My desperate pleas go unanswered.

Drake drops next to me, brushing an icy twist of hair from my eyes. "Babe, he's gone. There's no coming back from ... from *this*." He looks down at my Day God and I follow suit, taking in the grey, tepid skin and flat, watery gaze staring at nothing.

His lips are blue.

He feels just as cold as the marble ground I'm kneeling on.

Aero wraps his arms around me, his lips brushing the shell of my ear. "Dell, Drake's right ... there's nothing we can do for him now. Sol's dead. Why don't we move his body somewhere warm so we can start to mou—"

I stand, shove Aero off, and stomp away, dragging my floppy half-wing behind me—giving the others access to Sol as I let a small wash of power seep from my pores.

The only thing I want to *mourn* right now is the crown I just inherited by becoming a murderer.

"Stop telling me he's *dead*," I snap, stabbing them all with the best Beasty impression I can conjure. "I know he's dead, but I have a loose sun bun tether that needs its father to cling to. So for the last time, someone flash Sol to the world's rotten arsehole so he can marinate in some shit and I can try to bring him back! *Now!*"

My mates draw a collective breath before they all move toward my fallen Day God, giving me a wide berth as they mumble to each other in that ancient language.

I'm on fire again. Big deal. I needed them to see I'm not faffing around.

Also, it's fucking freezing.

Kal and Aero each wrap a hand around Sol's arms, peering at Drake then at the flaming mess beside him, before one of them tears open the Bright. They disappear with a strident clap of light and sound, leaving a Sol-sized stamp in the frozen blood.

I almost vomit all over it.

I look to Drake and shove my hand towards him, but he just clears his throat and ruffles his filthy feathers. "Babe ..."

Oh, right.

I tamper the flames and wrap my broken wing around myself so it's not dangling about.

Drake watches me for another beat, opens his mouth,

then shakes his head and steps in close. He pulls me against his chest and rips into the Bright ... leaving my father's body alone in the cold on a deserted throne room floor.

I wonder if anyone noticed the piece of my heart left lying on the ground next to him.

CHAPTER FIFTY-TWO
DRAKE

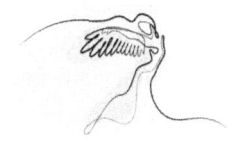

The smell of shit almost knocks me unconscious, despite the bog being frozen and dusted with snow. The pungent aroma drudges up memories of a wafer-thin girl who held my heart in her dying hands, making my feathers fluff around my chilly parcel.

I fucking hate this place.

"Are we supposed to ... dig him a hole?" Kal mumbles, juggling Sol's silver wing poised around his back while he scuffs the frozen muck with his boot.

My own wings tighten their grip around Dell as she goes stiff in my arms, and I wince. For someone so in tune with other people's emotions, Kal sure says some insensitive shit sometimes.

He does, however, have a valid point.

All we're going to achieve with this is a premature burial that smells like the aftermath of eating five-day-old leftover fowl. Sol and I had our differences, but I'm sure he wouldn't be on board with having his corpse buried in a heap of frozen crap.

Dell's got her eyes closed to the fact that there's nothing left inside the vessel hanging between Kal and Aero.

Nothing.

I felt Sol's energy siphon back to the sun as he lay beneath our girl; felt like I was bleeding out on that throne room floor right along with him. I went from thinking I was about to lose my mate and unborn child to losing an integral link in the chain of my very meaning for existence.

We'd prepared for this possibility, but the reality of it is ... well, *fucked*. It feels like falling with no end in sight. Seeing my mate dwelling on such futile hope? That's just bitter icing on the poisonous cake I'm being forced to gag on.

Dell wiggles in my grip and I loosen my hold, letting my hand trail her abdomen, every muscle in my body knotting the moment she slips away.

I clear my throat and bang my fist against my still-healing chest as my lungs tighten. Even a centimetre of separation between us feels like the space is stretched too thin.

I thought I'd lost her when she penned herself off from us, and if she pulls that shit again ... well, I can't be held accountable for my actions.

Dell leads the others out across the bog, finds a spot she appears to deem suitable, and tells everyone to stand back. She propels a plume of white flames from her motherfucking hands straight at the snowy surface of frozen shit, making a steamy puddle that ratchets up the reek we're all choking on ...

I guess that's one way to do it.

I try not to look too dismal as I watch that puddle bloom with false hope.

"There," she snips, shaking her hands out and painting a faux smile on her face that makes my hackles rise. "Nice, warm mud bath."

Don't, babe.

Don't give me that precious smile unless it's fucking real.

This mask she's wearing is enough to set my beast on edge. There's more to this picture than she's letting on, I know there is. I saw the struggle she went through while I was clawing along the ground, desperate to put down the monster myself.

I've been preparing for that task a shit ton longer than she has, and I detest that it's now weighing down her conscience and not mine.

I just want Dell to pour her pain onto my bloody shirt until she's empty enough to assess the damage ... but she's on a morose mission fuelled by grief, putting off a fall that's inevitable.

I help the others ease Sol's cold, lifeless body into the sludge, wedging him up against a lump of frozen shit. When I almost vomit all over him, it has nothing to do with the smell and everything to do with that hole in his chest that seems to stare at me, reminding me that he'll never get to hold his baby.

We let go of him, and all three of us breathe a soft sigh when his body doesn't sink. I doubt that would have gone down very well with our little mate who's giving us all a decent taste of her defensive growl.

Aero stands, wipes his hands on his pants, then plants them on his hips, and I can tell by his awkward stance that he's probably feeling about as lost as I am right now. "Well ... he looks pretty comforta—"

Plop.

"Fucking hell," Kal mumbles as I watch Dell wade towards Sol, dragging muddy wings behind her like big shit-nets.

I snarl, my beast roaring at me to sink my teeth into her and drag her out by her neck ...

For once, the fucker is on to something.

What if she drops below the surface and we can't find her

again? What if the world's sphincter decides to chew them both up for using and abusing its saintly shit? It's a fucking long shot, but I'm not one to take risks.

I'm just peeling back my lips, preparing to pounce, when she throws up another sparkly fucking *shield*, tossing the three of us backwards with the abrupt force. I land in a feathery heap, teeth bared, ready to draw the *one* card I have up my sleeve when Aero snaps his hand around my wrist like a shackle.

"*Don't.*"

I hiss at the daring bastard, wishing I wasn't dry as a husk so I could give his liver a little squeeze. "That's my *child* in there ..."

"And Dell's got a clipped wing," he sneers, flashing his canines. "And she's nearly as cold as Sol, for fuck's sake. Let her warm up and heal before we shatter this ..." he drops his voice so low even I can barely hear him, "this *illusion* she's hiding behind."

I grunt. So does my beast.

The man has a point.

"Fine," I mutter, snatching my arm back and dusting myself off. "But I have my limits."

She'll learn that.

"So do I," Kal grits out, staring daggers at her from his spot crouched on the ground with his shield-splitting sword drawn, his wings perched as if they're preparing to spear him straight through the sparkly shell.

The dexterous fuck probably landed that way.

I sigh, blindly plucking twigs and other muck from my filthy feathers while watching my girl marinate in a pool of rotten hope, cradling my brother the same way I sometimes cradle Sap to sleep.

That's what Dell needs: a snuggle from my wee fireball. Fuck, that's what we both need. That bouncy critter is my constant reminder that the world was once good and kind. When this dust settles, Sap will show Dell she has a family waiting in the wing, ready to give her something to fight for.

Dell rocks back and forth in her bubble, humming a tune I don't recognise, stroking Sol's face and smearing it with crap ...

He would be rolling in his shit grave if he knew she was suffering this way.

I study his pale complexion, wearing none of the golden glow the sun once fed him.

My skin crawls.

Someone really should have shut his eyes ... then we wouldn't be haunted by his flat, hollow gaze staring at sweet fuck all.

Lifeless.

I clear my throat, trying to tamp another dry retch, thankful that I can blame it on the vile stench. I hear Aero do the same while I watch Kal's eyes glaze over, as if he's using the spare time to store the painful shit somewhere deep where his beast can pickle himself in it.

Dell thinks this place will bring Sol back to us, but we're out here choking on the merciless truth: There is no magical bog that can restore the spark of life.

Death is final.

And so we wait for her to come to terms with the bitter taste of our new reality ...

Sol's gone.

CHAPTER FIFTY-THREE
DELL

"Come on, come back to me," I mumble into Sol's damp, frosty hair, wishing I had my little bag of potpourri to stem the overwhelming urge to vomit everywhere. "I know the prospect of all those dirty diapers in our future is frightening, but *you* planted that baby seed inside me, Daymare, so you don't get off the hook that easily."

A tingling sensation crawls up my wing, and I cringe when the bone snaps back into place.

I'd forgotten it was even broken. The pain paled in comparison to the raw ache inside my chest.

"Also, we didn't get a chance to discuss baby names. I know you're just rolling in your sunshiny grave at the possibility of me naming our child Solson or Soliday, but I'll do it if you don't pry yourself from your peaceful possie and throw me some better options."

He doesn't answer.

I sigh into his hair. "Honestly? I'm surprised you're not more anxious to dive into the world's boggy arsehole with me. This is a once in a lifetime opportunity. I know you love a bit of arse play ..."

He doesn't move.

I press my lips against his temple, swallowing the lump in my throat. "Look, I know you can be a brutal bastard, that you'll probably teach our child to swear before I do, and we'll disagree on every child-rearing decision, but I'm okay with that ... I'd rather disagree with you on *everything* than not have you to argue with at all."

I thread my hand down his chest, below the boggy surface until I feel the raw, spongy flesh of his gaping wound.

No, no, *nope*.

I snatch my hand away, shaking my head, trying to ignore the fact that this muddy trough I made seems to be shrinking by the minute and is no longer steaming. I'm not sure I'll be able to warm it back up without turning my little dome into an oven and giving Sol a hasty cremation ...

"Just a bit longer," I say through chattering teeth. "The sun made you, so the bog's probably just trying to figure out how to put you back together again. You just need to cure for a while."

Beasty looks up at me with wide eyes and probes me with her paw, her talons entirely retracted.

Does she want me to toss her a severed dick treat? Because she's shit out of luck. That's not the sort of thing I carry around in my back pocket.

I brush her off and focus on my holey Day God as a thick sheet of snow starts to batter the outer shell of my shield. Though the sound is soothing, I can't help but notice my patient mates start to shiver out there ...

Sol sure is taking his sweet time.

I try to ignore the tear that rips a path down my cheek when I blink. And all the ones that follow. "Look, you n-need to hurry up and come back, okay? It's cold, and ..." I clear my throat, "and I can't do this without you. I c-can't. And I don't want to."

I don't fucking want to.

I nuzzle his hair and try to draw on his scent, expecting my senses to spirit me off to the shack on his little island—to white sheets we never got to tangle between and cresting waves that salt our skin.

But all I can smell is shit.

Slowly, bit by bit, I'm losing every part of the man I love, and I can't help but wonder if this was how my mother felt when her mate began to slide into his shadows.

Helpless.

"P-please don't leave me to raise our baby without you ... *please*. My mother always put on s-such a brave face, but I would sometimes wake up in the middle of the night and hear her crying. At the time, I thought it w-was because I'd done something wrong ... but now I know it was because her heart was broken."

I hear the others mutter between each other, but I ignore them. I can't understand that language anyway.

"I d-don't want that for our baby. I don't. Please come back ..." I press my lips to his temple, puffing milky breath all over his face. "*P-please ...*"

Nothing.

The pool continues to shrink, along with my well of hope.

"I lost a father today, Sol ... one I n-never knew I had."

My mates stop talking, and I close my eyes, not wanting to watch them watch me unbandage this raw wound that will likely always be just a little bit septic.

"He called me b-beautiful before he died, and the words just sounded so ... *different* coming from him. Like they had this extra special meaning. That probably doesn't make much sense, but I can't really explain it any other way ..." I clear my throat, trying to persuade the lump to go away. "One thing I know for sure is that I refuse to let our child g-grow up without knowing how it feels to have your arms wrapped around him. Or her."

I fucking refuse.

And so I wait.

And wait.

And wait ...

There's a soft tap against my shield. I glance over, seeing Aero's whisky eyes peering in, his wings dusted with snow and perched high on his back.

"Dell, you're turning blue. We need you to come out now."

I shake my head, nuzzling back into the crook of Sol's neck. Perhaps I didn't make myself clear enough with the shield I've been fortifying since I got in here.

I'm not coming out. Not unless Sol comes out with me. Alive.

"Dell ..."

"N-n-no," I stammer, tightening my grip ... I think. My limbs have no sensation left.

Not that I care.

Come on, Alphie. Come back to me.

I brush off another probing beast paw. It's a bit like having a needy house cat living inside me.

"Babe ..."

Drake's solemn tone coils around me like a choker chain, snagging my attention, and it occurs to me that I should have used the soundproof shield ...

Something's not right.

I lift my head and stare into golden orbs that seem to have lost their lustre. He's standing on the frozen edge of my shrinking pool, his face set in stony resolve.

I narrow my eyes.

He tugs his wings in, then drops into the bog. It only takes two languid steps until he's just outside the boundary of my shield ...

"What are you d-doing?" I whisper, trying—and failing—to drag Sol through the thickening sludge ... *away* from Drake.

I don't miss the way his brow pinches.

"You're going to freeze."

The words sound more like an apology than a statement.

Unshed tears start to blur my vision, like my body's realising something my mind is trying so hard to ignore.

"I'm fine!"

He presses his forehead against my wall of defence. "You're not, Dell. You're a fucking ice cube, and my tolerance can only be stretched so thin."

Fat tears spill down my cheeks.

"G-g-go away," I mutter. "Leave us alone."

"Can't do that, babe. You know I can't."

My eyes flutter closed, and I turn to face the other way, ignoring the man I love. The golden link attached to my brittle heart tugs, making fresh tears well as I nuzzle Sol's stiff, frozen shoulder.

Now that my eyes are closed, I don't know if I want to open them again. It's a strange kind of peacefulness—one that slows your thoughts and makes you feel like time itself is creeping by ... which is kind of perfect for me since I don't want to go forward without him.

"Dell ..."

No.

"I wish for you to lift your shield and get out of this bog. *Now.*"

Drake's words fall over me like a sinister shadow, and I choke on a strangled sob. A warmth claims my body and soul before decimating entirely, leaving no prisoners aside from my ravaged heart and the bitter taste of failure.

My face twists into a scream, but no sound comes out

through my calloused throat as my shield drops without my permission ...

Sol is lifted while my limbs scramble to snatch him back. I can barely see through the sheen of tears, gritting my teeth while my body betrays my withered heart and tries to make me move.

"Get her out, Dusk. Before she hurts herself."

"Just focus on him!"

Something warm dribbles from my nose before my stiff limbs and wings are folded up. I'm swept against a warm body that's so at odds with the unresponsive bulk of my Day God that just got confiscated from me.

"Shhh ... it's okay, babe," Drake whispers, carrying me out of the bog and tramping towards the bank. His wings cloak us both like a thick robe that gives me no sense of comfort. "It's going to be okay."

It's not.

Someone sweeps a hand across my forehead. I pry my eyes open to see Kal's brooding face ... and I'm momentarily blinded by the fierce light radiating from flaxen wings wrapped around me.

What the ...

I blink, unsure whether what I'm seeing is reality or my mind's unusual response to the sour taste of betrayal.

My Sun Gods were already straight tens before ... but now? They're straight *glowing* tens.

Everything about them is more spectacular. Kal's leaking soft wisps of shadows that fall off him like tortured smoke, and I swear I can see the entire night sky in his eyes. Drake's thick, tousled hair bleeds a burnished, liquid radiance, and what little I can see of his skin looks even *more* golden. Aero's hair looks like a mess of rebellious flames, and he's swaddled in a rosy aura that's so beautiful it makes me want to weep ...

Wait a minute ... *wait a fucking minute.*

My heart leaps into my throat and tries to worm its way out of my mouth.

The wishes! The wishes are complete!

Before I have a chance to comprehend my own train of thought, I'm jabbing Drake in the guts with my elbow. While he's roaring from the shock, I use all this shitty lubrication to my advantage and slide out of his grip, duck some swiftly moving snatchy hands, and fall to my knees next to Sol who's spread out beneath a drooping tree.

The power surge will bring him back.

"Dell, what the flying *fuck* are you doing? You need to warm up!"

"The p-p-power boost," I rasp, throwing myself over Sol like a boggy blanket. "It's going to b-bring him back. I want to be the first thing he sees."

I grip the sides of his face and study his flat eyes, waiting for him to blink ... ignoring the foreign conversation my other mates are having under their breaths.

They probably think I'm crazy, but I'm not. This is the answer to all our problems, and I don't know why I didn't think of it sooner.

He's going to glow any minute now, then complain about the smell and ask how the fuck we ended up *here* of all places. He'll wrap me in his big, shit-covered wings, then drag me through the Bright, straight into a steaming bathtub that'll rinse away the evidence of all this pain.

I might even welcome him back from his grave with one of my famous blowjobs after I've warmed up a bit and can guarantee my chattering teeth aren't going to decapitate his cock.

Kal kneels beside us and brushes a thumb through the muck on my face, leaving a wisp of darkness clinging to my skin. "Little Dove, he's not coming back."

I shake my head and glance back at Sol's powdery eyes. "He will. Y-y-you'll see."

Kal sighs, muttering something in the language of the arsehole. Drake answers, his sharp, husky words making my skin prickle.

Pessimists.

Kal slides his hand down my body and folds my wings into my back. It feels quite nice until he begins to peel me off Sol ...

"*Stop!*" I shout, thrashing in his arms, but his grip only tightens and he's a shit ton stronger than I am.

"Little Dove ... don't make me put you to sleep. *Please.*"

"Just *do it!*" Drake roars. "Before she puts her fucking wal —*fuck!*"

Too late, Sunset.

"*Vej al de na viuala!*" Aero snarls as I grab Beasty by the scruff, noting she was mid-paw probe *again*. Perhaps she wants the reins?

Well, now's her chance.

I throw the bitch in control.

She seems to take a second to warm up to the idea before twisting in Kal's arms and growling at them all, showing them just how long and sharp our pretty canines are.

The three of them spread their glowing wings and I'm surprised my beast doesn't get distracted by all those handsome feathers.

"Put me down. *Now.*"

"Stop, Dell. This needs to *stop*," Kal thunders, his wings drumming a slow beat. "You need to think of the babies!"

"I fucking *am*," she sneers, slipping our hand down the front of his pants where the bitch grabs his nuts and gives them a squeeze ...

He grunts.

"Now, put me down."

I watch Kal's upper lip curl back from my place on the inside, pacing back and forth; thankful my beast isn't out there blowing shit up to satiate her mournful bloodlust.

"*Gluvi des ta ...*" Kal mutters through his teeth, eyes hardening as he sets us back down on top of Sol.

Beasty drops his balls, then flashes our teeth at the tightening snare of Gods. "You might want to back up."

Huh?

She curls around our Day God, nuzzles into the crook of his neck, then grabs me by the scruff with her feral teeth. I squeal as she tosses me back into my own body, almost causing me to vomit all over Sol from the displacement whiplash.

Well, shit. That's how that feels. No wonder the poor thing gets pissy at me sometimes.

I'm still reeling when my beast starts rooting around in my shadows which feels a bit like a dry dicking right in the pit of my soul. She turns to the surface with frail, ebony threads clinging to her whiskers, offering me a wad of steaming blackness as if it's some tasty morsel she's spent hours preparing and not something that resembles a pile of beast poo.

I blink at her. '*What is that? The last thing I need right now is more shi—*'

She starts to *whimper*, giving me those sad eyes again, shoving it at me like it's an insult to turn down her strange little shit-gift.

Fucking hell.

I scoop the dubious bundle and gasp when the wispy darkness falls away, revealing a searing orb of crisp, blinding *light*.

Tears well in my eyes because I know exactly what this is. Something I've been in denial about for most of my life.

My beast is parting with one of the first gifts my mummy ever gave me ...

> *She plucked a star from the sky above,*
> *Then set it in her daughter's soul.*
> *She asked it to watch over her*
> *And keep her daughter whole.*

I dig my fingers into Sol, clutching him so tightly I'm surprised we don't fuse together. And then I start to pour.
And pour.
And pour ...

CHAPTER FIFTY-FOUR
KAL

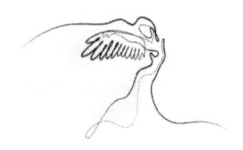

Dell's body contorts, her wings stabbing the air as she erupts like a tiny fucking *star*. Light pours from between her lips, her eyes, her nose, and I have to shield my face when she burns so bright it starts to scald my exposed skin.

I scream her name loud enough to taste blood, sending hot shards of power towards her, trying to get a gauge on her emotions ... but her walls are like pure darnium.

Impenetrable.

What are you doing, Little Dove ...

I'm trapped in the wake of her explosive energy, toes dug into the ground so I don't get tossed through the air—my beast a fierce, twisted blur pacing inside me.

We haven't felt this sort of raw, guttural power since we were born from the sun.

Drake and Aero's emotions are so loud it feels like my heavy heart is trapped in a vice.

Anger. Shock. Grief. Frustration.

The overflow puts knots all through my chest that I scramble to untie. But there's one main ingredient oozing off them—something so rare I can tell they don't know how to feel about it trapped inside their chests, fluttering about, making itself known ...

Something I've become accustomed to since I first held Cassian in my arms.

Fear.

"What's she fucking doing?" Drake thunders, his hand a claw digging into his pec while the other shields his face from the unforgiving light exploding out of her. He's on his knees, feet dug in the dirt, his wings trying to propel him towards our powerful, *stubborn* mate.

I have no idea.

Aero roars, and I catch a glimpse of him trying to inch towards her, his beast wholly in charge and actually making some progress, right before her light is snuffed out.

I'm assaulted by the most perfect stillness; void of sound, movement, trees, grass ... just a drab, grey space.

A clean slate.

Snow sifts down, doing what little it can to re-populate the gully that's been scraped clean of the residue.

There, at the epicentre of destruction, is Dell's small body folded over Sol—the floppy tip of her wing curling into the bog.

Most of the filth is gone, like it was burnt off by the force that just exploded out of her.

I sense a flicker of *disbelief* and draw a sharp breath, falling to my knees, watching Sol's arm rise from the ground and fold over Dell's body. His silver wing follows and I shake my head, scrambling for something ... *anything* to justify this miracle I'm witnessing.

Impossible. Fucking *impossible*.

She brought him back.

Sol groans and I choke on the sound, my sense of reality

tipping on its axis. He rolls to the side, opens his eyes, and I watch Dell's head flop back ...

Sol's eyes widen.

My heart stops beating.

I hear Aero thud to his knees.

"*No*," Drake groans, falling forward, hands fisting the dirt while he watches on with a face just as desolate as our surroundings.

I slap my hand across my mouth so I don't disturb the patient silence—my beast lapping at Dell's tether, keeping guard while we wait for her to breathe ...

Or move.

Or blink.

Her curls hang long and limp, reaching for the ground like spindly bones. Her skin no longer holds that pearly sheen. Her eyes are closed, and those plump lips seem to have bled their rich, red hue—perpetually parted, as if ... *as if* ...

As if her soul slipped from her body while she was still pouring that light into Sol.

I choke on my next breath, trying to convince myself of *anything* else while Sol's eyes become wild, electric pools that scour every surface of our mate. He draws sharp, sporadic breaths like he's forgotten how to breathe, and his hand flies to his chest ... swiping through the muddy remnants, searching for a wound we all know is no longer there.

He resorts to etching the flesh covering his heart with a clawed hand like the motion alone could hold himself together.

Keep her present.

Undo everything she just did.

"*This isn't real*," Aero wrestles out, his voice a dark, twisted thing that makes my skin crawl.

I should turn, see if he's okay, but I can't bring myself to look away from Dell folded backwards over Sol's arm ... waiting for her to give me something to cling to.

Trying to avoid being crushed by the compounding weight of my brothers' emotions.

My own.

The link on my heart tugs taut and I groan, my fingers sharp talons that dig into my chest as our tether begins to crumble, and all my worst nightmares peek above the surface of reality ...

My beast scrambles to catch all the tiny white pieces that flake off, trying to push them back into place ...

It's useless.

She's going.

Drake roars so loud my ears bleed, or perhaps that's just my body breaking apart without the roots of her essence holding it together.

Sol gives Dell a little shake, his eyes holding the smallest drop of hope that swiftly bleeds away.

I feel the devastating flood of heartbreak like an axe cleaving my chest clean open ...

Sol heaves a twisted moan, his hand sliding down her body and coming to rest over the gentle swell of her abdomen. The boulder of his helpless anguish drops on my chest with such force that I grunt from the impact.

And then he starts to scream.

CHAPTER FIFTY-FIVE
DELL

*R*ibbons of light cling to my limbs, trailing behind me as I flounder for something to grab hold of in this endless void of white ...

If my beast has plugged me into some strange, alternate version of the Bright like a useless knick-knack nobody wants but you just can't bring yourself to toss away, I'll skin the bitch and turn her into a pair of slippers.

I hear a song and spin so fast I swaddle myself with light. *My* song, sung in a voice that sounds like swims across a glassy lake and soft kisses that never fade.

It's a voice like warm, buttery scones that fall apart on my tongue. One that soothes a hurt until it's nothing but a distant memory ...

It's a voice I'd recognise anywhere.

Mummy.

I close my eyes and listen, absorbing ... *savouring*.

Making the most of this dream.

A sudden chorus of giggles gives the tune *life*—the sound both erratic and vivacious. I open my eyes and gasp when a glowing orb sneaks up from behind, skates right up to my face, and a little boy's voice *whispers something* I don't understand.

Seems my dreams have taken on the language of the arsehole.

Lovely.

I'm just about to ask the high-spirited orb to speak *normally* when the tiny thing giggles and shoots off through a cloud of fog.

Hmm.

I know this game. As it turns out, I'm rather good at it.

Hide-and-go-seek.

Guess he likes to play, too.

"Ready or not, here I come," I whisper, unable to stop the smile that splits my face.

I dash forward, dragging ribbons of light akin to the water weeds I used to scoop from the bottom of the lake. Piercing through a spray of mist, I'm bombarded by a *flurry* of orbs that twist and churn as if they're dancing ... or *playing.*

With me.

But just as quickly as they came, they disappear, shooting off through the haze together and leaving a trail of giggles.

Cheeky things.

"Hey, wait up!"

I follow them, pawing the mist—remembering how it felt to giggle like that.

Light and fluffy and whole.

The smog dissipates and I have to rub my eyes ...

There, nuzzled in the crook of a billowy cloud, is my childhood home.

Except it's *not.*

The apple tree out front is weighed down with fat fruit—their luscious, red skin shimmering. The surrounding fence seems to smile, inviting me towards the soft tune that's trickling out of a wide-open window.

I've never had this dream before ...

I float to the front gate and peel it open, missing the rusty *squeak* I'm so familiar with. I walk through wild grass until I'm standing at a pristine front door—the eggshell blue stark against the flawless white of the house.

My balled fist hovers over the surface ... but then I think better of it.

I'm not sure why I feel the need to knock.

The song stops the moment I touch the doorknob, and I hold my breath ... preparing for the pitfall that'll no doubt leave me curled over, waking with sweaty sheets and a hoarse throat.

Still, curiosity killed the whore.

I push the door open, welcomed by the smell of butterbread pudding and freshly stewed fruit. It feels like I've stepped into one of the brightest shards of my memories—except I can reach the handle now and there's a stranger peeling apples at the kitchen bench, looking out the window with a faraway gaze.

Her long hair is curly wisps of smoke that reach all the way to her hips, her flawless complexion stained peaches and cream.

She's wearing my mother's clothes.

I shake my head, trying to work out what my mind is up to.

The woman turns, her hand fluttering to her chest as I fall to my knees ...

Although I don't recognise that beautiful face from any of my memories, those eyes? *I'd recognise them anywhere.*

I spent years trapped in a dark room, kissing a rock the exact same hue.

River rock grey.

She kneels before me, her gaze searching mine, trembling hands rising to my face. The moment they settle, I watch a tear fall.

It takes the pad of her thumb skating across my cheek for me to realise I'm also crying—and not a gentle cry that makes no sound, but the heaving sort that splits you right down the middle.

Mummy.

"You—you've gotten so big, baby ..." she falters through a sad smile that makes my heart ache.

Is she not happy to see me? Perhaps *that's* the cruel catch of this dream?

I push the thought aside and nod into her hands, trying to blink away the haze of my tears. "You ... you look so different. So ... *whole.*"

Her watery smile warms, making her eyes shine. "Everyone's whole in this place, Little Dove ..."

My hand drifts to my chest ...

She's right.

My heart's no longer haunted by gaping wounds. And my mummy's white tether—the one which tore out of me after my father sliced her throat open—is now filling that hole again, fluttering with life.

Even *tugging* a little.

"I want to stay here forever," I whisper, folding my hand over hers.

The light in her eyes seems to shutter, but I mean every word.

I don't want to wake up from this wholesome dream to a reality where I'm curled over my dead mate with a hole in my heart and my father's death on my hands. A reality where my mother's face is still a smudge, and these floorboards are forever stained with a pool of her blood.

My heart flutters again, like it's just been hooked on a

fishing line, and I feel a warmth radiating from my ... *womb* of all places. Mummy and I glance down at the warm, buttery light pouring out of me, and I frown, sniffing back my overflow of emotions.

Well, that's new.

"I ..." *I have no idea what's happening.* "Sorry, sometimes I leak light, but not usually when I'm—" I look up to see my mother's twisted face, tears streaming down her cheeks ...

These tears don't smell like the ones that fell when she was sawing off my wings. These tears smell like *happiness*.

"Wh—why are you crying?"

I hate that I'm frightened to hear the answer. I hate that I automatically think something bad is about to happen.

She shakes her head, her gaze darting behind me for a second as heavy footsteps thump against the floorboards.

I don't turn around.

I can smell a botanical musk; I know who's casting me in his larger-than-life shadow.

Perhaps this is the cruel twist of this otherwise perfect dream? I'm about to watch the monster ruling my daddy's body slice my mother's throat again, knowing full well there's a tortured man beneath the surface, screaming for him to stop.

"I'm crying because they love you," she murmurs, tilting my head to kiss my tears away. "And because they *listened*."

Listened ...

I glance at the rich, creamy light *pouring* from my abdomen, twisting up my body, warming me ... and my heart winds in my chest.

I realise with a gasp that this is not a dream.

I'm here, with my mother and father.

Dead.

Meaning my mates ... my *babies* ...

"*Mummy*," I weep as my face crumbles, the slam of

comprehension making my head spin. I fall forward into her arms, trying to find some sense of comfort in the steady beat of her heart ...

But there is no beat, because her heart stopped working when her soul slipped out of her own body.

I curl up on her lap, trying to fit. But I'm not the child I used to be.

"It's okay," she coos, the words stretched far too thin. She runs her fingers through my curls, painting them with the motherly touch I never thought I'd feel again, and I hear the lyrical giggles of those little balls of light.

I open my eyes, watching them churn in a playful dance I could never grow sick of.

"I know why you didn't look back," I croak, feeling the heat take greedy sips of my soul.

She stiffens, and I bunch my hands into her clothing as if it could keep us wedged together.

"And I need you to know that you didn't fail me. Not at all. You were the best mummy I could have asked for, and I love you *so* much."

I hear her choke.

"I know, Little Dove. I know you do ..."

I slip further, losing sensation in my abdomen, my thighs, my chest—watching those balls brush against my mummy as if they find comfort in her touch ...

Hot tears stream down my face when I realise that's exactly what they're doing.

That scalding light takes big, ravaged gulps, then I can no longer feel the fingers brushing through my hair. I know it means that somehow my mates are bringing me back from the dead, but I have no idea what that means for my babies ... and I'm frightened to find out.

What if I've lost them? What if I've *failed* them?

"I taught your brothers to play hide-and-go-seek,"

mummy whispers in the voice she would use when she was trying to distract me. Like the times I'd wake in the middle of the night to the sound of her sobbing, and I'd ask what was wrong. We'd somehow end up talking about the stars ... or our chicken that never laid eggs and we later discovered was actually a rooster. "It's their favourite game. Playing it with them reminds me that you exist, somewhere, and that I didn't lose you after all."

"*Mummy*," I whisper, my body losing all sense of sensation as I begin to lift off her lap.

"Now I know it was all worth it, even if it means we have to spend eternity apart. I'll always love you, Adeline, and I'm so proud of the *woman* you've become."

I try to respond, but nothing comes out as I drift like a feather on a breeze. I scramble to grab hold of *anything* ... screaming '*I love you*' over and over and over again.

My father steps towards mummy curled on the ground, clutching *nothing*.

I scream louder.

He kneels, sweeps her into his arms, then smooths the hair back from her face.

I notice his soft features and grey eyes that no longer look burdened, and something settles back into place inside my chest ...

He's happy. *Whole.*

They both are.

He plants a kiss on her head, and a fat tear falls down my mother's cheek as she smiles up at him ...

Then ... nothingness.

CHAPTER FIFTY-SIX
DELL

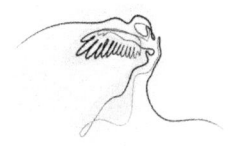

Waking is not a lazy, gentle thing; not when it feels like I've just been stuffed back into a shell that no longer fits, carrying a belly full of closure I'm not sure how to process.

My hand flies to my stomach ...

I unravel my essence from around my baby tethers, almost vomiting when I find them tucked at the epicentre, hanging off my heart. Still glowing. Still *safe*.

Strong little things.

I glance sidelong to the empty crater in my heart—a tombstone I refused to accept or even think about for years.

Mummy.

Suddenly, it feels like less of a raw, gaping hole ... more a scar that will always remind me of the precious years we had together, meshed somewhere between her terrors and my own.

Still, I try not to choke on my tightening throat. I may have some sense of closure and I may feel sick with relief that my sun buns are safe, but I now have *four* wounds in my heart, right next to my mother's ...

Four.

I open my eyes and squint at the luminous wing keeping guard over me like a big plate of armour. Feathers whisper and the glowing God whips up, nailing an arm on the other side of my body. His wings spread like he's gliding through clouds, and though the flop of dishevelled hair is trying to hide it, his electric-blue gaze is impossible to escape.

I let out a crushed moan that sponges all the bitter silence.

Sol.

My Sol.

He's *alive*.

"*Is it still there?*"

I feel my face fall from the snap of his anxious tone.

"Is *what* still there?"

"Our baby ... the *tether*," he grits, his voice cracking on the last word and making my heart fracture right along with it ...

Fuck.

How long has he been lying next to my body, curled up in his bed with holes in his own heart, wondering if our child survived? Three hours? Three days? Three fucking *weeks?*

"It's still there, Sol."

His features seem to melt and he draws a deep breath, as if it's the first to hit his lungs since I plucked him out of his sunny grave.

I press my hand flat against his chest, right above the absence of a wound that will likely taunt my nightmares for the rest of eternity. "Are the others okay?" I ask, watching his skin pebble in the wake of my skating fingertips.

"They're all *alive*, yes."

I nod, feeling the noose around my heart loosen as I chew the inside of my mouth, hating the feel of Sol's too-soft pillow under my head—giving such a false impression of comfort.

I'm not comfortable.

I'm so far from fucking *comfortable*.

My bones feel like they're trying to jut through too tight skin, my head spinning with an overflow of emotions—a turntable that *just won't stop* ...

One is impossible to ignore ...

Rage.

I push Sol and he rears back, giving me the space I need to sit up. His hands are shaking at his sides and I watch his nostrils flare ...

His brow jacks up.

I cock my arm, palm splayed, and drive it at his face, slapping him clean across his perfect cheek. His head stays snapped to the side, white hair dangling in his eyes. "*You left me*," I scream, my hand hanging limp. "You left *us*."

He lets out a low rumble and flicks the hair out of his face, paralysing me with a cerulean glare as strident as the midday sun. He lifts his chin, his upper lip curling back, and then my hand is rising again *without my fucking permission*.

How is he getting his power past my motherfucking walls?

"You're pissed at me because I value your life, my *child's* life, more than I value my own? *Really*, Dell?" My arm cocks back before swinging forward, slapping his cheek with a sharp *snap*.

"Sol, *stop!*"

He cocks my arm and I grit my teeth against the pull of his power, scouring my walls, trying to find the hole his compulsion must be slipping through.

No matter what I do, I can't stop the wave of assault he's forcing me to punish him with ...

Slap.

My palm throbs as he cocks my arm again. "*Believe* me when I tell you, your poison is unnecessary. I already *resent* myself for not being there to stop you from doing something as *stupid* as throwing it all away."

Slap.

"Sol, I said *stop!*"

Slap.

"Or what?" he thunders, crowing out a caustic laugh. "There's nothing you can take from me that I haven't already *lost.*"

I crunch my eyes shut, trying to ignore the tears that feel like blades slicing down my cheeks ...

"Don't close your eyes," Sol bellows, his voice blunt and threatening. "Don't close your *fucking* eyes again."

I open them, wearing my tears like armour as I face down my unhinged Alpha Arsehole who's struggling to alleviate his emotional boner. Truth be told, this is one sort of boner I'm not good at dealing with, either ...

"The world needed you, Sol."

I needed you.

Your baby needed you.

Don't even get me started on my vagina ...

"I had no *choice*. I had to at least tr—"

"No *choice?*" he snarls, and the rest of my words catch in the net of my throat. "Well, that's a steaming load of manticore shit. I took a spear to give you *choices*, then I made a wish for our child to live a long and happy life so that he or she could have *choices*. And then I woke up covered in *crap*, with you, the mother of my unborn child, lumped over me *lifeless*. I held you in my arms, trying to remember how to *breathe*, listening to my brothers scream as your tether turned to dust in their chests."

He launches forward, throws me back against the bed, wraps his hands around my wrists, and pins them over my head—my wings spread like a blanket beneath me.

"What are yo—"

"Do you know how long it took us to bring you back?" he sneers, his cold eyes so at odds with the hot breath fanning my face, smelling like desperation. *"Two minutes.* You laid there dead for *two fucking minutes* while Drake's baby tether withered by the second, and it was the longest two minutes of my life."

I shake my head, my hands curling into claws. "Sol, I—"

"You did have a choice. I made damn *sure* you had a choice. And you chose wrong."

I lift my head off the fluffy mattress and get my canines right up in his face. His eyes widen and his wings splay to their full span. "No. I chose *right*," I snap, fortifying my walls with an extra layer of adamant, patching up any potential holes he could possibly slip through again.

"You don't want to say that sort of shit to me right now, Dell." His grip tightens and I snarl, jerking my hips as if I could roll him off me ... or into me. One or the other. *"I've* got the upper hand."

I almost arch a brow.

Almost.

I guess he was too dead to see my beast turn an entire army into carrion. I'll let him keep his smoke screen, but first I need to straighten the kink in his emotional cock.

"You're here. *Alive.* I didn't fail this frozen fucking world I'm suddenly in charge of. You say I had a choice, but there is no world without you. No *me* and no son or daughter to carry your memory on. I made the *only* choice I had."

All the anger seems to drain right from his eyes. His face softens, as if I just peeled off the pinched arsehole mask he was protecting himself with.

"And what if we were too late?" he grits out, his voice cracking on the last word, the strong stance of his wings giving a little. Even his hands lose their rigidity, like the strength just bled out of him.

Fuck.

He's not angry. He's in *agony*.

"Sol ..." I wiggle my wrist free, take his hand in mine, and try to hide my shock when he freezes up over the contact. "Our baby is fine," I whisper, setting his palm over my heart. "How could it not be when its parents are both too stubborn to let each other *die?*"

His hand is a rock against my flesh, his body a mountain poised over me. Unmoving. Unblinking. Like he's caught in some sort of trance.

"This kid is made from strong stu—"

His lips break off my sentence, breathing in my words as he hungers over my mouth and tears at my shift. My body folds and I'm crushed against the mattress, as if he resents our very skin for the thin slice of separation.

He grinds his hips, his cock hard and ready to mute this hurt between us, and I can almost hear hushed thoughts with the beat of each feverish grind ...

I hate you.
I need you.
I love you.

I can taste the ashy grave of my own unheard words. The ones I spoke to a dead man when my heart was a rock in my chest.

"I love you, too," I pour, entombed by the ecstasy of this arcane reality.

He's here. He's alive. He can hear them now.

He makes a grating noise that gets under my skin and rattles my bones. It's robust, guttural, full of carnal heat—a proud, claiming sound that cushions my heart.

"I know," he rasps, like the words were ripped from his throat, and he whips back, leaving me breathless and panting.

He hovers over me; every rippling muscle looking like

they want to burst through his radiant skin. I try to move—to pull him back down on top of me—but I can't.

At all.

The only things I have control over are my lips, my tongue, my lungs, and my fucking *eyes* ...

"Sol ... *what*—"

My words catch when my legs spread *on their own.*

I glare between us with eyes bugging out of my head. "You shouldn't be able to do that. I have my walls up. I *fortified* that shit!"

He just grunts and hooks a finger in the hem of my nightie, dragging it up my thighs, trailing along my wet slit.

My eyes roll back, my body screaming for more of the delicious friction. "Somebody forgot to put underwear on me ..."

"You think I forgot?" he growls, brow twitching as he lets the hem fall to my stomach. I'm already a puddle of need when he pinches my clit, and a sharp *zing* snags me all the way to my belly button.

Fuck.

"This little pussy has been waiting so patiently for her punishment."

"Her punis—"

He pinches again, but harder this time, and I almost combust all over him. He soothes the hurt by sliding a finger inside, stroking that budding pleasure with tame, expert thrusts ...

I moan, needing to rock onto him but not being able to move a single *centimetre*. "More. I need *more.*"

"You'll get more, but only when I'm ready to *give* you more." He slips the offending finger into his mouth and *sucks* like I'm some sort of rare delicacy. "You're going to have to be *patient* for a change. Do you think you can handle that?"

Condescending jackass.

He sweeps up my foot and plants a kiss on my ankle, then the muscle of my lower leg, then the inside of my knee ... edging his way towards the coil of nerves between my legs.

All I want is to cuff his head with my thighs and force him to make a meal out of me ... but I'm putty in his hands.

"*Sol*, don't make m—"

He pinches my clit and sinks his canines right into the fleshy part of my inner thigh. I come apart with a sharp scream, pulsing around sweet fuck all as he draws on my blood and feeds on my submission.

My wings disappear and he suctions onto my clit with a glossy, red smear around his lips, watching me from the frame of my thighs as he nurses the high I can't seem to come down from ...

Every part of me has been lit with a ferocious hunger that will only be satiated once I taste the rich, coppery tang of Sol's blood.

He wipes his mouth with the back of a powerful forearm, surveying me while I try not to drool over all that skin ripe for the biting. "Still angry?"

I growl as he kneels between my legs with his pretty wings out. "Are you just going to sit there and look at me, Daymare?"

"Yes," he says with zero remorse, unbuttoning his slacks. He pulls out his big, angry dick, then gives it a white-knuckled jerk.

"You're not playing fair."

Dropping down, he nips the sharp blade of my hip bone, making the muscles jump and feather. "Really? And what are you going to do about it, *Sparrow?*"

He licks the hurt, then trails across to my belly button, planting a soft kiss that turns me molten. He looks up at me from his spot hovering over the discreet swell of my abdomen. "Burn me? Rip me up from the inside out? Give me all your pretty pain?"

"*Let me go.*"

Kissing up my ribs, he creates a trail of searing pleasure. "No."

I narrow my eyes. I know he needs control right now, but my canines are dripping venom down my chin so I'm not in a very philanthropic mood.

My shift is ripped clean down the middle, and he takes my nipple into his mouth, cupping my breast with a too soft hand. His lustrous skin is just as flawless as mine. *Too* flawless. It's a stark reminder that we've both been dead.

He drags the tip of his pointy finger along my lower lip, and I hold my breath, halting everything but the beat of my heart ... like a predator luring her prey into a trap.

He's so close I can almost *taste* him.

A finger trails down my canine, and I pride myself on staying rock fucking solid. "Good girl," he mumbles. "So *patient.*"

Sol can shove his patience lesson right up his Alpha Arsehole. He's about to discover just how *im*patient I am—and intend to stay for the rest of my immortal life.

"Patient girls get rewarded," he rumbles, dipping down to plant a kiss on my cupid's bow ... just as I snatch his bottom lip between my teeth.

I'm all about self-gratification.

His eyes widen and he lets out a low, throaty laugh that makes his dimple pucker and my heart ache ...

I'm not sure I've ever heard Sol laugh genuinely.

"You got me," he says, his voice shallow and raspy, and I hold him here—on the cusp of sealing our bond, trapped in the cage of his gaze like a prisoner of war.

He brushes his thumb over my peaked nipple. "But are you going to keep me?"

I bite into the soft, pliable flesh, making us both moan as that silver link digs into its wound on my heart. Our baby tether snuggles in tight, and Sol's hold on my body dissipates.

He drives into me, slamming our bodies together much the same way our souls just connected ...

I curl my legs around his hips, trying to find some form of closeness that will erase the memory of his flat gaze staring at nothing. "Don't you ever try to save my life again. I had it. *I fucking had it.*"

He grips my jaw, smudging blood across my chin—his shoulder a ball of muscle bunched by his head.

Eyes like the unforgiving ocean.

I don't notice I'm crying until his other hand comes up and swipes my cheek with a clenched fist—his low, threatening growl making my bones quiver.

It's not a gentle gesture. More like the tear has personally insulted him.

"I'll always be your shield, even when you don't need me to be," he scratches out, churning his hips.

I open my mouth to rebuke only for him to nail my jaw closed with the palm of his hand. "So how about you stop putting your life at risk and we'll call it even, hmm?"

He's pretending it's a question, but he's staring down at me like I'm his captive.

It's not really a question.

"*Fine*," I snip through my locked jaw, tilting my hips so the next time he slams into me it feels like he's stoking the embers of my heart.

Though I hate to admit it, his over-protective stance makes my hormones flutter a secret little love dance. Pretty soon he'll be pouring all that possessive energy into a tiny meld of both of us ... and I wouldn't have it any other way.

CHAPTER FIFTY-SEVEN
DELL

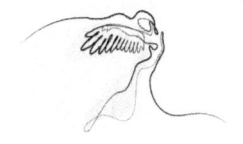

"*That* good, eh?"

I'm not sure what gives it away. Perhaps the fact I'm moaning more than I did while he was making my vagina gag around his cock?

I glug back an entire chalice of sweet, sparkly water and balance the goblet on his pec. "You really outdid yourself."

Dying is hungry stuff, and this colourful spread is exactly what my re-animated body needed. Also, Sol makes a great serving platter. I figured if I lumped all the food on his chest and straddled him, he couldn't flutter off and get himself killed again.

"Is that enough yet?"

His chin disappears while he inspects the remnants of the meal I was instructed to eat before he'll take me to see the rest of my ... *non-mates*. Turns out, I can devour half my body weight in meat and berries in less than three minutes flat.

"Finish the blueberries and we'll call it a wi—" Sol's mouth pops open and he starts to convulse, causing my remaining meal to scatter.

My heart drops right out of my arse as I watch all the

tendons in his body fight against the shell of his skin, his eyes rolling around in their sockets ...

Oh ... fuck. Did I not fix him properly? My star didn't come with a fucking manual!

My chalice clanks to the ground and shatters. *"What's happening?"* I scream, swiping a piece of meat from his nipple, patting his chest for any hidden holes. I peep at his cock to make sure I didn't damage it while I took his post-death virginity ...

"Sol!"

His entire body loosens and he huffs a sigh, then glances off the side of the bed to the mess of shattered crystal. "Fuck. Sorry."

Ahh ...

"What just happened? You looked like you were dying ... again."

I tried not to sound bitter.

It definitely sounded bitter.

His features soften and he combs his fingers through dishevelled hair, making my vagina drool over that popping bicep. "Drake was sending me a bolt of pain," he says on a yawn. "He's been doing it every half hour or so."

"Are you kidding m—" I try to scramble off him, but he clinches my waist and pins me down.

"Calm down, Sparrow. Don't tell him I said so, but it actually feels kind of good from this distance."

Lord have mercy.

"Why the hell is he doing that?"

He plucks a strawberry nesting against my crotch and takes a juicy bite. "I told them if they came anywhere near us until you'd bitten me, I'd compel them to twist their own ball sacks like a corkscrew."

My ovaries knot. Even my vagina tries to knit her little face shut. "Well. No wonder they're keeping their distance."

He almost chokes, his shoulders shaking as if he's repressing a laugh. "They're not. The moment one of them tries to fly off the sky platform," he shrugs, "I turn them right back around."

"You can do all that from ... from *here?*"

"Of course."

Fuck me, what have I gotten myself into.

Sol offers me a bite of his berry and I scrunch my nose. "No, thank you. That was practically bumping uglies with my vagina."

He shrugs and pops the rest in his mouth, making me want to ride his face.

"So ... are you back to full power?"

He nods, licking red juice off his fingers. "Your completed wish cycle was ... fruitful."

I'm rolled onto my back, feeling berries pop beneath my legs while he plucks a down feather from my curls. "You have no idea what you've signed up for, but there's no turning back now."

He pecks my nose with a kiss which feels like a brand of sympathy.

I'm missing something ...

He lopes off the bed like a feline, disappearing behind a door. "The unseasonable winter is still edging towards my kingdom. You should be warm enough in what you have on," he calls out, emerging in a pair of tight leather pants that hug his half-mast dick like a second skin, but his face quickly darkens. "Though I think you'll need another bath before we go ..."

I follow his gaze to the red and purple smear up my legs. "Nonsense," I mumble, sitting up. I don't want to spend any more time in that bath than necessary. The thirty second dip I had before Sol gave me my eating orders was enough to make my skin crawl. That tub brings back bad memories.

I grab the hem of my fresh shift that looks like smudged stardust, and put my teeth to the flimsy material—ripping off a wide strip I use to mop the mess. It's not until I slip off the side of the bed that I realise I took too much off the length ...

Oh well. Sun's out, clunge out.

Actually, maybe it's not appropriate. I did learn my common etiquette from a whore house.

I glance up to see Sol's eyebrow jacked so high it's almost jumping off his face. "I think I need some underwear ..."

He flicks the rugged hem of my refurbished nightie. "No underwear. You won't be wearing any for the foreseeable future."

Ahhh ...

"Then everyone's going to be seeing my *vagina*, Sol. How do you feel about *that*, huh?" I was hoping to make publicly exposed vaginas a thing of the past under my new rule.

"Nobody's going to see that sweet little succulent but us," he says, stalking towards me, those massive wings unfurling.

I wither under their dwarfing intensity.

"You're going to be under us, on us, or between us for as long as it takes to convince ourselves that you're actually *alive*." He pinches my chin, holding me hostage with the shackle of his gaze while his other hand slips around my lower back. "Do you have a problem with that, *Sparrow?*"

I feel my wings quiver inside me.

"Nope," I say, popping the 'p'.

"Good. Pre-warning, I don't know what you're walking into." He cracks a condescending half-smile, exposing that dimple again.

It's my new favourite part of him.

Hang on.

"Me? Don't you mean *we?*" I make a light grunting sound that's about ten percent attempted laugh and ninety percent nervous, awkward animal sound.

His thumb travels up my chin and over my bottom lip before dragging it down. "No. I mean *you*. My liver's going to get minced either way."

A heaviness settles on my chest ...

Actually, I'll be *disappointed* if mine doesn't get just as minced. I failed Drake's baby, failed *him*, and it's time to pay my dues.

Sol's hand tightens around my back before he rips a hole in the Bright, dousing us both in a spill of light.

We emerge on a massive crystal platform haunted by the strident sound of swords clashing. Sweeping columns arc from edge to edge with dense, sparkling material draped between them, creating large pockets of shade.

Towering at one end is a forever curling crystal wave that looks like the angry ocean itself. A throne is set in its barrel—the majestic structure carved from a colossal seashell, maintaining its natural spires and whorls.

It's the most beautiful throne I've seen, not that I'd tell the others that. They might take offence.

Speaking of which ...

Sol gives me a gentle nudge, and I stumble forward a few steps as Aero, Drake, and Kal stalk towards me—a deep gash across Drake's right pec knitting itself together before my very eyes.

Oh, boy.

Kal sheaths his sword in one fluid motion, the others tossing theirs aside. I'm trapped in a snare of narrowed eyes and scowling faces.

Sol just threw me to the wolves. So much for always being my *shield*.

I'm slapped with the scent of their anger and fear and ... my vagina smacks her lips.

Fuck.

Me.

Aero's eyes widen. "Oh, I fucking will."

"Easy, Dawn." The deep cadence of Kal's voice travels as if he spoke it through a megaphone.

I hear Sol thud to the ground behind me, and I whirl to see his strained face turning a deep shade of burgundy.

"I should have shaved your eyebrows off when you were dead, you silver *fuck*," Drake roars, and I watch Sol's entire body convulse. His wings twist upon themselves while his eyes roll around like marbles.

"Stop doing that, Drake! Now! Unless you want to find out what a flaming feather-finger is!"

Drake gets right up in my face, his burnished wings flaring as Sol coughs and splutters behind me. "*Done*," he grits through a locked jaw, then folds my head to the side, exposing the line of my neck and leaning in as if he's about to bite—

"Wait!" I push Drake ... which achieves sweet fuck all because he's a mountain.

"*Wait?*" he bellows, like he doesn't trust his own hearing. I snatch my hand away from Aero who was about to gnaw my wrist.

"*Yes*." I smush Kal's face away from my shoulder. "I ... I have something I need to tell you before you decide if you want to mate with me again."

Perhaps it's something in my tone, but everyone takes a step back as if they think I'm about to turn into a sizzling ball of emotion.

"Okay ..." Drake's brow pinches and he knots his arms over his chest, those bulky shoulder muscles popping.

I clear my throat.

Right.

My beast nuzzles under a shadow of shame and I don't even consider chastising her for it.

"It's ... it's about Sap."

Drake lifts a brow, his face seeming to light up, and it breaks my goddamn heart. "Fucking *finally*. You're ready to take on an active role in her parenting?" He cracks a crooked smile and my heart crumbles just a little more. "Honestly, I could really use the extra hands. The testy teens ar—"

"No, that's not what I'm talking about," I blurt, watching his face fall. I wrap my arms around myself, a feeble attempt to hold my splitting chest together. "Drake, my father captured her, and ... and ..."

"Dell, what are you talking about?"

I'm making this so much worse.

"He was trying to get me to break. I should have realised what he was up to when he set the girls on fire ... perhaps I could have given Sap more of a head start ... I don't know ..." I shake my head and sigh, dropping my arms. I lift my chin and look him square in the eye, watching him scratch his burnished stubble.

"No matter how hard I tried, I couldn't be who she needed me to be." My voice cracks on the last word and I blink, sending hot tears streaming down my cheeks. "I'm so sorry, Drake. I failed her."

He takes a step forward. "What do you mean you *failed* her?"

More tears zip down my cheeks as I prepare to break his big, golden heart. "He set Kyro on her. I heard the flames. She's ... she's *gone*."

I expect him to break apart—for his beast to rip through and churn my insides for failing his baby ...

But Drake just blinks at me, like he's trapped in the void of shock.

I know how that feels.

He takes another step forward, reaching out. "De—"

"No!" I snap, batting his hand, trying to work out why he isn't *punishing* me. I deserve whatever he gives; I'll take it, then get on my knees and beg for more. "Before you say anything else, I need you to know I don't want your forgiveness. Ever. I'll shoulder this guilt for the rest of my life. I understand if you can't bear to even look at me, let alone mate with m—"

He snatches my hand, dragging me towards the edge of the vast, crystal platform, and I have to jog to keep up as my heart leaves a trail of thundering beats. "What are you doing?"

"Putting you out of your misery."

Oh—*fuck*. A bit unceremonious, but ...

I nod to myself as I'm dragged along behind him, stealing a glance over my shoulder at my three other Sun Gods, wishing I had a chance to bone them one more time before paying my penance.

"Okay." A life for a life ... "I guess that makes sense."

Wait ... I'm worth *three* lives.

"*Ahh* ... maybe we wait until I've had the babies first though?" I screech, praying Drake will see reason and spare me eight or so months to pop his *other* child out first.

He stops and spins so abruptly I squish my face into his sternum. I rub my nose, hoping it's not broken ... before realising a crooked nose doesn't particularly matter when you're six feet under.

"First? Before what?" he thunders, and I wither under his all-pervading, molten gaze.

"Yyyy—" *yikes*. "You said you're putting me out of my misery. Sooo, before I ... *d-die?*"

Again.

Drake shakes his head as if he's actually *baffled* and

resumes our journey—the others trailing behind us with oddly calm demeanours. Aero even has a smile on his face, like he's going to take some sick pleasure in my impending doom.

His smile falls.

I squeal as I'm plucked off the ground and set down in front of Drake—his arms crossed over my chest. I try to make sense of what I'm seeing on that platform suspended between lofty towers glimmering in the midday sun ...

Kyro's lumped on it with leathery wings tucked against his back, and if it weren't for his twitching tail, I'd say he was asleep. But I guess it'd be difficult to nap with a drako the size of your hangnail gnawing on your face prongs like a feral game of tug of war ...

Sap's little snarls sound like the whirring wind, though Kyro's only reaction is to puff the odd plume of smoke from his full-moon nostrils.

My sob is spontaneous, and it's only when Drake's tightening grip starts to nag my aching boobs that I notice he's holding me up—that my knees have given way to the overwhelming sense of relief that's making me want to vomit meat and berries off the side of this platform.

"I ... I don't understand ..."

"That day on the field, you showed Kyro the first drop of kindness he's seen in fuck knows how long," Drake rasps against my ear, sounding almost *proud*. "Perhaps he saw how much Sap meant to you and it gave him the balls to go against his brutal conditioning?"

More tears slip down my cheeks as he pushes my hair off my shoulder and sinks his canines into the spongy muscle. My eyes squeeze shut and I cry out, absorbing the sweet sting of his commitment.

His teeth slide free and he manhandles my body until I'm trapped in his deprived embrace. "Don't you understand?" he mumbles, eyes blazing like the sun as he tucks a curl behind my ear. "You did save her. Fuck, you saved them *both*."

"I thought I lost your baby ..."

His thumb rolls my bottom lip down, piercing the pad with the sharp tip of my canine, causing us both to moan as my venom rushes into his body—stabbing that golden tether deep into the raw hole in my heart. Our baby tether tourniquets around our fresh link as Drake takes my mouth in a feverish collision that tastes like blood and leaves me breathless.

"It might just be me," Kal interrupts, "but that bantam spitfire has never looked happier."

Drake starts to rumble, peeling away from our kiss, and I look down at Sap still gnawing on Kyro's face; stopping every few seconds to waggle her body and taunt the huge, tolerant drako.

Drake huffs, brushing his hand across my lower stomach. "Yeah, well, she'll come crawling back when she needs her pound of lamb liver. And I doubt *Kyro* can rock her to sleep the way I do ..."

"Someone's jealous," Sol murmurs from the other side of Kal.

"Fuck off, ya big silver corpse."

I spin and slap Drake's broad, bloody chest. "Don't be a dick!"

He flaunts a sheepish smile. "Too soon? I'll try again tomorrow."

Kal plucks me off the ground and throws me over his shoulder before I get the chance to knee Drake in the junk. I let out a dense *oomph*, flashing my bits, my wings spurting from my back. They give Kal an upside-down cuddle, and I'm surprised the bastard can see where he's walking.

He slaps my exposed arse cheek. Hard. It feels so good I

almost beg him to do it again ... but a bit harder. And closer to my throbbing pussy.

He drops me to the ground a safe distance from the overwhelming mosh of male dominance and starts to jostle my ever-loving wings. "Just seeing for myself that we didn't miss any spots."

"What is *that* supposed to mean?" I ask, getting manhandled by his calloused fingers.

He doesn't answer, his face pinched in concentration.

I tap my foot while he clinically spreads my wings, scrutinising every single feather while Sol, Drake, and Aero advance.

Patience has never been my virtue.

Kal's half-turned away, making sure my wing folds in all the right places, when I strike—sinking my teeth into the back of his arm like a fucking snake.

He whirls, glaring, and I catch a line of blood rolling down my chin, then suck my thumb to savour the residue. He inspects my little viper bite, wings exploding from his back—puffs of black smoke falling off the fluffy feathers. "That's the first time I've ever been caught off guard ..."

"I don't like being ignored."

I also don't like having holes in my heart.

Kal laughs, low and dark and grating, then cocks his head to the side and sets his *black* eyes on me. *"Run."*

Ohh ... *shit*.

My stomach flips and I explode into action, the thrill sharpening my senses and turning me into a feathery sprinting *machine*.

I am swift.
I am speed.
I am—

A cloud of blackness swarms me, and I'm enveloped in

warm limbs, skating lips, and the sense of a feathery cage that makes me feel *safe*.

"Nice try ..." a dark, chilling voice rumbles, and it's all around me; *through* me. It's my pulse and the breath in my lungs. "But not fast enough to escape *me*."

My head is tugged to the side and I smile, folding into the virile body keeping me steady. Kal's canines pierce the stretched flesh of my neck, his lips hot on my skin as a black tether drives into my heart—like the roots of an ancient tree weaving deep, anchoring in place ...

The dark storm dissolves, his canines withdraw, and I open my eyes, staring up into a star-flecked gaze that makes me weak at the knees. I lift my hand to cup his sharp jaw ... and squeal.

I'm.

Fucking.

Glowing.

"What ..." I clear my throat, inspecting a long tendril of hair that looks like coiled *sunlight*. "What *exactly* did you do to me?"

Drake lets out a deep, rolling laugh, and I spin, stabbing my glare at three smirking arseholes standing with their arms crossed over bare chests. "We pieced you back together with sunlight."

"*You wh—*"

Fucking hell.

I glance sidelong at my splayed, *glowing* wings, then down to my hands, my feet, my legs ...

Fuuuucking helllll.

I stumble into the middle of the Sun God circle, hearing Drake and Kal chuckle while I lift the hem of my already short dress and ... *fuck my life.*

"*You gave me a glowing vagina!*" I stomp my foot and for some reason I start to glow *brighter*.

I stare at my hands, getting angrier by the second, while getting brighter and brighter and *brig*—

"I would stem that wrath if I were you, babe. Any anger, sadness, or anxiety only makes the sunlight work harder to hold you together. And makes your little baby barn glow ..." they all cock their heads to the side, "*brighter.*"

"And your arsehole, too," Sol rumbles from behind me.

I'm about ready to skin some Sun Gods and turn them into a pelt with down pillows to match.

"And what does this mean, exactly?" I sweep my hands down my glowing body with one hand, trying to shield my eyes with the other, and nearly blind myself. "Aside from the fact that I'm never going to be able to sleep again because I look like a fucking Fae orb."

I'm pissed.

I have a hard time sleeping already, and now I resemble the sun. I wouldn't be surprised if some motherfucking planets start orbiting me.

"Stop stressing," Aero says, cupping my cheek. "You only glow in direct sunlight. See?"

His wings emerge and sweep over me, creating a pocket of shade. My glow almost disappears entirely.

"Oh," I whisper, getting a little distracted by all those pretty feathers. "Guess I'll never be able to complain about any of you slipping one in the wrong hole ..."

"I never miss my target," Sol states, turning my vagina molten.

He really doesn't.

"While we're on the subject, your newfound glow also means we can ping you." Kal chucks in, and that gets my fucking attention. "We placed the trigger somewhere near your clit. Hope you don't mind. It seemed like a good idea at the time ..."

"What's that supposed to me—"

Something deep in my belly *zaps*, like plucking a lute cord ... but in my fucking *vagina*. All I can see is rippling velvet and distant prickles of light as I'm struck with this overwhelming flood of wanton *need*—the reverberations pooling in my core and making me want to dry-hump the air.

"What the hell was that?" I pant and notice I'm clutching Aero's *big* ... oh, no, it's actually his arm.

It happens again though this time it's all soft pinks and auburn tones and the overwhelming sense of thirst for my own blood. I slither down Aero's body, onto my knees, biting my tongue in a desperate effort to stem this compulsive desire.

Someone chuckles.

I don't know who it is, I just know it isn't *me*.

The *thing* happens again and all I can see is *gold*. Then *silver*. Then *black* again.

My vagina's slipped off into vagina heaven while my beast reclines on a shadow, flossing wisps of black from between her fangs. What a bitch.

My body winds forward, my disloyal wings palping one of my Gods while I ride that bitter, unobtainable edge of an orgasm—unable to form coherent words as my inner thighs become slick with arousal.

Screw this.

I throw my walls up, fortifying those bastards so they're nice and strong, but the delicious torture doesn't let up.

At all.

"She's trying to use her walls," Aero says with a light chuckle.

Are they defective? I worked so hard on them! I feel like I just lost the keys to my sin bin, and I don't feel good about it.

The pinging stops.

Aero helps me up once the aftershocks finally subside.

"Yes, they are defective. On us. Which I personally think is a vast improvement."

"You've got to be shitting me," I rasp, trying not to blush from the overwhelming scent of lusty vagina while my knees clank together.

Sol gets right up in my face. "That's your penance for giving your life to save me. Happy re-birthday," he rumbles through a condescending smile that's about to earn himself a one-way ticket straight to my sin bi—

Fuck.

Aero chuckles.

"You're all enjoying this far too much!"

Sol plucks me off the ground, wraps my legs around his trim hips, and strides towards his throne. My traitorous wings give him a bit of feather-finger while I twist and turn in his hold, waiting for the next ball to drop. "What are you doing?"

He plants me on his pretty throne, walks backwards down the shimmering steps, and cocks his head to the side. "Trying it out for size."

I clear my throat and smooth my hair, my toes swinging an inch above the ground. I'm pretty sure I'm flashing the four Gods now staring up at me. "I think it's a bit big ..."

Aero climbs the stairs and drops to his knees right in front of me, giving me a crooked smile, his wings floating down behind him like a red, orange, and peach coloured carpet.

"Ahh ..."

He wraps his hands around my thighs and cleaves them apart, the flushed flesh of my core right in his face. His lips curl at the corners, hands sliding up the insides of my legs and leaving a prickly trail ...

"What are you doing down there, Sunrise?"

He holds my gaze and swirls his thumb around my clit,

making my breath snag. "I'm on my knees for my Queen." He licks a hot line up my slit and I throw my head back as he thrusts his tongue inside me.

I knew I liked this throne.

I crack my heavy lids, seeing Kal, Drake, and Sol with their arms crossed over their chests, watching with smooth, content smirks stamped across their faces.

"She looks good up there," Sol mumbles to Kal, and his wings get a fluffy boner.

"Are you ... buttering me for extra ... gold vagi—*ohmygod*—stars, Solstice?"

Aero laughs between my legs, making me moan from the organic tickle that feels *amazing*.

"You've already given me your star, Sparrow." He thumps his chest with a closed fist, and I swear another piece of my heart slips back into place.

Aero's tooth scrapes across my swollen nub, and I break apart, curling my fingers into his hair, turning to fucking liquid. He kneads me until my body turns floppy, then pulls back and gives me a smoky grin. "I can't wait to serve you up on *my* throne ..."

He rises like the morning sun, a sheen of *me* glistening on his lips. "What colour is it?" I ramble, filling the space with words when all I really want to do is dig my way into his heart again.

He grips the back of my neck, tilting my head until my throat's a stretched line of needy flesh. "You'll just have to wait and see." His lips skate from collarbone to ear, his other hand gripping the globe of my arse cheek.

He draws a deep breath, like he's sipping on me, and my skin prickles all the way down to my pebbling nipples. "You smell like moss, teardrops, and sweet apples. And it's my favourite smell in the entire *fucking* world."

I let out a deep, throaty moan as he sinks his canines into

the canvas of my flesh. I'm breathless, my hands claiming claws when he finally pulls away, those amber eyes seeming to dig into me.

"Don't make me wait any longer, Dell ..."

I lean forward and taste me on him, then sink my own teeth into the soft flesh of his lower lip—causing that final tether to snap into place on my heart, right where it belongs.

It doesn't make me whole. My heart will always be scarred with the loss of my mummy, the daddy I never knew I had, and everyone else I've watched fall victim to this unraveling world. But I've come to accept that there's a battered beauty to my brokenness ...

My heart might feature my pain, but it also highlights the brightest moments of my life—like waking up to see my mother's smile every single day for the first four years of my life; sitting on her shoulders, plucking ripe apples from the top of the tree, feeling like I was on top of the world.

My father, waist deep in the lake, reaching his arms out for me while his heart hammered a fearful tune; and the sweet smell of his relief when I glided up against his chest.

The moment he told me I'm beautiful.

The sight of my parents together, happy, *whole*, without the burden of everything they'd once lost ...

And my Sun Gods, who reminded me of what it means to love and be loved—who made me part of their family and lifted me onto their *own* shoulders ... giving me the courage I know I'm going to need to make this world a better place.

CHAPTER FIFTY-EIGHT
DELL

TEN MONTHS LATER

*T*he doors look just like they do in my memory—a large face staring down at me with secrets locked behind its clenched jaw. I clear my throat and flatten my hand against an engraved cheek, then push, listening to the creak of burdened hinges.

I try to ignore the wetness on my face brought forward by the sharp, unsavoury scent as I clap my hands—sending a small bead of power to the many Fae orbs dotted around the room.

The entire place lights up.

My hand flutters to my chest and I hold it there while Beasty steps up like a valiant steed—as if she's preparing to take the crippling weight that just settled on my shoulders.

I appreciate it, but I've been avoiding this place for far too long.

I need to do this on my own.

Another tear darts down my cheek while I try to clear my throat of the swollen lump—my constant companion for the past two months. They say it's normal; all the crying and the

CHAPTER 58

endless, overwhelming emotion. That it will eventually subside ...

Well, I call bullshit.

The only things subsiding are my sanity and personal hygiene, and unfortunately, there wasn't much of the former to begin with.

I float between the cluster of jars, studying the immortalised names and sleeping faces, remembering the little voices tittering to each other as they played hide-and-go-seek through the clouds.

I don't want this to be a sad place. My brothers may not be here, alive ... but they're with *her*—perpetually suspended in the childhood that was everything to me, so I know they're happy. How could they not be?

My attention catches on a gilded plaque and my lungs flop against my ribs ...

I stop moving. Stop breathing.

Amias.

Did my father choose his name? Did my mother? Did they choose it *together*?

I sketch each letter on the inscribed plate before I sweep my gaze to the immortalised child ...

His chubby cheeks are dusted with sandy freckles and a single dimple, his white wings curled around him like the petals of a rose bud that never got the chance to bloom.

"Amias," I whisper, cradling each syllable, offering them to the world like a gift.

A smile warms my face, and although it hurts to be cast because it's shaded in heartbreak, it's also dusted with *hope*.

I hear heavy footsteps as someone draws close. "Dell?"

My heart flips at the sound of Aero's honeyed voice. I swipe my face with the back of my hand and turn.

"Hey ..."

"You okay?"

TEN MONTHS LATER

I nod and his features soften as he chews up the space between us, his shoulders bunched around his ears. "All these years and I had no idea this place existed," he murmurs, looking at anything other than the jars cluttering the room.

"I think that was the point. Perhaps he felt like he was keeping part of them alive? Once you voice these things ..."

Aero clears his throat. "It becomes so much more real."

I catch his gaze and almost drown in it. "Sorry I didn't tell you I was ready to face ... *this*. I was walking and I jus—"

"I know," he says, tapping his temple, and I note the dark scallops under his eyes.

He looks tired.

"I *am* tired."

Noticing something brownish-yellow that's smeared across his shoulder, I swipe it off, smell my hand, and instantly regret it.

"Well, shit."

I wipe the offensive substance on my shift, adding to the conglomeration of ... *everything*. He's already losing sleep. He shouldn't have to smell like crap, too.

"Speaking of which," Aero murmurs, as if treading thin ice. "You're ... *required*. I'm sorry, I know you needed a moment to yourself. We stretched it out as long as we could ..."

"Let's be honest," I say, stifling a yawn, "*alone time* doesn't really exist anymore."

He threads his arm around my back and tucks my head under his chin. I nuzzle into him despite the fact that his shoulder still reeks like poo. It's not often we get a minute alone, and I want to enjoy what little we have left of it.

"What's that?"

I glance over my shoulder in the direction he's pointing. *Ahh ...*

"That's a wall, Aero." I feel his brow. "You feeling okay?"

CHAPTER 58

He jerks back and snatches my wrist, pulling my hand away that probably still smells like shit.

"It does. And that's not *just* a wall," he says, half dragging me forward. It's not until we draw closer that I see the recess pressed into it ...

Huh.

I peep into the alcove and look to the left, seeing foreboding stairs snaking down into the darkness. "Any idea what could be down there?"

Aero's chest brushes my back, his hand threading around my waist. "I honestly don't," he mumbles over top of my head, and I frown, taking the first step into the gloom.

"Well, I guess we're about to find out."

Knowing my luck, it will probably lead to some ancient, naked being with perfect tits who likes to sniff my neck, steal jerky, and has a questionable taste for Fae flesh.

"What's *that* supposed to mean?" Aero asks with a bite to his tone, trailing me as I wind around the spiral staircase that goes on and on and fucking *on*.

"Eh, nothing important. What is it with Gods and long, dark stairways?" I ask, running my hand along the stone wall lest I tumble all the way into the abyss of this seemingly bottomless pit.

Aero grunts, which I barely validate as an answer.

We round on a dead end stoppered by a large, white door lit by a single Fae orb bobbing above it, highlighting the carved pair of wings in the middle—splayed wide and proud and pillowy.

They're the same size as my baby ones.

"It's like they're guarding the door," I whisper, tracing them with the tips of my fingers. I glance down at the worn handle, grabbing hold of it ...

"Are you sure, Dell?"

"Nope."

TEN MONTHS LATER

I swing the door open, releasing a strident stream of light that floods the hallway. I squint, stepping forward once my eyes adjust ...

A sharp sound slips out of me while I try not to crumble.

"*Aero* ..."

"I'm here, baby."

The vast room doubles as an internal garden, protected by sweeping panes of glass that showcase a spectacular view of snow-dusted Sterling. There's a silver stream threaded between rocks; soft grass and plump, fleshy moss cushion the floor. Purple flowers hang from vines woven across the uneven stone ceiling, and bushes dot the ground dressed with fluffy, white roses that don't seem to realise it's the middle of winter.

There's a sturdy tree that twists around itself, wearing huge knots and a gnarly expression. Its distorted limbs shelter a worn timber seat and a crystal coffin that reflects the light pouring in through the windows ...

My tongue turns to chalk in my mouth.

Inside the coffin is a nest of brown sludge cradling pallid bones barely cresting above the surface. And perhaps it's because I loved her with every beat of my baby heart, but I instantly know who they belong to.

I fall to my knees, sinking into a tuft of moss, my lungs battling crisp, clean air that's suddenly *suffocating*.

Aero places his hand on the coffin, peering at its contents. "He buried her," he rasps. "In—"

"In mud from the bog," I whisper, blinking away the tears blurring my vision.

"He thought he could—"

He doesn't finish the sentence, so I finish it for him. "Bring her back. He thought he could bring her back."

And he built her a living, breathing shrine.

The realisation fills my lungs with stones. I remember a

CHAPTER 58

time when I stewed in the world's arsehole, praying for it to heal Sol and bring him back to me.

"That must be why he sometimes smelt like the bog. Perhaps he replaced the mud often, and the remnants clung to his shield ..."

The comment flays me because I know he's probably right.

It makes it all the more heartbreaking.

Aero rubs his face and offers me a hand. I allow him to pull me up so I can look into my mother's hollow gaze ...

At least I know where she is now. I can visit her, talk to her; tell her about all the good things in my life. Be close to her whenever that hole in my heart hurts ...

"I think the really cruel thing is that his beast allowed him to hope," I whisper, and Aero tugs me closer, bandaging me in his rosy essence.

"Hope is our greatest vulnerability; it can be empowering ... or crippling."

I skate my fingers across the cold face of the casket. "His beast used it as a weapon."

"But it didn't stop Edom from hoping, Dell." Aero hooks a finger under my chin and lures my gaze. "It brought him to you."

I offer him a small smile that feels tight on my face. "I know that now ..."

I just wish we'd had more time.

That's the thing about loss; it's unavoidable. Inevitable. If you run from it, cut yourself off from it, you also miss the things that have the potential to make your heart *swell*.

And I have so much of that.

So much that I barely have time to sleep. Or eat. Or pee. And I can't even remember the last time I brushed my hair. Honestly? I'm barely functioning ... but my heart is full, and I wouldn't have it any other way.

TEN MONTHS LATER

I yawn.

"You're tired," Aero growls, like it personally offends him. "Honestly, Dell, you should accept more help. Have you given any more thought into the we—"

I throw my hand up, stamp my finger to his lips, and castrate that suggestion before it has a chance to sow its seed. If I've learnt anything over the past year, it's that Sun God seeds are resilient. "I don't want a wet nurse, Morning Glory. I can do it mys—"

A familiar tingle blooms in my armpits—like millions of tiny pins stabbing deep into my sensitive flesh before traveling around my breasts to my tight, stinging nipples.

I look down, hearing Aero sniff the air as I cup my boobs. "I'm leaking."

"Oh, I know. We'll take the shortcut."

"Wait!" I screech, wiggling out of his hold and reaching for my slippers.

"What are you doing?"

I dismiss Aero's disrespectful tone, drag the drab things off my feet, and stuff them between us; ignoring the dense aroma that wafts up from that one time I stepped in some bog water and they got a little jammy. "I don't want my slippers to fall off in the Bright and get lost forever! Do you know how long it took me to break these bad boys in?"

"The past seven and a half months," Aero answers with a flat tone that suggests he has it in for my slippers.

I scowl. He's bang on the clitoris, like always.

A smooth smirk curls his lips, but then his nostrils flare and he glances down at my dowdy second feet. All the pride bleeds right off his face, and I swear his rosy aura dampens a smidge. "Honestly, Dell, I think it would be a fitting way for them to go. Those things smell like arse."

I clutch them harder. "So do you, Breakfast. But I'm not throwing *you* away. Now hurry up."

CHAPTER 58

We land on a fluffy rug right next to a hearth with a belly full of fire crackling away, making the large room feel almost cosy.

It would be idyllic if it weren't for the shrill squawking.

Times two.

I glance at my wide-eyed Dusk God perched on the arm of a seat in the corner, to our daughter arching off him, arms and legs flailing as if someone's attempting to exorcise her. Kal's holding Amias, bouncing him up and down, pacing the room like a pro ...

Too bad it doesn't seem to be working.

"Where's Sol?" I ask, tossing my slippers next to the bed.

"What?" Kal smirks, the stars in his eyes twinkling. "You're not still mad at him for eating your cold, leftover bacon rind?"

I wave him off, tucking a matted curl into my dreary mum bun. "Water off a dick's back. My hormones can be unreasonable sometimes. For once, I was being the arsehole, not the other way around."

Kal seems to choke on his own spit.

Yeah ... too bad Sol wasn't around to hear that because I won't be caught dead repeating it.

I press my fingers over my nipples in an attempt to stem my flow, but the material's already sodden. "Goddammit. Not again." I glance down at twin wet patches and flick the straps off my shoulders, leaving the soiled shift in a heap on the ground.

I'll pick it up later.

Maybe.

"Dell ..." Aero groans, likely because I forgot to put underwear on this morning.

I spin, walking backwards towards the bed as my gaze is

TEN MONTHS LATER

drawn to the swelling bulge in the crotch of his tight leather pants. "Sor—"

A large arc of milk hits Aero square in the face, his hand flying to his eye. "Not again ..."

I wince. That's the fourth time this week.

"Marion said it's a good moisturiser, so rub that shi—ugar in."

"*Dell*," Drake warns, cradling our chubby, pint-sized kraken close to his chest and looking far too delectable. "I'm about to lose some skin here. Not that I mind! But those boobs look really ... fudging ..." he clears his throat, "*ready.*"

He means *huge*, but he knows I'm sensitive about them since *The Incident* two weeks ago. I had my eyes screwed shut while trying to change my shit-smeared top, so as to not disturb my semi-sleeping state, and I fell face first into a plate of cake I'd stashed next to the bed.

I still ate the cake.

Off the floor.

While I cried.

"Well, now you know how it fudging feels."

"Language," Drake growls, and I narrow my eyes on the gruff bastard who's *literally* covering our daughter's ears like I'm going to poison her mind with my foul mouth.

"*I said fudging!*"

I stalk towards my feeding nest—a pile of pillows stacked on the bed in the shape of a horseshoe. It's the place I've spent the past two months permanently propped whilst being constantly gnawed on.

Turns out, Faelings are born with teeth—teeth they use to *nibble* on their parents and strengthen that familial bond ...

Go figure.

Our daughter's wings explode from her back, prodding Drake in the eye with the gold tip of an otherwise white feather. I smirk, settle into my nest, and give him grabby

CHAPTER 58

hands. "Here, give her to me. Her wings only come out when she's about to get *really* bitey."

Drake makes a chiding sound. "That ship has sailed, babe."

I try to contain my amusement.

Amarii snarls as he pries her tiny teeth off his pec and nuzzles close, whispering in her ear—words I only *just* manage to catch over the sound of her yowling ...

"Des ve heil, shasken da."

I love you, beautiful one.

My language lessons have paid off, at least enough for me to pick up the really important stuff ...

Drake places her in my arms and she snuffles about until I pinch my breast and shove it in her mouth. A hollow silence settles over the room ...

Strange.

I glance up to see Kal curled over Amias with a big smile on his face while he lets him chew his pinkie finger, and my heart explodes.

"Nice trick," Drake huffs, glancing down at the graffiti marring his pec that will take at least three days to heal. Even for him. My nipples know from experience.

"I've had practise," Kal mumbles, edging towards me. He glances up through half-lidded eyes, oozing paternal devotion, and I swear my empty womb does a summersault. "Are you ready, or would you like me to hold on to him a bit longer?"

Fuck.

Me.

That's all the dirty talk I'll ever need.

I glance down at my other nipple spurting milk all over the comforter. "Marion did say I'll end up with wonky boobs if I don't feed them evenly ..."

I hear a door shut and the woman herself brushes into the room, wearing a bun so tight it smooths her face. "And

TEN MONTHS LATER

Marion knows best." She struts over, placing a glass on the bedside table and a cloth over my shoulder. She clicks her tongue at Kal and reaches out. "Quick, before he falls asleep without his fill."

He frowns, removing his finger, and Amias starts to wail again. Marion plucks him up then manhandles my spare boob into his wide-open mouth.

Everyone breathes a collective sigh ... except me.

My poor nipples.

"So," she huffs, readjusting my hold so Amarii's pretty little wing isn't batting me in the face every time she swallows. "Where's the grumpy one gone? I want to introduce him to a sleeping tonic."

"I was wondering the same thing." I stifle a yawn that mutates into a hiss when my daughter decides to give my areola a piercing. "*Ouch!* Goddamn it! Not again ..."

"Language, babe! For fudge sake!"

I roll my fucking eyes at the soon-to-be eunuch. "I'm allowed to say *goddamn*. I was damning you for destroying my breasts and turning me into a fff"—his eyes narrow—"*fudging cow*."

He sinks onto the bed, tosses a throw over my naked bottom half, and starts to massage my feet as his golden aura thrums with a captivating static. "You could stop breastfeeding," he suggests with a roguish smile that makes his dimple pucker. "The sooner you go back into heat, the sooner I can put my seed in you again."

"I. Will. Cut. You," I whisper slow and deadly calm.

"It's my turn next, anyway."

I gape at Aero spread across the chaise with a leg swinging over the side—crunching into an apple. He throws me a wink, and I almost reach into my bedside cockie jar and toss one at his smug-ass face.

CHAPTER 58

It's like he has zero regard for the safety of his own testicles.

"Fudge off," Kal huffs, lifting the glass of water to my lips which I accept graciously. I might just reward him with my Holy-Birthing-Grail for standing up for my poor, exerted uterus. "Night comes after day and dusk. I'm next in line."

I spit water all over the two unsuspecting children cushioned up against my boobs.

"Why am I the only one in this room who seems to care about my traumatised perineum? It's because I'm so good with my mouth, isn't it?" I knew all those free-for-all, superior blowjobs when I was too pregnant to handle more than just the tip would come back and bite me in the cunt one day.

Aero chokes on his apple as Marion tuts, slapping Kal across the back of the head—which looks ridiculous considering she's less than half his size. She dabs my sodden babies, breasts, and face with a spit rag, then shoves Kal out of the way and offers me more water. "Honestly, I don't know how she handles the four of you."

"Oh, she handles us very *fudging* well." Drake throws me a wink, melting my anger and making me go all gooey inside.

Marion thumps him over the back of the head with the cloth on her way past, probably picturing her twilight years being eaten up by squawking Sun God spawn, though I can see the ghost of a smile on her lips as she breezes out.

Drake rubs his head but his eyes are *smoldering* ...

Looks like I'll be taking a big, golden dick tonight. If I can keep my eyes open.

Doubtful.

Maybe I'll suggest the dead cow position; that way if I fall asleep midway through, he still has a chance to finish.

Sap trudges in from the spare room with a face smudged in carrion, and I watch Drake's face light up. "Hey, little one ..."

TEN MONTHS LATER

She leaps onto the bed, licks Drake right in his eyehole, then flops into my lap, smelling like roast liver.

I smile.

She likes it there—the perfect spot to keep an eye on her babies. She's also a convenient hot water bottle.

"So," I say, giving Sap a scratch between the wings. "Where *is* Sol?"

I glance up in time to see my three Gods share a knowing *look*, and my heart tries to leap right out of my chest. "What is it?"

Kal clears his throat and steps closer to the bed. "Cassian arrived with news while you were taking a walk. Sol went to follow up ..."

Fuck.

Cassian with news could only mean one thing.

Up until I gave birth, I'd been the one overseeing Kal's kingdom—lovingly dubbed the Kingdom of Dreams by those who've visited in the past ten months.

I think it's fitting.

The terrace pools are constantly filled with diluted shit from the bog, creating enough space for up to a hundred Fae to soak in at any given time.

I spent the first five months of my pregnancy scouring the world for survivors—for women broken more than just mentally—offering them the use of the pools. Everyone I found accepted the offer, aside from Leila ...

She wanted to go last, and I understood why. I decided not to be crowned Queen for the same reason; refusing to take something so sacred until everyone else is made whole again ... at least physically.

I hear the Bright rip open and Sol comes storming through the balcony doors. Our gazes collide; those hard features softening as my chest caves at the sight of him.

I hate it when they go off on their own. Marion says it's

CHAPTER 58

the hormones, I say I'm haunted by those gaping holes in my heart.

He stalks towards me, shaking off the snow. "Didn't they just feed?"

I refuse to dignify that question with an answer.

"Is there something wrong with the pools? Or the bog? Did we run out of shhh—ugar?"

Sol stretches over me and kisses my nose, ignoring Sap's little snarl as he plants another on our son's chubby cheek. He brushes his hand over Amarii's head, then gives Sap a scratch behind the ear which softens her sound. "Nothing's wrong."

"Then, what? You know I hate being left in the dark. Just because I'm lactating every thirty minutes and I can't sneeze without a little pee dribbling out doesn't mean you get to hold out on me!"

"Babe, calm down ..."

I narrow my eyes on Drake. "Don't tell me to calm down while my nipples are getting chewed on."

He swiftly continues his deep muscle massage.

Fuck yes, that's the stuff.

"What's going on at the pools?"

Sol clears his throat and knots his arms over his chest. "Leila just got in ..."

"Oh ..."

My shoulders drop, losing all their rigidity, and I realise they've been tense since I dragged that blade across my father's throat ...

It's over.

It's actually over.

Part of me wants to vomit; another part of me wants to cry; and then there's the part of me that wants to do something entirely removed from both those things. Something so foreign I'm not even sure I know how to do it properly anymore ...

I look down at my children, sound asleep and nuzzled up against each other.

Safe.

Both proof that light can spawn in even the darkest places.

A smile splits my face ... and then I start to *laugh*.

It ends up slipping out so naturally, I couldn't have caught it if I tried.

I lift my gaze, seeing my mates watching with wide eyes and faces drawn of colour, and I make a silent promise that my children will hear this sound so much they grow sick of it.

I know we still have a long way to go, that the world's still choking on the memories of my father's poisoned reign ... but perhaps people can begin to heal now that the evidence is no longer carved into their bodies?

"We did it," I chime, barely recognising the sound of my own voice.

"No, Little Dove," Kal rasps, wiping his face with the back of his arm. "*You* did it."

CHAPTER FIFTY-NINE
SOL

ONE YEAR LATER

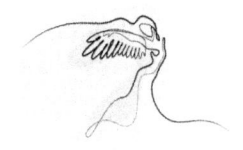

"Maaa ma. Boooob. *Maa!*"

I hang my legs off the bed, wincing from the brutal chill of the floor while I rub the attempted sleep from my face.

"Maaa! *Boob.*"

Looks like I'm not the only one struggling tonight.

I stride towards the crib and see Amias staring up at me with eyes like steely ocean pearls. He's wide the fuck awake—his hands gripping the bars of the crib like a jailbird, his silver-tipped wings shimmering in the slice of moonlight cutting through the gap in the curtains.

"Boon, it's the middle of the night ..."

He gives me a big smile that makes the dimple on his chubby cheek pucker, and I feel my heart wind around his little finger. "Dadda," he chimes, giving me grabby hands before losing balance and falling to his arse ... making Amarii grouse in her sleep beside him.

Fuck.

If he's not careful, he's going to wake his sister, then we'll all be screwed.

ONE YEAR LATER

"Boob bo—"

"*Tas, tas* ..." I pluck him up, getting a face full of wing. "You don't want to wake the siren. Believe me."

He usually sleeps through her midnight tantrums.

I don't.

Tucking him close, I snatch a throw off the end of the bed and head towards the balcony doors. The chill might persuade him to snuggle into me and fall back to sleep without chewing Dell's tit for comfort.

She needs her rest. Tomorrow's a big day, and I know she's nervous.

I fold his wings, swaddle him in the woollen throw, then step out into the brisk air. My own wings push out and sweep around us both as I tighten my hold, blowing hot huffs into his hair.

This sheltered balcony is unburdened by the snow that hasn't stopped falling since the Long Dawn, and I sink into a lounger, letting my boy soften onto me so he's absorbing all my body warmth.

"Maa, ma," he mumbles, wiggling his hand free and slapping my chest like a drum, his fluffy curls glowing against the black velvet night.

"She's asleep, Boon. Just like you should be. You're supposed to be the well-behaved one, remember?"

He grips my nipple, almost ripping the thing right off, and I can't help but smile through my wince as I press a kiss to the crown of his head.

He's strong ...

I nudge him up so his head is resting in the crook of my neck, then close my eyes and start to whisper-sing the song that's been haunting my subconscious for the past two years ...

She made her daughter's hair from moss,

CHAPTER 59

Plucked her eyes from a riverbed.
She wove her skin from water's fall,
Then painted her lips an apple red.
She formed her curls with coiled vines,
But forgot to ask them to be tame.
She smeared them with soft clouds instead,
Then prayed she'd love them just the same.
She plucked a star from the sky above,
Then set it in her daughter's soul.
She asked it to watch over her
And keep her daughter whole.
But the Faeling did not weep or stir
Or breathe upon the lips that kissed.
So, she rolled her up in sunshine,
Then stole a smile from the sun's eclipse.
But still the child did not move,
And so she fell upon her knees.
The mother reached inside herself,
And gave her heart to sow the seed.
And though her daughter was made whole
With pieces of the world's bouquet,
The mother knew deep down inside
She was never meant to stay.
Her eyes would sink to the riverbed,
Her lips would bleed their hue.
Her skin would fall back to the lake,
The moss would take its due.
But perhaps the sun would be so kind
To love her daughter anyway.
And it would piece her back together
In her own mosaic way.

It feels good to get the words out—give them shape. Perhaps the reason they've haunted me was because I kept them trapped right next to the memory of Edom carving a fresh ward into his skin. One which could have taken my son if Dell hadn't set her father free from his beast before she gave birth.

What-ifs ... I fucking hate them.

My arms tighten and I notice Amias drifted off while I was singing. Now the real mission—transfer the little nipple biter back to bed without waking him up.

Maybe I'll just sleep here with him ...

"Sol?"

My eyes pop open—seeing Dell looking down at us from her spot by the open door, her hair a waterfall of sunshine that rolls all the way to her hips.

My next breath snags in my throat.

Her shift may be long and brushing her toes but, fuck me, it does nothing to hide all her curves and dips.

She's *perfection*.

I intend to spend the rest of eternity deifying that flawless body and reminding her how *good* it feels to be alive.

"I was hoping you'd sleep through ..."

She takes a step closer, and I can hear her heart hammering much faster than usual ...

"*Sparrow?*"

"Where did you hear that song?"

I go very, very still.

I'd hoped to avoid telling her this—didn't want her to know some lingering part of me bore witness to her pain while I clung to her with everything I had ... until those final wispy threads of energy dissipated.

I didn't want to drag her back into the raw well of emotions I'm still clawing my own way out of.

Death has a way of fucking with you.

Life after death feels like a dream you're frightened to wake up from.

CHAPTER 59

"It was the last thing I heard before my energy was absorbed by the sun," I admit, and I hate how weak my voice sounds. But that feeling of our mate bond—of *Amias'* bond being torn from my dying heart is the reason I'm always the last to fall asleep at night.

I'm afraid to lose moments that could be spent just *looking* at them because I know how quickly it can all be ripped away.

"And you ... you remembered it?"

How could I forget?

I nod and her features melt.

"Who had the idea to piece me back together with sunlight?" she rasps, and the way her voice whittles down almost lures my heart right out of my fucking chest.

"Me."

She blinks, sending a tear darting down her cheek. "My mother made up that song ..."

I nod again, brushing a hand over our son's wing, making him wiggle in his sleep.

I'd figured that out ...

She clears her throat, watching me disentangle from the lounger—doing my best not to disturb our little Boon. I use my wings to herd her into our pocket of warmth.

Her hand slides around my back, leaving a trail of prickly skin. "I miss her, Sol."

I know, Sparrow.

"She saved you," I whisper as she tilts onto her tippy toes and presses a butterfly kiss to our son's dimple.

"No. They both did."

CHAPTER SIXTY
AERO

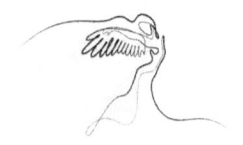

'I'm going to have buns of steel by the time I reach the top of these stairs.'

My lips curl at the corner.

Your buns are already fucking glorious, baby.

"Did she let you see the dress?" Drake asks Sol, who shakes his head, then plants a kiss in his son's mass of curls. Silver tipped wings are fanned across his chest while the kid uses his glossy shoulder plate as a pillow ... unlike Amarii, whose hands are sunk into Drake's generally perfect mane while her wings churn the air.

She's only ever docile when she's asleep or playing with Sap—who's currently pacing back and forth in front of the dais, hackles up, hurling smoke balls at anyone who dares put a toe past what she deems a respectable distance from her babies.

Nobody's scared, but she doesn't know that. She thinks she's the most terrifying drako in the world right now; picturing herself just as big as the black one lounging behind us, still smelling like his last meal: charred lava monster.

"She wouldn't let me see the dress either," Drake grumbles, wincing when his daughter uses his eye socket as a foothold to scale his head. "She said she wanted it to be a *surprise* ..."

All three look at me and my eyes widen. "Don't ask me, I've got no fudging idea. She must have organized it while I slept."

They frown and sway their attentions back to the crowd. I really wish they'd stop using me as a fucking Dell-decoder.

"I call dibs to take it off her," Kal murmurs, and I roll my eyes.

Fucking bro code. "That one doesn't count."

"Fudge off, it does. Don't be a sore loser. Bro code was your idea," he says on a smirk that makes me want to jab him in the nose, though he'd probably see it coming.

"Because I usually have the upper hand," I drone, scanning the sea of High and Lesser Fae squeezed into the throne room, hoping to catch even a glimpse of their new Queen.

I'm trying to drown out the masses because there's only one train of thought I want to follow ...

'This dress is giving me vagina chafe. Nobody likes vagina chafe, least of all my fucking vagina.'

Ah, there she is.

"She coming?" Sol snips.

"She decided to take the stairs rather than use the Bright," I mumble, watching people shift and fidget.

Sol swings his full attention to me. "But she *hates* stairs."

Oh, I know.

"So, she's stalling," Drake grinds out, and I sigh, starting to sweat in my armor despite the brisk chill.

"Do you blame her?"

Kal clears his throat, his wings rustling as Kyro puffs smoke at us from his spot behind the throne. "People are getting restle—"

The door cracks open and the entire room draws a

collective gasp. Even the internal chatter lulls, as if the woman standing at the neck of the room has literally siphoned the thoughts right out of their minds.

"Good fucking *God*," I whisper, fanning my wings. It's taking everything in my power not to bite down on my knuckle at the sight of her.

Her hair is long and loose, falling to her hips in careless waves, harboring its own natural glow from the sunlight fused with her life force. She has a touch of kohl across her lids and a shimmer on her cheeks.

She's wearing a blood-red gown that bleeds over the curves of her body and pools at her feet; redefining the color she wore while her body was defiled time and time again ...

A bold choice.

The *perfect* fucking choice.

Her gaze meets mine and my back straightens. Not only am I looking at my better half in every way, but what I see staring back at me is straight confidence.

That shit can't be fabricated.

"No wonder she took the stairs," Kal says beside me, and I clear my throat, wishing I could readjust my pants without drawing attention to my raging cock.

The entire room bows, cleaving a path to the throne we carved from a massive river rock the exact hue of the one she values in her special box.

She lifts her chin, squares her shoulders, and sways down the aisle; her heels tapping against the marble. *'Don't vomit, don't leak all over your dress, don't trip ...'*

If she did, I'd catch her before she hit the ground.

A cape hangs off her hips, trailing behind her—a ribbon of red creating the illusion that she's painting the floor in her wake.

She's owning her past, present, and future ...

I commit every breath, every step, every *blink* to memory.

Right now, everything is as it should be; Dell walking towards me with the world bowing at her feet.

She passes through a slice of midday sun, lighting her up like a beacon, and her wings emerge to a sea of gasps.

"Fudge me," Drake rasps as she takes the last few steps towards us, drops to a kneel, and sets her hands on her knees, palms up—her gown dribbling down the steps behind her.

I swallow. *Hard.*

'You like that, Big Man?'

It's taking everything I have not to drag her through the Bright, tear that dress right down the middle, and stuff her fuller.

I nod to Kal who steps forward, holding a white pillow with a crown set on its belly. It's small but intricate, pressed from a crushed star. Light bounces off its ethereal design, making it glimmer with its own heartbeat.

"This was your mother's," I whisper, hovering it over her head.

Her breath halts, she looks into me, and I swear my heart almost beats right out of my chest.

'You didn't tell me about this ...'

We had secrets too, baby.

I wink at her and a tear darts down her cheek that she doesn't swipe away. It sets my fucking heart on fire.

The girl I met on that cliff was too afraid to show her pain. She thought it made her weak, but she's never been weak a day in her life.

I lower the crown, committing her to an eternity of servitude I know she has the strength to shoulder.

There's a beat where the world seems to still before her lashes sweep up and she peers at me with glittering eyes ...

Even her mind gives away no secrets.

"It's beautiful on you."

Her face splits into a blinding smile that looks like it was peeled straight from the sun, and it makes my heart ache for all the right reasons.

She starts to rise, and the crowd erupts—a roaring welcome for the mosaic Queen who took on the crumbling world that broke her, then used fissured fingers to piece it back together.

We step to the side and watch Dell ascend towards her throne.

THE END

Thank you for reading!
I hope you have enjoyed Dell's journey through this imperfect world ... a world that still has so much left to explore.

Although Dell has found her happily ever after, for some? The journey has just begun.

Please enjoy the epilogue from Cassian on the next page.

Keep in the loop by joining my reader group here:
S.A. Parker Reader's Group

CHAPTER SIXTY-ONE
CASSIAN

I stick to a slab of shade behind a pillar at the edge of the room, watching Dell cradle that tiny, sleeping drako who finally passed out.

The shadows shield me from sight, their ardour akin to a cold lover's embrace ...

"Cass?"

I clear my throat, wipe wisps of black off my shoulders, and step into a slice of light—though I pause when I see the small child trying to clamber out of my father's arms ...

Fuck no.

I spear my hands between us, as if they could shield me from the metaphorical shit I'm about to get tossed in. "No fucking way."

"But Dell thought it would be a nice idea. Make you feel more involved ..."

I cock a brow.

He gives me a hopeful smile.

"No."

His face drops. "Cass, it's only for a moment. She doesn't cope with all the noise, and she can't help but ... *compete*."

"You're not helping your case," I mutter, resisting the urge to cover my ears and block them both out.

"Just ... take her out to play in the snow until we finish up. You know she loves the snow."

I don't know that, because I've been keeping my distance. That's not my family up there on the dais ... it's *his*.

"Where's her father? Why the fuck can't *he* take her?" I glance around, trying to spot the big, golden bastard. The kid squawks louder and the aureate band around her pupils' throbs.

"He's busy discussing borders," Dad yells over the racket. "And don't let Drake hear you swear in front of his daughter. He'll turn you into a eunuch, then make you eat your own cock."

I screw my face up, stuffing my hands in my pockets. "You know I don't do ... little people."

"She's your stepsister."

"Emphasis on the *step*. That thing's your problem, not mine. We don't share blood and, unlike you, I'm not pussy whipped by her mother."

Dad gives me the signature scowl that suggests I'm crossing into cunty territory. "You're not too old for me to send you to your room for being a dick ..."

"Like I'd complain. Why don't you just ..." I wave my hand around like a magic fucking wand, "*happy* her?"

"Dell would have my balls for breakfast. She doesn't want to mess with their emotions, and you know exactly where I stand on that."

I grunt.

"Look, I'm not asking, Cass. We all have to play our part. Like it or not, you're a member of this family. And all the crying is making Dell's tits leak, so ..."

Fucking hell.

I shake my head, thrusting my hands at him, trying to

dissolve the picture he just slammed into my mind. "Give her here, for *fudge* sake."

Dad gives me a watery smile as he palms the child off, her rebellious hair making the poor thing look like she's been dragged backwards through a bush.

She's a storm in a thimble.

The moment I pull her against my chest, she stops crying. Instantly.

I scowl.

"Well," Dad says, doing nothing to hide the shock in his tone, which is a bit fucking insulting. "That settles that. You're in charge of your stepsister."

I open my mouth to sling something sharp at him, but he's already tearing through the Bright. He reappears on the dais next to Aero, some important people I haven't bothered to learn the names of, and Drake ... whose wings are spread to their full span. His chest is puffed and he's eyeing me like a viper, probably picturing the many ways he's going to fry my nuts and feed them to his golden spitfire.

He pokes his fingers at his eyes, then at me, and I sigh, bobbing the kid on my hip like a bag of grain; doing anything I can to stop her from crying again.

I glance down as I weave through the crowd, aiming for one of the side doors. "Guess it's you and me, Kid."

It's much quieter in the courtyard outside, the crisp air biting my skin in a pathetic attempt to cool the fire in my veins.

"Baaa, ba ba," she coos, wrapping her mouth around one of my buttons. I shake my head and drop onto a stone bench that's tucked well away from the celebrating roar.

If I'm honest, it's nice to have an excuse to get out of there —even if that excuse is a little thing with a volatile temper and questionable taste in chew toys.

Actually, Drake would skin me alive if I let his daughter choke on a button.

I pry it away, then place her on the ground between my knees. She uses her tiny, gold-dipped wings to balance, takes two shaky steps through the snow, tips forward, and makes a hole so deep I lose sight of her.

"Shit!"

I fish her out, dusting her off while she uses pincer fingers to pluck bits of snow from her curls—her face bunched with concentration. The wind stirs her hair and that lower lip wobbles when her ringlets keep flicking out of reach ...

It's going to be really inconvenient if she starts crying again.

I scan the courtyard twice for extra eyes before I push my wings out. They cast the patio in velvet darkness, and the kid's eyes double in size as her mouth pops open.

I give them a stretch and I've never seen her so still ... just as still as my fucking lungs.

Strangers don't get to see my wings.

Ever.

Exposing them while Edom was alive would have put a target on my back, or so Dad drilled into me when I was young. Old habits die hard and now, I'm saddled with limbs that feel like they should belong to somebody else.

I curl them forward with a *whuff*, forming a hollow protected from the wind—but she's lost interest in the snow.

Her fingers tickle a tapered, blood-red tip, sending shivers scuttling up my spine. She glances up from her spot trapped in my shadow and smiles so wide I taste ash.

"That smile's too pretty to waste on me, Kid."

Something scratches my conscience and I drop my wing an inch, tucking Amarii against my chest when I catch sight of a woman standing not too far away, watching us ...

She's striking—like she was pieced together with only the most regal features. Her hair is oil running down the long lines of her body, her round face pale like the moon, contrasting bold lips that look like someone sucked all the colour to the surface of them.

I should hide my wings, but that would mean exposing the kid. My instincts tell me that's a very bad idea ... logic supported by the woman's *black* eyes.

My fire roils, answering a call I can't see or hear, and the snow begins to eddy.

Amarii growls ...

I glance down, seeing her staring up at me with swirling eyes that are fucking disarming. I quickly avert my gaze and peek over my wing, but the woman's gone. All that's left is a bad taste in my mouth and dainty footprints that will soon be filled in by the snowfall.

Water starts to leech up my legs, and I realise I just turned half the balcony to mush. Unconsciously.

Dad would have a fit.

"Boooob. Boobbb," the kid hollers, hanging off a fist full of my jacket, salivating over my pec while her irises teeter between gold and black ...

I didn't sign up to get gnawed on.

I tuck my wings away and am halfway across the courtyard when she starts to snarl like a rabid wolf. I've never been more thankful to see Dell and her lactating tits than when she bursts through the door—chewing on something that smells like potpourri, hands only half-covering the wet patches bleeding down her bust.

Fucking hell ... I'm going to need therapy.

"Thanks for holding her off while we finished up," Dell gushes. Literally. Those wet patches are only getting bigger.

I hand her the kid, averting my gaze in a desperate

attempt to give her some privacy while her errant wings scoop around the child.

Little growls taper into suckling sounds.

I try not to look as awkward as I feel while Dell's gaze scours my scalding skin. "I keep hoping it'll let up …"

Clumps of snow collect on the banister despite the fact that it *should* be the middle of summer, and I consider telling her I've been hoping the same. But then I just … don't.

"You don't have to bother making small talk with me."

Admittedly, the comment scalded my tongue. Sometimes I just can't stop myself from being a cunt.

"Look, Just because your father and I are—"

I clear my throat, *knowing* she's about to say something that will make me want to hang myself with my own cum tract.

She sighs, bouncing up and down in my peripheral. "Cassian, you're family …"

It's lost on me.

I don't fit in the puzzle of their perfect family picture, but that's not their fault. They want more; I'm not capable of more.

I don't *want* more.

I turn from the stormy view, stuff my hands deep in my pockets, and head back inside so I can pretend to check on my Electi. It's only once I'm confined to the shade, leaning against a column and doing my best to blend with the scenery, that I realise how far I overstepped.

Dell deserves better than what I just gave her. She's dealt with too much shit to have to cop mine on top of it all. But in so many ways, looking at her feels like glancing in a mirror I've been trying to avoid for years …

So, I've landed somewhere on the island of indifference—where I can be a bit of a cunt in the hopes nobody notices I'm innately flawed.

Dell and I may have our parallels, but we're also polar opposites.

Life shattered Dell, but somehow, she was able to draw those pieces back together and mould herself into something formidable.

I was born broken—missing the bits that seem to make other people *feel* properly. But why would I want them? I've seen a world rot because of one man's broken heart.

I'm better off with an empty chest. You can't break something that was never there in the first place.

Perhaps that makes me a monster, too?

All the more reason for me to stay the *fuck* away from their happily ever after.

ACKNOWLEDGMENTS

Chinah, I'm so blessed to have you as my editor. You lived and breathed these words with me for an entire year; helped me puff **soul** into them.

Thank you for pressing pause on your life to help me grow A Woman's Worth to its full potential. Thank you for showing my characters so much love, devotion, and understanding. Thank you for always squeezing the best out of me —for pushing me to take my writing to the next level.

Thank you for believing in me.

The Editor & The Quill

Brittani, thank you for the endless hours spent brainstorming, polishing, researching ... so much more. Thank you for your constant stream of encouragement.

Thank you for your friendship—for turning nocturnal for me when you could tell I was reaching my limit.

Thank you for **being there** for me.

Mum and Dad, you are a pillar of support and have always urged me to follow my dreams.

Thank you for **everything**.

Philippa, thank you for always checking in, and for making sure I've got the tools (or just the quiet space) I need to get the job done.

Thank you for your endless love and support.

Josh, thank you for the hundreds of tacos you delivered to me throughout the past year. Thank you for loving me, and for encouraging me to follow my dreams.

Thank you for our life together.

Lauren, Angelique, and Talarah, thank you for your ongoing support. For loving these characters and making me feel such incredible validation.

Most of all, thank you for your wonderful friendships—I'm so lucky to have you ladies in my life.

Nana, thank you for inspiring me with your creativity, and for showing me how strong and independent a woman can be.

I love you, and not a day goes by that I don't miss you.

SPAWN OF DARKNESS SERIES

A Token's Worth
A Feather's Worth
A Lover's Worth
A Woman's Worth

ABOUT THE AUTHOR
SARAH ASHLEIGH PARKER

Sarah is New Zealand born and lives in the Gold Coast, Australia with her husband and their three children. She discovered her love for the written word early on, devouring book after book and creating her own stories in her spare time, winning various competitions throughout her school years for her quirky imagination.

Recently, she has been able to fully immerse herself into writing, being at home with three young children and an unquenchable thirst for creativity.

And so, with the timing being as good as it ever gets, and the passion and determination of a woman possessed, Sarah threw herself into becoming an author. Juggling an eclectic mix of manic writing, editing and proofing sessions, child rearing, homemaking and everything else life throws around, she somehow makes it work.

Sarah's preferred genres are adult fantasy romance and contemporary romance.

Printed in Great Britain
by Amazon